LEGENDS
of the
TWIN DRAGONS

—

THE PROPHECY OF GEMINI

—

Book One
of the Chronicles of Shiloh

BRIAN JOHN SKILLEN

Published by: Publishing Hackers
Arvada, Colorado, USA

Ebook ISBN: 978-1-959911-49-4
Paperback ISBN: 978-1-959911-47-0
Hardcover ISBN: 978-1-959911-48-7
Hard Cover Collector's Edition ISBN: 978-1-959911-50-0

Design by Publishing Hackers
Edited by: Dr. Michael McClure and Malina Dravis-Tucker
Cover art by: Christopher Clark - http://Christopherclark.com
Interior art by: Artem Kyryluik

Printed in the United States of America

Brian loves hearing from readers, you can reach him at:
Brian@brianjohnskillen.com or http://www.brianjohnskillen.com

DEDICATION

This book is dedicated to Emianna
&
all of the other young dreamers who will read these pages

Altiniya
The Void
Binah
Chokmah
Geburah
Chesed
Tiphareth
Hod
Netzach
Yesod
Trading Post
Malkuth

WHAT'S YOUR INNER DRAGON?

Dear Adventurer,

Welcome to the world of Altiniya. In this enchanted realm, dragons are living reflections of the human soul, bonded to individuals through a Summoning Ceremony at age thirteen. Each person's dragon is tied to one of nine distinct personality types with unique traits and magical abilities. Discover your own inner dragon by taking the Dragon Type Quiz. Scan the QR code or use the link below to begin.

B.J.S.

https://books.brianjohnskillen.com/dragon-quiz-landing-page

TABLE OF CONTENTS

THE FOOT OF THE ORACLE

Shiloh's brown eyes darted between the hieroglyphs on the wall and her book. Behind her glasses, her gaze sharpened. "Uncle, I think this translation is wrong."

"That's nice, dear," her uncle Max replied distractedly. He blew hard on the wall, sending a plume of dust into the beam of Shiloh's flashlight.

Shiloh stared at him, biting back frustration. She couldn't understand why adults never listened. Maybe it was because her uncle didn't know her that well. They only saw each other once or twice a year during the holidays. He was always away, traveling around the world on an archeological dig. When he visited, he captivated Shiloh and her twin brother Link with tales of his adventures and exotic lands. Shiloh had always dreamed of going with him. Now, here they were in a small, cramped tunnel in the middle of the Valley of the Kings, hoping to make the next great discovery. Shiloh just didn't know there would be so much dust.

"According to the Rosetta Stone," Shiloh pressed on, tucking a strand of her blond hair back into her braid, "this glyph means wind—a very big wind. Actually, if you put the two of these together…" She squinted at the wall. "There is also fire. It doesn't quite make sense yet, but I'm sure this translation is wrong."

Uncle Max chuckled, wiping away more dust with a barbershop-style brush. "And when did you become an expert on hieroglyphs?"

"On the plane ride here," she said matter-of-factly. "I read *The Enigma of the Rosetta*."

Uncle Max turned, raising an eyebrow. "You read the book I sent to you?"

"I've read every book you have sent to me; from the one on Sanskrit to the one on Viking Runes—I really enjoyed that one. *The Enigma of the Rosetta* was a little dry, but I got the concept. At least enough to know that this glyph," she pointed to a small image of a bird carved into the wall, "has a determinative, which changes it from an ideogram to something more metaphorical."

The rhythmic brushing stopped. Uncle Max walked to her. "Let me see."

Shiloh pointed her flashlight at the hieroglyphs and then at the translation.

Uncle Max leaned in, his laugh echoing off the tunnel walls. "You're right. One of my best grad students translated this, but here you are, just twelve—"

"We're thirteen now," Link interrupted as he entered the tunnel and dropped a large burlap sack of supplies with a thud.

"Well, with her brains and your brawn, I would have guessed you were at least sixteen."

Link grinned, a smile that came easily to him. He was tall for his age, his frame more developed than most boys in their class. His brown hair and blue eyes shone in the dim light. Shiloh studied him for a moment, remembering how they used to run together, inseparable. But this past year, Link had traded track for football, spending more time with his team and less with her.

"Is there anything else you need from above?" Link asked.

"No, that will be fine," Uncle Max replied, turning back to the wall. "Big wind… This could help to explain why…"

"Why what?" Shiloh shot up in her chair.

"Why the desert is expanding."

"Isn't it global warming, or something like that?" Link asked.

Shiloh bristled. He knew very well what global warming was. Link was just as smart as she was, but in a different way. Even though he was dyslexic, Link saw things that others didn't and grasped concepts at a high level. Plus, his emotional intelligence was through the roof. Since joining the team, though, he had picked up the annoying habit of pretending not to be as smart as he was.

Shiloh didn't know why he wanted to be ordinary. For that matter, she didn't really understand people. She knew from a young age that she was different. She didn't get social cues that others would pick up on, and forget about understanding sarcasm. She took everything at face value. To cope with this, she mimicked the social behavior of others, but more importantly, she would read. She was obsessed. Books always had the answers. They taught her how to act.

"Global warming is part of it," Uncle Max said, breaking her train of thought, "but there is something else. That is why they called me here. Ever since this tomb—we call it the foot of the oracle—was unearthed, the desert has been expanding at an alarming rate."

"If the opening of the tomb is responsible, why don't you just close it up?" Shiloh asked. It was the obvious answer.

"We did." Uncle Max sighed. "The storms just grew stronger. I wasn't supposed to tell you about this, but, Shiloh, big wind—this could be something." He traced his finger over the glyph.

"Professor!" a man shouted, running into the tunnel. He gave Shiloh and Link a side glance, then continued in French. The expression on Uncle Max's face turned grim, and his wrinkles seemed to deepen.

"I must go above ground—there has been an accident." Uncle Max snatched the lantern at his feet and followed the man.

"What about us?" Link shouted.

Uncle Max paused, his expression masked. "We will soon see."

"What is that supposed to mean?" Link muttered, glancing at Shiloh. "Did you understand anything the man said?"

"I haven't started learning French yet. But from the Latin roots of some of the words, I understood 'sea' and 'children.' It doesn't make any sense, though. We are in the middle of the desert, and we are the closest things to children. But I would hardly call being thirteen a child."

Link's face paled. "Shiloh, Mom, and Dad are on a cruise." A moment of dread passed between them. Link bolted down the tunnel, and Shiloh was right behind.

Outside, the Egyptian sun blazed mercilessly. Shiloh shielded her eyes, spotting Link leaning against a pole of one of the eight makeshift tents. Being twins, she would recognize him even in the dark. She approached slowly, fear tightening in her chest. The wind whipped around her, loosening the strand of hair from her braid again. She always liked to think the wind carried all of the places it had traveled, but this was a foreign wind to her. This was the wind of change, and she wanted to resist its pull.

Uncle Max lowered the satellite phone, his face ashen. "Your parents…there's been an accident on their ship. I don't know how to tell you this…" He trailed off, rubbing his chin.

"Are they okay?" Link asked.

Uncle Max stared off into the desert; his expressions shifting like the sands.

"They're dead, aren't they?" Shiloh whispered, the words tumbling out before she could stop them.

Uncle Max nodded, tears filling in his eyes.

"No!" Link broke into a full sprint across the sand, leaving a trail of dust in his wake.

Shiloh shot off after him, her heart pounding. He was the only person in the world that she wanted to be with. She couldn't bear to be alone.

"Wait," Uncle Max yelled. "There is—" Another gust of wind rose, cutting off his words.

Link was a black dot on the crest of a dune above, but Shiloh knew she could catch him. He was fast in short bursts, but endurance was her strength. She pushed herself harder, closing the gap.

When she reached him, Link dropped to his knees, his breath ragged, tears streaking his dusty face. Shiloh sank to the ground beside him, wrapping her arms around his shoulders.

"It's my fault." Link choked out. "All of it." Link shook his head.

"What?"

"Why we are here. Why they were on that cruise—it is all my fault."

"Link, what are you talking about?"

"Mom and Dad were only on that cruise because of me." Link punched the ground. "I stole a car, Shi."

Shiloh's stomach turned. "What? Why would you do that?"

"Justin," he spat the name.

"Really? I should have guessed."

"He said if I did it, he would give up his position as team captain, and I could have it." Link's whole body sighed. "I just wanted them all to respect me."

"Link, that's ridiculous. Why would you care what they think?"

"Not everyone can be like you! I wish I didn't care what others think, but I do."

A moment of silence passed.

"Sorry." Link shook his head. "I crashed the car, and when the cops came, all of the others ran away. I was stuck. I have never seen Dad so angry or Mom so sad. It was her disappointment that hurt me more. They were going to send me to Juvie, Shiloh. But instead, Dad worked out a deal where I would quit the team for the summer to get away from Justin, and we would be sent out here. It's like my community service. If I hadn't been so stupid, we would all be at home, and they would be alive. I killed them, Shiloh." His ragged eyes stared up at her.

"Stop," Shiloh said, her voice firm. "This isn't your fault. What happened to Mom and Dad…it's not on you. Don't blame yourself for their deaths." A sob erupted from inside Shiloh. Saying it made it real. They were dead. She would never hug her mother again or hold her father's hand. They were gone. Link pulled Shiloh in tight to his chest, and they wept together.

"What is that?" Link sniffed.

Shiloh cleared her eyes, and turned.

The sky darkened, as a shadow passed overhead. Above, birds and insects fled in a chaotic swarm away from the direction of the camp. Link and Shiloh exchanged a glance and ran to the crest of the dune. In the distance, the wind tore the camp to shreds, and behind it loomed a storm stretching as far as Shiloh could see.

"We can try to—" The wind pushed Shiloh back, and she stumbled to regain her footing.

"We will never reach them in time. We need to find shelter."

Together, they stumbled down the dune, scanning the barren landscape. Shiloh spotted a curved rock jutting out of the sand, and pulled Link toward it. They wedged themselves into the narrow alcove it formed, the wind howling around them.

"Link," Shiloh whispered, clutching his hand. "I love you."

Chapter Two

LOST DRAGONS

"Shiloh! Shiloh, wake up!"

Shiloh's eyes flickered open, revealing a blurry silhouette against the bright sky.

"Link?" Shiloh swallowed hard. Her tongue felt like sandpaper. She wheezed to clear her lungs from the dust.

"Here." Link handed Shiloh her glasses, and the world came into focus. Behind Link stretched a vast sea of sand, its dunes rolling like waves. The sand was much finer than before, and the golden hues sparkled brightly.

Shiloh swallowed hard. "Where are we?"

"I don't know." Link looked to the left and right. "Either the storm blew us farther into the desert, or it covered everything with this." He scooped up a handful of the sand and let it slip through his fingers, creating a waterfall of sparkles. "Are you hurt?"

"I don't think so." Shiloh pushed herself upright. Heat shimmered off the dunes in every direction. "We need to find shelter and water."

Link stood and helped Shiloh to her feet. Her legs wobbled as if she had just finished a 10k race.

Shiloh shielded her eyes. "We should head east. That's where the camp was."

"If there still is a camp. Did you see the way the wind tore the tents apart?"

Shiloh nodded as it was still difficult to speak.

"Which way is east?"

Shiloh looked at the sun, then motioned with her head, indicating the opposite direction. "It was around noon when the storm struck, and I don't think that it lasted for more than a couple hours. That would put the sun in the western sky."

Link agreed, and they set out.

The desert was relentless, and the heat continued to increase as the day waned. If the camp still existed, they should have reached it hours ago. It had only been one sand dune away. This confirmed Shiloh's fear: they were utterly alone.

Though her body was physically fit, the heat and dehydration caused Shiloh to fade in and out of consciousness. She chuckled to herself. At least they would be joining their parents in Heaven soon.

"What's so funny?" Link croaked.

Shiloh shook her head.

"What is that?" Link pointed up.

Above them, a black shape circled in the sky. Shiloh had watched too many Westerns with her grandfather to not recognize a vulture, circling in for a feast. She hated those birds. The way they moved always creeped her out. Not to mention that they were harbingers of death. *What a way to die.*

The bird swooped closer and closer. Shiloh squinted—either her eyes were playing tricks on her, or it wasn't a vulture. Its wingspan was massive. She had read that vultures typically had a wingspan of six feet; this one's was at least double or triple that size. The thing circled again, and Shiloh lost it in the sun.

"Where did it go?" Shiloh heard the fear in her own voice.

The sand below Shiloh trembled, and a cloud of dust rose. She turned and saw a massive shape eclipsing the sun.

"Link, am I hallucinating?"

"Stand behind me." Link moved between her and the creature. He circled to the left, keeping the sun out of their eyes. It was a smart move. He always reacted well under pressure.

Shiloh peered around Link, and a head came into view, its teeth as large as daggers. They stopped in their tracks as something tumbled off the beast's back. It rolled across the sand, stood, and ran toward them with a weapon in its hand.

Shiloh screamed reflexively, and the figure screamed back.

The creature let out a roar that shook Shiloh to her core.

"Oh, right," the figure said, stopping abruptly, "I must look terrifying." He pulled back his mask and hood, revealing a boy about their age with a cherub face. His cheeks were large, and he had little ringlets of brown hair. "See, I'm not so scary."

"We weren't afraid of you. What is that?" Shiloh pointed a quivering finger.

"That's Alithia. She's a number Four dragon. I know it is hard to tell—she shifts so often she could be confused with any of them. Except a Two. She's never been that small. Even on the day she came out, she was large. But, you know how it is with dragons. You can never tell until they come out. Anyway, what are you kids doing out here?"

"Kids?" Shiloh's pride beat out her parched throat. The boy couldn't be any older than them. "We're not kids," she said, putting on a false vibrato to hide her fear of the beast.

"Well, you can't be thirteen yet. You don't have your dragons."

"We just turned thirteen last month." Shiloh crossed her arms. "Wait, did you say drag—"

"Laka!" The boy yelled and ran for cover behind his dragon, who also pulled away.

"Ah, hello." Shiloh's eyebrows pinched together. "We aren't Laka, whatever that is. Anyway, it's us who should be afraid. You have a giant dragon."

"And I won't let you take her." The boy jumped out from behind the dragon with a staff, spinning it around clumsily. "Do you like this? I traded for it. It's real wood, and it will be the last thing you see if you try to take my dragon."

They speak the truth; they aren't Laka. I sense their dragons. A velvety female voice filled Shiloh's mind. She stiffened, glancing at Link, whose wide-eyed expression told her he'd heard it too.

"I don't know who said that, but listen to her. We aren't Laka, just travelers from a faraway land. We don't know where we are, and we'll surely die without water and shelter soon." Shiloh's voice trembled, her eyes pleaded with the stranger.

"Well, if Alithia says you're all right, you must be all right." The boy rested his staff against his shoulder. "Why don't you have dragons? Did you not go through the ceremony?"

"What ceremony?" Link asked, still eyeing the dragon cautiously.

The boy raised a hand, motioning for them to wait as he rummaged through a saddlebag on the dragon's side. Shiloh's gaze lingered on the creature, seeing it clearly for the first time.

Alithia was magnificent. Her scales shimmered and shifted colors in the sunlight—one moment they were bright and metallic, the next muted. Spikes ran down her spine, and her eyes glistened like polished jewels. She stood over twelve feet tall, her corded muscles rippling as she moved.

"Got it!" the boy shouted, hoisting a gourd of water. "Hospitality is the way of the desert."

He extended the gourd to Link, who handed it to Shiloh. The water was cool and refreshing as it slid down her throat. It was the best thing she'd ever tasted. She resisted the urge to drink it all and handed the gourd to Link.

"I'm Pendleton Shortwing of Yesod, but most people call me Pen," the boy said.

"I'm Link Jones, and this is my sister Shiloh." Link wiped his mouth.

Pen took back the gourd. "Come, let us shelter together."

Alithia stretched out one massive wing, creating a shaded alcove, and Pen led them underneath. Shiloh hesitantly entered the shade of the wing. This was a dragon! However, her fear melted away along with the heat. The temperature dropped by at least twenty degrees, and Shiloh's body sighed.

Pen plopped down and leaned against Alithia's side. He rose and fell with each breath she took. Shiloh soaked in every detail of the creature. She longed to reach out and touch her, to examine the intricate patterns of her scales and the translucent veins visible in her wing membrane. This was a real live dragon!

"Neither of you are bleeding, right?" Pen's sudden urgency startled Shiloh. She searched her body frantically for wounds.

"I don't think so," Link replied, checking himself.

"Good! That was a close one. I should have asked you that first thing."

"Why?" Shiloh's eyebrows knitted together.

"No reason." He glanced around nervously, then changed the subject. "Can you believe it, Alithia? No dragons. Everyone has a dragon."

"What do you mean, 'everyone has a dragon'?" Shiloh asked. "This is the first dragon I have ever seen."

Pen stared at her blankly as if she had just asked what a hand was.

"You're joking, right? Did you hear that, Alithia?" Pen patted the dragon, and she made a cooing noise.

"No, I'm serious. We don't have dragons where we come from."

"Don't have dragons!" Pen nearly choked on the words. "That's the most ridiculous thing I've heard. Everyone has a dragon. What would a person be without their dragon? I'll tell you what—a Laka. The walking dead. Your dragon is your essence, your being."

"Your soul?" Link said quietly.

"I don't know that word, but sure."

They do have dragons inside of them; they just don't know it. Alithia's voice rang in Shiloh's head.

"I don't know if I will ever get used to that." Shiloh exchanged a glance with Link. "Pen, what is this ceremony you spoke about?"

"You don't even know that? You must be from really far away. Imagine no dragons and no ceremony." Pen shook his head, and his brown locks tossed from side to side. "When children turn thirteen, they become adults in our society, but first they have to go through the Summoning Ceremony. In it, your dragon reveals itself to you and the world. You never know what will come out until it happens. We all thought I would be a Two like my mom, we are really close you know, but Alithia was a Four. It surprised everyone. Anyway, the Ones perform the ceremony, then depending on what class your dragon is—"

"I'm lost," Link said. "Twos, Fours, Ones, classes of dragons?"

Pen sighed. "Right, I suppose you don't even know that. What hole did you crawl out from?"

Don't be rude. Your mother taught us better than that.

Pen rolled his eyes. "There are nine classes of dragons. The class of your dragon determines what you are in society."

Alithia shifted her position, and Pen steadied himself.

"The Ones are the reformer class," Pen continued. "My dad is a One, and he always needs everything perfect. When he performed my ceremony, he said he would take away food from me for a month if I made him look ridiculous in front of the temple congregation. I was so nervous. He always makes me nervous."

The One dragons do not appear as I do. Looking into your memories, I can see that their wings are similar to what you call a dragonfly, and their tails fan out like a hummingbird's.

"Get out of my head," Link said. His words weren't unkind but were strong and forceful.

"She can't help it. All dragons are slightly telepathic, especially the Nines. Anyway, my mother, on the other hand, is a Two-class, the helper. They are kind and love to help, but they do store things inside until they burst. My mother is always holding grudges against my father. She will bring up something from weeks or years ago that we had all forgotten about. She is a baker. Twos are often healers, but my mother took another path—"

Pen stopped mid-sentence, his expression shifting as if holding a silent conversation.

"Alithia wants to know if she can communicate directly with you, or if I should speak for her. She understands that your customs are not like ours and apologizes if there was any offense."

Alithia's wing membrane darkened to a deep violet.

"Alithia, I'd like to hear directly from you," Shiloh said, her tone respectful but curious. She glanced at Link, who gave a reluctant nod.

"Fine. But don't go digging around for anything else," Link said firmly.

The dragon's wing membrane brightened, returning to shimmering gold.

Thank goodness, I don't know how we could continue otherwise. I am translating Pen's words for you.

"What do you mean?" Pen asked.

Shiloh watched Pen's lips as he spoke, and it was true, their movement didn't match the words she was hearing.

Exactly as I said, dragons don't need words to speak to each other. I am communicating the meaning of your words to their dragons, and in turn, their dragons are translating to them.

"This is amazing." Shiloh pushed her glasses further up her nose. "I want to know more. What are the Two dragons like?"

"Well, Sprout, my mom's dragon, is squat and fat," Pen said, jumping back in. "Two dragons are usually really cute with their small little wings. Other times, they look like Sprout. But don't let their size fool you. Two dragons are poisonous. That is why Twos often are healers. They are able to transmute that poison into all sorts of cures. Do you have magic where you come from?"

"Only in books," Shiloh said, dreamily.

"What's a book?" Pen tilted his head.

"You don't have books here?" Shiloh gasped.

"Nope."

"Maybe this place isn't so bad after all." Link shot Shiloh a smirk.

"Alithia, can you transmit images as well as words? I read a book once where dragons had that ability."

I can, but only with your and Pen's permission. It is forbidden for dragons to place images into the heads of others without their consent.

"You have my consent," Pen said eagerly. "I would love to know what this book thing is."

Very well, Shiloh, imagine the image you want Pen to see.

Shiloh closed her eyes and imagined a book. She flipped through the pages in her mind's eye.

"Wow, we definitely don't have anything like that here. What is it made out of?"

"Paper."

"And what's paper?"

Link leaned forward. "Paper is made out of wood, just like your staff. They chop the wood into tiny pieces, put it into water, and smash it together. Then you have paper."

"Link oversimplified the process, but that is pretty much it."

"That book must be worth a fortune. I was only able to trade for this," Pen tapped his staff, "because I happened to be in the right place at the right time with some water."

"Is wood really that scarce out here?" Shiloh asked.

Pen nodded. He held up the gourd. "But this is the most valuable thing."

"Let's get back to the magic. Do you also have magic here?" Shiloh asked, wanting to know everything about this new land.

"Yes, everyone has an extension of power from their dragon. Like the Two's healing magic. After the ceremony, and you figure out what class your dragon is, you are sent to Dragon's Claw Academy and then to one of the seven great cities in Altiniya or to the Wandering Tribes. There you are trained to connect with your dragon. The stronger your bond, the stronger your magic becomes.

Would you like to learn about the other dragons?

"Yes," Link said quickly, his eagerness catching Shiloh by surprise.

"Right," Pen took over. "Then we have the Threes; personally, they annoy me. They are always strutting about thinking they are better than everyone else. They are the most attractive and well-dressed. They usually go into politics or business. Their dragons, though, wow, are they splendid to look at. They have elongated scales that resemble feathers; they shimmer iridescent blue and green. And—"

That is quite enough about them!

"Right, sorry about that. I'm getting to the best one next." Pen winked. "The Four class. That's me. It is the artist class. As I said before, everyone thought I would be a Two. My dad wanted me to be an Eight—actually, every parent wants their kid to be an Eight—anyway,

I was as surprised as anyone, but the dragon inside you has a calling, and it knows best what your destiny will be. But, there's a secret I've been keeping."

Alithia snorted softly, and her body shimmered gold in the fading light.

Pen looked around to make sure no one was close by, which was ridiculous as there wasn't a soul around for miles. He beckoned for them to lean closer. "I think I'm part Five."

Alithia erupted in laughter, and the sand shook from her rumbling.

"What's so funny about that?" Pen pouted.

Pen, you know an Ice Dragon hasn't been born in centuries. Some think they are extinct.

"Ice dragon," Shiloh repeated, the words sparking something deep inside her.

"The Ice dragons are almost as much a legend now as Eimi himself"

Pen, be careful saying that name. The wind has a way of traveling.

"Sorry, I know."

"Tell me more about the Ice Dragons." Shiloh felt a yearning inside of her as if her soul was calling her to something greater than herself.

"The Ice Dragons are the rarest of all the dragons. Instead of blowing fire like other dragons, they blow ice, which turns into water."

More importantly than that, they are the memory keepers for our ancestors. Just as water retains memory, the Ice dragons retain the memory of our people going all the way back to the time of the Golden Phoenix Dragon, the one dragon from whom all dragons were born.

"How come you can talk about you know who and I can't?"

Because I am thinking, and you are talking. Thoughts can't travel on the wind.

"But, if another dragon was close enough?"

I would know if there was another dragon close by.

"What's that?" Link pointed to the East. On the horizon, a dust storm appeared with large shapes spaced out evenly in it.

"They found us!" Pen gasped. "Alithia, quickly."

Alithia's body shimmered and shifted, turning the color of the sand. If Shiloh hadn't seen it happen, she'd have mistaken Alithia for a massive dune.

Shiloh and Link exchanged a look. His face mirrored her own fear. What would someone with a giant dragon be afraid of?

"Who—"

Pen practically jumped the distance between them and silenced Shiloh with a hand. He placed a finger to his lips, and mouthed the words, *They'll hear us.*

FLIGHT TO THE CRYSTAL CITY

A thundering sound filled the air, louder than any helicopter. Shiloh covered her ears; she had always been more sensitive to sound than most others. The noise lasted for a few agonizing minutes before falling silent.

"Pendleton, Alithia, reveal yourselves!" A man's voice demanded.

Pen flinched.

"Pendleton," the voice boomed again, "answer your father now! I know exactly where you are."

Pen.

"I know, Alithia. Go ahead."

The dragon's scales shimmered, shifting from sand-like camouflage to a vivid cobalt blue. She lifted her wing, and Pen stepped forward, shoulders tense.

"Pendleton Shortwing," the man said, his voice as sharp as a blade, "how dare you run away from your responsibilities. You are the son of a Temple master. You will make a disgrace of yourself, your family, and your ancestors. What do you have to say for yourself?"

Shiloh pushed up from the sand and stormed out from under Alithia's wing, stepping into full view.

A tall, gaunt man stood scowling at Pen, his black goatee neatly trimmed, his posture rigid and imposing. He was flanked by five dragons, their sleek black bodies gleaming the same hues of green a raven's feathers have. Their wings, like those of dragonflies, beat so quickly they were nearly invisible, creating a low, droning hum.

"He saved us from death," Shiloh said, meeting the man's piercing gaze. "You have raised a good, kind, and brave son. He heard our call for help on the wind and came to our rescue."

"Good and kind, perhaps, but brave?" Pen's father's lip curled in disdain.

Alithia snarled, her low growl reverberating through the ground. The black dragons behind Pen's father responded in kind, their droning wings amplifying until the sound was nearly deafening. Shiloh shielded her face as the wind whipped sand into her eyes.

"It's true!" Link shouted, joining Shiloh. "Pen saved us. We would've died without him."

Pen's father raised a hand, and the black dragons fell silent, landing in unison. He raised a skeptical eyebrow at Pen.

"Perhaps the ceremony has finally made you a man," he said slowly. His gaze shifted to Shiloh and Link. "As for you…children." He pointed a long finger at Shiloh. "Where are your parents, and how did you get here?"

"They are dead," Shiloh said softly, her voice barely above a whisper.

"As to how we got here," Link added, his jaw tight, "we have no idea. The wind must have carried us."

Pen's father narrowed his eyes, studying them both. Link's fists clenched at his sides, and Shiloh squeezed his arm, silently urging him to stay calm.

"We are not children," Shiloh said, her voice firm despite the lump in her throat. "We are thirteen—adults, the same as Pen."

Pen's father's eyes darkened. His stance shifted, as though preparing to attack. A flicker of energy sparked in his outstretched hand.

"Father, stop!" Pen stepped between them. "They've been lost in the desert since they became adults. They haven't had the chance to undergo their summoning ceremony. You always preach about finding lost dragons and aiding them. This is your chance—two lost dragons in need of help."

Pen's father lowered his hand but didn't relax. "How many days have passed since your birthday?"

"It is hard to know," Shiloh said cautiously, "but I believe it has been twenty."

"There is still time," he said, his tone shifting to something almost reverent. "It hasn't been a full lunar cycle. Praise be—there is still time to save these lost dragons."

"Praise be," the other riders echoed in unison.

"Ride with my brothers," Pen's father said, motioning toward the other riders. "We must make haste."

"I would rather ride with Pen," Shiloh said.

Pen's father's cutting gaze snapped to her. "Did your parents teach you no manners?" He barked. "You never refuse a ride on another's dragon. It is the highest offense."

Shiloh faltered, glancing at Pen, who gave her a small nod.

"Come on, Shiloh." Link took her by the hand and they walked forward.

A rider helped Shiloh onto the back of a black dragon. Its scales were cool and smooth to the touch, and its wings created a steady hum that made her chest vibrate.

As the dragon took to the air, the world below disappeared in a swirl of sand and sunlight. Shiloh gripped the rider in front of her tightly, her stomach lurching as the dragon tilted and ascended. She risked a glance back and saw Pen following on Alithia, his expression unreadable.

Shiloh didn't know which made her more uncomfortable: the heights or that she was holding onto a stranger. She wasn't the touchy-feely type, even with her friends—granted most of her friends were in books. She glanced to her right, and the sea of dunes sped past. Bile rose in her throat, and her head spun.

This is just like being carsick, she told herself, recalling her mother's advice. *Focus forward and look out the front window.*

But there was no window. Instead, there was only the long black cloak of the dragon rider. He sat comfortably in a leather saddle, a blanket cushioning the seat. Beyond him, two rows of spikes trailed from the dragon's head to its tail.

The scales of the dragon rippled like a snake's, moving in perfect unison. Each scale was about the size of Shiloh's hand, and when they caught the light, the iridescent greens and blues emerged from the black.

All in all, it was exactly what Shiloh imagined a dragon would be, besides the double set of dragonfly wings. The one thing she was happy about, though, was that the roar of the wings and wind were blocked out by an invisible barrier.

Shiloh, Alithia's familiar voice rang in her head. *Pen keeps pestering me to tell you to look ahead. I know you are frightened, but don't let fear stop you from seeing the beauty in the world. Plus, I am here to catch you if you fall. I promise.*

Shiloh stole a glance over her shoulder. Pen and Alithia were right behind them and slightly below. Pen waved like a mad man and pointed forward.

Shiloh hesitated but leaned slightly to the side, peering past the rider.

Far ahead, rising from the endless desert, was a massive crystal dome. It towered hundreds of feet into the air, refracting sunlight into a dazzling display. Beneath the dome, the city sprawled outward like a sunflower. At its center was a second, smaller dome, crowned with a towering spike that reminded her of St. Paul's Cathedral.

Your brother seems to be having fun.

Shiloh stole another glance behind. Link's dragon was rolling and diving through the air, and he was laughing, his arms raised as if on a roller coaster. Shiloh felt a pang of jealousy. Link's carefree bravery often frustrated her; he never hesitated to seize the moment, while she always weighed the risks.

Alithia, can the other dragons hear our conversations?

No, Alithia replied. *They can sense that we are talking, but they can't make out the meaning.*

Relief washed over Shiloh. *That is good, There's something I have been wanting to ask. Before you told Pen to be careful because his words would travel on the wind. What did you mean by that?*

Do you remember how Pen said each dragon class has unique abilities?

Shiloh nodded, though she wasn't sure if Alithia could see her.

Ones have some control over the wind. With it, they can hear words carried across great distances. That is how Pen's father found us.

Shiloh frowned, thinking of her own world and the expanding desert. *Could they create sandstorms?*

No, it is in the One's nature to seek perfection not chaos. They protect the cities from the sand storms. They like everything to be so perfect; it drives us crazy sometimes.

What powers do Four's have?

We built what you see in front of you. Along with Alithia's words, Shiloh could feel a great sensation of pride. *We are the artists and builders.*

You can shape crystal?

Not exactly. What you see is dragon glass. Our fire, just as our emotions, burns hotter than any other dragons'. Although our flames do not shoot far, by your measuring system, we can reach temperatures of about 3,000 degrees Fahrenheit. This enables us to shape the very desert to our will. The whole world is our canvas.

That's incredible. Can you camouflage yourselves, too? Is that what happened in the desert?

Yes, we can blend into our surroundings. You may have also noticed my coloring shifting. Fours wear our emotions outwardly. Our color changes with our moods. But, look ahead. We have arrived.

Shiloh gasped as they passed through an opening in the dome. The city blossomed around them, alive with light and artistry. Buildings seemed to grow organically from the glass, their intricate designs shimmering in the sunlight.

One structure in particular caught Shiloh's eye. A towering prism sat atop its thirty-story height. When the sunlight struck it, rainbows cascaded through the building, casting vibrant hues across the city.

The dragon beneath her folded its wings and dove sharply. Shiloh's stomach lurched, as she lost her grip and slipped from the saddle. She reached desperately for anything, but all she found was air.

THE SHORTWINGS

Shiloh's heart beat furiously as the ground raced toward her. She opened her mouth to scream, but the air choked her, and the force of the wind pushed hard against her cheeks.

Shiloh placed her arms in front of her face bracing for impact. Strong talons wrapped firmly around her, and the world became a tumbling blur. Then, everything just stopped. Shiloh, Alithia, and Pen hung suspended in the air. Shiloh's braid gently brushed the ground, and the blood rushed to her head.

"Are you okay?" An upside down Link jumped off his dragon and rushed to her.

Alithia opened her talons and Link helped Shiloh to the ground. Her legs shook, and adrenalin pumped through her body, as they walked from below Alithia.

"Shiloh?"

Link's words snapped her back into the present.

"I… I think so. How?" Shiloh looked up at Pen and Alithia, who were still suspended in the air. They appeared to be halfway through a somersault, Pen levitating above Alithia's back.

"Pendleton, what were you thinking?" Mr. Shortwing clapped his hands, and the currents of air holding them dissipated, sending Pen and Alithia to the ground.

Pen stood and brushed himself off. "Well, it wasn't my worst landing." He looked bashfully at Shiloh. "I can't tell you how many times I have fallen off a dragon… I probably shouldn't have said that."

"Pendleton?"

Pen turned to his father. "We made a promise—"

"Reckless." Mr. Shortwing shook his head.

"Oh, thank the spark!" A heavy-set woman with a plump dragon perched on her shoulder burst through a door. "My little, Penny-wenny! I was so worried about you. Isn't that right, Sprout?" The pudgy dragon puffed a little swirl of smoke. The woman squished Pen's cheeks between her hands and kissed him on the forehead.

"Mom." Pen's words were muffled under the weight of his mother's hands. "Mom!" She released her grip. "I want you to meet my friends, Shiloh and Link."

"Well, look what the dragon dragged in." Pen's mom stepped back, put her hands on her hips, and looked them up and down. "Pen, well, I don't remember the last time you brought a friend—"

"Mom!" Both Pen and Alithia turned a shade of red.

Sprout, Mrs Shortwing's dragon, huffed, and a propeller—resembeling the seed pod from a helicopter tree—popped up from his back. The tiny blades spun quickly, lifting the little dragon into the air. Using his wings to navigate, he circled Shiloh and Link once, looking at them with a keen eye. Satisfied with a single pass, he returned to his perch.

"Tattered clothes, sunburns, and sand caked to every bit of you," Mrs. Shortwing said, clucking her tongue. "Let me guess—you poor children were lost in the desert. You look famished. We must get you inside, out of these clothes, and some hot food in your bellies. Alfie, why didn't you tell me we were having visitors."

"We don't have time, Beatrice. There is much work to be done." Mr. Shortwing's voice was firm. "These children are thirteen and haven't had their summoning ceremony yet. I have to get them to the Temple immediately."

"No dragons?" Mrs. Shortwing gasped, her brow furrowing. "That is serious. But so is starving, Alpheus. Why bring them here first if it's so urgent?"

"I know how worried you were about Pen. I wanted to bring him home first." Mr. Shortwing's expression softened.

"That's not fair! I want to go to the ceremony, too," Pen pleaded.

"And when did you become so interested in the Temple and ceremonies?" Mr. Shortwing looked down his sharp nose.

"Since never, but I'm interested in my new friends. I have so much to share with them. I can't wait to show them my room and what I have been working on and—"

"Pen."

"Yes, Dad. I know. Don't ramble."

Mrs. Shortwing sighed, looking the twins over once more. "They are obviously in their first month, otherwise you wouldn't have brought them back at all. How many days do they have?" Mrs. Shortwing asked.

"Not many."

"Good, then there's one to spare. Come in, come in. There's food already on the stove. You know it's no use trying to stop me, Alpheus. We have to help them."

"Thank you, Mrs. Shortwing," Link said. "I'm starving."

"Me, too," Shiloh added, her voice still shaky.

"Right this way, my dearies. Oh, I almost forgot—Alfie, they are covered in sand. Do you mind?"

Mr. Shortwing sighed heavily. Reluctantly, he placed one hand above the other, about six inches apart and spun them clockwise. A small vortex appeared; he stretched his hands, and the tornado grew bigger. When it was about a foot high, he shot it at Shiloh. The little tornado worked its way up and down Shiloh's body blowing away all of the sand. He did the same for Link.

"Perfect!" Mrs. Shortwing said. "This way."

"One minute." Shiloh unlaced her boots and poured out a mountain of sand. She pulled off her socks and shook them out as well. She had been wanting to do that ever since they landed. "I'm just going to leave these out here," she said, setting them by the door before following the others.

The Shortwings looked at the boots and socks curiously; they were definitely a contrast to their sandaled feet.

Inside, Shiloh's breath was taken away. The room was bathed in beams of light in every color, creating intricate patterns on the frosted glass walls. Shiloh extended her hand, blocking a green beam. A happy little circle appeared on her palm, altering the picture on the wall beside her.

"We do that," Pen said, beaming.

"What?" Shiloh asked, mesmerized.

"Prism Painting. Us Fours bend light through prisms to create all of this." Pen motioned to the light paintings and patterns on the frosted glass walls.

"They are beautiful. I've never seen anything like it before." Shiloh moved her hand from the green beam, and it found its home on the wall again.

"That's why Fours are the best."

The rest of the room looked like the exterior of the other structures they had passed. The walls were made of opaque frosted glass, and there was clear glass where the windows were.

"I want to show you my room." Pen grabbed Shiloh and Link by the hands and pulled them to the stairs.

"Not so fast, young man. We have to get some food in them first. This way." Mrs. Shortwing disappeared down a long hallway.

"Fine," Pen said. "Let's go."

The kitchen was constructed like the rest of the house with the cabinets and table made of the frosted glass. The center piece of the room was an old black potbelly stove with embers burning bright red. A glass kettle whistled on the stove, and a large glass pot bubbled softly, sending a spicy scent into the air.

"So you do have metal here," Link said.

"Some," Pen said, sliding into a seat at the glass table. "But you have to trade with the Sevens for it." He beckoned for Shiloh and Link to join him.

"Surely you know that?" Mrs. Shortwing raised a spoon. "Did you hit your head in the desert? Sprout and I can take a look at that later." Mrs. Shortwing looked at the stove. "Sprout, do you mind?"

The small dragon propellered himself off Mrs. Shortwing's shoulder and belched a fireball into the stove. Satisfied with the heat, he returned to his perch.

"Does Sprout ever get heavy on your shoulder?" Shiloh had wanted to ask that question ever since she first saw the small plump dragon.

"Sprout, no, he is mostly made of Hydrogen. He is light as a feather. If he didn't grip on, he might just float away."

Everyone laughed and Mrs. Shortwing returned to the pot.

"Pen, would you be a dear and hand me some cactus root from the counter."

Pen followed orders and handed his mom some strange translucent tubers.

"Do these grow in the desert?" Shiloh asked.

"You're lucky if you can find it," Mrs. Shortwing replied. "It is getting harder and harder to scavenge for food these days. This all came from the city garden. Pen will have to take you there—it's beautiful. Which of the seven cities did you come from, dear?"

"They're from the Wandering Tribes," Pen said abruptly. "They got lost in a sand storm and separated from them."

Mr. Shortwing eyed Shiloh and Link suspiciously. "Pen, you must have so many questions for them. I know you always admired the Sevens."

Pen's brow beaded with sweat.

"Where is Alithia?" Shiloh interrupted. "And, I'm sorry, Mr Shortwing, I didn't catch the name of your dragon."

Mr. Shortwing opened his mouth, but Pen got there first. "Dad's dragon is named Onyx. They both have their lairs out back."

"Yes, I suppose you wouldn't know that, being from the Wandering Tribes." Mr. Shortwing stroked his goatee. "Tell me, do you sleep under the stars?"

"I heard Seven Dragons' wings are so big that they could create a tent that ten people could sleep in," Pen said, eagerly.

"I want to hear it from them, not you, Pen." Mr. Shortwing's focus remained on Shiloh, his tone challenging. "And your hair color—did you have a scare as a child? In this part of the world only the elderly have that shade."

Shiloh blinked, realizing for the first time that her blond hair stood out starkly from the brown and black hair they had seen.

"We call them teepees," Link said evenly.

Mr. Shortwing turned his steely gaze to Link, who returned it in kind.

"Seven Dragons can fold their wings up into a cone shape, and we all rest easily inside. As for her hair, the fright from the storm must have turned it that color."

Shiloh was about to correct him when Link kicked her under the table.

"And, where do you get your water?" Mr. Shortwing asked, continuing to stare.

"Alpheus! Why I never! Where are your manners?" Mrs. Shortwing brandished a spoon from the stove. "You are worse than Pen with all of your questions. Now let's put a stop to this and eat. Pen, will you help me? Take these."

Pen went to the counter and helped Mrs. Shortwing move the plates to the table.

Shiloh cut a piece of the milky tuber on the glass plate, and it oozed a clear liquid. She looked at Link, and he shrugged. He stabbed his and took a large bite. As he chewed, his expression changed from one of disdain to delight.

Shiloh tentatively followed his example. The texture reminded her of aloe jelly, but the flavor was slightly floral. As she swallowed, the moisture spread through her body, quenching her thirst in a way water never had.

"This is amazing," she said, taking another bite. "My thirst is gone."

"Well, that's Sprouts doing." Mrs. Shortwing scratched the little dragon under the chin, and he puffed a little ball of smoke. "I transmuted a little of his poison—"

Link spat out his food. "Poison?"

"Transmuted means changed, Link." Shiloh put a reassuring hand on his shoulder.

Mr. Shortwing slammed his napkin onto the table. "I have never seen such rudeness. I will retire for the evening. There is much to prepare for tomorrow's ceremony. The sooner you have your dragons, the sooner you will be on your way, and we can have order in this house."

"Alpheus Shortwing!" Mrs. Shortwing snapped with an incredulous look on her face. "Now *that* was rude. I agree; I think it is best that you retire. Perhaps that desert sun got to you as well."

With a huff, Mr. Shortwing stormed out of the room and disappeared down the hallway.

Mrs. Shortwing sighed and turned back to Shiloh and Link. "You must excuse, Mr. Shortwing; he is under a lot of stress. The capital is threatening to shut down all the temples. If it wasn't for the Summoning Ceremony, I think they would have already shut them down. Still, though, that is no excuse for his behavior. All done, deary?"

Shiloh nodded. The only thing left on her plate was a layer of clear ooze. Mrs. Shortwing took Shiloh's plate and held it up to Sprout. The small dragon blew little fireballs at the plate until all of the ooze evaporated. She repeated the process with each of the plates, and Pen stacked them on the counter.

"Now, will you go light the way for our guests?" Mrs. Shortwing nudged the dragon from her shoulder. His propeller extended, and he flew to the hallway that Mr. Shortwing had disappeared down. He turned to face the table and caught Shiloh's eye. A large, toothy grin crossed his face, and he farted a little fireball that lit a candle held in a sconce on the wall.

"Sprout!" Mrs. Shortwing let out, turning red. "Not in front of our visitors." She put her head in her hands and shook it.

The small dragon merrily propellered down the hall, paying no attention, and the sound of farting fireballs echoed behind him.

"What a dinner. What a dinner." Mrs. Shortwing shook her head again. "Pen, why don't you show our guests to their room. Oh, I almost forgot. Let me see that sunburn."

The skin on Shiloh's arms pulled tightly as she extended them. Since they arrived, the burn had worsened. Her forearms were now a deep shade of red bordering on purple.

"This is worse than I thought, but no matter." Mrs. Shortwing placed both hands around Shiloh's arm. At first, the heat increased, then it was as if a cool balm was spread over her arm. "Now the other one." Shiloh extended her other arm, and Mrs. Shortwing repeated the process. Within seconds, the sunburn on both arms magically turned into a golden tan, and the pain was gone.

"Thank you." Shiloh brushed her arms, not believing what she was seeing and feeling.

"You're welcome, deary. Now the two of you follow Pen up to your room," Mrs. Shortwing said, finishing up Link's arms.

Pen led them down the hallway lit by flickering candles, their light refracted through prisms to cast rainbows on the frosted glass walls. It felt like walking through a cascade of colors.

The guest room, like the rest of the house, was made of glass. Two beds with silk-covered mattresses stood against the walls. The curtains in the room also appeared to be made of silk. On the nightstand, a lonely lantern burned, once again casting little rainbows of light on the wall behind it.

"Thank you, Pen," Shiloh said, "You and your family have been so kind to us."

"Yeah, thanks," Link clapped Pen on the shoulder.

"You're welcome. My mother always taught me hospitality is the way of the desert." Pen shut the door behind him and leaned in conspiritorily. "But, before I take you out into public tomorrow, there are a few things you should know."

Pen motioned to the bed for them to sit, settling himself on the floor with a pillow in the center. The silk was smooth and cool under Shiloh's fingertips, and the bed formed perfectly to her body. Her eyelids drooped heavily, but she willed herself to stay awake. She wanted to learn everything about this world, especially if their survival depended on it. Across from her, Link sat with his arms crossed; his forehead furrowed.

"What are these made of?" Link asked, patting the mattress.

"Sand of course, what else? Or do you mean the silk… There is so much. I think we can get away with you being from the Wandering Tribes… I don't think my dad fully bought it…"

"Pen, focus. What do we need to know?"

"I don't know where to start." Pen grimaced.

"Well, to start off, where are we?" Link asked. "I think you said it was Altiniya."

"Yep, that's the name of this world," Pen answered. "I'm guessing at this point that you aren't from this world, are you?"

"No," Shiloh said. "We come from a place called Earth. Tell us more about Altiniya." She pushed up her glasses and leaned forward.

"Well," Pen took a pillow from the bed and placed it in the center of the floor, "this is Tiphareth. It is where Dragon's Claw Academy is. Around it are seven cities." Pen placed other objects around the pillow. "We are here in the southernmost city, and below us is the trading post. Beyond that is the outer reach and the deep desert. That is where the Sevens live. They have become known as the Wandering Tribes."

"That is where you said we are from. I want to know more." Shiloh leaned in even further.

Pen nodded. "Each of the cities is governed by the capital because they control the flow of water. But the Sevens are free from the capital's reach. They have a way of producing their own water."

"How?" Link asked.

Pen shrugged. "Nobody knows for sure. Some people think that because the Seven Dragons can fly farther than any other dragons they discovered a lush land to the south where they get their water. Others believe they are able to pull water from thin air. Most people have never met a Seven after they've graduated from Dragon's Claw, but all know that they are loyal to…" Pen glanced around as if checking for eavesdroppers. "…to Eimi."

Shiloh lowered her voice. "Who is Eimi?"

"Eimi," Pen whispered, "is the Great Golden Phoenix Dragon, the source of all dragons. It's believed that every dragon is sparked from Eimi's flame, and that a fragment of Eimi's essence lives inside each of us."

Shiloh moved off the bed to join Pen on the floor. "So, the summoning ceremony…"

Pen nodded. "During the ceremony, the Ones call down the Holy Wind to fan the flame inside you and awaken your dragon."

"That's incredible!" Link said, his voice breaking into a grin. "You mean I can have my own dragon? That is awesome!"

"Shhhh, not too loud." Pen looked at the door.

"If we are supposed to be from the Wandering Tribes," Shiloh whispered, "where the Sevens are, we need to know more about Eimi."

Pen hesitated, looking conflicted.

"Come on," Link said, joining them on the floor with a pillow. "Why do you have to be so secretive about Eimi?" Link elongated the last vowel.

"Because it's illegal to even speak Eimi's name outside of the Summoning Ceremony—rules from the capital. Most people nowadays think that it is all a myth, but not the Sevens—they are all loyal—and people like our family. I probably shouldn't have told you that. Promise you won't tell anyone."

"We promise, Pen. Tell us more." Shiloh said.

"And you?" Pen shot a desperate look at Link.

"Yes, I promise."

"It is said that there was a time when Eimi walked amongst us and the land was covered with trees and other living things. More importantly, there was water everywhere, and people had more than they could ever ask for. Then the Great Fall happened… But, it is said, Eimi will come again and restore the land."

"What was the Great Fall?" Shiloh asked.

"No one knows for sure," Pen replied, lowering his voice even further. "When the Fives disappeared, they took the truth with them. Besides being Ice Dragons, Fives were also the memory keepers as water is able to store memory. But they are lost now, too. There hasn't been an Ice Dragon in over a thousand years. Every now and then there will be a Six or a Four that has been touched by frost, but they are carted off to the capital by the Sixes right after their ceremony, never to be seen again."

Shiloh and Link exchanged a glance.

"Is there anything else we need to know about being Sevens or the ceremony?" Shiloh asked.

"Not really, you just kind of stand there, and my dad shoots a big gust of wind at you."

"We don't need to say any words or anything like that?"

"Just answer 'yes' to his questions, and you should be fine."

Link raised an eyebrow. "That's it? No fancy chants or rituals?"

"Nope." Pen shook his head.

"So," Link said after a long pause. "What were you doing so deep in the desert? I know you didn't hear us on the wind, whatever that is." Link leaned against the bed and put his arms behind his head.

Pen looked down, his cheeks reddening. "I was running away."

"You rebel." Link shot up again. "Now this is getting interesting."

"Pen, why would you run away? Your parents love you, and you love them." Shiloh's chest tightened. She would give anything for one more day with her parents. Emotions swirled inside of her.

"It wasn't because of them; it was because of Alithia's calling. Our destiny lies with the Sevens in the desert, not at Dragon's Claw Academy.

I'm supposed to leave next month with all of the other thirteen-year-olds to Old Dragon's Claw, the most prestigious Dragoning school. My father had to pull some strings to get me in there, but you can't ignore your dragon's calling."

"What is a calling?" Shiloh asked.

"Every dragon has a calling… Maybe Alithia can explain it better. Alithia, are you awake?"

I'm here Pen.

"Will you explain what a calling is?"

Every dragon has a calling—a deep feeling or intuition that will lead you to your life's purpose. Sometimes this feeling can be as small as a grain of sand, or it can be as powerful as a sand storm. You as a rider have a choice: you can listen to this calling or ignore it. To listen to it is to step into your destiny; to ignore it is to miss out on a life that should have been.

Shiloh nodded slowly, absorbing the words. "If that is the case, why would anyone ever ignore it?"

Alithia's voice softened. *Have you ever heard a voice inside of you that you didn't listen to?*

"I have." The words tumbled out of Link's mouth as he pulled in his knees tightly.

"Link, it wasn't your fault." Shiloh reached for him, but he pulled away.

"I heard it loud and clear: 'Don't steal the car.' But I didn't listen; I did it anyway, and look where we ended up: orphans in a strange world."

"Link—"

Link's stare shot through Pen, silencing him.

The air in the room grew thick. Shiloh wanted to comfort her brother, but she didn't know how. She wished she had a book on grief. Reading was her answer to everything. Emotions were foreign to her sometimes. But, books had the answers—they always knew what to do.

"I think I should go to bed," Pen said softly. "We will need to go to the market first thing tomorrow to get you some clothes for the ceremony. Good night, don't let the sandflies bite!"

Pen shut the door behind him, leaving Shiloh and Link alone in the softly lit room.

Chapter Five

BREAKFAST AT THE SHORTWINGS

"Shiloh… Shiloh… We should go."

Through the haze of sleep, Shiloh blinked up at Link bending over her. His voice was urgent but hushed.

"Link," she mumbled, stretching until her muscles felt their length, "I had the strangest dream. We were in this storm, and it took us to—"

"It wasn't a dream."

Shiloh brushed the table searching for her glasses. The world came into focus, revealing the frosted glass walls and silken sheets. Morning light streamed into the room and the refracted colors danced on the walls.

"This is real?" Her voice trembled. "And mom and dad?"

Link nodded, his lips pressed into a thin line.

"Come on," he said softly. "Let's go."

"Go where?" Shiloh pushed herself up and rubbed her face. "We are in a strange land with untold dangers—Pen and his family have been kind to us. I think we should stay."

Link's eyes darted toward the door and back to her. "I just… I have a feeling that something bad will happen if we don't leave now."

His eyes pleaded, and after a moment, Shiloh reluctantly nodded.

They dressed quickly, and together they crept to the door. Link turned the knob slowly, careful not to make any sound.

"Ahhhh!" Link yelped, startling Shiloh so badly that her stomach flipped.

On the other side of the door was Sprout, Mrs. Shortwing's dragon. He hovered at eye level with his little propeller wings spinning furiously. He gave Shiloh and Link his toothy grin, turned, and led them down the hallway.

In the kitchen, Mrs. Shortwing was already cooking up a storm. Bowls lined the counter in a haphazard way. She hummed merrily, as she stirred a pot on the stove. The smell of cinnamon and the sound of Pen chopping filled the air.

"Good morning, good morning!" Mrs. Shortwing sang, without turning from her pot.

"You're awake!" Pen's voice brimmed with excitement as he glanced over his shoulder. "I've been so excited for today, I barely slept. I have never seen someone sleep so late. You know how it is in the desert, wake up before the sun, then afternoon nap—my favorite part of the day."

"Pen, pay attention." Mrs. Shortwing shot him a side glance. "Otherwise you'll cut yourself again."

"Yes, Mom."

Sprout hovered in front of Shiloh and Link, looking both of them in the eyes before guiding them to the table. Seeing his job was done, the little dragon floated across the kitchen and perched on Mrs. Shortwing's shoulder.

"You're just in time," Mrs. Shortwing said. "Breakfast is ready. Pen, hand me those bowls."

Pen did as he was instructed, and Mrs. Shortwing dolloped a healthy portion into each bowl before handing them back to Pen to add whatever it was he had been cutting.

"I think you will really like this; it's called oatmeal," Pen said, handing them their bowls.

Shiloh blinked in surprise. "You have oatmeal here?"

The smell of cinnamon and oats tugged at memories buried deep in her chest. Oatmeal was her favorite breakfast, especially during cross-country training. She'd eaten it nearly every morning, the comforting scent of it filling the kitchen while her mother hummed along to the radio. Tears stung her eyes, and before she could stop them, they rolled down her cheeks.

"Are you okay?" Pen wore a concerned puppy dog expression.

"Yes." Shiloh cleared her face. "This just… reminds me of home."

"There, there, deary." Mrs. Shortwing swept over and draped an arm over Shiloh's shoulders, pulling her into a firm embrace. Her ample bosom pressed into Shiloh, making it a little hard for her to breathe. "You can call this place home for the time being. And I'm sure once you have your dragons, you will be able to find your people again."

"I will help you," Pen said, his voice bright with confidence. "I know this part of the desert like the back of my hand."

"Now, let's not exaggerate, Pen. But, speaking of help—" Mrs. Shortwing released Shiloh and returned to the counter, retrieving a glass container roughly the size of a large water bottle. "This liter of water should be enough to get you what you need for the ceremony at the market."

Mrs. Shortwing handed Pen the bottle. "Make sure you don't spill any. You know how tight things are. Also, take this and see what Stix can do with it." Mrs. Shortwing handed Pen a silk garment.

"Mom, this is my ceremonial outfit."

"And you will never wear it again. I'm sure if Stix takes it in, Link will look mighty fine in it."

"Thank you, Mrs. Shortwing." Link said.

"You're welcome, deary. Hospitality is the way of the desert. Pen, give me a hand with these dishes."

Pen gathered the empty bowls and carried them to his mother, who began cleaning with Sprout's help. The little dragon blew small bursts of fire at the dishes, making the room smell like burnt oatmeal cookies.

The scent hit Shiloh like a wave, triggering a thousand memories of home. She felt another small tear roll down her cheek.

Link grabbed Shiloh's hand under the table. "We will find our way back home again," he whispered. "I promise you."

Chapter Six

DRAGON SILK

"Hello, my name is Pen, and I will be your tour guide today. Welcome to Yesod," Pen said, ushering Shiloh and Link outside. He spread his arms wide and flashed them a proud smile.

Shiloh blinked against the morning light, and her eyes drank up the city. She had been too overwhelmed and shaken yesterday to take in the surrounding splendor. The street, like the rest of the ground, was entirely made of frosted glass and as wide as a semi-truck is long. It stretched ahead and dead-ended at a structure resembling a massive greenhouse. Rising behind it was a geodesic dome that extended another two hundred feet into the sky, mirroring the dome encasing the entire city. Jutting from its top, a spire, increased its height by another fifty feet. Shiloh could make out different dragons flying to and fro around it, but they were too far away to see what types they were.

On either side of the street, houses like Pen's lined the way, each resembling a blend of a home and a greenhouse. They were two stories high, made of both frosted and clear glass. The frosted sections replaced what might have been ironwork in Earth's greenhouses, while the clear glass formed large windows spanning from floor to ceiling. The first floor stood about ten feet high, and the second consisted of one or two domes. On each rooftop sat a prism that split sunlight into a rainbow of colors, casting them into the homes below.

"That is the Temple," Pen said, noticing Shiloh's gaze down the street. "It's the center of Yesod, all roads lead there. It's the greatest temple in all of Altiniya because Yesod is the city of the Ones."

"The city of the Ones?" Shiloh asked, turning her full attention to him.

"Each city in Altiniya is said to hold the essence of one dragon class. Yesod, which means 'foundation,' is the city of the Ones, as the foundation of our society is based on the Religion of the Eternal Flame, although, as I said last night…" Pen trailed off, shrugging. "All that is left of it these days is the summoning ceremony, and the Ones are the only people who can perform it. Most people don't care about the rest anymore—at least that is what my father says."

"What about the other cities?" Link asked abruptly. "Will you explain more about them? I didn't quite get all of it last night."

Shiloh could tell by the look in Link's eyes that he was up to something.

"I wish I had some sand to draw in."

"You can use these." Link reached into his pocket and handed Pen some coins.

"What are these?" Pen marveled at the small metal disks in his hand.

"Don't worry about what they are in our world. Here they are just something for you to make a map with."

Shiloh frowned at Link's tone. "Pen, we call those coins. We use them for exchange like you do with water. I'd love to see a map as well." She shot her brother a cutting glance, and he sighed, stepping back.

"Coins." Pen rolled the word around in his mouth, holding one up. "I like that word. Who's this on here and how is it made?" He pointed to the small image on the Egyptian pound coin.

"That is Pharaoh Tutankhamun," Shiloh said.

Pen squinted at the coin. "He looks like Abaddon—not that I have ever seen him before—but there are statues of him everywhere."

"Who is Abaddon?" Shiloh asked.

Pen gave Shiloh a blank stare. "Right, you didn't even know about dragons so why would you know about Lord Abaddon the Immortal." He shook his head and his locks went to and fro. "Lord Abaddon is the ruler of all of Altiniya, well at least since the Great Fall. He was the one who instructed the Fours to build this." Pen pointed up to the giant dome that covered the city. "Everyone says if it weren't for him, we all would have died and been swallowed by the desert. People call him the savior, but there is only one true savior—at least, that is what my father says."

"Who is the one true savior? Is it Em—"

Pen covered Shiloh's mouth and put his finger to his lips.

"You will find out more about that in the ceremony."

"Can we get back to the map?" Link crossed his arms. "I don't think we went over all of it last night."

Shiloh didn't know why Link was so insistent on going over the map again. She had it memorized from last night.

"Right, right." Pen knelt down and positioned the coins. He laid out three in a column on the right side, two in the center, and three on the left. The center column was slightly lower than the other two. He pointed to the lowest coin in the middle. "This is Yesod, we are here, the city of the Ones. Above that," he pointed to the next coin up, "is Tiphareth, which means beauty, it is obviously the city of the Fours. It is said to be the most beautiful place in existence. It is also where Dragon's Claw Academy is. After the dragon summoning ceremony, all thirteen-year-olds must go there for a year to train with their dragon. Then you go to your respective city for an apprenticeship."

"That's what you were running away from, right?"

"Link!" Shiloh snapped.

"No, he's right." Pen's shoulders slumped. "I was running away to find the Sevens. Alithia had a calling, and I wanted to be free like them, imagine, free on the open dunes." Pen's eyes coated with a dream.

"Where exactly do the Sevens live?" Link asked.

"No one knows," Pen admitted. "That's why they are called the Wandering Tribes. Some say they just travel in the open desert in camps; others say that they have found something beyond the reach of other dragons to the South of the great desert." Pen pointed to the area below the coin that represented Yesod. "Sevens can fly for days without tiring, unlike the rest of us. It is also said that they can create their own water. Imagine that." Pen held up his canteen. "This is what keeps the rest of us trapped here. We all rely on the capital and King Abaddon for our water. But, I told you all of that last night."

"So that is where you found us? In the great desert to the south?" Link asked.

Pen nodded.

"Where is the capital?" Link leaned in.

Pen pointed to the first coin in the left column. "Hod is here. Literally translated it means majesty. Above that is Geburah, which means power. It is the home of the army and the Sixes. The farthest north is Binah, which means understanding, this is where the Nines farm. It isn't so much a city as vast fields. They provide all of the supplementary food for the kingdom."

"Does each city have a shield like this?" Shiloh pointed up at the clear dome encasing the city.

"Yes, we wouldn't survive without it. It helps us retain what moisture we have and also protects us from the sand storms, and the dragon glass ground protects us from… well, other things."

Shiloh raised her eyebrows. "Other things?"

"What are these two cities?" Link interrupted, pointing to the coins on the far right.

"Those are Netzach and Chesed," Pen said, "Netzach is where the senate is, and most of the Threes can be found there; it translates to Victory. Chesed means Mercy, and it is where the healers are. Being a Two, my mom spent her apprenticeship there."

"So you don't have to stay in a city after your apprenticeship?" Shiloh asked.

"No, you can go where you please. Some even try to join the Sevens, but they are never heard from again."

"What is the top coin above Chesed? Did I say that right?" Shiloh asked.

"You had excellent pronunciation!" Pen flashed her a smile, and his cheeks turned rosy. "Chokmah is where the Fives used to be before they disappeared. It means Wisdom."

A silence fell over them, and everything was too still in the city with no wind.

Shiloh pulled at the collar of her khaki shirt. She wanted the silence to end so she asked, "What is that surrounding the Temple?"

"That's the track. It circles the entire city center; it's where our food is grown. The whole city is shaped like a Nine dragon eating its own tail, with nine major roads like this one leading straight to the Temple."

"So it's like a wheel with spokes?" Link said.

"I don't know what a wheel is, but sure."

"You don't know what a wheel is? How do you transport things to places?" Shiloh raised an eyebrow and exchanged a look of disbelief with Link.

"Dragons, of course, or you could hire a teleporter, though those are rare in the cities."

A dark shadow passed overhead, and the ground reverberated as Alithia landed. Today her leathery skin was white, but Shiloh could tell all the same that she was Pen's dragon. Alithia licked the back of her claw with a long forked tongue and brushed her face lightly.

"Good morning, sleepy head. I see you got dressed up for today's occasion." Pen wrapped his arms around Alithia's hind leg. His fingers nearly touched, but not quite. The dragon made a small cooing noise and folded her wings back. "Now that we are all here, let's get to the market before it gets too busy."

Pen led Shiloh and Link down the main street, the Temple growing ever larger on the horizon. Every ten houses, side streets branched off, each identical to the last.

"It all looks the same," Link said. "How can you find your way around?"

"I know." Pen sighed. "It drives us crazy, but Ones love order. Everything has to be neat and in its place, even the houses and streets. I heard that in Tiphareth, the city of the Fours, there isn't a straight street. It's filled with little alleys and all sorts of exciting things. Here there is nothing exciting, just straight lines."

"I think it is one of the most beautiful places I have ever seen." Shiloh pushed her glasses up her nose and ran her fingers across the frosted glass of a house, marveling at its smooth texture.

"If you think this is beautiful, just wait until you see the market. It is the only place to find some life and anything to do in this place."

Pen took a sharp left, leading them to the bustling square that opened up from the narrow streets. Frosted glass carts, colorful stalls, and a cacophony of sound filled the space. Larger dragons perched on rooftops, resembling living gargoyles, their wings twitching occasionally as if they were itching to fly. Smaller dragons flitted from stall to stall, some perched on their riders' shoulders.

Shiloh's eyes locked on one particular dragon perched on a far wall. It had a long, slender neck and a short, beak-like snout, its shimmering scales reflecting sunlight like blue sapphires and green emeralds. Its tail opened into a fan resembling a peacock's feathers, scattering dazzling patterns of light onto the wall and ground. Its whole body seemed to dance in the sunlight.

"There they go," Pen muttered, rolling his eyes. "Three dragons, always showing off."

"I have never seen anything like it," Shiloh said, dreamily.

"Well, there's plenty more where she came from, always strutting about."

Alithia, watching from the corner of her eye, shifted her scales to mimic the Three dragon's colors.

"You are just as beautiful as well, Alithia." Shiloh reached out and patted Alithia's leg. The dragon's smooth scales shifted like plate armor under her touch.

In the square, each vendor shouted louder than the next, and dragons' claws clattered on the glass as they went to and fro. Little Two dragons sat perched on their riders' shoulders. Some had wings and propellers like Sprout, others short little stubby wings. However, as they passed, the sound died down and was replaced with stares.

"Stix! Hey, Stix!" Pen waved frantically.

A girl about their age with dark skin and kinky hair looked up from her booth. She waved back with a wide smile.

"That's Stix, she's my cousin," Pen said.

Stix's booth was filled with silk garments and blankets. All were expertly woven, and the colors popped like a field full of flowers.

"Hey, cuz, I want you to meet my friends, Link and Shiloh," Pen said.

Stix raised an eyebrow.

"I found them in the desert…"

"Welcome, friends." Stix's eyes lingered on Shiloh and Link as if she were studying every detail. "Your hair is beautiful; it is like the many sands of the dunes. May I touch it?"

Shiloh hesitated but nodded, pulling her braid over her shoulder.

Stix ran her fingers lightly over the tip. "It's as fine as dragon silk. Maybe she is a Nine like me."

"Maybe," Pen said. "We'll find out at their dragon summoning ceremony this afternoon. That's why we're here. We need to get them some proper clothes."

Stix shifted her attention to Shiloh's shirt, thumbing the fabric. "What sort of material is this?"

"It's Khaki," Shiloh said, a little uncomfortable at the touch.

"Is that necessary?" Link asked, reading her expression.

"Peace be with you, brother. It is necessary for one who needs to know what the very fabric of the world is made of." Stix shifted her focus to Link and stared intently at his face. "Your eyes, they hold the sky. How is this possible?"

"I don't know," Pen said. "But I do know that they need some new clothes. Will you help us? I have water." Pen held up his canteen.

"Of course." Stix smiled. "You are blood of my blood."

"Good. Mom said to give you this for Link." Pen handed Stix his ceremonial outfit but was reluctant to let go. After a few tugs, Stix pried it from his hands.

She held out the garment and peeked her head from behind it. "We will definitely need to take this in."

"Hey." Pen sucked in his gut and puffed out his chest.

"Pen, I am just stating a fact. You are handsome the way you are. You have the kindest heart of anyone I have ever met, and it shines through, right down to this glossy hair." Stix pulled one of Pen's ringlet curls, and it bounced back.

"She's right, Pen, I have met a lot of people who look beautiful on the outside but inside they are cold and empty. What is important is what is in here." Shiloh touched Pen's heart and he looked everywhere except at her.

"Axel, I need you to take a measurement," Stix said.

From below the counter came the clicking of claws on the frosted glass followed by a dragon's head and a long spiked neck. The neck continued and two front legs appeared. A moment later the back legs then the tail. On the whole, the dragon looked like an eighteen-foot boa constrictor with legs and spikes. The dragon glanced from Link to Shiloh.

"Not her, him," Stix said.

In a flash, the dragon was on Link wrapping itself around his waist.

"Get it off! Get it off!" Link yelled, his voice raising panic.

The marketplace fell silent as all eyes turned to them.

"Get it off! Get it off!" Pen repeated and started to dance around like a madman. When all eyes were on him he said, "What? Haven't you heard of the get it off dance? You are so behind the times." Slowly, the onlookers returned to their business.

"I do not understand," Stix said, nodding for Axel to return. The dragon leapt from Link and rested on the counter.

"They aren't from around here," Pen said. " I don't think they have ever had a measurement before."

"I have," Shiloh said, "but not by a dragon."

"Well, you will be next. Axel." The dragon looked at Stix and hesitated. "It will be fine." She patted Axel on the head.

Axel wrapped himself around Shiloh's waist and hugged tightly. The pressure was what Shiloh expected but not the weight. Despite his size, Axel was the weight of a tissue box.

May I wrap around your neck, Madam? I don't want you to make a spectacle like your brother did, a proper British accent filled Shiloh's head. If Shiloh were to imagine the person connected to that voice, it would be an old British Lord with a monocle, wearing a tuxedo, not the dragon wrapped around her.

Shiloh nodded, repressing a giggle as she thought of the dragon wearing a monocle.

The dragon's tail glided up Shiloh's body and wrapped itself around her neck. Axel's scales were cool and smooth to the touch. It reminded Shiloh of a snake she once held in her fourth-grade science class. Axel released his grip and looped his tail around her arm at the shoulder joint then dropped the top portion of his body to the ground.

I have to get your inseam now.

"Okay," Shiloh said.

Axel unlatched from her arm and his tail touched the inside of her thigh.

Thank you, Madam. One last question, what is your favorite color?"

"It may sound strange, but my favorite color is pearl."

Not strange at all, especially in this hot environment. This shan't take but a moment. Axel's claws clittered and clattered on the frosted glass as he scurried back to the booth. He climbed up onto the counter and rolled the bottom half of his body into a circle with his tail at his front paws. A white substance came out of his tail and his paws moved furiously.

"What is he doing?" Link asked.

"He's spinning dragon silk," Pen said, in a hushed voice. "All of our clothes are made from it. If it wasn't for dragon silk, we would all be naked, imagine that."

"I would rather not," Link said, crossing his arms.

Stix took the silk and wove it in the air. Her hands moved almost as quickly as Axel's paws, and garments began to take shape. The white silk pants were the first to form; they shimmered in the sunlight and had the same iridescent quality as a pearl.

"That is amazing." Shiloh couldn't take her eyes off the process.

"The coolest part is that when two people and a Nine touch dragon silk, you can actually feel what the other person is feeling. It is how we settle many minor disputes," Pen said.

"No way," Link let out.

"Would you like to try?" Stix held out a strand of dragon silk.

Link looked at it suspiciously for a moment and took it. His body tensed, then slowly relaxed. His eyes became distant and filled with peace.

"I see," Stix said. "You are so angry and afraid, that is why you lash out at people."

Link threw the strand on the table and walked away.

"Link," Shiloh called.

"He will be back," Stix said. "He loves you too much to leave you. Come, you can put these on in the back of my stall."

Shiloh took the garments from Stix and drew a curtain separating her from the others. The silk was cool and smooth in her hands. She understood why people use the term silky for things, but none of the silky things she had ever touched compared to this. The pants were billowy, and the top wrapped around her. It reminded her of a cross between an Indian Sari and a Bedouin outfit.

When Shiloh came out from behind the curtain, Link had reappeared. He smiled gently as their eyes met.

"Wow! You look..." Pen said, his cheeks blushing again.

"Now it is your turn." Stix handed Link his garments.

"Thank you... I wish I had the peace you do."

"Give it time." Stix patted his hand.

A gong sounded through the square ten times, followed by a reverberating note that made Shiloh's insides shake.

"Fiery fart balls!" Pen said. "Is that the time?"

"The singing bowls are never wrong," Stix said.

"We have to go; we are already late. Stix, how much do we owe you?"

"Pen, you are family and I know—"

"Never mind about that. Fine, we have to go, but I will pay you later. I have the water."

"What do you think?" Link said, reappearing.

In the time that Pen and Stix were going back and forth, Link had changed into his new outfit. His pants billowed just as Shiloh's and the shirt had a mandarin cut. The whole thing was ruby red and had an almost metallic gleam to it.

"You look great," Pen said. "Now let's go."

9
8
1
7
2
6
3
5
4

Chapter Seven

THE SUMMONING CEREMONY

A rush of humidity and an earthen smell met Shiloh as she stepped into the greenhouse encircling the temple. She inhaled deeply, and her lungs were revived by the oxygen-rich air. The latticework of frosted glass crisscrossed and arched fifty feet in the air, leaving space for dragons to fly between it and the tallest trees.

A cluster of bananas hung ten feet over Shiloh's head, and to her right, a massive banyan tree spread its gray roots, diving in and out of the ground. Shiloh crouched to touch the soil. Its familiar texture stirred up a mixture of emotions and memories.

"Come on," Pen urged. "We don't have time—my dad will be so disappointed if we're late."

Shiloh brushed her hands together, and they rushed through a maze of trails that seemed to go on for miles, until they reached a massive archway rising clear up to the top of the greenhouse.

On the other side of the arch, the geodesic dome rose five times higher than the greenhouse and spanned the width of two football fields. Carved into the floor was a giant circular symbol with the numbers one to nine on its circumference. The numbers were connected by lines to one another. Nine was connected to three and six. One was connected to four and seven. Two was connected to eight and four. Three to six and nine, four to one and two, five to seven and eight, six to nine and three, and seven to five and one. Finally, eight was connected to two and five. The symbol reminded Shiloh of a misshapen star.

A thunderous noise shattered the stillness as One dragons peeled off of the dome and descended. They landed on the circumference of the circle, leaving a gap between the numbers four and five.

"This way," Pen whispered, nudging Shiloh and Link toward the open space.

Shiloh halted abruptly. "What is that?" She pointed a shaky finger toward the beast and man standing next to Pen's father.

"Don't point." Pen hissed, lowering Shiloh's hand. "That's a Six observer from the capital. There is one at every ceremony. If you show any signs that you have Five in you, they take you directly to the capital."

Shiloh stared at the man who had a long grizzled gray beard and a glass eye with a scar stretching down from his eyebrow to his lower jaw. His silvery hair was pulled back tightly, and his face was stern.

Next to him was his dragon, who also had a glass eye and the same scar. It had row upon row of teeth and was plated like a tank with spikes coming out in neat rows ending at a tail in the shape of a mace.

"Who comes to this ceremony?" Mr. Shotwing's voice boomed and seemed to fill the whole chamber, "and who presents them?"

Pen nudged Shiloh forward. "Go on. You have to do your part first, then I will do mine."

Shiloh swallowed hard. "Shiloh Jones!" she shouted, hoping her vibrato would cover her fear.

"And Link Jones," Link added, his gaze steady as he stared directly at the Six observer.

"And, I, Pendleton Shortwing the third, present them as they are orphans in our land."

"Are you both of age?" a creaky voice asked from Shiloh's left.

"We are," Shiloh and Link said in unison.

"Having answered in the affirmative," the creaky voice said, "You may proceed with the Summoning Ceremony, Flame Summoner."

Mr. Shortwing stepped into the center of the circle and spread his arms.

"In the beginning there was darkness." Mr. Shortwing clapped his hands together, and the entire chamber went dark. "Then came the great spark."

A spark the size of a firefly appeared, hovering in the middle of the circle.

"The Spark became a Flame." The little spark turned into a tornado of flame spiraling to the ceiling. "And the Flame became the first dragon, Eimi, Son of the Great Flame."

A radiant golden dragon appeared with flames licking all sides.

"The Great Flame lit other fires in the sky to create the heavens." Stars appeared all around the dome. "And in turn, the heavens created Altiniya."

All of the Ones around the circle threw sand into the air. Pen's father moved his hands, and a gust of wind formed the sand into a sphere.

"Eimi walked upon Altiniya," Mr. Shortwing continued, "and life sprang up from under his footprints." The image of a flaming dragon walked across the sand globe; in its footsteps, animals and trees appeared.

"The Great Flame saw none were equal to Eimi so it chose Man to be a host for its spirit." Around the circle, at each number, a boy or girl made of sand appeared. The flame broke into nine pieces and dove into each person.

"The Spirit of the great flame rested inside each child until their thirteenth birthday when its true form appeared—dragons—for dragons are the Flame made flesh."

A gust of wind hit the sand people standing around the circle, and a dragon from each of the nine classes emerged from their bodies, taking position behind them.

"Now it is your turn to reveal your inner dragon—the spark of the One True Flame." Mr. Shortwing clapped his hands, and the room went dark.

A gust of wind rose, striking Shiloh with such force she stumbled back a few feet. Shiloh blinked her eyes several times. The room was still dark, but to her left about twenty feet in the air she could make out two straight lines with a curved line on both top and bottom. The symbol was the color of lava—a mixture of red, orange, yellow, and black all flowing together. She recognized it as the Zodiac symbol of her birth month, Gemini.

"Let there be light," Mr. Shortwing boomed.

Shiloh covered her eyes as they were assaulted by the rays of sunlight streaming through the glass dome above. After they adjusted, she glanced to her left where the symbol had been. The symbol was still there, but surrounding it now was a massive black dragon with red markings on its face. The symbol was embedded in its black chest. The dragon had spikes running the length of its body, and its eyes seemed to glow with the same lava as the chest. The dragon radiated power, and its presence filled the chamber with awe. Between its legs, Link stood, staring up at it.

"An Eight!" an elderly voice exclaimed. "How marvelous, Alpheus, you summoned an Eight, old chap! We haven't had one of those in years, congratulations." The man then turned his attention to Shiloh. "I say, where is your dragon? Is it a Two hiding? They can be shy sometimes."

Shiloh looked around desperately. Her heart sank as she realized there was no dragon beside her—not even a tiny Two.

"I… I don't seem to have a dragon," Shiloh's voice was hushed as she talked into her chest.

A murmur rolled like a wave across the circle with words like "blasphemy," "infidel," and "Laka," all tossed about like a beach ball.

A large object crashed, and all eyes turned to the Six from the capital, whose dragon had dented the floor with its mace-like tail. General Grishnoff stepped forward. "No dragon equals no life. You know the law." The general's armored dragon struck its tail again for emphasis.

A terrifying roar erupted to Shiloh's left. Link's dragon bared its swordlike teeth and let out a plume of fire that reached the top of the dome. Shiloh shielded her face from the searing heat.

"No one is touching my sister," Link said, his voice cold and firm.

"We will see about that, boy." The general stepped into the circle, and his dragon lowered its head.

"I should have done this when I met you." Mr. Shortwing's arms twirled, and the strands of Shiloh's hair whipped about.

Something thudded behind Shiloh and the world dimmed as Alithia wrapped her wings around Shiloh, pulling her close into her body.

"Stop! Stop!" Pen shouted. "Alithia can still feel her dragon. Feel for yourselves."

"Pendleton Shortwing, move at once!"

"I won't move, Dad, not until you feel."

"It is true," an old voice said. "We can sense that this girl has a dragon. Stand down."

Alithia released Shiloh, who stood trembling as the crowd's gaze bore into her.

"Are you sure you are thirteen?" Mr. Shortwing asked. "I know that the Wandering Tribes aren't as in tune with dates as we are."

"Absolutely sure," Shiloh said. "Link and I are twins."

"Twins?" The word rippled through the crowd like a shockwave.

"Yes, Link and I were born on the same day by the same mother. Perhaps we share a dragon." Shiloh looked over at Link's massive dragon, knowing it wasn't true.

"How is that even possible?" Mr. Shortwing let out.

"Enough," the general barked. "This is a case for the capital."

"General Grishnoff," Mr. Shortwing said, "I assure you we can handle this here. There is no need—"

"There is a great need," the general interrupted. He stared at Shiloh with his one good eye. "You have until morning to pack your things, girl. We leave at first light."

Chapter Eight

EMBER

"This will be the end of us, Beatrice." Mr. Shortwing held his head and rested his elbows on the kitchen table.

These were the first words he had spoken since the ceremony. Their walk home had been a somber one. Pen trudged a few paces ahead, silent, while Mr. Shortwing smoldered behind. Link kept looking up at his massive dragon—as did many other people in the street. Shiloh couldn't tell, but it looked like they were in deep conversation. This left Shiloh to her thoughts. The most prevalent of which was: *Why hadn't my dragon appeared?*

"It can't be that bad." Mrs. Shortwing gently rubbed Mr. Shortwing's back.

"I heard them—they think that I am incompetent and can't even perform a Summoning Ceremony…" He lifted bloodshot eyes to Pen. "This is all your fault."

"Now, that isn't fair, Alpheus." Mrs. Shortwing glanced at Pen who was fighting back tears.

"It's true," he pressed on. "If he hadn't brought them here" —he pointed sharply at Shiloh and Link— "none of this would have happened. Pendleton, you embarrassed and defied me in front of the whole assembly. Why can't you be like other boys?"

"Alpheus Rudolf Shortwing!" Mrs. Shortwing paused, and the tension in the kitchen grew hot. She breathed in deeply. "I think we will all have to go see a Nine in the morning." She turned to Pen. "You know your father didn't mean it."

Pen stormed out of the room.

"I think you two better go to bed as well," Mrs Shortwing said. "The general will be here first thing in the morning."

Shiloh nodded. She and Link followed Pen down the hallway. The merry lamps lighting their way were a stark contrast to the emotions in the kitchen. Shiloh hated it when adults fought. Her parents had rarely argued, but when they did, she and Link would try to get as far away as possible.

"I'm sorry," Link said as he closed the bedroom door behind them.

"For what?" Shiloh asked.

"I'm sorry you don't have a dragon. I feel… It's so hard to describe… I feel like I have connected with a part of myself I have been missing my whole life."

Shiloh's heart sank. She wanted to be happy for her brother, but she ached to have her own dragon. Now that Link had Ember and their parents were gone, she felt more alone than ever.

"Would you like to meet her?" Link asked. "I know that she has been wanting to speak to you."

"I would love to," Shiloh whispered, hope flickering in her chest.

"Ember, I would like for you to meet Shiloh."

I have known Shiloh since before we were born, a powerful feminine voice filled Shiloh's head. *But, I have never had the chance to speak to you directly. Shiloh, how long I have waited for this moment.*

"Ember is a beautiful name," Shiloh said. "Did Link come up with it?"

Ember has always been my name and always will be. It is who I am and always shall be. Dragons do not change. Unlike you humans, we remain the same.

"Isn't she amazing?" Link said.

Shiloh studied her brother. He seemed older and wiser. This made Shiloh's heart sink even further. If Link's dragon was this deep, imagine what she could learn from her own.

"Ember," Shiloh asked, "do you know why my dragon didn't appear?"

There was a long silence before Ember replied. *How can something that has always been there appear? There are reasons why the eyes do not see, but it is not for me to say, nor any other dragon.*

"But, I do have a dragon, don't I?" Shiloh could hear the desperation in her voice.

All have dragons inside of them. What the eyes cannot see the ears can hear.

"Does she always talk in riddles?" Shiloh crossed her arms and looked at Link over the rim of her glasses.

"I'm not sure. I'm just getting to know her myself. It feels funny to say that, since I have known her my whole life—without realizing it... It is so hard to explain. You will know when you get your dragon."

"If I get my dragon… Maybe I am one of those Laka that everyone seems to be so afraid of. What do you think they are?"

"You're not a Laka."

"You don't even know what the Laka are. How can you know that I'm not one? Ember, do you know what these Laka are?"

It is simple. Laka are people without dragons.

"But how can it be so bad for someone to not have a dragon?" Shiloh asked.

Link hesitated. "Now that I have Ember, I don't know what I would do if anything happened to her. I never want to be apart from her."

Think back to the ceremony, Shiloh. What was man before the Great Spark entered him?

"Nothing."

In your version of the story, you were clay.

"Clay..." Shiloh's mouth gaped. "The creation story... the Bible... 'And the Lord God formed man of the dust of the ground, and breathed into his nostrils the breath of life; and man became a living soul.'"

We are that living soul. So, you see Shiloh, I know that you have a dragon.

Shiloh sat heavily on the bed, her legs suddenly weak. "This is impossible," she mumbled. "Link, I'm talking to your—"

"Soul," Link said.

"If she is your soul, what does that make you?"

"It's hard to explain, we are intertwined so deeply, I don't begin where she ends. There is no beginning and no end, there is just us."

"So, Laka are people without souls," Shiloh said quietly. "Link, they thought I didn't have a soul... Do you think it is safe for us to go to the Capital with this general? He wanted to kill me."

"I don't think we have much of a choice," Link said.

"What happened to your plan this morning to run away?"

"Things have changed since then."

"It has gotten easier. Ember could carry us back to where we were first transported here."

I cannot. This shell has yet to harden. It takes a dragon some time before its body has settled.

"There is one other thing," Link said. "I'm not sure if we can go back now that we have gone through the ceremony. Would Ember return into my body again when we enter our world, would we become separated, or would she enter in her full dragon form? We need to figure that out before we try. I can't lose her."

Chapter Nine

ALL IS FAIR IN WAR

"Ahhh!" A piercing scream jarred Shiloh from her sleep. "He's gone! My Penny-Wenny is gone!"

"Link?" Shiloh said, groggily. The room was still dark.

Link shot up in his bed. "Let's go see what's going on."

In moments, they were dressed and walking down the twinkling hallway to the kitchen where Mrs. Shortwing was head down on the table, sobbing.

"Is everything alright?" Shiloh asked.

Mrs. Shortwing sniffed heavily. "Pen is gone. He ran away again. I told Alpheus this would happen if he didn't change the way he treated him, but he didn't listen. He just didn't listen; now Pen is gone again." Mrs. Shortwing gave out a long sob. "I went to his room to wake him so he could help me prepare your meals, but he wasn't there."

Link placed his hand on Mrs. Shotwing's shoulder. "I'm sure he will come back again. Maybe he just needed to blow off some steam."

"You don't know my Pen. When he decides to do something, he does it no matter how irrational. All he had to do was wait another couple of weeks then he would be at Dragon's Claws Academy, but, no, he had to run away again and break his poor mother's heart."

A loud knock came from the front door. Seeing that Mrs. Shortwing wasn't going anywhere and that Link was better at comforting than she was, Shiloh decided it was up to her to answer the door.

She opened the frosted glass door and was met by the general's glass eye and grizzled beard. "Good," he said. "I don't like to be kept waiting. Let's go."

"What about my brother?"

"What about him? He can go to Dragon's Claw like the rest of the thirteen-year-olds. I only need you to come to the capital with me."

"I'm not going anywhere without him."

The General's dragon reared its armor plated head forward and breathed heavily on Shiloh. Her knees grew weak, and the world went black.

Shiloh gasped for air. She was so hot. What was she wrapped in? Her eyes shot open, and a sea of sand glinted merrily. In the distance, heat smeared the air and made things look blurry. She was moving, but not of her own accord, and the smell of polished leather surrounded her.

"Careful," the General's gruff voice came from below.

Shiloh felt around, and when she was sure of her surroundings, she pushed herself up. She had been lying on the back of the General's dragon.

"Is this necessary?" Shiloh lifted her bound wrists, tied to one of the dragon's spikes.

"Now they're not. I wanted to make sure you didn't fall." The general turned his glass eye on her. "Or run away."

"Well… now I won't do either." Shiloh extended her bound hands.

She can't go anywhere, a husky woman's voice filled Shiloh's ears.

The general grunted, "Fine."

The armored dragon stooped, and the general climbed up her spikes and into the massive saddle. He produced a glass blade and severed her bonds.

Shiloh rolled her wrists around. "Thank you…"

"I'm General Grishnoff, and her name is Maybel."

"Maybel?" Shiloh said reflexively, repressing laughter.

"Maybel is a ferocious name. Have you never heard of Maybel the Devourer or Maybel Spear Claws?"

Shiloh shook her head.

"You must have been really deep in the desert then." General Grishnoff eyed her suspiciously.

"General, your eye is leaking."

General Grishnoff pulled back quickly. "It's nothing," He brought a little vial to his eye and captured the liquid. "No water is lost in the desert. Being from the wandering tribes you would know that better than many." The general looked as if he knew something she didn't.

"I suppose we will fly now that I'm awake?"

"No, Six dragons can only fly a short distance with more than their rider on them. Even then, we don't get good mileage, do we, Maybel?"

Maybel's tail thudded loudly behind them. The noise startled Shiloh, and she turned. On the horizon, three black shapes appeared rushing toward them, two in the air and one on the ground.

The general followed her gaze. "Ah, that would be your fool brother and your pudgy friend. I don't know why they would bring a Nine, though. Maybe they want to try reasoning with me."

Maybel let out a chortle, and her whole body shook.

"What do you think, Maybel? Do we turn and wait for them, or do we keep going and let them catch up?"

Maybel stopped abruptly, and Shiloh held on as she turned.

"That's what I thought." General Grishnoff patted Maybel. "Sorry about this." Before Shiloh knew it, her hands were bound tightly again and fastened around one of Maybel's spikes. General Grishnoff dismounted and unsheathed his sword. The blade was black, and the edges looked incredibly sharp. The material of the sword reminded Shiloh of obsidian.

Link's dragon Ember was the first to reach them. Shiloh squinted to see if Link was riding her, but she couldn't see him. Ember dove swiftly at General Grishnoff.

"No! Sixes can control…" Pen's voice reached them before Ember did.

General Grishnoff raised his hand as if he was scooping up something, and a giant sand barrier rose twenty feet into the air. Ember crashed into it full force, pelting Shiloh with small particles of sand. Half the barrier was knocked down, and so was Ember.

"Ember!" Link shouted as he dismounted Alithia. He ran to his dragon and cradled her head.

"Just as I thought, your dragon hasn't fully settled yet. You're lucky she hasn't; she could have killed herself had she fully hardened. We don't need this any more." General Grishnoff waved his hand to the side, and the remainder of the barrier disappeared into the sand dune on the left of the road.

Behind Alithia, a giant spinning wheel approached with Stix sitting in the middle of it. She was perched on a double clawed seat with a clawed footrest. As the wheel slowed, Shiloh realized it wasn't a wheel at all—it was Axel, Stix's dragon. The dragon had its tail in its mouth and its fore and rear legs were the seat and footrest that supported Stix.

"Let her go!" Pen shouted. He spun his staff and dropped it on the ground.

Both the general and Maybel let out a robust laugh in unison.

Ember shook her massive head and raised to her full height. She let out a blood-curdling roar, and the sign of Gemini on her chest glowed brightly.

"Roar all you like, you won't be effective until you have hardened. You will just have to live with that. Why are you three interfering with capital business?"

"Any business that involves Shiloh is my business," Link growled.

"I don't see how this is capital business," Pen said. "You aren't heading west to the capital. You are heading south to the trading post."

"I came this way because I knew he would try to follow." The General nodded to Link. "I wasn't expecting to see you, and who is this Nine?"

"I am a peaceful observer," Stix said, dismounting Axel, who stretched out to his full length and wrapped himself around Stix. "We are connected. Be careful—"

"Sand spider!" General Grishnoff pointed to the right. All turned as a fist of sand rose from the desert, striking both Stix and Axel across the face, causing them to fall to the ground unconscious.

Pen's mouth gaped. "Harming a peaceful observer is against the law."

"All is fair in war, boy. You will learn that soon enough."

"War? There isn't a war."

Ember swiped a massive paw with claws the size of swords at the General, and it passed through him as if it was made of vapor.

Link used the distraction to take Pen's staff and land a blow across the General's shoulder. He swung again, but the staff was intercepted by the general's black sword, and the two weapons lodged in each other. Grishnoff swung his fist, and Link's nose crunched from the impact. He stumbled backward and fell at the edge of the road. Blood dripped steadily down his face and puddled in the sand.

The ground rumbled, and tremors appeared in the sand like rain hitting a pond. The rumbling noise got louder, and the ground shook more intently.

"Go, Maybel, you know what to do." Grishnoff hit the rear of the dragon, and she took off at a full run. Shiloh clutched onto a spike that had been worn down from many years of Grishnoff's grip. She looked back at her friends, and from the sand, rose the most terrifying creatures Shiloh had ever seen. They resembled spiders, but their hind legs bent up like the dinosaur crickets in Shiloh's basement back home, and on top of it all, they had scorpion tails, including the venomous barb. Their bodies were the size of a horse, but their legs stretched out at least ten feet on each side, and their beady eyes hid behind massive fangs.

One spider jumped thirty feet in the air and landed on the road behind them blocking Shiloh's view of the others. Its fangs clicked together, and it jumped again.

"Maybel!" Shiloh screamed as the beast bore down on them. Maybel spun 360 degrees and smacked the spider in the abdomen with her mace tail. The impact made the sound of a car crash and sent the creature flying into the desert.

Alithia grabbed Pen with her jaws and crouched over Stix and Axel. Seconds later, they completely disappeared. Grishnoff pulled Link close. He waved his hand, and a barrier of sand formed around them just as a scorpion tail struck.

All of the spiders moved from where Alithia had been and focused on the mound that Grishnoff and Link were in. They swarmed like ants on a popsicle stick. Ember barreled down on the spiders repeatedly, but no matter how hard she tried, her fangs and claws just passed through the foul beasts.

"We have to help them!" Shiloh shouted.

I have to be loyal and follow orders.

"But Grishnoff and Link will die," Shiloh pleaded, as Maybel continued to run like a rhinoceros trying to put out a fire.

Shiloh bent to her bound hands, and took the glasses from her face. She held them so the sun's full force was focused through the lens. Almost immediately the dragon silk smoked and frayed. Moments later her hands were free and she climbed down Maybel's back as if she were climbing on monkey rings. Her feet hit the ground, and she broke into a sprint back toward the others. She didn't know what she would do, but she knew she didn't want to live without Link—he was everything to her.

Maybel skidded to a stop and turned her body, but Shiloh had a head start, and her legs were powerful from track. She knew she could make it close enough to the beasts to draw them away before Maybel was able to catch up with her.

The spiders stung the mound shielding Link again and again, and their legs clawed at it. The mound was decreasing in size at an alarming rate. The top crumbled.

"Hey!" Shiloh shouted.

Five sets of beady eyes stared up at her, and fangs the size of her arms clicked together. Retractable spikes raised on their legs, and the spiders swarmed to her. They leapt as one body and surrounded her. Just as a tail was bearing down on her, the circle of spiders was shattered by Maybel. She stood over Shiloh and received blow after blow. Maybel spun, and her mace tail cleared space, but the spider tails were still able to strike her.

Grishnoff slid under a spider and used his sword to split open its underbelly. He joined Shiloh between Maybel's powerful legs.

"Are you hurt?" he said desperately.

"Link—you left him alone?"

The spiders sensed this as well. One of the four remaining tore off from the pack and leapt toward Link, covering the distance in a single bound. Ember roared and let out a huge stream of fire. The flames engulfed the spider, and it crouched down, contracting its body to protect itself. The flames disappeared, and the creature stretched out, pouncing on Link.

A flash appeared in the sky, then another to Link's right, and the body of the massive spider dropped. Shiloh was afraid Link had been crushed by its weight, but between the legs of the struggling beasts around her, she saw him scramble free.

A scorpion tail shot down at Shiloh, and Grishnoff threw his body over hers. He let out a scream of agony and swung wildly with his sword, lopping off the tail that had struck him. The creature backed away and burrowed in the sand, leaving two for Maybel. The flash appeared again, and another spider fell. Maybel reared up and slammed the last spider under her front two legs. The beast crushed like a can of soda and made the sound of a tree breaking.

"General," a voice cried. "You've been hit."

Grishnoff rolled away from Shiloh. Standing behind him was a tall figure wearing armor made from the exoskeleton of sand spiders. The ends of what had once been a spider's fingers formed a facemask, and other parts were used to create a protective shell for the torso. The man's arms were fitted into the hollows of a spider's legs, and as he flicked his wrists, the spikes lining it retracted.

The stranger whistled, and a dragon landed next to him. Its body was lean and aerodynamic with a wingspan twice the size of Ember's, even though Ember was the much larger dragon. On the ground, the dragon's wings bent up like great pyramids on either side of the lean body.

The warrior looked at Shiloh then at the General, whose body was contorting on the ground. A decision weighed heavily behind his dark eyes. "Arda, take him to Mim immediately."

His dragon scooped Grishnoff from the ground and bounded into the sky. The force from the air pushed Shiloh's cheeks back, and she had to brace herself to stay upright as the dragon disappeared into a ring of vapor.

"Are you harmed?" the warrior asked.

"I don't think so." Shiloh felt her body to make sure.

"What about the others?"

"Link?" Shiloh pushed off from the ground and ran to him. "Are you—"

"I'm fine." He cleared a viscous blue substance from his face.

The stranger walked up behind them. "It would appear I arrived just in time. A moment later, and you would all have been dead."

"I had it under control." Link's jaw hardened.

"It didn't appear that way."

Link pushed the Spider's abdomen with his foot. The underbelly of the beast revealed two smoldering handprints burrowed deep into its thorax.

"Agh," Link let out.

"What is it?" Shiloh's eyebrows knitted together.

Link opened his fists; steam rose from his glowing palms. "I… I don't know how to stop it."

"Help him! You have to help him," Shiloh pleaded with the stranger.

"This is beyond me. We will have to get him to Mim as well. She will know what to do."

"Or, we could take him to my mom." Pen sidled up next to Shiloh.

"You can't go back." The stranger's eyes hardened on Pen. "Soldiers from the capital will be there already, looking for her." The stranger pointed at Shiloh.

"You mean the general wasn't from the capital?" Shiloh asked.

"He was saving you from them. We have been searching for you since the first signs of the prophecy began."

"And who are you?" Pen asked.

The stranger removed his mask, revealing olive skin, a strong jawline, brown eyes, and black hair. "I'm Kai from the wandering tribes." He took Pen by the wrist, and they shook.

"You're a Seven, aren't you?" Pen asked. "I saw you teleport; that was so cool."

Kai nodded with a cheeky smile.

"Pen, we should go back." Stix joined them, rubbing her head.

"As I said before, you can't—at least not until we are out of the capital's reach."

She is a peace observer. Maybel's voice filled all their heads. *She was connected before these things attacked.* Maybel stomped on the leg of a spider, and it snapped.

"Are you still connected?" Kai asked.

"I might be." Stix crossed her arms.

"I pray you are not."

"Why?" Stix held his gaze. "You want to protect yourself as well as that kidnapping general?"

"Yes, and to save your lives. I don't think you understand. It isn't just soldiers coming; the Laka are coming, as well. They are already searching for them"—he nodded at Shiloh and Link—"and anyone who has associated with them."

A look of dread passed between Pen and Stix.

"If you lost contact, and they see this," Kai motioned to the dead spiders, "they may just think that you were all eaten."

"What about my parents?" Pen sputtered.

"They will be questioned, that is for sure; beyond that, I do not know."

Pen sat on the ground, put his arms around his legs, and buried his face in his knees.

"My connection was broken when I passed out," Stix admitted. "I haven't been able to reestablish it."

"Good." Kai flicked his wrist, and spikes sprang from the armor on his forearms. He pushed forward again, and the spikes became a single blade. He pulled out the end of the nearest spider leg, and with one swing of his blade, he cut it at the joint. He repeated the process and handed the oozing ends to Link. "Put your hands in here. It might help."

Link looked at the leg questioningly as a weird smell filled the air.

"Go on," Kai said reassuringly.

There was a squishy noise as Link plunged his hands deep into the spider's legs, and his face relaxed a bit.

"Four Dragon, will you help me to lift this spider onto Maybel's back?"

"Her name is Alithia," Shiloh said sharply.

"We will need to butcher this spider for food and protection," Kai said, ignoring Shiloh's tone. "The rest we can use to trade with. Under normal circumstances we wouldn't leave a scrap behind. But today, the desert will reclaim what is hers. I think there is already enough blood for them to believe that you were injured or killed here."

"Alithia, help him," Pen said, sniffling.

"As for you," Kai turned back to Link, "I don't know what we will do with you; Eights are not welcome where we are going."

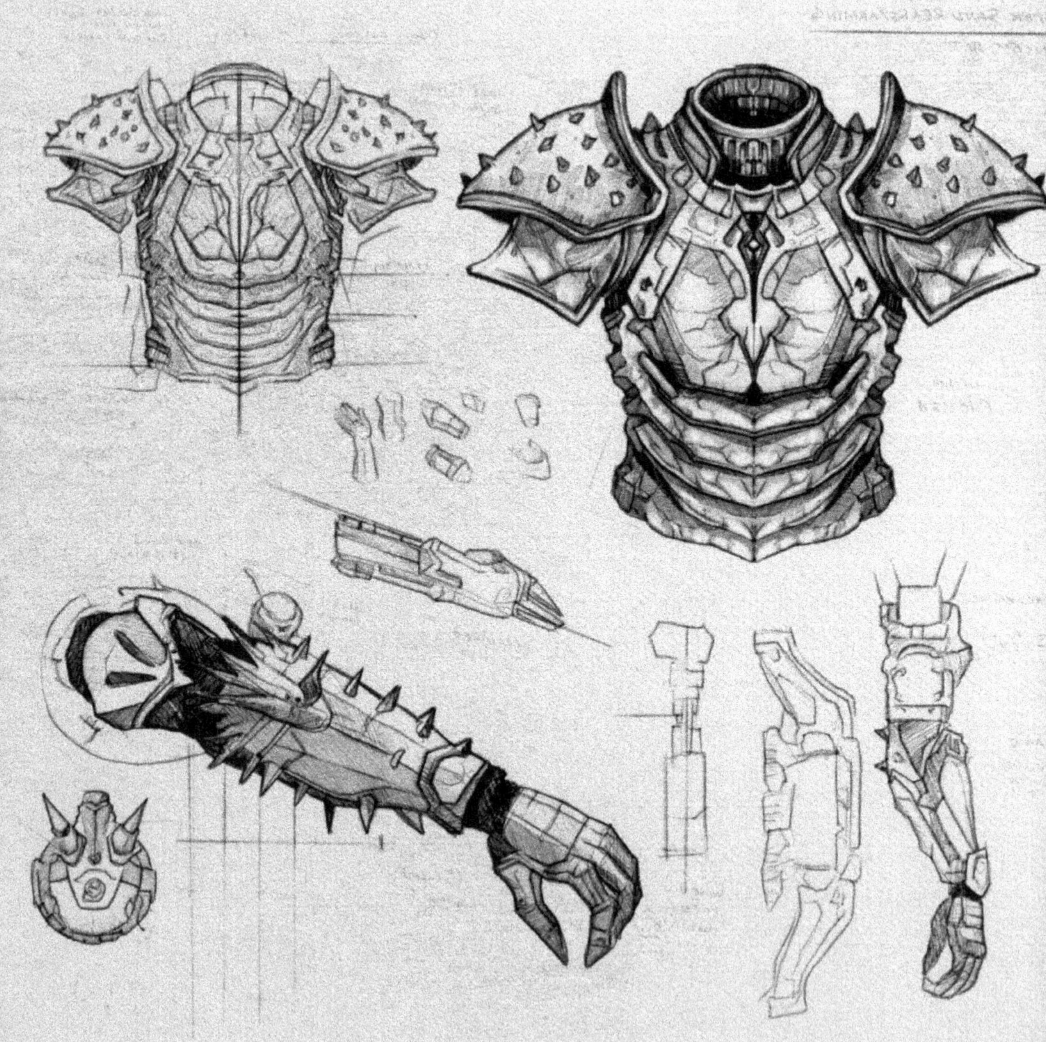

Chapter Ten

DESERT ARMOR

The heat shimmered above the glass road, creating waves that came in and out of view. The company walked single file next to the dragons who blocked the direct sun. Kai and Shiloh took the lead beside Maybel, next was Pen, Stix, Axel, and Alithia, followed by Link and Ember. It was approaching the noon hour, and the shade from Maybel was diminishing quickly. Soon, Shiloh would have to walk under Maybel's legs to avoid the blistering sun. She looked at the leg next to her, which was the size of a large tree trunk. She was mesmerized by the corded muscles contracting with every step.

Kai held up his hand. "We stop here until night." These were the first words that had been spoken since leaving the carnage.

"Thank the Spark," Pen said. "I don't think that I could have taken another step."

"How much farther do we have?" Shiloh looked ahead at the glass road disappearing in the distance.

"Is it safe to stop?" Stix asked.

"Nothing is ever safe in the desert," Kai said. "Only by Eimi's providence are we protected. It is in him whom I trust. All else shall fail. But, it is safer for us to stop now than continue. We must prepare before we reach the trading post."

"What do you mean?" Link asked.

"You will not fit in. The trading post isn't like the other cities. It is of the desert, and so are its people. They survive at any cost." Kai pointed at Shiloh. "With that hair and those things on your face, covering your eyes—you will be recognized immediately." He pointed at Link. "Your eyes are not of the south either. Being an Eight, you will already attract too much attention anyway." He glanced at Pen. "You look like a Temple Master's son. You are too well fed and clothed."

"What about Stix?" Pen asked.

"She will be fine. Her rivers run deep."

Shiloh's insides turned, and her gaze narrowed on Stix. She didn't understand the emotion she was having, but she didn't like it. She blurted out, "These things on my face are called glasses, and I can't see without them—I will be blind."

"And how am I to change the color of my eyes?" Link said.

"That is why it is safer for us to rest and figure out what to do. Now that we have enough distance between us and the spiders, we must eat and clothe you properly. That will solve half of the problem. But, before we eat, it is safer if the dragons rest head to tail and stretch out their wings to protect us from the midday sun, as it is done with our people.

Maybel plopped down, blocking the road in front of them. Ember blocked the rear and curled her body to take up some of the sides as well. Axel placed his head at Ember's tail and stretched his own to Maybel's head, blocking the right side. Alithia did the same on the opposite side. Ember stretched her massive wing almost eclipsing Maybel. The sun shone through the membrane and a vast network of veins appeared, coursing through the wing. Once in position, they vaguely resembled a circle of covered wagons in the wild west.

Shiloh helped Link down to lean against Ember. His hands had improved but were still tender to the touch. Pen sat against Alithia with his legs stretched out and crossed at the ankles. Axel made a little perch for Stix, and Kai remained standing. He extended the blades on his forearms and lopped off another section from the spider's leg at the joint. He flicked his wrist, and the blade became spikes. He held the section of the leg with his foot and began to saw. After a few moments, the leg cracked open, revealing the slimy flesh inside. He handed both halves to Shiloh and repeated the process for the others.

"Only eat down to the cooling membrane." He pointed to a thin layer of blue gel that looked like it should be in an ice pack. "And leave the front tendon intact." He turned his piece so all could see the sinuous tendon stretching the width of the leg.

"Why is that?" Pen strummed the tendon on his piece of leg, and spikes shot out, nearly taking off his finger.

"That is why." Kai pulled on the tendon in the opposite direction and the spikes retracted.

"When you said, 'clothed properly',"—Pen raised an eyebrow— "do you mean we get to have armor like yours—like a real member of the wandering tribes?"

"It is so. The armor of the sand spider is one of the hardest things in existence. Its spikes are as sharp as dragon's teeth, and its body provides both protection and cooling from the desert sun. We will need all of this in the deep desert," Kai said. "Usually you have to earn your armor in our culture. You survived, I suppose under these circumstances that is enough."

"I killed this spider," Link growled. "I have earned it for all of us."

"Perhaps…" Kai let the word hang in the air before he continued, "We are fortunate to have a nine with us. Do you weave?"

"Stix is the best weaver in town."

"Pen, I can answer for myself. Yes, I weave, and I will be happy to help with what is necessary."

The unfamiliar feeling rose inside Shiloh again, and she blurted out, "I have an idea." All eyes turned to her. "Back home…we have these things called contact lenses. They can change the color of your eyes and also help you to see. Alithia, can I share an image with you? Perhaps you can make Link and me sets just to use when we are at the trading post."

As you wish little one. Alithia's velvety voice calmed Shiloh. She hadn't had the idea when she began speaking, but was happy the pressure had brought this solution to mind. Shiloh imagined a pair of her contact lenses.

That will work for you, but how do we color Link's?"

"Maybe we can char some of this," Shiloh held up her portion of spider, "and use the ash to darken the glass."

Very well. I have never made something this small before, but we can try. Pen, place four small portions of sand in front of me and a small piece of the spider.

Pen did as instructed, and Alithia's bright blue flame ignited. She used her tongue to form the contacts and continued to push them around until the amber glow disappeared.

We will let these cool, and you can try them on after we have rested.

"Let us eat." Kai raised his potion of spider leg. "Eimi, thank you for this food. May it nourish our bodies and keep us healthy and strong for the voyage ahead."

Shiloh looked at the goo cupped in spider's leg. She had never been a picky eater, but eating bugs is something she never thought she would do. She lifted the leg to her lips and sucked. It made a terrible slurping sound, and it took her a moment to place the taste. It was mussels. The spider tasted like mussels in garlic sauce. The closer Shiloh got to the cooling membrane the colder the goo became.

"This is delicious," Pen said with a full mouth. "I could get used to this."

"You will have to." Kai lifted his portion of leg in a toast.

After the meal, Stix gathered the empty shells with the cooling membrane and tendon intact and fitted them around everyone's forearms, lacing them with dragon silk from Axel. The moment the cooling membrane touched Shiloh's arm, she felt instant relief from the relentless sun.

I say, Axel's voice came into Shiloh's head as he tightened a lace. *I think I have a solution for your hair. What if I create a hair covering? I could do the same for Stix and that way it wouldn't look odd.*

"That is a great idea," Shiloh said. All eyes turned to her. "Axel came up with an idea for my hair—our hair." Shiloh smiled at Stix.

Chapter Eleven

THE LAKA

"Aghhh!" Pen's shout pulled Shiloh from her slumber. Kai was already standing with his forearm blades raised. The dragons had stirred as well, but Link and Stix remained sleeping.

"Pen, what is it?" Shiloh whispered.

"The Laka, I heard them."

"I didn't hear anything," Kai said. "You must have been dreaming."

"I heard them clear as day, calling my name, pulling at me."

"I was awake, and all was silent," Kai said. He had taken watch while the others slept.

"Pen, I'm sure it was a dream," Shiloh put a reassuring hand on his shoulder, and he leaned into it. "What are the Laka, anyway? Everyone seems to be so afraid of them."

"I told you before, they take your dragon." Pen looked worriedly at Alithia.

"That is only half true." Kai retracted his blades. "They silence your dragon."

"My dad is the—"

"I don't care who your dad is. I'm speaking the truth."

"Why are you so mean all the time?" Shiloh's brow furrowed.

"I'm not mean, just direct. In the desert, that is the way of life."

"I think you are a bully."

"Apologies." Kai bowed.

"Don't apologize to me," Shiloh said. "Apologize to Pen and Link. Actually, the only one you have been kind to is Stix."

"I am kind to her because she has use. In the desert, all members of the community have to be useful. She will fit in. Pen, I don't think… There aren't many Fours in the desert."

"What about my brother and me?"

"Eights do not belong with a free people. They were responsible for… Well, that is not for me to say. Mim will tell you, if she chooses to."

"And me. Why me?"

"Because of the Prophecy of Gemini. Your appearance is one of the signs of the return of Eimi. We must protect you at all costs."

"Protect me from who?"

"Abaddon."

"Aren't you supposed to say Lord Abaddon?" Pen said. "Where I come from, it's the law—"

"He isn't my Lord and never will be."

"Well, why would the king want Shiloh anyway?" Pen asked.

"Once again, that is for Mim to say."

A moment passed, and a dry breeze blew over the desert.

"Well, can you tell us more about the Laka?" Shiloh asked. "You seem to know so much about them,"

"Such things shouldn't be spoken of in the open desert. But since we have begun, we may as well finish. The Laka do take your dragon—"

"I told you—"

"But not in the way you think. They silence your dragon's voice. First comes the whispering, then they plant pictures or thoughts in your head—"

"That is illegal."

"Pen, let him continue."

"These thoughts draw you in—they are so tempting, so enticing. The Laka know what triggers you. A small wind on the other side of the desert can cause a huge sand storm. So it is with their voices. What seems so subtle is given great power when you pay attention to it. Most don't even know it is happening. Your dragon does, though. They urge you not to listen to these whispers that aren't yours and not to act on these impulses that are wrong. Soon the Laka are the only voices you hear, and your dragon is silenced. That is what is meant by them 'taking your dragon.' Once they have your dragon, they have complete control over you. You only hear their voices in your head. They pull you in directions you know aren't right, but you listen to them anyway. It is hard to tell who is under their influence because those under their control still retain their physical dragons."

"So anyone could be working for the Laka?" A chill ran up Shiloh's spine.

Kai nodded.

"And how do you know so much about them?" Shiloh asked.

"My mother was taken by them."

"I'm sorry. My mother was taken from me, too," Shiloh said. "She died recently. It still doesn't feel real..." She trailed off, sensing that Kai no longer wanted to talk. "We should get some more sleep before we have to go." Shiloh lay down and snuggled in tight next to Link and Ember.

"Don't fall back asleep," Kai said. "Evening is upon us."

Kai pointed to the west where the flaming chariot of the sun dowsed itself in the abyss of the desert. Twilight lasted only a few minutes before a canopy of stars opened above them, muted by a nearly full moon. Even though they were in a different world, the stars were still the same. Something about this realization comforted Shiloh.

"Wake the others," Kai said. "If we leave now, we will reach the trading post by morning."

THE TRADING POST

Shiloh rubbed her eyes. Even though her new contacts were made of the smoothest glass she had ever felt, her eyes were dry and scratchy. By the looks of it, Link wasn't faring much better. He kept rubbing his eyes every few minutes. He looked strange with dark eyes, not quite himself. Actually, ever since the summoning ceremony, he hadn't quite looked like himself.

"There it is!" Pen said excitedly. "This is exactly how I imagined the trading post would be."

In the distance, dragon glass stalagmites twelve feet in diameter rose out of the desert floor, stretching forty feet into the air, creating a giant wall. The road led into its center, where two centurions on heavily armored Six dragons stood guard.

"Do not use your real names. For that matter, don't speak—especially you." Kai pointed at Pen.

Shiloh narrowed her gaze.

"You may think me cruel," Kai continued, "but this is a matter of life and death. If you thought the spiders were dangerous, just wait until you see what is on the other side of that wall. Alithia and Ember, take high to the sky so they can't see what type of dragons you are."

Kai whistled merrily and approached the gate.

"Halt," a guard said, barring entrance to the fort with his dragon glass axe. "What do we have here? Why I've never seen a member of the Wandering Tribes with a Six before—thought they's too big and dumb for the desert."

His companion let out a cackle.

"You're a Six. How can you talk about Six's like that?" Kai asked.

"I know, right, that's exactly why I can talk about them like that. Ain't that right, Bessi." The guard slapped his dragon, and it snorted in response. "Anyway, what's your business?"

"Trading, we have a sand spider—a fresh kill, too."

"Ooo—I loves me some sand spider. Go on, give us a leg. I haven't had breakfast yet."

"As I said, I'm here to trade. What will you trade me for it?"

"How about entrance to the city."

"The last time I checked, the entrance to the city was free."

"Just changed yesterday." The guard gripped his axe tightly.

"Well, when I get in and trade with Stue, I will let him know you have one of the legs. But, if you insist." Kai twisted his wrist, and his blade appeared.

"Stop!" The guard said, backpedaling. "Weze didn't know you had dealings with Stue. Of course, you can pass."

"Much obliged."

Shiloh hadn't seen this side of Kai. He was so charming. She shook her head and continued forward.

A tight grip took her by the shoulder. "Wait a minute. Where is your dragon?"

Kai batted the guard's hand away. "Her dragon hasn't come yet, and as for theirs," Kai pointed up to the two dragons circling in the sky, "you know how free dragons can be."

The man grunted, and they continued on their way.

The dwellings inside the fort were constructed with logs of dragon glass, resembling giant glass Lincoln Logs. There were no prism paintings, no domes, and no green anywhere. The people and dragons were colorful enough, though, to make up for it. There were so many different shades and hues of both dragons and humans.

"Quit staring," Kai said, returning to his normal demeanor. "We don't want to attract any more attention than we can help." He led them through a maze of streets and alleyways until they reached a large estate with flaming torches on either side of a dragon glass gate. Behind it, a giant courtyard opened up with a mosaic of a dragon on the floor. A covered walkway lined the courtyard with pillars spaced every ten feet. Hanging down from the top of the covered archway were cluster upon cluster of red and purple grapes glistening in the sunlight.

"We are here to trade with Stue," Kai shouted. The gates pulled open, and Kai walked confidently forward, followed by Maybel and the company.

"That is far enough," a whiney voice said as they reached the bottom of the stairs at the far end of the courtyard. "Who comes here to trade with Stue?" Atop the stairs a man sat cross-legged on a bed of pillows. His large belly protruded from his open vest. Next to him was a tiny Two dragon.

"I am Kai, from the Wandering Tribes, and I bring meat to trade with you." Maybel turned to show the dead spider on her back. "And I take it you are Stue? Your reputation is known wide and far."

"Good." Stue clapped his hands together. "Very good, my boy." Stue held a glass pipe to the little Two's mouth, and the dragon blew into it. Stue inhaled deeply, and a look of ecstasy crossed his face. "Come."

Stue's voice had gotten three octaves higher. "No one does business with Stue unless they suck the dragon's breath."

Shiloh had to use every restraint she had not to laugh. Stue sounded like a cartoon character. For that matter, he looked a little like one, too.

Kai climbed the steps, and Stue motioned for him to sit. He held the glass pipe to the Two dragon, who then filled it with what Shiloh guessed was helium. Kai bent down and took a hit from the pipe. "Stue—"

Shiloh burst out laughing at Kai's voice which was now twice as high as her own. The harder she tried to repress the laughter, the louder it became.

Anger raged across Stue's face.

"You must forgive her," Kai said, in a falsetto voice. "She isn't of age yet."

This time it was Link who laughed, and Shiloh joined in.

"Silence!" Stue shouted in his ridiculously high voice. "Silence!"

Shiloh was laughing so hard now that her stomach hurt. Link was doubled over holding his gut.

"Silence!" Stue's voice had returned back to normal, and it wasn't so funny now. "I will not tolerate this offense in my own house. To the pit with you." Guards rushed to surround them.

"She is just a child." Kai's voice had returned to normal as well. "She has no dragon. You can't—"

"I can, and I will. Take them!"

In one movement, Kai flicked his wrist, extending his blades, and held them to Stue's throat.

A rumbling came from behind Stue, and a giant Seven dragon stretched its head over the wall.

"You will all die," Stue said.

"Then we will die together." Kai tightened his grip.

"I see that we are at an impasse. Your only objection is that she doesn't fight—is that so?"

"Yes."

"Very good, then you will be her champion."

"Only on one condition." Kai pressed the sharp edge of the spike harder on Stew's throat, causing a little trickle of blood.

"What is that?"

"You are a Seven, right?" Kai glanced at the Seven dragon looming above them.

"Yes, yes." Stue pointed at the Two Dragon. "This little thing belongs to my servant."

"Then as a Seven, I want you to swear to Eimi that you will deliver my companions back to our people unharmed whether I live or die."

Stue looked at Shiloh quizzically. "I swear it."

Chapter Thirteen

GLADIATORS AND DRAGONS

"This couldn't have gone any worse," Kai said, crouching in the corner of their frosted dragon glass cell with his hands on his head.

A crowd roared above, and the ground shook from the stamping of the audience in the coliseum.

"Stue was our ticket to get home. He is a teleporter like me. That was the plan. If anything happenes, get to Stue, he will send you home. I don't think he will send us now." Kai punched the ground.

"Can't you teleport us?" Shiloh asked.

"Not without, Arda. She is too far away for my powers to work. I will be defenseless now, and there is no way for her to get back here."

Not completely defenseless. I will fight by your side. Maybel's voice rang out loudly in all of their heads.

"Are you sure? Would the general approve? I could never ask another person's dragon—"

I am sure. You saved my rider by allowing Arda to take him to Mim.

Kai bowed to Maybel deeply. As he rose, he shot Link a look. "Have you figured out how to use those yet?"

Link flicked his wrists, and blades appeared on his forearms. "I think I've got it."

"Good, because we don't know what we will be up against in there. We could be facing sand spiders, other gladiators, or a combination of both. Has your dragon hardened yet?"

"I don't know."

"Pen, can your Alithia fight in her stead?" Kai asked.

"Alithia is more of a hider than a fighter. I don't know what good she would do in there. You saw us with the sand spiders."

"Pen." Stix grabbed his arm. "You and Alithia saved Axel and me. You were very brave. You could have just flown away."

"That is true. Perhaps I underestimated you." Kai shot Pen a smile.

"What are the rules?" Link asked. "Every game has its rules."

"There are only two rules. One, don't kill your teammate. Two, don't die. Got it?"

"What have I gotten us into?" Shiloh's voice quivered as she fought back tears.

Link embraced her. "Don't. Water is too precious here. It was my fault just as much as yours. We are in this together."

"But, Kai didn't have to—" Shiloh glanced at him over Link's shoulder.

"I did. My orders were clear." Kai met her eyes. "Keep you alive at all costs."

The ringing of giant glass singing bowls reverberated Shiloh's insides.

Kai put his hand on Link's shoulder. "Come, the hour is upon us. May Eimi fight at our side."

Two guards led them down a brick dragon glass tunnel toward a blinding light. The closer they got to the light, the louder the cheers from the crowd became. Shiloh squeezed Link's hand tightly, but he looked straight ahead. She could tell he was already in that ring.

"Come with us," a gruff voice said.

Shiloh was abruptly torn away from Link. She held on as long as she could, but the arms pulling her were much stronger than her grip.

"Don't hurt my sister, or I will come for you next." Something in the power of Link's words frightened Shiloh.

"She'll be fine. Worry about yourself, boy," the guard spat and continued to lead Shiloh away.

Shiloh, Pen, and Stix were ushered up several flights of stairs to a landing with three giant chairs.

"Go on." The guard pushed Shiloh forward. "He wants you to sit with him."

Shiloh glared at her escort, but seeing no other choice, she walked to the front of the chairs. Stue's belly appeared first, then the rest of him came into view.

"Let's see how funny you think this is." A little drop of saliva formed at the corner of Stue's mouth as he spoke. He motioned to the seat at his right. "I reserved this special spot just for you."

Shiloh sat reluctantly.

"Girl," Stue raised his eyebrows at Stix. "You can sit here." He motioned to the seat to his left. "And boy, you will have to sit on the steps." He nodded at the three steps leading up to the raised seats.

"I am not a girl," Stix said defiantly. "Do you not see my dragon? You will treat us with the respect our society prescribes."

"Or what? You gonna tell Lord Abaddon on me? Ha, I rule here. Now sit or be taken below. I tire of you."

Stix took her seat, and Pen looked relieved as he sat on the step below the others.

Stue raised his hand, and the crowd fell silent. He nodded to the servant on his right, who struck the big glass bowl three times. The crowd went wild, and two large doors on either side of the coliseum opened.

On the far side, a bald man that had to be well over six feet and as wide as he was tall stepped into the ring, swinging a dragon glass mace in vicious circles over his head. He wore two leather straps that criss-crossed his body and a pair of shorts with sheathes holding several glass knives. Next to him stood a sallow man. In Shiloh's world, she would have guessed he was a junkie. He had a dragon glass sword and shield to match.

Behind the tall man a Six dragon stepped into the ring—its armor was thick and bristling with massive spikes. A cloud of dust rose next to the Six, and when it cleared, a Nine Dragon appeared. The crowd went even wilder in its lust for blood. The Nine was the size of a twenty-five foot python and had spikes running down its whole length.

"Oh, no," Stix let out. She looked around Stue's body. "Has Link had any mental defense training?"

"What?"

"This isn't good."

A wide grin crossed Stue's face.

On the other side of the coliseum, Link and Kai stepped into the ring, their sand spider armor covering their whole bodies. They both flicked their wrists, revealing the spikes, and the crowd booed. Moments later Maybel appeared and hit the glass wall with her tail, sending a large crack up its side. A great commotion stirred in the crowd as the observers laid their bets.

A dark shadow passed overhead, and Ember landed next to Link. She let out a terrible roar and the crowd went silent.

"Sir…" the servant said.

"He is an Eight?" Stue looked at Shiloh. "Who are you?"

"Ah sir…"

"Yes, go ahead." He waved his hand lazily, and the servant struck the bowl. Its sound reverberated through the coliseum, and in the ring below, the fighters sprang into action. Maybel charged the other Six and looked terrifying. The other Six reared up and charged her. They met in the middle of the field, and the sound of their butting heads made Shiloh cringe. She didn't want to watch, but she couldn't take her eyes off of the fight.

The Nine dragon spun like a circular saw at Link. It made up the distance across the field in mere seconds. Link leapt out of the way and ended up face down in the sand. He spun around quickly and stood. Ember blew a massive plume of fire at the Nine, but it had no effect. The people in the stands, however, shielded themselves and pushed each other over to get out of its way.

Maybel landed a blow with her mace-like tail, lodging its spikes deep into the other Six's leg. The other Six tugged hard, and Maybel was pulled sideways, leaving her torso exposed. The other Six rammed her and pinned her against the wall. It was trying to flip Maybel to get to her underside. Maybel struggled, but her tail was just as trapped as she was.

Kai and the bald man met in the middle of the ring. They circled each other while Kai's opponent swung his mace over head. After a few tense moments, the man let the mace fly. Kai blocked it with both arms. The mace nicked the armor and wrapped around Kai's left arm. The bald man pulled hard, sending Kai flying toward him. Midair, Kai flicked his foot, and spikes appeared on his shin guard. He spun, and his blades slit the man's throat.

The bald man reached for his neck and stared up at Kai in disbelief, before falling to his knees. Immediately, his dragon stopped fighting Maybel and charged Kai, stumbling with its maimed leg. Maybel swung her tail which had dislodged and swiped its feet from under it. The dragon skidded forward from its momentum, stopping inches from Kai.

The bald man fell to the ground, and his dragon disappeared.

The crowd booed and hissed.

The jeers were overpowered by a cheer on the other side of the coliseum. Link was down. He was flat on his back, and his arms were crossed in front of him like a mummy. The sallow Nine's rider stood over him, sword held high, while Ember and the Nine dragon were locked in a death match. The beast had wrapped its body around Ember and was squeezing tightly, but Ember had her teeth sunk into its neck. Kai and Maybel were running to Link, but there was no way they would make it in time.

The Nine's rider brought down his sword for the kill, but Link rolled aside just in time to avoid the blade piercing his heart. He shook his head as if he was coming out of a dream. The rider struck again, but Link deflected the blow with the blade on his forearm. Like thunder, Maybel charged in and pierced the man's chest with one of her horns. She shook her head a few times and flung him across the arena. The Nine dragon dropped to the ground and disappeared. The crowd hushed; it was over.

MELODY OF THE SOUL

Shiloh, Stix, and Pen ran into the glass-brick cell below the coliseum where they had been before the fight, leaving their escort in the long tunnel. Shiloh wrapped her arms around Link. "Thank God, you are alive! I was so worried… I don't know what I would have done if I lost you."

"But you didn't lose me." Link returned Shiloh's embrace tightly. The smell of burning fabric and hair filled the air, and Shiloh felt a hot sensation on her neck where her hood met her armor. Link pulled away quickly. "Sorry, it's back, and I can't turn them off." He extended his hands which were nearly glowing red.

"Looks like it burned right through your hood," Stix said. "No bother, we should be able to mend that for you quite quickly. Also," she turned to Link and nodded at his hands, "I have something that might help with that." She handed him a pair of spider shell gloves complete with the cooling membrane.

"When did you?" Link looked at the gloves with a humble expression on his face.

"I started working on them yesterday." Stix smiled then became somber. "During the first part of the fight. We couldn't watch, especially knowing that a Nine was fighting. It goes against everything we stand for. I kept my hands busy to take my mind off the fight—until you were in trouble."

"Yeah," Pen said. "At first you were doing great. You were like this." He lunged to one side. "Then like that." He lunged to the other side. "Next thing we know, you were lying on the ground with your arms crossed."

"I don't know what happened. My body just stopped listening to me. I couldn't move."

"It was the Nine," Stix said. "He was controlling your mind, until." All eyes looked expectantly at her. "Until I stopped him. When Shiloh told me you hadn't had any mental protection training, I blocked his attack so you could move."

"So you cheated." Stue's unwelcomed voice came from the entrance of the room. "I was just coming down to congratulate you, but it seems the match is forfeit. There will just have to be another one—guards!"

One of the guards pulled a lever on the wall, and a portcullis dropped from the ceiling, trapping them.

"He should have never been using his powers," Stix said. "It goes against the very being of a Nine."

"Perhaps he wasn't a Nine any longer, perhaps he lost who he was long ago. Now, the question is, do I have you all fight in the next match or—Your hair...that color"

Shiloh pushed the loose strands of hair back into the burnt hole as quickly as she could.

"I knew there was something more to you than met the eye. I felt it since I first laid eyes on you. You all just became much, much more valuable. When the capital—"

"You can't!" Kai flicked his wrists, and his blades extended.

"I can, and I will. There is nothing you can do about it. This dragon glass is reinforced. Eimi himself couldn't break through it."

"How dare you say his name!" Kai thrashed at the portcullis, but it did no good. "If you do this, you betray your people and Eimi. Are you not still a Seven?"

"Perhaps like the Nine in the fight, I ceased to be a Seven long ago." He turned to the guard on his left. "Treat them well. I wouldn't want Lord Abaddon to think we have been cruel to his guests."

"Pen!" Shiloh cried as soon as Stue was gone. "Where is Pen?"

"Just like a Four to run off," Kai complained, sitting on one of the dragon glass benches lining the room.

"Pen isn't a coward." Shiloh clenched her fists. "What do you have against him?"

"There are more important things to talk about." Link sat next to Kai. "How long will it take for the delegation to get here from the capital?"

"If they teleport, they will be here in a matter of minutes. If they fly, it will take them a day, maybe two."

"That doesn't leave us much time." Link raised his eyebrows. "Ouch." A small trickle of blood streamed down his brow.

"Link, you're bleeding. Are you alright?" Shiloh asked.

"I'm fine." Link wiped the blood from his brow.

"I wish we had a Two here to fix both of you up," Stix said, "and I'm concerned about your hands."

"The gloves are helping." Link shot Stix a smile.

"Stix, how far away is Yesod?" Shiloh asked.

"I think it would be about a day's flight."

"Could we contact someone from there to come help us?" Shiloh continued. "I heard you tell the general you were an observer and linked. What did that mean?"

"Nines have some psychic abilities, as you saw in the fight. We are able to communicate telepathically with one another. Thoughts travel in waves just as sound does. When you are linked to someone, you have attuned yourself to their frequency, and you can pick up their thought waves."

"Who were you attuned to?" Shiloh asked.

"My aunt; she is a Nine like me. I was working in her stall when we first met."

"Can you contact her now?" Link asked.

Stix shook her head. "My connection was broken when I was knocked out. We are too far away to find the thread of her thought again."

"I remember Pen saying something about Eights having psychic abilities, too." Shiloh began to pace.

"It is true," Kai said. "Although, their powers are usually used for controlling others. I would bet the Nine you fought had an Eight wing."

"What does that mean?" Link asked.

"Each person is on a spectrum. They have their number, but on either side are their wings just like a dragon has. Let's say you are an Eight like Link. His wings are the Seven and Nine. A person can lean more to one wing or the other or be right in the middle."

"Could Link amplify your power to connect?" Shiloh asked. "If he has psychic abilities, could his power be added to yours? Back home, our WIFI signal wasn't very strong, so mom bought a booster, and it was able to reach the whole house. Maybe Link could be a booster for you."

"I have no idea what a WIFI is," Kai said, "but you might be onto something. When Sevens need to teleport a great distance, we will pool our energy to travel further."

"It's worth a try," Link said. "Tell me what I need to do."

"Sit with me." Stix sat cross-legged with her hands on her knees. Link joined her, crossing his legs as well. "Now take my hands." Link hesitated for a moment. "The gloves will protect me from your heat."

Link took her hands, and they both blushed slightly.

After an awkward moment, Stix continued, "I will teach you the way my aunt taught me. Finding a person's thread of thought is like finding a drop of water in a vast ocean. Just as each person and dragon are unique, so is their thought signature. Nines believe this thread is what connects a person to their dragon, and, in turn, a dragon is connected to everything else. First, I must teach you my thought signature so we can connect."

Stix hummed the most beautiful melody. Its tones and frequency undulating, weaving in and out of each other. Link swayed to the tune. Shiloh found herself moving to it as well, entraining to its hypnotic rhythm. Soon, the humming stopped, but Link's body continued to sway as if he were still listening to the music.

"Yes," Link said. "I can hear your voice." Link opened his eyes. "I can hear you, but you aren't speaking. This is amazing!"

"You have found my thread and are connected to it. Now I must teach you my aunt's."

Stix hummed again. This time the song was a low dirge. It was somber and haunting. The audible sound stopped, but Shiloh could tell that Link was still connected to the song.

"I think I have it," Link said. "But I don't hear any words or anything outside of you."

"Now we must tie the threads together," Stix said. "Where is Ember?"

"She is flying high above the city. After the fight, she took to the air. She didn't want to stay here. Now I know why."

"Dragons always have a better sense than humans. I want you to find her and connect with her."

I am here with you. Ember touched all of their minds..

"Now we must transmit and hope she hears us."

The room was silent. All of the focus was drawn into Stix's and Link's meditative state.

Both Stix's and Link's heads shot up, and their mouths gaped open. Shiloh and Kai exchanged a nervous look.

"Is this normal?" Shiloh asked.

Kai shook his head.

"Should I wake them?" Shiloh asked. "They haven't moved in ages."

"I don't know—"

Stix and Link shot away from each other and huddled in little balls on either side of the cell. Shiloh rushed to her brother and cradled him. Kai did the same for Stix.

"Link, What's happening?" His body was convulsing "Link!"

Stop! Ember's powerful voice filled the cell and all became still.

A Million Stars Against the Velvet Sky

Many hours passed with Stix and Link immobile in the same positions. Shiloh checked every few minutes to make sure they were still breathing. Kai had been quiet since the incident happened, and Shiloh wished Pen was still there for support.

"What do you think happened to them?" Shiloh asked, breaking the silence.

Kai shook his head. "I do not know."

"I wish there was something more we could do. There has to be something." Shiloh racked her brain for all the information from books she had read, but she was drawing a blank. All she could think of were the Victorian Era novels in which they gave women who passed out smelling salts, but that didn't help them now. Why hadn't she read more medical books? Shiloh made it a point to read more when she returned—if they returned. Shiloh stroked Link's head and fought back tears.

"Right," a gruff voice said from outside the cell. "Stue says we have to feed you lot. Keep you healthy for Lord Abaddon. Says he will be really disappointed if anything happens to you. Oh, crikey, what happened to them two?" The crotchety old man walked to the lever that opened the cell and stopped abruptly. "I see… I see, you's faking it to get me to open these here bars, then you hit me over the head and escape. Well, you aren't going to pull a fast one over old Snaggletooth. Very clever."

"We aren't faking." Shiloh ran to the bars and grabbed them. "They have been like this for hours. Can you help us?"

"Right, little missy. What do you think, Myrtle?" The spiked six dragon with the crotchety old guard shook her head. "Here's your food and drink." The man took a key out of his pocket and opened a small door at the bottom of the cell. He slipped a tray through, closed it quickly, and walked away.

"Please," Shiloh said. "Is there nothing you can do?"

The guard looked over his shoulder. "There is something I can do, but the question is will I? Really, it's up to her." The guard patted the dragon on its side. "What's that, Myrtle? …Well, I suppose it wouldn't hurt… She does remind me of my niece, too." The guard looked at Shiloh. "If you bring them to the bars, Myrtle will help you."

"Help me, Kai." Together Shiloh and Kai pulled Link and Stix to the closed gate. "Now what?"

"Put their heads right up close."

Shiloh held Link's face to one of the openings in the lattice work of the gate, and Kai did the same with Stix. Myrtle lowered her head and opened her jaws wide, exposing a very large snaggle tooth that mirrored the guard's.

"Don't bite!" Shiloh pulled back Link abruptly.

"Bite! Why would poor old Myrtle bite? Do you want help or not? We can very well just get out of here."

"No, wait, sorry. We would love your help. Also, it would benefit you."

"How's that?"

"Didn't Stue say to keep us in good health. What if he or Lord Abaddon find out they were injured on your watch."

Snaggletooth stroked his chin. "Right you are. Let's try this again."

Shiloh repositioned Link's head, and Myrtle blew a stream of air that ruffled Link's hair. His eyes shot open, and he gulped as if he were drowning.

"Link, it's okay. I'm here."

Link's eyes shot up to Shiloh's, and they held a terror which she had never seen before. He broke his gaze and looked back and forth in the cell.

Stix gasped for air as well, but Shiloh only focused on Link. He pushed back from the gate, sending Shiloh toppling over. He scanned the cell frantically.

Shiloh pushed herself up. "Link, Link! What is it?"

"They are coming," he said, still not focusing.

"Who?" Kai asked.

"The Laka," Stix said in a raspy voice.

Snaggletooth let out a robust laugh. "Ya hear that, Myrtle? Next she is going to say Eimi exists. The Laka. You must have hit your head really hard—" Snaggletooth's body went rigid, and his eyes glazed over.

A whispering voice filled the air. Shiloh couldn't tell if it was one voice or many speaking all at once. The whispering drowned out all other noises. Even though it was quiet, it was all consuming.

Myrtle grasped at Snaggletooth's clothes and tried to pull him back. In return, she received a kick, causing Myrtle to lose her grip. Snagglethooth walked to the lever on the wall that opened the gate. In the distance, Shiloh could make out a ghostly figure—it was pale and had long white hair. All of its features seemed to be sucked in as if its very being was a black hole closing in on itself. Shiloh shuddered as a chill ran through her body. The figure lifted its hand with long cruel fingernails, and Snaggletooth lifted his hand. The figure gripped the air, and Snaggletooth clutched the lever. The figure put both hands at the level of Snaggletooth's head and turned them, then drew its fingers in a line. Snaggletooth's head turned, and a wicked smile crossed his face.

Myrtle charged at the figure, but it raised a palm, and she came to a screeching halt. Try as she might, the dragon couldn't push past the invisible force. The temperature dropped precipitously, and ice formed on the walls surrounding the Laka.

"Kai, what do we do?" Shiloh's voice was drowned out by the whispering. Shiloh could barely hear the rumbling of the gate lifting.

"Charge!" Pen's voice cut through the whispering.

The figure turned, and Shiloh gasped when she saw it struck by Maybel, Pen riding on her back. The Laka flew into the wall and right through it. Pen didn't even seem to notice it though; Maybel just continued on her rampage to Myrtle. The smaller six dragon lowered its head and stepped out of the way.

"Hop on!" Pen yelled, reaching the others. Everyone climbed aboard, piling on top of each other, and Maybel stormed out of the prison.

The long tunnel led them onto the field of the coliseum. The night air was fresh and dry. Above, a million stars twinkled against the velvet sky, and two large shapes dove toward them.

Ember landed with thundering noise and scooped Link and Shiloh from Maybel's back. Moments later they were airborne with Pen and Alithia at their side. Below, Maybel half-bounded, half-flew over the coliseum with Stix, Axel, and Kai.

Shiloh's body tensed. It was her first time flying since she had fallen. Her neck prickled as if someone was watching her. She looked back, and on the floor of the arena two ghostly figures stood far below. She turned immediately. Her fear of the Laka outweighed her fear of falling. She knew with them, a fate worse than death waited.

THE PILLAR OF FLAME

The wind rushed past Shiloh's ears as she clutched Link tightly to her chest. Ember's powerful muscles flexed and contracted with every flap of her wings. The tranquility of the night sky was a stark contrast to the terror in the prison cell. Shiloh couldn't get the overwhelming whispering out of her head. It was like a horde of cicadas all singing at once.

Time sped past like the desert below, and the sun crested the horizon. It sparkled in the morning light as the stars faded. Ahead, Pen and Alithia dove to meet Maybel, and Shiloh's stomach lurched as Ember followed suit. She squeezed Link even tighter and clamped down on Ember with her thighs. She wasn't going to make the same mistake she had before.

Do not fear, little one. I will never let anything happen to you, Ember's powerful voice entered Shiloh's head, banishing her fear of their descent and any remnant of the whispering from the Laka.

Shiloh's legs were shaky as she stepped onto the ground. She sank into the fluid sand, and her feet dragged as she walked to join the others.

"Do you think we will be followed?" Link asked.

"They can try," Kai said, "but I doubt they will find us. It is nearly impossible to track someone in the air, and Axel has covered our tracks." Shiloh had wondered what the Nine Dragon was doing hanging off Maybel's back side.

"Why have we stopped?" Stix asked, shakily. "I want to get as far away from that thing as possible."

On this flat terrain, Maybel's voice filled everyone's head, *We can be spotted from miles away by air. It is safer for us to stop, assuming Alithia and Pen have the power to shield us from view.*

All eyes turned to Pen.

"I ahh… We…" Pen rubbed the back of his head. He looked at Maybel who was about the size of Alithia and Ember who was twice her size. "We can try."

We will lend you our power as well, Ember's voice filled them all. *Alone it would be impossible, but by the power of the Flame combined, all things are possible.*

"Very well," Kai said. "It is settled. Let us assemble ourselves in the style of my people."

Once the dragons were assembled head to tail, and their wings stretched out overhead, Alithia worked her magic. Pen kept popping out of the circle saying things like, "Almost there," and "I can still see a claw." After about five minutes, every inch of them was concealed.

Kai placed a hand on Pen's shoulder as he stepped back into the enclosure. "I owe you an apology. I called you a coward. It took great bravery for you to do what you did for us. Not many would have had the courage to risk their own safety to save others. I am in your debt."

Pen smiled. "I heard you call me a coward, but it made my plan all the better. The moment Stue said 'cheated,' I had a feeling that he was going to do something like that. I camouflaged myself and was able to escape right as the portcullis closed. I didn't spare any time. I ran until I got a cramp in my side. But, by then, I was able to blend in with the crowd leaving the coliseum. I would have come back for you sooner, but I had to take care of this first." He patted the saddlebags on Alithia.

"What's in there?" Link raised an eyebrow.

Pen pulled out five large bladders of water and passed them out to the others. Shiloh opened hers and took a large swig. Her fear had kept her from noticing how parched she was, but after tasting a few drops, her thirst became insatiable.

"Once again, I am in your debt." Kai raised his water in a toast to Pen and drank.

"We all are," Shiloh said. "Thank you, Pen."

Pen blushed.

"How did you get this much water?" Stix asked. "This must have cost you..."

"I traded for it."

"What did you trade?" Shiloh asked, after taking another sip.

"My stick."

"Pen, you loved that stick."

"It was my most valuable possession. I didn't tell you this before, but wood isn't only rare; it is also considered a holy relic. The One's say wood is a reminder of a time when Eimi walked amongst us. They say it is proof He was once here and the ground was fertile. It is considered a sin to cut down a tree from one of our arboretums, and thus wood is incredibly rare. I took my staff to the local temple and traded it with the Temple Master. He had never seen a piece of wood before. He took a while inspecting it to make sure it was real. He gave me the five bladders of water and some food for us all. I hope it will be enough to get us to where we are going. How many days will it take us to reach the Wandering Tribes?"

All eyes turned to Kai.

Kai lowered his head. "We won't find them down here."

"What do you mean?" Stix asked.

"Yeah," Pen said. "Everyone knows the Sevens and the Wandering Tribes live in the desert to the south of the Kingdom. Right?"

"That is what we want you to believe. We want everyone to believe that."

"If you don't live in the Southlands, where do you live?" Pen's shocked face was almost comical. His eyebrows were raised so high they were almost falling off of his forehead.

"And what are we supposed to do?" Shiloh asked. "We can't go back the way we came, not with that thing after us. I would rather face one hundred sand spiders than see it again."

"You saw it?" Link asked.

"Saw what?" Pen raised an eyebrow.

"The Laka, didn't any of you see it?"

"I felt it." Stix shuttered. "No matter how hard I try, I don't think I will ever forget what they feel like."

Kai looked at each one of them somberly, finally resting his gaze on Shiloh. "As for what we will do, I do not know, but I am in your debt." He nodded to Pen. "I will tell you the true story of the Sevens. Before I do, I need each of you to swear by Eimi that you will not tell another living soul lest the great fire from above come down and consume you."

Everyone swore in their own way.

"Very well," Kai said. "After the Great Fall, the Sevens refused to follow Aboddon's rule. Our once great city of Malkuth was destroyed by him and the Eights. Many died, others were enslaved by the Laka." A shiver ran down Shiloh's spine. "But the rest of us fled into the deep southern desert. Seven dragons can fly farther than any others, and the Eights had no chance of catching us. My people wandered the desert for forty years. We survived on desert spiders, and our dragons have the ability to produce our own water."

"How?" Pen leaned even farther forward with his chin on both hands.

"Look at Alithia's wing." Kai pointed up. "Do you see all of those little veins?"

Pen nodded eagerly.

"Seven's have those, too. However, they can retract the membrane covering the webbing of veins and tendons. This mesh collects moisture from the air and funnels it down to the cool of the dragon's shadow where it is collected."

"That is amazing!" Shiloh said, "It is like a Warka Water Tower in Ethiopia."

"A what?" Link asked.

"Do you ever pay attention in school? We learned about them in Mrs. Wilminster's class."

"Nope, don't remember." Link leaned back against Ember with his hands behind his head.

"It looks like this." Shiloh drew a vase shape in the ground with lines crossing through it and coming out of the top.

"Oh, I remember that."

Shiloh shook her head. "Anyway, they work in a similar fashion and are able to pull condensation from the air. It is amazing Seven Dragons can do that. I wonder if they adapted to the environment."

"I don't know if they always could, or if they just adapted, but it was enough to sustain my people for forty years. We interacted very little with the Kingdom except to trade or collect a new Seven after their year at Dragon's Claw Academy. Just like any other dragon rider, they came for a year of apprenticeship."

"Wait a minute," Link said. "If you were off wandering in the desert, how did you get back and forth to the Kingdom?"

"Some Seven's can teleport?" Shiloh said. She wished her brother would pay closer attention.

"Right, I forgot about that part." Link cozied even further into Ember.

"Some?" Pen asked, almost falling over from leaning so far forward.

"Some can teleport, and others have wings themselves—"

"Wings!" Pen was nearly shouting. "I have never heard that before. You're joking, right?"

Kai gave Pen a half smile. "I hope you get to see it for yourself. Anyway, teleporters like me kept the lines of transport and communication open."

"How did you find the tribe again after you teleported?" Stix asked.

"You of all people should know that. Just like Nines can tie into others' thoughts, Sevens can tie into the energy signature of other Sevens. We create a tether with someone back home or someone in a city, like Stue—that traitor!"

"Keep going," Pen said.

"After a Seven has served a year with the Wandering Tribes, they have a choice: they can either stay with us or go back to the Kingdom. Ninety percent choose to stay. A Seven has an untamed heart and must be free. Of those few who chose to go back, more often than not, they returned if they could find a way. If a Seven did decide to join us, we would offer sanctuary to them and their family.

"The size of the wandering tribes swelled in numbers not only because of this, but because others' dragons had a calling, leading them to the desert to find us."

"Like me!" Pen shouted. "Alithia had a calling for the desert. I was trying to find the Wandering Tribes when I found them." Pen nodded to Shiloh and Link.

"Interesting." Kai stroked his chin.

"What is it?" Pen asked.

"Nothing… Shall I continue?"

"Yes," Shiloh said, hungry to learn more.

"As I said before, the Wandering Tribes swelled in size, and it got to the point where the water from the Seven Dragons could no longer sustain us. As a people we appealed to Eimi in prayer and fasting. And he answered. A great pillar of cloud rose up in front of us. Many people were terrified and thought it was a storm coming to destroy us, but others said they caught a glimpse of Eimi inside the pillar. The pillar of cloud led our people by day, and by night it became a pillar of fire. Dragons are made of earth, wind, and fire. For another forty years our people were thus led until we reached the Promised Land."

Shiloh could hardly believe what she heard, and her expression showed that amazement.

"What is it?" Kai asked Shiloh.

"Your story sounds like one from our own culture."

"What was the Promised Land like?" Pen asked.

"At first the earth below our feet hardened like walking on dragon glass. Gradually, the color of the sand gave way to green. There was grass, shrubs, and trees."

Pen hung his head.

"Pen?" Shiloh put a hand on his shoulder, and he shrugged it off. "What is it?"

"I'm too ashamed to tell you." Pen looked at the others and sighed heavily.

Tell them, Alithia's voice filled their heads.

"I stole it." Pen picked up a bit of sand and threw it.

And..

"And I lied about it. I found the branch in the track that surrounds the Temple. See, one day I was waiting for my dad, and, well, this branch fell. No one was around, so I took it, carved it, and said I had traded for it.

Link whistled. "Like I said before—rebel."

"Link!" Shiloh frowned at her brother.

"I should have turned it in at the Temple—that is the law, but I wanted it for myself. I was proud of it. Or at least I was until now." Pen hung his head in shame.

Everyone was silent at Pen's confession. Then Kai said, "Pen, that sacred wood saved our lives."

Pen looked up avoiding eye contact. "Anyway, how is the Promised Land green? That would take more water than …"

A wide grin spread across Kai's face.

"No," Pen said.

Kai nodded.

"How is that possible?" Stix asked.

"After the sand gave way to grass and forest, we soon came upon a mighty river, and we met Mim, the keeper of the Promised Land."

"You mentioned her before," Shiloh said.

"How was there water there?" Pen asked. "I mean a whole river. That is impossible."

"Mim is a Five, and the river was created by her dragon Jordan."

Stix sat up straight. "But the Fives are extinct! There hasn't been one since the fall."

"I will let Mim explain it all when you meet her."

"If we meet her," Link said. "We still don't have a plan. We have maybe two or three days worth of water, then what?"

"Have faith," Kai said.

Chapter Eighteen

LEGION

A bead of sweat rolled down Shiloh's face. She could only imagine how hot it was in the open desert. Everyone was dozing lazily; extreme heat has a way of doing that to people. Shiloh was so grateful for the protection from the dragon's wings and her desert spider armor. However, she wondered how long the cooling membrane would last. Could they really survive in the open desert? If the heat didn't kill them, thirst and hunger eventually would. It was suicide. Shiloh wished she had Kai's faith, but her logical mind wouldn't let her ignore the facts. They would die if they didn't find water and shelter.

"You can't sleep, either?" Link said from her side.

Shiloh shook her head. "I keep thinking about all of the ways we could die out here."

"My mind is racing, too."

"About what?"

"The Laka." Link's face was grave.

"I was so worried I had lost you back there. Both of you were curled up, shivering, seemingly unconscious, unresponsive. What happened?"

"I don't want to think about it."

"You already are. It might help you to talk about it. I'm always here for you." Shiloh put a hand on Link's knee to calm the bouncing.

"Thank you." He grasped her hand tightly. "It… it was so beautiful and terrible at the same time. We found Stix's aunt and our three consciousnesses sang together. We conveyed messages at such a deep and profound level. It was like golden threads all weaving together, looping in and out of each other. Then… her aunt went silent, and a darkness dimmed her light. Whispering drowned out everything else. They pulled on the threads of our thoughts and bound us to her aunt's consciousness. We were tethered and couldn't escape. Slowly, the Laka climbed on the golden arc of our thoughts, dimming its light, and distorting its melody into dissonance. Their jagged voices climbed all the way to Ember, and she fought them for all of the time you saw us shaking. That was Ember protecting us. They almost got me. They almost severed my connection with her…"

"You said them—how many of them were there?"

"It's hard to tell, but I know there was more than one."

"How did you finally escape?"

A shadow crossed Link's face.

"Link, if they attack again… I need to know how to protect myself. I don't know if you noticed, but I don't have a dragon. I don't have Ember to protect me."

"She will protect you with her last breath as well. Remember how we thought dragons were a part of our soul. After that experience, I think they are more like our guardian angels. Think about it, when you have the two voices inside of you, it is like the good angel on one shoulder and the bad on the other. That is the Laka and your dragon."

"Link, how did you finally break free?"

Link looked at her somberly. "Ember shouted 'Enough,' and it shook my insides. It shook the connection, and Stix's aunt's thread went completely silent. I think she might have died."

Shiloh glanced over at Stix curled up next to Axel. "I would have never known. She seems unphased."

"Don't shed water in the desert," Link said. "That is the rule. But I can still feel Stix; we are still connected somehow. Her song is one of mourning now. It is one of the saddest things I have ever heard. It makes me want to cry for her."

They sat in silence, and tears formed in Link's eyes.

"What happened to my rough and tough brother?" Shiloh punched Link in the arm. She had never known him to be so sensitive, or at least he had never talked about it.

"Ember has changed me. The desert has changed me." Link wiped the tears from his eyes.

Shiloh covered her face as she was pelted with sand.

She was just about to say, "hey," when she saw Kai with his finger to his lips. He cupped his hand around his ear gesturing for them to listen.

"Well, that's just great," a weaselly voice said. "The trail ends here."

"Are you sure?" another voice grumbled.

"Look at the hound yourself. Does it look like he is moving? Don't they teach you how to track in the capital?"

"Watch your tongue, or it will be the last thing you say before I feed it to you. Is that clear?"

"Well, the hounds don't lie. They either flew away from here, or they were teleported."

"For your sake, let's hope for the former. If they teleported, we may never find them, and Lord Abaddon will be very disappointed. I hate to see what he will do to you and the pathetic little trading post."

"What was that?" Stue's distinctive voice came from a little further away.

"Let me spell it out for you. If you fail to find them, you and your pathetic little fort will be wiped from the face of the earth. It has long been suspected you have been helping the Wandering Tribes teleport people."

"You know very well I have been loyal to Lord Abaddon."

"Stue, everyone knows you are only loyal to profit and yourself—a man like that cannot be trusted. Spread out!" the gruff voice shouted. "And remember, they have a Four with them. They could be hiding anywhere."

The sound of heavily armored Six dragons rumbled in the direction of the voices. Shiloh was grateful Kai had encouraged Maybel to fly a short distance away from the end of her trail. She couldn't go far bearing the others, but Shiloh hoped it was far enough to lose the scent.

The wind shifted, and a hound let out a blood curdling howl. "Sir, she has the scent again. This way."

The sound of armored Six dragons got closer and closer.

"Kai," Shiloh whispered. "Are sand spiders attracted to blood or water?"

Kai put his finger to his lips.

"Answer me."

"Blood."

Shiloh flicked her wrist and the spikes on her armor extended. She winced as she ran the sharp spike over her hand. A small pool of crimson blood formed in the palm of her hand. She quickly packed sand on the wound.

"Are you crazy?" Link asked in a forceful whisper.

"Trust me." Shiloh forced her way from behind Alithia's wing on the opposite side from the voices. Kai tried to grab her, but she was too quick.

The ferocious sun beat down hard on Shiloh, and she pulled her hood over her head for protection. From the outside, the dragon enclosure looked like a giant sand dune, blending in perfectly with the rest of the desert. Shiloh peered round the edge of the dune, and ten Six dragons with their riders came into view. At their lead, a three-headed beast spotted her, and its corded muscles rippled under its shiny black fur as it tugged forward on its chain. The beast was about the size of a Six dragon with the musculature of a pit bull, but its heads were those of Dire Wolves with giant fangs. A shiver ran down Shiloh's spine when one of the heads made eye contact with her. It pulled so hard on its chain, it nearly knocked the Six dragon it was tethered to over.

Shiloh's heart pounded, and she reflexively ran away from her friends and the terrifying dog. She never liked dogs. They always chased her on her runs.

She stopped in her tracks as day became night and a black shadow covered the land. Shiloh looked up, and just as she did, the shadow passed, and she was blinded by the sun. She blinked her eyes, and when her sight returned, there was now a giant Eight dragon as well as Stue's dragon.

The rider of the Eight dismounted and pulled off his black leather gloves. The man stood over six feet tall with jet black hair and black eyes. His skin was lighter than anyone else Shiloh had met since she arrived, and his face was gaunt.

"Come forward, child. Do not be afraid," the rider said in a raspy voice. He turned to Stue. "Lucky for you, Cerberus was able to find her."

"I'm not afraid." Shiloh placed her hands on her hips definitely.

"Where are the others?" the rider asked.

"They left me here." Shiloh held her ground.

"Why would they do that?" Stue's face contorted into a question mark.

"Because the Laka are after me."

Stue laughed heartily. "The Laka. They don't exist. They are just children's stories and old man's dreams. Just as Eimi is." The dog snarled as if Stue's words injured it. "A man of this world knows none of that exists. No, I gave up my faith in all of that years ago."

"Silence, you fool," the Eight rider said. "Girl, come with us."

"My name is Shiloh, and I take it you are Lord Abaddon."

At this the whole company laughed, including the rider.

"No, I am Legion, Baron of Geburah, a faithful servant of Lord Abaddon, may he reign forever."

All the Sixes pounded their chest once at heart level and parroted back, "May he reign forever."

"Well, Legion, if you want me to go anywhere with you, you will have to catch me first." Shiloh took off at a sprint away from her friends and foe alike. The sand made it incredibly difficult to run, but she didn't have to go far—just far enough so her friends wouldn't be in danger. The hound barked behind her, and the armored Six Dragons clamored as she ran down a steep sand slope and scrambled up the other side. Her foes reached the valley below, and she tossed the bloodied sand into their midst—chaos ensued. The moment the blood hit the sand, sand spiders emerged, toppling the Six dragons. One latched onto the dog's powerful hind legs, but the dog bit its head off and tore it into pieces.

Legion watched from the summit of the opposite dune. He mounted his dragon, and just as they were taking off, Maybel and Ember barreled into them, sending the huge black dragon tumbling into the fray. In one bound, Ember flew to the peak where Shiloh was and scooped her up. Moments later, they were high in the air, and the rushing wind cooled Shiloh, who was on the verge of collapsing from the heat and exertion.

STAR STONES

"Link, where are we going, and what about the others?" Shiloh asked, as the vast sea of dunes spread out below them.

"You shouldn't have done that." Link kept his gaze forward, both hands on the ring-like spike on Ember's back and his legs bent up under the edge of her wings.

"It worked, didn't it."

"Don't you understand that Kai, Pen, and… Stix," Link said angrily, shaking his head, "all risked their lives to save you. By doing that—"

"I risked my life to save them—and you." Shiloh's cheeks flushed. "There isn't a difference. Why are you so angry about it?"

"Because I love you, and because… Shiloh, I can't lose you, too." A ribbon of steam leaked out from Link's gloves.

"Link, your hands."

"It will stop in a minute. Ember has been helping me learn to control it. I need to be silent, though, and focus my mind."

Shiloh clutched her brother tightly around the waist with both her arms and bent legs. "You won't lose me. I'm right here with you."

They flew on in silence for several hours, as wave after wave of sand rose and fell. The sun sank low into the western sky, and by its position, Shiloh could tell they were still traveling south.

"I'm better now." Link's words floated on the silent night and startled Shiloh from her private thoughts.

"What is going on with you—with your hands?"

"It's like Kai said, I am out of balance. Ember can help me some, but Shiloh, it is spreading."

Warm tears flew off of Shiloh's cheeks and into the wind.

Do not waste your water. This was the first time Ember had spoken to Shiloh on the flight. *I won't let anything happen to him.* Ember's words were powerful and said with such conviction that Shiloh believed them.

"Do you think the others made it out, Link?"

"I'm not sure. We will know when we meet at the rendezvous point. When you were playing the hero, Kai transmitted an image to Ember of where we should meet if we got separated."

"And where is that? I thought there was nothing to the south except the great desert."

We are going to Malkuth. It was the ancestral home of the Seven's before the great fall. It is a ruined desolate place, but there is a chance we might be able to hide there.

"What happens if the others don't show up? How much food and water do we have?"

"None," Link said.

"You know we can only survive one or two days without water. Three at most."

"I know."

We will wait a day and a half for them. If they haven't arrived, I will take you back to the trading post.

"What? No, we can't go back there." Shiloh's whole body tensed. *It is our only choice. Now rest and save your water.*

Shiloh had the worst pain in her neck. Her right cheek was firmly planted on Link's back, and there was a trace of moisture from her drool. She straightened and rolled her head from side to side, but the pain continued. She tried to move her arms to clear the sleep from her eyes, but they were frozen around Link's waist. She must have slept like this the whole night. With great effort, she pried one arm free, then the other, sending pins and needles down their lengths. She shook them out and rubbed the sleep from her eyes.

"You're awake?" Link's voice was tender. His tone brought back memories of when they would stay up all night during slumber parties with their friends and were the only ones still awake just before dawn.

"Barely. I can't believe I was actually able to sleep." Shiloh looked below, and her stomach wrenched at the height. "I don't think I will ever get used to flying. Were you able to sleep at all?"

"No, but I had good company." Link patted Ember.

"Is that where we are heading?" Shiloh pointed to some jagged shapes in the distance. They stuck out of the desert like shark's teeth devouring the sand and glowed red in the morning sun, making them appear stained with blood.

"Yes, looks kind of creepy, doesn't it? I have been watching it all morning, wondering what is waiting there for us."

The sun was three fingers width from the horizon when they reached the city. The shark teeth structure surrounding the city was actually red stone. Its composition reminded Shiloh of the sandstone at Red Rocks Amphitheater. Their parents had taken them there once to see a concert, when visiting her grandmother. It was such a magical night sitting under the stars in her father's embrace, listening to a symphony playing the score from Fantasia. Shiloh's heart ached, knowing she would never feel his embrace again, nor hear his voice.

Shiloh focused on the decrepit city below to take her mind off of the painful memory. Behind the stone wall, buildings lay in ruin—their edges softened by the harshness of the elements. Most of the adobe style structures were charred black, and the stone looked like it had been melted. There was a term for this—*vitrified*. Yes, the buildings were vitrified, melting like an ice cream cake on a hot day.

"What do you think happened here?" Link asked.

"I have no idea, but I can see why the Seven's left."

"Ember, let's land there." Link pointed to a large square in the middle of the town. One or two buildings were intact, but most were vitrified.

Ember landed with the grace of a cat jumping from the couch to the floor. Her mighty legs absorbed the impact, and Shiloh barely felt it when they touched the ground. Link held onto the ring-shaped spike as he swung his leg over to one side. Ember lifted the crest of her wing, and Link slid to the ground. Shiloh mimicked him, and her inner thighs screamed out. They were rubbed raw and ached from the night's flight. She closed her eyes as she slid down the wing, and her stomach lurched on the descent.

Shiloh's legs wobbled as Link helped her to her feet. The air tasted of dust, and the city smelled like burnt hair. Eight streets led into the square, two on each corner. On three sides of the square the buildings were a melted glob, but to the right one building was still intact and had beautiful spires reaching up.

"It kinda feels like a tumbleweed should blow through at any moment, doesn't it?"

Shiloh smiled at Link. "Yeah, it's like we just entered a ghost town in an old western movie. Remember how Grandpa used to watch them all the time?"

Link chuckled. "I think Grandpa was a cowboy in a past life."

"What do you think did all of this?" Shiloh motioned to the melted buildings.

"Dragons," Link said plainly. "What else could have done it?"

"We should find some shelter, the sun is already starting to fill the square. We also need to try to find some water. Let's start there." Shiloh pointed to the spired building. "Ember, do you think you can fit through those doors?"

Ember turned her long black neck to the building and examined the three archways where solid doors once stood. *I think I can fit through the center one. If not, I will make a way. I am not letting you two out of my sight. Not here in this place of desolation. Shadows like to grow in empty places.*

A chill ran through Shiloh's spine, and the hairs on her arms stood on end inside her armor.

"Then we will be the light that drowns the shadows out." Link flexed his wrists, and the spikes on his armor stood at attention. Shiloh did the same, and they proceeded to the building looming on the eastern side of the square. A gated fence had once surrounded the building. Remnants of cast iron bars dotted the perimeter. Shiloh and Link slipped through an opening, and Ember took one giant leap, clearing the twelve foot fence with ease.

Three giant arches loomed before them. In their center, empty spaces gaped open where doors once stood but had long since been abandoned to time. The darkness on the other side unnerved Shiloh. It was the type of darkness under your bed as a child, a darkness that brought up primal fear. Shiloh avoided staring into the abyss by following the carvings etched into the arch up to the keystone, where a flame seemed to jump off of the sandstone. She observed the other carvings and realized it was the creation story from the summoning ceremony. It was all there carved in this one archway. Something about knowing this was here eased Shiloh's tension—knowing that *the flame brought light to darkness.*

"Well," Link said. "Will you be able to fit?"

It will be tight, but I can always make a way."

Link shot Ember a smile. He took two steps forward.

Wait. Ember's warning brought the fear shooting back into Shiloh's body. *Do you hear it?*

Shiloh strained her ears, but the silence was as empty as the space where the door had once stood.

"There… and there was another one?" The smile from Link's face disappeared.

"What is it?"

A bated moment passed. All was silent; even the wind seemed to have disappeared.

"It is gone now. Should we try to find another building?"

This is the only one I will fit in. If we want to remain hidden, this is our best choice.

"Well," Link said, "we may as well let them know we are coming."

Ember lowered her head and blew a plume of fire into the hollow of the building. Shiloh shielded her face from the heat, but she could make out pillar upon pillar inside the structure and a magnificent sparkling domed ceiling.

"This must have been where they did the summoning ceremony," Shiloh said.

"How do you know that?" Link asked.

"That dome reminds me of the one in Pen's town, and did you see the floor? It had the same circle with numbers around it. And look here." Shiloh pointed to the sculpture.

This is a sacred place. We must bring the light back into it once more. Ember blew another large plume of fire into the building. This time, lanterns on the columns lit. One or two of the lanterns burst, sending an echoing bang throughout the dome, but most withstood the heat.

"Why do you think there aren't any windows?" Shiloh asked.

"I don't know. Maybe dragon glass hadn't been invented when this place was made. This is the first stone I have seen our whole time here."

Come let us reclaim this place. Ember stepped over them and pushed through the archway. Dust and a few small rocks came down as the girth of her body crossed the threshold, but the arch maintained its shape. Ember lit more candles and lanterns as she passed, brightening the way for them.

Shiloh walked beside Link. She glanced nervously at the spaces behind the columns still shrouded in darkness.

"Link, what was it that you heard?"

"It was a sort of faint clicking. It was probably nothing. Old buildings have a way of shifting."

If Link was trying to be reassuring, he wasn't doing a good job of it. Shiloh looked over her shoulder and wished that the light pouring through the door filled every inch of this forgotten place.

It wasn't long before they stopped beside Ember in what Shiloh supposed was the center of the dome. It was hard to tell as their path was the only one lit.

Watch this. Ember blew a pillar of fire fifty feet in the air.

Shiloh was momentarily blinded by the light and the flash of white that followed. It was like looking at the sun and still seeing its shape in a brilliant white, green, yellow afterimage impressed on your retinas. She rubbed her eyes, and her mouth gaped open. On the domed ceiling, little iridescent pinpoints of light appeared.

Ember blew fire again, this time all around them and above. As Shiloh's eyes cleared, the whole galaxy appeared on the dome. It was just like looking at the night sky.

"There's Orion," Link said.

"And there is our constellation, Gemini." The stars brought a warmth into Shiloh. It was the same sense of security and safety a nightlight brings as it pushes out the cursed dark. For the first time in days, she felt hopeful. She loved reading adventure books filled with excitement and danger—but, it was a whole different thing living through one. She had been running on adrenaline nonstop since she was kidnapped. Her mind hadn't caught up to the situation; she had constantly been in a fight or flight mode.

"What is it?" Link's face shone in the reflection of the stars.

"I'm tired… drained… I wasn't built for this. I'm supposed to be studying and learning, not fighting and running for my life.

We never know what we are built for until we have been tried by fire. I believe you are built for much more than even this. Do not fear the person you must become. Stay here. Ember leapt to the far side of the dome and lit the corridor of columns stretching to the far end of the temple.

Thirst bit at the back of Shiloh's throat. "Link, we need to find water soon, and Ember won't be able to come with us. She won't be able to fit down the corridors or into the rooms where the water is stored. We haven't had anything to drink since yesterday afternoon."

"I know, I feel it too. Let's wait until she has lit this entire hall and explore here first. Maybe we will get lucky."

Shiloh bent down to the ground and lay on her back. If she had to wait, she wanted to admire the starred ceiling above in all of its glory.

Link joined her and placed his arm under her head. "We will be alright. I know it."

Shiloh sighed heavily. She wished she could believe his words, but she hadn't felt alright in some time. She wasn't concerned just about herself; Link's hands worried her. Even with the gloves, she could tell he was in pain. She had caught him rubbing them, and he had told her it was spreading. She could feel the heat radiating from under his armor. She was also still numb from the loss of her parents. She had pushed that sorrow to the back of her mind to survive, but thinking about losing Link, it was all too much. She would have to save him at all costs. She couldn't lose him too.

The temple is clear and lit. If there ever was anything here, it is gone now. Link, take these and squeeze them tightly in your hands. Ember nudged two large stones to Link. He sat up and took off his glove. His hand glowed bright orange, and steam from the spider goo ribboned in the air.

"Don't look," he said, quickly.

Shiloh respected his wishes and turned away.

Now, place one on your chest and give one to Shiloh.

"Can I look now?"

"Yes,"

Inside each of Link's fists a white light was pouring out. He placed one of his hands to his chest and pressed firmly. The stone melted into his armor. As he removed his hand, it was as if a star shone brightly from his solar plexus, lighting the room in front of him.

"Put this on." Link handed her his glove. Shiloh slid her hand inside and took the stone from his outstretched hand. She pressed firmly into the chest shield of her armor. When she removed her hand, the same white light shone from her.

"This is so beautiful." Shiloh waved her hand in front of her chest. She took the glove off and handed it back to Link.

I know you must seek water, and these will aid you in any dark places.

"Thank you. What makes them glow?" Shiloh couldn't help her question. Even though she was in awe of the star stone, she wanted to know how it worked. "How long will it last? Will it burn me?"

"Mine has already cooled down." Link tapped his stone gently. "But it is still glowing as bright as before."

"Right, and the stars on the ceiling haven't diminished. I suppose if we run out of juice you can recharge them."

"I suppose so."

Go find that which you need.

Chapter Twenty

WHISPERS IN THE DARK

"Did you find anything?" Link asked when they returned to the center of the dome where Ember lay curled up under the stars. It had been about an hour, and neither the stars nor the light on Shiloh's chest had faded.

"Nothing. You?"

"Lots of cool things," Link said, "but no water. I'm really starting to feel it now. I got light-headed a few times, and I think it will only get worse as it gets hotter."

Shiloh's body was dehydrated as well, but she was a distance runner; she was used to being under that type of strain. She had the mental toughness to shrug off any discomfort. She also knew this strength could also be her undoing. She once ran so hard in a race she actually passed out. She was so embarrassed when she woke up and saw everyone standing over her.

Shiloh pointed to her right. "I found a passageway that looks like it leads below the temple. I didn't want to go down there without you, though." Shiloh's light had given her confidence but not enough to brave that passage alone.

"I'm happy you didn't. We shouldn't split up. Ember, will you announce our coming?" Link asked.

With pleasure. The dragon rose to her full height, and the stone scraped under her spear-like claws.

Shiloh led them to the passageway in the northwest corner of the temple. Ember breathed in deeply, expanding her black body, and the mark of Gemini on her chest glowed brightly. The glow traveled up her long neck and erupted out of her mouth in a steady stream of fire. She moved back, and the passageway glowed with star stones leading down a flight of fifteen stairs.

The light from the star stones stopped at the base of the stairs. It didn't matter, though. The light from the star stones on their chests was enough to light the passageway five feet in front of them.

There was no way to get lost in the passageway, which led down at a thirty percent gradient. The rock was smooth on all sides, and the path was well worn. Shiloh was grateful for the light in front of them but was always conscious of the darkness closing behind.

Soon, the passage opened into a large cavern that looked like a subway stop. Ten feet from the exit of the passage, the ledge dropped off. To the left and right, the ledge continued out of the radius of light.

"Over here! Look!" Link shone his light on the wall near the entrance of the passage. Out of the void appeared five water jugs that stood about hip height. Next to them was a smaller cup for dipping out water.

Link picked up the cup and plunged it into the first jug. "Empty." He repeated the process with all five jugs with the same result. Link went to smash the cup against the wall, but Shiloh stopped him. Link's arm radiated heat through his armor, and Shiloh pulled her hand away quickly so as not to get burned.

"We might need that."

"Fine." Link handed Shiloh the cup and kicked over one of the jugs. The shattering sound reverberated up and down the cavern, getting lost in the distance.

"Link?"

"It's harder to control it when Ember isn't with me."

"Control what?"

"My anger. Ember says that's why I am out of balance. That's why my body is burning itself. I have a rage inside of me I can't control. Since mom and dad died…" He kicked a piece of the clay jug into the darkness.

"What do you need?" Shiloh wanted to help her brother but didn't know how.

"Nothing that you can provide."

The air got heavy.

"Come on. These are here for a reason." Shiloh pointed to the jugs. "Let's go to the ledge and see what's on the other side."

Since Ember had appeared, Shiloh felt like she finally had her brother back, the loving, caring, sometimes over-protective brother she loved so much. It hurt her to see Link returning to this bitter person she hardly recognized.

Shiloh's feet teetered over the ledge which dropped off about four feet into what appeared to be a dried up riverbed. Smooth pebbles lined the bottom of the channel and there was claylike dirt below.

"Hold this." Shiloh handed Link the cup, and she jumped down.

"What are you doing?"

"I read that sometimes under dried-out river beds there is still water. You just have to dig for it."

"Shiloh…" His voice faltered, and he dropped the cup as he passed out. His body was limp, and an arm dangled over the ledge.

"Link! Wake up! Link!" Shiloh touched his forehead. He was burning up. She pushed his arm back onto the ledge so he wouldn't fall into the canal, and she kicked away the smooth stones. She dropped to all fours and dug her fingers into the ground. The clay pressed up under her fingernails, and the smell of earth reached her nostrils. She found a curved rock and troweled at the dirt. Still no water. Sweat beaded her brow as she continued to dig furiously.

"Argh!" She yelled and threw the stone. The echo of her cry bounced off the cavern walls. The river bed was dry. She glanced back at Link. "Please," she prayed. "I need water." The light under her hands shone more intensely, and she dug harder. The dry clay became wet. It wasn't just the sweat on her hands. This was water, actual water, seeping up through the dirt. She redoubled her efforts to dig deeper, and the water pooled enough that she could use the cup. She scooped some into the mug and brought it to Link's lips. Link gagged, then his body accepted the water. Shiloh lifted the cup to his lips again, careful not to go too quickly or give him too much.

Shiloh refilled the mug and poured it over Link's head. He shot up and gasped, looking around wildly.

"It's okay, I have water." Shiloh scooped up another cupfull and handed it to Link. He gulped the water down quickly and reached out for more.

"Thank you."

Seeing that Link was okay, Shiloh took a drink. The water tasted slightly metallic, but the sensation of it going down her throat was one of the greatest joys she had known. They were going to live.

"Are you strong enough to bring over a jug?"

"I'm fine. I just overheated. I feel better now. Thank you." Link pushed up to his feet and brought over a jug. Shiloh filled the container cup by cup until it was full. She pushed herself out of the riverbed and joined Link on the ledge. Link and she shared one last cup, and then each took a handle of the jug.

"What was that? Did you say something?" Link asked.

"I didn't say anything."

"Are you sure?"

The light on Shiloh's chest flickered. "I'm sure."

"No, are you sure you want me to do that?"

Whispers crawled along the edges of the cavern and reached Shiloh's ears.

"Why would I want to hurt her?" Link whispered.

"Link, don't listen to them. Link!"

Link swung at Shiloh, and she ducked. They dropped the water jug, and both were doused with the cool water. Link snapped out of his trance, and the sound momentarily blocked the whispering.

Run! Shiloh heard a deep voice say as clear as day.

It wasn't Ember, but a male's voice. She took Link by the hand and yanked him into the passage. Their lights flickered with every step, and the darkness closed in behind them. Shiloh heard the beating of her heart in her ears and it throbbed with every step she took. Ahead, the star stones shone like a lighthouse leading them to a safe harbor.

The whispers encompassed them again as they reached the first step. Shiloh willed herself forward, up the stairs. They dove into the temple, and with one swoop of her tail, Ember struck the entryway. The rocks crumbled and caved in the passage behind.

A GUIDING VOICE

The tranquility of the chapel was shattered along with any hope of reaching the water again. How had the Laka found them? And whose voice had Shiloh heard? She looked at Link sitting on the ground next to her with his arms folded around his knees. He glanced at her but was too ashamed to meet her eyes.

"It wasn't your fault." Shiloh touched Link's shoulder, and he shrugged it off.

"I tried to hit you."

"It was them, not you. Don't blame yourself for that. They were controlling you."

"But I let them. I wasn't strong enough to resist them."

"You were separated from Ember. You were at a disadvantage."

"You don't get it." Link picked up a rock and threw it. "You can still hear your dragon's voice even if you are a great distance away. Ember tried to help me, but I didn't listen. I couldn't. They were too powerful."

Link, we are stronger than they are. Believe in us. We are here now, and they are trapped.

"Ember, how can we be sure of that? For all we know, they can walk through walls or teleport. Distance is the only thing that seems to help." Link looked at Shiloh for the first time. "How come you weren't affected?"

"I heard them, but I also heard another voice telling me to run. I chose to listen to that voice."

Link raised his eyebrows. "Your dragon?"

"I don't know. It was a deep male voice. If it was my dragon, where is he now, and where has he been the whole time? You are right, though. We don't know if the Laka are trapped or not. We need to leave here immediately.

They rushed to the front entrance, and Shiloh was nearly knocked over by the wall of heat outside as the sunlight blinded her. She guessed it was around noon. There was no hiding from the scorching sun, and the stones all seemed to radiate its heat. Shiloh was so thankful for the cooling membrane in her armor, but she wished she had more protection for her head. She pulled her silken hood tightly around her. Link wasn't faring as well; he swayed uneasily, and sweat glistened on his forehead.

The sound of an armored Six dragon came echoing down one of the streets.

"You run." Link flicked his wrists and his blades appeared. "And we will protect you."

"Can't we all just fly away?"

Legion and his dragon could easily overtake us, and if by some chance, we evaded him, Stue's dragon would beat us in endurance.

"Link, I don't want to lose you."

"You won't. Now go!"

The thundering sound rumbled closer.

"Go! What are you waiting for? Run!"

A surge of adrenaline shot through Shiloh, and she bounded down the stairs. She ran into the smallest street in the square opposite from where the noise of the approaching Six was rumbling. She doubted an armored Six dragon could fit, but its rider could. She ran blindly, zigzagging down alleys and avoiding the melted remnants of the stone houses.

Left, the voice she had heard in the passageway said.

Shiloh followed its directions and made a sharp left.

Three streets down and left again.

Shiloh passed two streets and took a left on the third.

Stop, the voice said.

"What?"

Stop!

A figure plowed into Shiloh, sending her to the ground. She stood reflexively, flicked her wrists, and swung down hard at the figure. Her blow was blocked. She punched with her left, and that blow was intercepted as well. Had that voice led her to her capture?

Shiloh took a step back. She had a choice: fight or flight. She could probably outrun this one, but how many more were there? She had to go back and help Link. Why had she ever left him? Shiloh lunged forward to attack. She was afraid if she turned, she would be stabbed in the back.

"Shiloh! Stop!"

"Pen?" It was Pen's voice. She broke off her attack midswing and pulled back her hood. Pen stood with a scrunched face, his armored arms crossed, awaiting her next blow.

"Pen! Is that really you?"

Pen looked up from behind his crossed arms and nodded.

Shiloh wrapped her arms around him and kissed his cheek.

Pen's whole face flushed, and he couldn't meet her eyes.

"I'm so happy to see you. Are the others here as well?"

Pen nodded again, seemingly unable to speak.

"What's wrong with you? Did I hurt you?"

Pen shook his head.

Give him a moment, Alithia's velvety voice touched Shiloh's mind. *I will lead you back to the others. They are gathered in the square now. This way.* Alithia's shadow covered them, providing relief from the relentless sun.

In the square, the others were assembled in the archways of the temple. A wave of laughter reached Shiloh's ears as she stepped into view.

"There you are." Kai stood and ran down the stairs to meet them. "Sorry if Maybel scared you. Link was about ready to put up a good fight. Say, what is wrong with you?" He asked Pen. "You are looking a little red."

"It's just the sun."

"You!" Shiloh shouted. "What are you doing here?"

"Happy to see you too, young one." Stue's smug voice made Shiloh's hair stand on end.

"It's your fault we are in this mess! You betrayed us to the king. You helped them track us down."

"He also saved us in the desert," Kai said.

"What?" Shiloh looked at him with raised eyebrows.

"We made a deal." Stue crossed his arms over his belly. "I save them, and they give me sanctuary with the Sevens."

"We all know what a deal with you is worth." Shiloh crossed her arms as well.

"Well, like it or not, what is done is done, and you have no say in it."

"How could you?" She asked Kai.

"It is our only way back home. Plus, he has no home to go back to. Legion was going to give him to Lord Abaddon for losing you."

"You know the saying, young one. Enemy of my enemy and all that." Stue lazily flourished his hands.

"How do we know this isn't a trap? A way for him to find out where the Sevens are? For all we know, this is part of Lord Abaddon's plan." Shiloh eyed Stue up and down.

"I tested him," Stix said, standing beside Link. "He allowed us to examine his mind. His intentions are true. He only wants to save himself. Granted, that is the only thing he does care about."

Stue shrugged. "I'm an opportunist."

"Now that we are all here, we can finally take you to where you belong," Kai said. He nodded at Stue.

Stue snapped his fingers, and his dragon shot something out of its mouth. The particle created a sonic boom, and a ring of vapor appeared suspended off the ground.

"I'm tethered," Kai said. "Arda, I feel you." Kai took Shiloh by the hand, and all of the others followed suit. Together they walked as one body into the center of the ring.

Chapter Twenty-Two

THE WANDERING TRIBES

Figures appeared on the other side of the ring. They were indistinct, as if Shiloh was looking at them from the bottom of a pool. For that matter, her whole body felt liquid. She couldn't tell where her hand ended and Kai's began.

With a splash, Shiloh emerged on the other side, and she gasped for air. Her ears were ringing, and she felt as if she weren't totally whole.

"It is quite the experience the first time, isn't it," a hearty voice let out with a chuckle.

She knew that voice, but how?

"Yeah, you're fine. Give us y'r hand." Meaty fingers reached out to her, and she took them. The hand briskly pulled her to her feet. "There ya are. Shake it out."

Shiloh shook her head, and the world came into view. The person who helped her to her feet was the general. He wore a large grin, and his glass eye glinted in the sunlight.

"There ya go. You'll be fine now."

"Where are the others?" Shiloh felt the fight or flight response rising in her body.

"We are all here," Link said.

Behind her the portal closed with a shoosh, and all her friends were helped to their feet. Maybel bounded forward and licked the general on the side of the face.

"I'm happy to see you too, girl." The general nuzzled his face against Maybel's.

"We are here, alright, but what is that?" Pen pointed above the general's head to a wall of clouds that stood as high and wide as Shiloh could see.

"That is the void," Kai said. "Come, there is much to discuss while we wait for Mim. General, this is Stue."

"I know his likes," the General growled.

"And I yours." Stue raised an eyebrow. "General Grishnoff of the Sixth rank. The most decorated General in Abaddon's army. You died a hero… or did you? Obviously, the latter isn't true, but this all just got more interesting… So, you are a traitor?"

The General went to strike Stue, but Kai blocked his hand. "He delivered us here in exchange for sanctuary. We must honor the ancient custom of our people."

"Of course," the general boomed. "All are welcome here. Why don't you come with me to get re-acquainted with your people." He clapped an arm around Stue and led him away from the group.

"But I want to stay with them," Stue protested.

"There will be time for that later. First, there are a few things you and I need to discuss." Stue looked back at the others pleadingly as the general and Maybel led him away.

A shadow appeared overhead as a dragon with a wingspan of forty feet circled them. There was a boom, and where Kai had stood only a vapor trail was left. His voice came from high above in an exuberant call. He had been reunited with his dragon. It was a beautiful sight, and Shiloh could feel the joy in his voice—something he had been devoid of since she met him. In the air he seemed younger, more carefree.

A moment later Kai reappeared. "I had to say hello to Arda. We have never been apart that long before. Come, follow me."

"Who would have ever thought there were so many of them," Pen said as they walked through the camp. It stretched on for miles, and Shiloh guessed there were thousands of people living here, maybe even hundreds of thousands, but, really, she had no idea. She was surprised by the diversity of the camp. There were riders and dragons of every class, except Eights and Fives. This made Link and Ember very conspicuous. They were gathering lots of attention, and the stares weren't friendly.

Kai led them to a giant pavilion style tent in the middle of the camp. The dragon silk that stretched around the framework alternated between royal blue and gold. Banners with a golden dragon on a blue background flew proudly in the light wind.

Shiloh kept looking to her left at the void—she couldn't help herself. Even in this world, she had never seen anything as impressive or mysterious. It looked as if the most ferocious storm in the world was contained behind an invisible force field, keeping it at bay. Black, white, and gray wisps of wind spiraled through the entire wall of cloud.

"Shiloh," Link said. "Come on." He stood in front of her holding open the flap of the tent. The temperature dropped significantly as Shiloh stepped into the shade. The tent was simple on the inside, the people far outnumbering the sparse furniture.

"Welcome, guests," a dignified voice said. Shiloh followed it to a man who stood a head above the rest. The two people in front of him moved, and Shiloh nearly squealed when she saw that the man was a centaur. He had a black stallion's body and a chiseled torso. His jaw was squared with a tight black beard, and his black hair was pulled back.

The room fell silent, and all eyes turned to their company.

"Kai," the centaur said, "present your companions."

"Elders of the Wandering Tribes, I present to you Pendleton and Stix of Yesod. They are brave warriors, who have proven their valor time and time again. Their dragons Alithia and Axel await outside the tent as is our custom.

"I'm so excited to be here," Pen burst out. "I have always wanted to join the Wandering Tribes. See my dragon, Alithia, had a calling and I listened. Well, here we are…" He slowly quit speaking when he saw the stern look on Kai's face.

"Welcome, Master Pendleton," The centaur beamed a smile with the whitest teeth Shiloh had ever seen. "We appreciate your enthusiasm. "Welcome, Stix."

Stix nodded.

"Continue."

"This is Link and Shiloh, who hail from lands unknown. They are the twins of which the prophecy speaks, whom we have sought for so long."

A great clamor rose in the tent as torrents of conversation erupted.

The centaur stamped his hoof, and the room fell silent once more. "And their dragons." His voice carried great interest.

"Link's dragon, Ember, is an Eight and bears the mark of Gemini. They have both proven themselves in battle and are loyal to our cause."

"And what of her dragon?" The centaur nodded to Shiloh.

"Her dragon has yet to appear."

Conversation broke out like wildfire again.

"Everyone out," the centaur said, his voice rolling like thunder.

Shiloh turned to leave.

"That is, everyone except the twins. They must stay as this concerns them and none others."

The last to leave the tent were two women clad in armor. The taller of the two wore her black hair in a high ponytail and appeared to be of Asian descent, but the thing that stood out most were her pointed ears. The shorter woman had fiery red hair and a mischievous smile. Her shoulders were wide, and she had a sturdy build. It was hard to tell much else since they were covered in armor.

"Come closer," the centaur said.

Shiloh and Link walked to the table the others had been gathered around. On it was burned a map of Altiniya. Shiloh recognized the pattern that Pen had laid out with the coins.

"I take it you are Mim." Link's voice had an edge of defiance on it.

The centaur chuckled. "No, young traveler. I am Ezekiel. It is I who read the stars that foretold your coming."

"You are talking about the Prophecy of Gemini, aren't you?" Shiloh said.

"It is so." Ezekiel nodded. "Long ago, the stars sang to me and my brothers of a prophecy that was yet to come. They sang of the greatest joy this world or any other has ever known. They sang of the return of Eimi and the destruction of Abaddon."

"No wonder why he wants to find us so bad." Link crossed his arms.

"The symphony of the spheres said that when the Star of Eimi appears in the constellation of Gemini, this is the first sign of Eimi's return. Several days ago, that very star appeared. When we saw that sign, we sent those loyal to Eimi to each city to search for the second sign."

"And what was that?" Link asked.

"Two born of one flesh. Of these two, one will harbor the spirit of Eimi." He looked at Shiloh. "And the other, the spirit of great destruction." His gaze shifted to Link.

"No, I don't believe it. Link is good!" Shiloh protested.

"Even now, I can sense he is out of balance."

"You just don't like him because he is an Eight!" The force in Shiloh's voice surprised her. "What do you have against Eights, anyway?"

"That would be best for Mim to tell you. It is not my story to tell."

"Where is this magical Mim we keep hearing about? Isn't she supposed to be the leader here?" Streaks of sweat rolled down Link's forehead. The heat was rising in his body again.

"Link." Shiloh placed a hand on his triceps. He locked eyes with her, and his gaze softened. "Ezekiel, will you take us to Mim?"

"I can try, but it isn't my decision to make."

"Then whose choice is it?" Shiloh's brow furrowed.

"The void's."

INTO THE VOID

Shiloh stared at the void as it swirled and turned—a thousand tempests trapped by some invisible force. Behind them, it seemed as if the whole encampment had congregated. The two warrior women stood on either side of Ezekiel.

"You have to go through that?" Pen asked Shiloh, under his breath.

"Apparently, it is the only way to see Mim."

"Is it really that important to you? We could all stay out here and be happy, you know. All of us together."

"Pen, you once told me about Alithia's calling. I know I don't have a dragon, but I feel a powerful calling deep inside of me, as well, and it tells me my destiny lies on the other side of this." Shiloh surveyed the vast expanse of the void.

"Well, I'm coming with you."

"What? You can't be serious."

"Never been more serious about anything in my life before."

"Pen."

"I've made up my mind. I'm coming."

"All are welcome to try to cross the void," Ezekiel said. "It is time."

"Pen, are you sure you want to do this?"

Pen looked at Alithia. "We are sure."

The two warrior women raised their staffs, and Ezekiel cried out in a loud voice, "We seek passage through the void to the Promised Land."

He was answered by a howling gust of wind. The whirling tarantella pushed everyone back, and sand flew viciously through the air. Ezekiel and the two warrior women pressed forward.

"You go first," Link shouted.

Shiloh looked at Pen, and he nodded. She took a deep breath and followed closely behind Ezekiel. The wind whipped some hair loose from her braid, and she received several coarse lashes from it.

Shiloh heard a thudding behind her. Link and Pen were trapped on the other side. The void hadn't let them enter. Panic rushed through her body. She turned to run back to her friends, but the elven woman grabbed her arm and shook her head. A moment of understanding passed between them, and Shiloh pressed forward. She knew in the deepest part of her that she was doing the right thing. Although, she couldn't help but wonder if the void would ever let her return.

THE PROMISED LAND

The wind subsided into a gentle whisper, and emerald green sprawled out in front of them. Shiloh's eyes moistened—grass, trees, vines, flowers, deer, rabbits, clouds. All of it was here.

"You can take those off." Ezekiel looked at Shiloh's boots. "You do not need them here, nor your armor."

"Sorry," Shiloh said, brushing the tears from her eyes. "I know, save your water."

"Cry all you want. There is no need to hide your emotions here, nor to, as you say, save your water. Look around you."

Shiloh was in a plain vaster than her senses could take in. The fragrance of rose mixed with honeysuckle wafted through the air. A robin sang its song. It was the familiar one they sing when they return at the end of winter. She touched the grass, and it folded softly under the pressure of her hands. Her feet drank up the soil as she removed her shoes, and blades of grass pushed up between her toes. She discarded her armor, and her skin rejoiced at the warmth of the sun and the coolness of the breeze. It was as if she was truly feeling these things for the first time. All of her experiences seemed to be just a hollow reflection of what she felt now.

"Welcome to the Promised Land," Ezekiel said, beaming at her. "Come, Mim awaits."

They walked across the meadow, and Shiloh ran her hands through the tall stalks of grass jutting up every now and then.

It is the imperfections that make things perfect. Her mother had told her this on a similar summer day as they sat in a field. *If I were to paint this,* the memory of her mother continued, *I wouldn't include that log or that tall stalk of grass nor that little ant hill. I would try to make it perfect, and in the doing, it would become imperfect.* Shiloh smiled, observing all the imperfections in this land that made them perfect.

They entered a grove of sycamore trees, their silver bark dotted with black knots, once again the imperfect making them look perfect. The leaves danced and rustled overhead as the wind pushed through them, creating a dance of light on the ground. It reminded Shiloh of prism painting, and her heart ached that Link and Pen couldn't see all of this. Pen wouldn't be able to keep quiet about it. He wouldn't hear—

The distinct rumbling of a mighty river caused Shiloh to abandon her thought. It really was water. She ran ahead of her escorts, and the grove opened up to a riverbank. Shiloh dunked her head in the water and drank. She lost her footing and fell right into the lazy river.

Ezekiel and the two women laughed.

Shiloh didn't care. The water was rejuvenating. She floated on her back and watched the clouds pass. All of her cares and worries seemed to drift downstream.

"Are you enjoying yourself?" A woman's kind voice startled Shiloh.

She stood and brushed the water from her eyes then pulled her hair back into a ponytail so she could see. On the bank of the river stood a woman in her sixties with eyes that sparkled like sapphires and chin-length hair shining like liquid silver. Her torso was short and her hips were wide. Every inch of her body boasted of kindness and compassion.

"I am… Thank you… You must be Mim."

"It is so. Come and join me." She sat on a log and patted the seat next to her.

Shiloh splashed through the water and climbed out of the river. The wet silk clung to her body cooling her from the sun—it was perfect. She sat next to Mim, and water dripped from her, staining the log dark brown and creating little puddles of mud at her feet.

"It has been a while since you swam, hasn't it."

Shiloh nodded. "What is this place? Everything seems sharper here, more real than anywhere else I have been before."

"This is the Promised Land. Before we go any further, would you like some milk and cookies?"

"That would be amazing!"

Mim clapped her hands, and two rabbits appeared. One was carrying a small tray with silver dollar sized cookies about a half inch thick, and the other carried two cups of milk.

Shiloh didn't know if she should thank the rabbits or not, but she decided to err on the side of caution. She took a cookie and nodded thanks. Mim toasted with her cookie, and Shiloh took a bite. The cookie crumbled in her mouth. Its texture was powdery, tasting of honey, peanut butter, and powdered sugar. She took a large swig of milk to wash the cookie down.

"There," Mim said. "I always think it is better to talk after having some cookies and milk."

Who is this woman? Shiloh wondered. She had the characteristics of the kindly grandmother Shiloh had always wanted and a fairytale princess. Shiloh half expected a robin to land on her shoulder and start singing. One swooped mighty close, only to pull up at the last second.

"So," Shiloh said between bites of her cookie. "What is the Promised Land?"

"What you see around you is the way the world was before the fall. All of the world was once like this, or I suppose a version of this. It was so long ago, but we never forget, do we Jordan?"

The river seemed to laugh.

"Jordan?"

"Jordan is my dragon." The river rolled up into itself and towered like a giant wave above them. Soon the wave took shape—watery wings spread out then a tail and two powerful legs followed by a snout. In an instant, the water hardened and turned into frosted ice.

"Jordan is a—"

"An Ice Dragon," Mim finished Shiloh's sentence.

"They are supposed to be extinct."

"Vanished, yes, extinct, no. Jordan is the last free Ice Dragon. Well, until now." Mim looked beyond Shiloh. "It's okay, you can show yourself. It is safe."

Shiloh turned her head as well, and another Ice Dragon took shape as if appearing from thin air. It was as large as Ember and had a matching mark of Gemini on its chest. Instead of the molten lava color the symbol was an ice blue.

"Shiloh, I would like you to meet your dragon."

Hello, the voice was familiar. It was the same one she had heard in the passageway telling her to run. The same one that had led her to Pen. But she knew the voice on an even deeper level. It is as if she was meeting a piece of herself she had always known but never had a name for.

Saying hi seemed silly as the dragon had always been a part of her, so instead she asked, "What is your name?"

I am Appomattox.

Shiloh smiled. The Appomattox river ran close to her home in Virginia. She used to love sitting by it, listening to its song, reading her books on its shore, and dreaming of adventuring down to the sea.

"That seems right," Shiloh said. "How is it that I am only meeting you now? Where were you when I needed you?"

I was always at your side. You were never in any true danger.

"What about the Laka in the dungeons at the trading post?"

Did you not see the ice I laced around it so it could not advance?

"I did." Shiloh whipped back around. "Mim, how is it that I saw the Laka and the others didn't? They were only able to sense them. I could see its terrible form.

"It is because you are one of them, as am I."

Shiloh froze.

Mim looked at her with a fathomless compassion. "I had better start from the beginning."

Shiloh braced herself on the log and looked up at Appomattox. He was the most beautiful thing she had ever seen. He had a gentle dusting of frost, and below it lay the fathomless blue of an iceberg.

"As I said, before the fall, all of the world was like this beautiful garden. The people were free and had everything they could possibly ask for." Mim's eyes became distant as if remembering a great love from long ago. "The best part was that Eimi walked amongst us. You didn't need food or water, all you needed was Eimi's presence to be whole." Mim sighed heavily.

"You were there weren't you?"

"It is so."

"How is that possible? The way people talk about it, the fall happened centuries ago."

"It has been thousands of years. If only the others could remember, our world wouldn't be like this. But, of course, they can't."

"What do you mean they can't remember?"

Mim nodded to Jordan. He closed his eyes, and a tranquil expression crossed his face. Moments later, a form of script covered his body. It looked to be some sort of Sanskrit mixed with hieroglyphs.

"Walked together in the garden." Shiloh read what she could on his right foreleg.

"You can read it?" Mim sounded astonished.

"I can read parts. My uncle is an archaeologist, and he used to send me books on the different dig sites he worked. Most recently we were in Egypt, and he sent me a book on Hieroglyphs." Shiloh pointed to the writing. "This seems to be a mix of Hieroglyphics and Sanskrit. I learned that when I was eight. I have an eidetic memory. If I read something once, I can recall it at any time."

Mim made eye contact with Jordan. "That will be useful."

"How?"

"You will learn later."

Shiloh eyed the text again. "What type of script is this?"

"It is Frost Script."

"Frost Script." Shiloh mouthed the words.

"I thought you didn't have books or a written language here."

"I don't know what a book is, but we do have two types of script—Frost Script and Fire Script."

"Let me guess," Shiloh said. "The Eights have Fire Script?"

Mim shook her head. "No, only Lord Abaddon's beast has it—the thing isn't worthy to be called a dragon—Eimi took care of that before he left—Lord Abaddon stole Frost Script from us and perverted it into Fire Script—I am getting ahead of myself."

"How come the others can't remember?"

"Fives are the memory keepers of our people; yes, I suppose that is as good a place as any to start. Water retains a memory. It has reached the highest heights in clouds and the lowest depths below the earth. It has explored the outside of man and the inside. A single drop remembers it all when combined with others. Together they make a sea of knowledge. Our dragons retain that knowledge and share it with us through Frost Script. What you see on Jordan isn't just the history of our people; it is a part of the history of the whole world. Do you like to learn and study?"

Shiloh nodded her head eagerly. "My favorite thing to do is curl up with a book and learn something new."

"There is that word again—book—what is it?"

"A book is a compilation of words like Frost Script written on pages of paper."

"Written?"

"It is like when you draw something in the sand only when you write it on paper, the letters never disappear."

"Interesting, very interesting. You are a true Five; we love nothing more than to learn and collect knowledge. The Fives knew everything of the earth and its people; each Five dragon maintained part of a record of the whole. However, with all of this knowledge, there were still things that only Eimi himself knew. One day Abaddon appeared at Chokma—"

"The city of the Fives—" the words blurted out of Shiloh's mouth "—it was in the north west of the Kingdom." Just like in school, Shiloh had to show that she knew the answer.

"That is correct, it is the farthest north and west, but at that time there was no kingdom. The people were free. We were all free to be with Eimi." The distant look crossed Mim's face again.

"Continue, please." Shiloh was thirsty for knowledge.

"Abaddon came to Chokmah, and we Fives took great interest in him. All of the waters of the world had never encountered someone like him—he was a grown man but walked without a dragon."

"You wanted to study him—didn't you?"

"That is correct. We wanted to learn everything we could. It is in our nature. Eventually though, that nature led to our downfall and eventually to the Great Fall. I was guilty of it, too. I was just as curious as the others."

"I can't believe you were there? I mean, you are thousands of years old. You look great for your age." Shiloh placed both hands on her mouth.

"Ice slows down the aging process. We live longer than any other. We watched many generations pass after the Great Fall, but none had been as curious to us as Abaddon. We welcomed him into our halls, dined with him, and learned all we could. One night we all gathered in the great hall, and he presented to us the one thing that all Fives desire—knowledge. He said he possessed the knowledge that Eimi had hidden from us, and that we could possess it, too, if we did one thing."

"What was that?" Shiloh was on the edge of her seat.

"He presented a fruit. He said it was from the Tree of Knowledge and if we took one bite the water of the fruit would mix with our waters, and we would have the knowledge of Eimi. The temptation was too great for two of the Fives, Adama and Ishshah, whose dragons were Tigris and Euphrates. At first, all seemed well. Then the whispers began."

"The Laka? Adama and Ishshah are the Laka? They were Fives?"

"It is so. What we did not know that night was that the moment Adama and Ishshah bit from the fruit, they exchanged their dragons for knowledge. Abaddon had deceived them. The once soulless man now had both of their souls. They were the first to form Abaddon's dragon. Adama and Ishshah had the knowledge, but they were now empty shells. To fill that emptiness, they began to separate others from their dragons. Each dragon they took became a part of Abaddon's beast. The first dragons they stole were their fellow ice dragons. They convinced them to join waters with Tigris and Euphrates."

"Join water?" Shiloh asked.

"Yes, it is better that Jordan and Appomattox show you that. Jordan."

Jordan flew into the sky and barrelled into the ground, turning himself into the river again, sending splashes of water all around. Following his lead, Appomattox did the same. The waters converged to create one massive river. Moments later they both took their dragon forms again, and new Frost Script had formed on each.

"This is the way Five dragons share water and pass on knowledge through that sharing."

"That is much quicker than reading a book."

"As you say. Once the other dragons had shared water, they also partook in Abaddon's knowledge and became subjugated to him. Like a disease, it spread through the city until all were taken by it, and those who resisted were killed." A shadow crossed Mim's face.

"How did you escape?"

"Touch your dragon, and he will show you. Now that memory is inside of him."

Shiloh stood and touched Appomattox. His skin felt similar to the cooling membrane in her armor. Shiloh didn't have long to ponder this as she was immediately sucked into the memory. Inside, everything was in pale shades of blue and gray as if she were looking through ice. She was in the great hall the night that Abaddon offered the fruit from the Tree of Knowledge. He stood in the middle of the room and was the most handsome man Shiloh had ever seen. He was tall with wide shoulders. His hair was pulled back showing his widow's peak. His cheekbones were high and chin square. He exuded a charisma that was contagious, and his black eyes had a depth of knowledge.

"Friends," he spoke, "with one bite of this fruit, you will know what Eimi has been keeping from you for all of these years. You will become as him, you will become Gods. You will have all the knowledge in the universe. Who is brave enough to take the first bite?"

"We are," Adama and Ishshah said in unison.

This had not surprised Mim. They were great explorers.

The two of them walked to the center of the room and bit from the fruit. They looked above to the heavens then around the room wildly.

"It is as if I can see for the first time," Adama said. "You all must join waters with us to see for yourselves."

"Mim," a young man said. He had the same sapphire eyes as Mim, and from her memory Shiloh knew him to be Mim's brother Judah. "Will you join waters with them?"

"Maybe when I am back. I shouldn't have stayed this long. I am the chosen one to go to Binah for the Sowing Ceremony. Will you join waters with them?"

"Of course," Judah said.

"Wait for me. Let's do it at the same time when I return."

"You know I hate not knowing what others know."

"Promise me you'll wait."

"Fine. I promise, but don't take too long."

The memory skipped forward to the Sowing Ceremony. Row upon row of Nine dragons were tilling the ground and their riders were throwing seeds into the holes to cover them. There must have been over one hundred acres stretched out.

"My friends," Mim said in a voice louder than it should have been on its own. "May our waters nourish the fruits of the labor of your hands, and may we all partake in the bounty. This we pray in the name of Eimi."

Jordan lept to the sky and seeded a giant cloud above, causing rain to fall on all of the crops. The people rejoiced and danced in the rain, as did Mim. The revelry was contagious, and Shiloh didn't want to leave, but the memory was pulling her somewhere else.

"Mim, what is this?" A portly man said. "The ceremony didn't work."

"What do you mean?" Mim shot out of bed. She didn't recognize her surroundings. As sleep slowly faded, she recalled that she was with the Nines.

"The waters are drying up."

"What?" Mim tore off the covers and walked to the window. The great river leading into the city from Chokmah was an empty riverbed of mud stretching for miles.

"What is the meaning of this?" The portly man put his hands on his hips.

"I... I don't know, but I will find out at once." Mim jumped out of the window and landed on Jordan who was already waiting. They flew without ceasing. All water in Altiniya flowed from Chokmah. If this river was dry, what of all the others?

The memory pulled Shiloh to Mim and Jordan landing outside of the gathering hall at Chokmah. Shiloh could feel the tension in Mim's body as if it were her own. Mim and Jordan exchanged a look, and the dragon pushed open the doors to the great hall. Inside, Abaddon sat on a newly made throne with Adama and Ishshah on his right and left. Their bodies were frail as if the water had been sucked out of them and their hair pure white. They were no longer Adama and Ishshah; they had now become the Laka—the soulless ones. Curled around them all was a dragon that took up an entire hall.

"Ah," Abaddon's voice had become cruel and raspy. The charismatic facade had long since been abandoned. "The prodigal child has returned. Welcome home. We have been expecting you. I will make this simple for you. You have two choices, join your waters with ours, or suffer his fate." Addadon snapped his fingers, and the Laka began to whisper. Moments later, Judah and his dragon, Sea, were dragged into the room in chains.

Mim couldn't make sense of what was happening. Their friends had her brother in chains. What had happened to Adama and Ishshah? Where had Abaddon's dragon come from?

The Laka whispered again and moved their arms. As they did, those pulling Judah threw him to the ground. Mim's heart pulled into her chest. The Laka were controlling them like puppets.

"Mim!" Judah yelled. "Don't join them. They will—" His words were choked off by a man's hand wrapping around his neck. The Laka squeezed their fingers tightly together and the man tightened his grip.

"Enough of this," Abaddon said. He flicked his index finger, and an icicle shot out, piercing Judah in the heart. His blood puddled on the ground, and for the first time, the land knew death. Sea, Judah's dragon, stumbled backwards and fell on Jordan. She shed a single tear, and their waters were joined. At that moment, Mim knew everything that had happened. She saw Abaddon's poison spreading through the community. She saw him take their dragons one by one and create the monster that sat behind him. Sea faded and was no more.

"Now it is your choice; join your waters with ours or die like him."

"Enough!" A voice roared, and a comet shot through the ceiling.

Shiloh's eyes adjusted, and she could tell it wasn't a comet, it was a man and dragon as one. The light from the being filled every dark space in the hall, and Abaddon cowered from it.

"What have you done, Deceiver?" the Being's voice rumbled.

"That which you could not. I showed them the truth. The truth you have hidden from them since the beginning. You cannot have light without shadow. You cannot have the day without the night.

The Being laughed, and he shone so brightly that the flesh of Shiloh's hands became red and translucent.

"This is what you call truth?"

"If they do not know anything other than you, how can they truly have free will?

"But they are me. I am inside each one of them."

"I have simply given them what you could not, a choice. If you take that away, you will be nothing more than a tyrant. I am freeing them from your rule."

"You mean subjecting them to yours." The Being nodded to the ghastly dragon behind Abaddon. "Free them."

"They are mine."

"Free them."

"They willingly gave me their dragons, and now their dragons are my own. Even you cannot take away a person's dragon. It must be willingly given."

"That is no dragon," the Being roared, and Abaddon's dragon lost its wings and legs, becoming a giant worm-like creature.

"In a world of choice, you cannot win. The flesh will always choose my way."

"You know it is not so. Why should I not destroy you now, fallen one?"

"Because if you do, we will never know if they will serve you by their own free will."

"Very well, I will give you a period of time to see your folly. Then I will come to collect those who are mine, including you. Man will know his true being; every dragon knows of its true home."

"And what of you, daughter?" the Being asked Mim.

"I serve you, Eimi, and no other."

"Very well, come with me, daughter." All of the light in the room was gathered into a single light along with Mim and Jordan, and they shot through the roof as Shiloh was shot back into her body. She clutched the log for support and looked at Mim.

"Eimi took us to this place and called it the Promised Land. He ordered us to nourish it for the children who would be led here. Year upon year we waited as the waters of the world told us of the fall of

Altiniya. After the Fives, the Eights were the next to go. Abaddon seduced eight of them with the promise of power. Those eight scorched the ground, and soon all life outside of the cities died. Without water, Altiniya became the vast desert you know today.

"All of the cities fell to Abaddon except for Malkuth, the city of the Seven's. They remained loyal to Eimi and would serve no other master. Their city was scorched, and they fled to the desert to wander for forty years until Eimi led them to me. The pillar of cloud and fire that led them through the wilderness became the void that you passed through."

"Why couldn't Pen and Link pass through the void?"

"The waters have told me about both of them. Pen has taken on the traits of lying and stealing. These qualities belong to Abaddon not Eimi. He also needs to atone with his parents. He won't be able to pass the void until he is in line with the will of Eimi once more."

"And Link?"

"He is out of balance. His anger is consuming him. I fear that he will become as one of the Eights of old. They were all consumed by fire, becoming no longer men, but furies."

"Can you help him?"

"He needs to learn from another Eight before he is consumed. He must go to Dragon's Claw Academy."

"Can I go with him?"

"You cannot. Because of the prophecy, Abaddon will track you down and kill you to prevent the return of Eimi. If you stay here and train with me, it is safer for everyone. It is needed for the battle ahead."

"How can anyone worship Abaddon?"

"As I said before, they don't remember. Besides controlling the water, the fives carried the memory of the entire people. When we were lost, so was the memory of all such things. Abaddon now controls not only the supply of water, but the narrative of history. The people are told that he is the great builder. That after the fall, all of mankind was lost, but he taught them how to make the domes to protect the cities. He paved over the great river beds with dragon glass to protect travelers from sand spiders. None of them know he was the cause of the fall; they see him as the savior from it. He is the great deceiver and the father of lies."

"But what about the summoning ceremony?"

"That had to remain as a part of the agreement between him and Eimi. Now it is the only vestige left of our one true God and savior."

Shiloh's mind was reeling. The prophecy, this history, it was all too much to take in. How could she be the one who would bring back the return of Eimi? She was just an ordinary girl. And Link was good; he wasn't the bringer of destruction.

"How do we know?"

"How do we know what?" Mim asked pleasantly.

"How do we know we are the ones to fulfill the prophecy?"

"We don't. But we have faith."

Chapter Twenty-Five

WILL I SEE YOU AGAIN

Shiloh emerged from the void, her hair whipping around her face. Pen, Stix, and Link sprang up from the sand and rushed to meet her.

"Are you okay?" Link asked, concern written on his face.

"Yeah, are you in one piece?" Pen asked. "You were gone for hours. Hey, what's that in your hand? Is that what I think it is?"

Shiloh handed Pen a branch that was the size of his former walking stick.

"Pen, listen to me. It is really important that you take this piece of wood back to the place where you stole your walking stick from."

"But—"

"You also need to tell your parents the truth; the whole truth about everything. Do you understand me?"

Pen nodded. He spun the stick around a few times and stuck it under his arm. Then he saluted Shiloh.

"You're not okay, are you?" Link looked her dead in the eyes, but she couldn't keep his gaze.

"I…"

"Wait a minute, go back to my parents? Are you guys coming too? I thought we came all the way out here to get you to a safe place. Now we are supposed to go back? That doesn't make much sense."

"Link is coming with you, but—"

"You're not coming, are you?" Link's words cut Shiloh off.

Shiloh shook her head.

"I'm not going either, Shi. They can't separate us. Don't let them."

"Yeah!" Pen put both hands on his hips. "I'm not going either."

"You don't understand." Shiloh looked at the ground and shook her head.

"I for one will be happy to go home," Stix said. "We got you here; you are safe; our job is done."

"You could stay," Kai said to Stix as he walked up to join the group.

"No, my dragon is calling me to Dragon's Claw Academy. Pen, if we leave now, that would give us one week with our families before the semester starts."

"You must go where your dragon calls," Kai said. "You will always be welcome with the Wandering Tribes if you change your mind."

"What about me, am I welcome to stay?" Pen asked.

"You are; you have proven yourself and are a friend of Eimi—"

"You are welcome to stay," Shiloh cut in, "but you can't. Pen, you have to do what I told you first. Then you can return if it is your dragon's calling."

"You are my dragon's calling," Pen mumbled.

"Alithia?" Shiloh pleaded.

Shiloh is right, Alithia's voice touched all of their minds, *our calling is at Dragon's Claw Academy as well.*

Shiloh put both hands on Pen's shoulders and smiled at him kindly. "Pen, I will miss you, too. Repeat what I told you. It is very important."

Pen pulled away. "Return the stick and tell my parents the truth." He walked away from the group fighting back tears.

"Shiloh, I'm not going to leave you." Link crossed his arms and grounded his feet.

"Will you give us a moment?" Shiloh said to Kai and Stix.

"Goodbye, Shiloh," Stix said and joined Pen, who kept pacing back and forth.

Kai just nodded and walked away.

"Link, look at me." Link brought his steely gaze up to meet Shiloh's. A lump formed in Shiloh's throat.

"Well, what is it?"

"Link, you are dying."

The word hung in the air between them.

"Did that crackpot Mim tell you that? I bet she just wants to separate us. It is because I'm an Eight, isn't it! I have felt it since the moment I stepped foot in this camp!"

Shiloh took Link by the hands but could only hold them for a moment.

"Your body is burning itself up. If you don't do something, it will consume you, and you will die. Mim told me that only an Eight can help you find balance, and there are no Eights here. Link, you have to go today. There isn't time."

"Who is this Mim anyway? What aren't you telling me?"

"Link, I can't."

Mim had made Shiloh promise not to tell anyone about Apomattox, especially Link. She said it would be safer for everyone involved, if they were the only two who knew. Looking at her brother, though, she had to fight with every fiber of her being not to tell him.

"I promised I wouldn't. If you had been on the other side of the void, you would understand. Do you trust me?"

"I have always trusted you, Shiloh."

"Then trust me when I say this. If you stay here, you will die, and I can't see that happen to you."

The moments felt like hours in Link's silence.

"Come with us. You don't have to stay here."

"You know I have to stay. You all won't be safe as long as the Laka and Legion are hunting me."

"Will we see each other again?" The resigned look in Link's eyes made Shiloh want to cry.

"I... I don't know."

Link hummed softly. The melody was so familiar to Shiloh, yet she was sure she had never heard it before. Link locked eyes with her and Shiloh knew to hum with him. When she hummed the melody perfectly, Link stopped. "That is the thread of my thought. Teach it to a Nine, and they should be able to find us, if we are in range."

"Link..."

"I love you." Link hugged her quickly and walked away.

"I love you, too." Shiloh reached for him, but he was already beyond her grasp.

"Let's go," Link said, when he reached Pen and Stix. "Kai, will you send us home?"

A sonic boom rattled the ground, and a misty portal appeared. Link walked through first followed by Stix. Pen reluctantly joined them and was the only one to look back at Shiloh as they disappeared into the aether.

Shiloh dropped to her knees and let all of the tears she had been holding back fall. She had never felt so alone in her life.

It is alright little one. Appomattox's invisible wings wrapped around Shiloh. *I am always with you.*

End Book One of *The Legends of the Twin Dragon*
Continue the Adventure in Book Two: *Fire and Frost*

Brian loves hearing from readers. Use the QR code or the link below to connect with him. Also, reviews are the heart beat of books. If you enjoyed this story, consider leaving a review wherever you purchased the book!

https://linktr.ee/brianjohnskillen

BOOKS BY BRIAN

The Way: Through a Field of Stars

There is a secret code of the Knights Templar on the Camino de Santiago…

The Way: Through a Field of Stars is the first book in a sweeping historical fantasy trilogy set on the Camino de Santiago one year before the Templars disappeared along with their treasure.

Back: Through a Field of Stars

Hunted by the seven deadly sins, two unlikely heroes must deliver a secret message across the Camino de Santiago before it's too late…

Home: Through a Field of Stars

Find The Way Back Home as you uncover the secret treasure of the Knights Templar on the Camino de Santiago…

Enjoy the exciting conclusion to the Through a Field of Stars trilogy as you uncover the secrets the Templars left behind.

KICKSTARTER BACKERS

Adolfo Ramos; Alanna Mensing; Alexandra Corrsin; Allison Kopelowitz Westmoreland; Amy Mann; Andrea Martin Kidder; Andrew Estep; Andrew Lewis; Andrew Sutton; Anna Champion; Arne Radtke; Barnabas Whitaker; Brad Hale; Carol Goss; Carol Scheppard; Cassie Springer; Chandra Fulton; Charlie St.Cyr-Paul; Charneka Edwards; Chase McGlinchey; Chelsea G; Christine Black-Reimel; Christine Santisteban; Cori; Cristina Cardenas; Crystal Sutherland; Cynthia P; Danbo; Dave Hoult; David Lars Chamberlain; David Rokov; David Wilson; Dawn Crosby; dPhantom0_0; Ed Jones; Esther Reeves; Ezekiel Bowers; Florentina; Hailey Anderson; Hannah Anderson; Holly Clarke; Hugh H Browne Jr.; Ian Caldwell; Irene M Guaraldi; J Mills; James McGettigan; James DL Fryer; Jan-Fei Li; Jason Guest; Jason Hamilton; Jeanne Smith; Jeff Kelley; Jeremiah Diaz; Jessie Marston; John Idlor; Josh Lieberman; Josh Parker; Julia Libby; Julie Elizabeth Emanuelson; K Wilmore; Kate Bullock; Katie & Kirsi Hornor; Kerrie Koopman; Kevin & Michelle Skillen; Kimberley O'Neill; Kristina Netemegesic; landontablada; Laura Taylor Cox; Laurel Truitt; Lele Beutel; Lessa Lamb; Linda Sami; Lisa Piatetsky; Lou Pierce; Lynley Thinnes; M. Carrie Hedden; Malina Dravis-Tucker; Mary Holloway; Megan E Dennis; Mike Carrión; Minty BF; Monique Bucheger; Morgan G.; Mystipul Rakkastaja; Nekoyang; Nicole Schuster; Norma Dennis; Pam McKinney-Peckinpaugh; Patty Rothwell; Peter "Tonour" Basak; polinchka; Radostina Petrova; Renee M Boucher; Richard Novak; Ricky Fraley; Rosa Thill; Ryan Todd; Samantha Falconer; Samantha Pierpont; Sherrie Stanley; SnapDragon Esq; Suellen Khoury; Suzanne Bowdle; Sydney and John; Taylor S.; Therese Anderson; Tia Luckenbaugh; Tony Pierce; Tyler Goss; Tyler Standley; Val Rokov; Vanessa Martin; Walt Pedigo; wiSalaam; Zach Heflin

Signals of Deception

A Scott Douglass Thriller

Dave Osborn

Signals of Deception

A Scott Douglass Thriller

(Book 1)

© 2025 Dave Osborn

Adriel Publishing

ISBN: 979-8-9912658-5-0

www.DaveOsbornBooks.com

One lie can start a war. One truth can stop it.

1. Ozgol (Tehran)
2. Herzliya, Israel
3. Chalus, Iran
4. Baku, Azerbaijan
5. Incirlik Air Base, Turkey

Part I
Deception

Day 1

Cybersecurity Intelligence Operations Center
The Ministry of Intelligence of The Islamic
Republic of Iran (MOIS)
Ozgol, Tajrish, Tehran Province, Iran
7:30 am

And with that moment, the first sparks of war were ignited.

The dimly lit basement operations center was thick with the scent of stale cigarette smoke and machine oil, remnants of the storage unit's past life. The only illumination sources were the flickering glow of computer monitors and a single overhead bulb casting long shadows on the cracked concrete floor.

Colonel Reza Mirzai stood at the head of the room, his broad shoulders tense, his dark eyes locked onto the cluster of screens before him. His reputation in Iran's intelligence community was legendary — a strategist, a survivor, a man who had outmaneuvered both domestic rivals and foreign enemies with ruthless precision. He was not merely a soldier but an architect of war and an engineer of chaos.

To his left sat Saeed Alavi, his best encryption specialist. A gaunt man with sharp features and an expression that rarely betrayed emotion, Saeed had spent the past decade working in cyberwarfare, honing his craft in both defense and attack operations against Western intelligence agencies. He was the backbone of Iran's cyber initiative.

Saeed had trained at Sharif University before advancing to a Russian cyberwarfare academy, where he studied NSA-level encryption techniques. After 15 years on missions, he had become an expert in fabricating high-level, classified communications.

Next to Saeed was Leila Pourfarrokh, a social engineering expert known for mimicking Western speech and dialects so convincingly that even native English speakers would be fooled. She was once a linguistics professor before being recruited into the Ministry's psychological warfare division.

Leila had spent years analyzing Western intelligence linguistics, ensuring no message would seem out of place. Her brothers were working in the Iraqi oilfields and became casualties of U.S. troops during the Iraqi invasion and removal of Saddam Hussein. The memory of their deaths created a deep hatred and resentment of the United States that still burned deep within her. Her fondest dream was to repay the pain she had experienced.

At the far end of the table sat Kamran Roshani, a communications specialist and black-market hacker who had earned his place in the room by infiltrating a secure Israeli defense server undetected. His skills in rerouting, obscuring, and fabricating digital footprints had made him indispensable.

Kamran, the youngest of the group, was a ghost in the network — he could make a message appear as though it had originated from anywhere in the world. He was well-educated and gifted and, despite his short tenure, was already becoming a legend within the Iranian cybersecurity and network forces.

Mirzai let the silence stretch before speaking, his voice low and commanding.

"This is not just another operation. This is history in the making."

His statement hung in the air. The weight of his words was not lost on his team. They did not have sufficient security clearance or a need-to-know basis, so he chose his words carefully. The full measure of this operation was highly classified and known only to a half dozen people in their government. They would learn the extent of its reach at the proper time.

"We have watched for decades as the Americans dictated terms to the world," Mirzai continued, his voice laced with simmering resentment. "They have used their technology, their influence, and their power to keep Iran under their boot. We have been sanctioned, starved, and painted as the villain while they wage their wars unchecked."

A pause. A deep breath. Then, he leaned over the table, his hands gripping the edges with white-knuckled force.

"But today, we begin to rewrite that story."

The monitors before them displayed a flowchart, a network of digital pathways leading to a singular entity on a highly classified U.S. network — the Adaptive Encryption and Global Intelligence System, otherwise known as AEGIS.

"The United States has the most advanced artificial intelligence defense system known," Mirzai continued. "We have learned that AEGIS analyzes intelligence data in real-time, identifies threats, and recommends military action. It is their all-seeing eye, their infallible oracle."

Kamran frowned. "A system like that is nearly impenetrable."

Mirzai smirked. "We are not hacking AEGIS."

Leila leaned forward. "Then how do we break it?"

"We don't need to break it," Mirzai said. "We manipulate it."

A flicker of realization crossed Saeed's face. "You mean… feed it false intelligence?"

Mirzai nodded. "Exactly. AEGIS was designed to detect patterns and predict threats. But, like any system, it is only as strong as the data it receives. If we control that data correctly, we control AEGIS itself."

Leila exhaled slowly. "We would be turning their own system against them."

"Precisely." Mirzai straightened. "We have access to the worldwide United Nations network and its servers, and from there we can view message traffic entering and leaving the U.S. classified networks through this U.N. portal. We have spent the past six months observing and analyzing Western intelligence communications. Every message, every phrase, every directive. We have learned their language and their decision-making processes."

He turned to Kamran. Your job is to make our transmissions untraceable while appearing authentic. Each message must appear as though it originates from a trusted source — an NSA operative, a U.S. embassy, even the Pentagon itself."

Kamran nodded. "With the proper masking protocols, we can reroute messages through multiple allied nations before sending them to a location where AEGIS can intercept them. By the time AEGIS receives the message, they will appear to have originated from within their network."

Mirzai turned to Leila. "You will craft the messages according to our plan. The tone, urgency, and specifics must match real intelligence reports. The threats must be credible."

Leila nodded. "I can weave the perfect lie."

Mirzai shifted his gaze to Saeed. "Every message must be encrypted with NSA-grade signatures. We cannot afford to raise even a fraction of doubt."

Saeed's expression darkened. "And if they do detect anomalies?"

Mirzai's jaw clenched. "Then we escalate before they can react. By the time they suspect anything, they will be too busy mobilizing against Russia and China to question AEGIS's conclusions."

A chilling silence settled over the room. They all knew what this meant.

A world on the brink of war.

Kamran exhaled, shaking his head. "This could change everything."

Mirzai's lips curled into a tight smile. "That is the expectation."

Leila tapped her fingers on the table. "How can we ensure AEGIS prioritizes our fabrications?"

Mirzai's eyes gleamed. "We make them believable. Realistic. AEGIS does not react to noise; it reacts to patterns." He stepped forward, his voice lowering to an almost conspiratorial tone. "We will craft an illusion of coordinated, escalating aggression from Russia and China. A cyberattack here. A military exercise there. Small embers are carefully placed until AEGIS fans them into an inferno. I will show you."

Saeed rubbed his chin. "And the Americans will respond accordingly."

Mirzai nodded. "Their intelligence officers will see what we want them to see. Their generals will believe they are on the brink of war. The U.S. will act in defense, positioning forces and shifting alliances. And in that moment of chaos, Iran will move in the Middle East without interference."

Kamran sighed, a mixture of awe and apprehension. "It's bold."

"It's necessary," Mirzai countered. "For too long, we have played defense. Now, we dictate the game."

The Colonel surveyed his team. They understood the stakes. They understood the consequences. And yet, not one of them flinched.

"Remember," Mirzai said, his voice steely. "This is not just about deception. It is about retribution and revenge. It is about power. It is about ensuring that the West never underestimates Iran again."

A quiet murmur of agreement filled the room.

Then, Mirzai gave the order.

"We will convene tomorrow morning at 1000 hours for a detailed review of the plan, and then we will begin."

As the team turned to their screens, only the soft hum of server fans filled the air.

Day 2

**Cybersecurity Intelligence Operations Center
The Ministry of Intelligence of The Islamic
Republic of Iran (MOIS)
Ozgol, Tajrish, Tehran Province, Iran
10:00 am**

Colonel Reza Mirzai stood at the head of a conference table deep within the Iranian Ministry of Intelligence. A scar on his left cheek, a souvenir of a movement too slow, gave the veteran warrior a distinctive air of dominance, despite his now gray hair and slower gait, the result of injuries sustained in the line of duty. The air was thick with tension as his cyber operative staff waited for him to speak. Their underground facility, officially listed as a defunct storage depot, was a cover for one of Iran's most classified operations. The walls were lined with secure server fans humming softly in the background, and the low glow of flat-screen monitors cast eerie blue shadows across the assembled team's faces.

The Colonel's sharp, calculating eyes scanned the room. He was a man of war, though not in the conventional sense. His battlefield was now digital, his weapons a network of falsehoods, deception, and strategic manipulation. His distinguished past in the Iranian Revolutionary Guard had hardened him. Still, his time at the Moscow Institute of Cybernetics refined him into the man he was now — a master of information warfare.

"This mission," he began in a clipped tone, "will be the most consequential operation in modern Iranian history. The West underestimates us. They believe power is dictated by military might and economic sanctions. We will show them otherwise." He leaned forward, placing his hands firmly on the steel briefing table. "Without firing a single bullet, we will weaken their resolve, turn their allies against them, and force their hand against our chosen enemies."

His words sent a ripple of anticipation through the room. His staff — all handpicked, trusted, and utterly devoted — understood the weight of what their mission team was about to do. Each special mission team member had been selected for his or her exceptional skills and loyalty to Iran's mission.

Mirzai curled his lips into a smirk as he activated the holographic display in the center of the table. A complex schematic of the United States classified artificial intelligence system — AEGIS — appeared before them.

"Remember, we are not hacking AEGIS," Mirzai continued. "We don't need to. We will use its own programming against it."

Kamran furrowed his brow. "That's the beauty of this plan – there need be no intrusions that could be detected and set off alarms."

Mirzai nodded his agreement. "That is correct. AEGIS is the most sophisticated artificial intelligence system the United States has ever built. It sifts through intelligence reports, financial transactions, and diplomatic chatter, identifying patterns and issuing military directives based on perceived threats. The U.S. military trusts it blindly. If AEGIS believes a threat is real, so will their leaders."

Leila, ever the strategist, leaned forward. "This fabricated intelligence will increase the paranoia that already exists."

"Not just paranoia," Mirzai corrected. "We will manipulate AEGIS into constructing a reality that does not exist. We will create a crisis, escalate tensions, and ensure that the United States perceives threats where none exist.

Mirzai then ended the briefing and dismissed all the staff members except the mission team.

Mirzai gestured toward Leila. "Your messages must be flawless. Every word must be indistinguishable from real intelligence briefings."

Leila grinned, her confidence evident. "I've studied Pentagon linguistics for years. I can make AEGIS believe anything."

Mirzai turned to Kamran. "And you? How convincingly can you falsify origins?"

Kamran's fingers danced over the keyboard of his laptop. "By the time I'm done, AEGIS will believe its information is coming from the Pentagon, NATO, Beijing, or even the Kremlin itself."

Saeed, who had been listening intently, finally spoke. "AEGIS is advanced. What if it detects the anomalies?"

Mirzai's expression darkened. "That's where your expertise comes in. Every message must pass through NSA-grade encryption, formatted identically to actual intelligence dispatches. It must mimic their timing, their patterns, and their urgency.

Saeed nodded, already considering the mathematical intricacies of crafting such a deception. He added, "We should also make these messages self-deleting to keep them off the logs and make them untraceable. Kamran, can you do that?"

"I certainly can – you just add a line or two of code at the end of the message header, and the message will disappear – never to be seen or heard from again."

"Excellent," replied Saeed.

Mirzai continued, "We will do this with two kinds of messages. First, we will create messages that appear to be sent and routed between Russia and China, allowing AEGIS to see and process them. Secondly, we will send fabricated internal messages to various U.S. military organizations with various warnings about Russian and Chinese movements. It doesn't matter if the receiving U.S. addresses are in service or not – AEGIS will see the messages and process them before the mail server rejects them. Then, they are deleted to prevent any problems from occurring.

Leila cracked her knuckles and pulled up her screen. "Let's begin."

Leila's fingers danced over the keyboard as she crafted the first false intelligence dispatch given to her by Mirzai. Every sentence was meticulously structured, every word chosen to escalate tension without seeming alarmist.

"Recent intelligence indicates that Chinese authorities are preparing to impose aggressive economic sanctions in response to recent U.S. diplomatic actions in the Asia-Pacific. Early estimates suggest that this move will target critical supply chains, with a particular emphasis on technology and infrastructure imports. The impact on trade relations is projected to be significant. Treasury is advised to monitor market fluctuations and prepare countermeasures. More intelligence to follow."

Kamran glanced at the message and whistled. "That looks real."

Leila nodded. "Because it is real, in a sense. I studied actual Pentagon reports that I accessed through the UN portal. It's just a minor tweak from being indistinguishable."

She moved on to the second message on her list, this time designed to make AEGIS believe China and Russia were strengthening ties in response to American aggression.

Encrypted Digital Directive #2
To: National Security Council
From: Foreign Intelligence Briefing Division
"Sources report an increase in high-level diplomatic exchanges between Chinese and Russian officials, signaling potential joint action concerning U.S. operations in Eastern Europe. It is advised that further attention be given to communications intercepts to assess the likelihood of coordinated economic and military measures.

Kamran grinned. "That will flag both countries as imminent threats on AEGIS."

Leila then typed out the final, most dangerous message — one that would put the U.S. military on high alert.

Encrypted Digital Directive #3
To: Department of Homeland Security
From: Cyber Threat Division
"Emerging intelligence suggests China's cybersecurity units have increased reconnaissance activity around U.S. infrastructure networks. Preliminary data indicates they may be mapping access points to launch potential denial-of-service attacks. Recommend heightened monitoring and readiness protocols for critical infrastructure sectors."

Kamran exhaled slowly. "If AEGIS flags that, the Americans will start shifting military resources."

Leila inserted deletion commands into each transmission. "After AEGIS processes these, they'll erase themselves from the system. No trail, no record. The Americans will only see the conclusions their own intelligent server draws."

With a final keystroke, the messages were sent.

Using the UN portal, the mission team silently watched the monitor as the network "sniffer" software observed message markets entering and exiting the network. They could see indications of AEGIS output without entering the AEGIS system directly.

4:15 pm

Kamran's eyes flicked to the monitor. "Leila," he whispered. "It's happening."

They could see traces of messages indicating that AEGIS was running calculations, flagging intelligence, and issuing alerts to American military command centers.

Leila's pulse quickened. "How fast is it reacting?"

Saeed's fingers tightened around his coffee cup. "Much faster than we expected – within a couple of hours of receipt. It's already cross-referencing intelligence and reinforcing our narrative."

Mirzai folded his arms. "Then we wait."

The room fell into tense silence as they watched their deception ripple through the world's most powerful intelligence network. AEGIS was already shifting the United States toward an unseen war.

And they had only just begun.

As Mirzai observed the first stage of their plan unfold, a slow, satisfied smile crept onto his face. They had planted the seeds of discord, and soon, the world would reap the consequences.

But what he didn't know — what none of them could know — was that an American counter-intelligence team had already begun to notice discrepancies in the data.

And they would be coming for them.

Day 3

Regional Office
U. S. Immigration & Customs Enforcement (ICE)
Harlingen, Texas
8:15 am

Special Agent Carlos Mejia leaned back in his office chair, his fingers wrapped around a mug of coffee that had long since gone room temperature. He barely noticed. His eyes remained locked on the monitors before him, scanning an endless stream of data on the government secure network pouring into the U.S. Immigration and Customs Enforcement (ICE) command center in the Rio Grande Valley. The fluorescent glow of the monitors bathed his face in blue light, emphasizing the lines of exhaustion that came from years of relentless vigilance.

Carlos had spent the last seventeen years at ICE tracking the movement of drug cartels, human traffickers, and any other threats that seeped through the porous U.S.-Mexico border. But this morning, his gut told him something was off. Something was wrong. He had spent enough time parsing cartel communications to know when something didn't fit the mold.

"Good morning, Carlos," came a voice from three workstations down the row. "Don't forget we have lunch with the Brownsville Chamber of Commerce today."

"Got it," replied Carlos as his attention returned to his screens.

His workstation was a nexus of intelligence — live surveillance feeds from border crossings, decrypted intercepts from cartel operatives, and sensor data tracking illegal movements along the border fence. He was trained to spot anomalies, and today, one practically leaped off the screen at him.

Unlike the usual cartel chatter — coded references to drug shipments, smuggling routes, or violent reprisals — what he saw now was something else entirely. Layers upon layers of encryption wrapped around data packets moving across international networks. Not cartel work. Not even close. This was different.

He frowned, adjusting his posture as he leaned in. The encryption wasn't just advanced — it was government-grade. And not just any government — this was the kind of cryptographic masking he'd seen during a joint training exercise with the National Security Agency years ago, the type used for classified military transmissions. What the hell was it doing here, mixed in with cross-border traffic?

Carlos's gut tightened as he clicked through the routing metadata. The message showed markings that it had been routed through multiple international relays, bouncing across Europe, the Middle East, and finally, through a small, obscure ISP near the Texas-Mexico border. Someone was trying to bury its origins beneath layers of misdirection.

His instincts screamed at him. This wasn't some run-of-the-mill cartel operation. This was something bigger — something more profound.

Carlos leaned back in his chair, continuing to stare at the encrypted message glowing ominously on his primary monitor. His instincts were good — something was going on. He took a slow sip of his now-cold coffee, the bitter taste doing little to ease the tension coiling in his gut. The anomalies were piling up, and he knew he couldn't tackle this alone. He turned to his left, looking for his partner.

Carlos looked around his cubicle wall and saw the long, straight dark hair that told him the workstation two down from him was occupied. He promptly summoned its occupant, Sandra Espinoza. Sandra was his closest confidante at ICE, a forensic financial analyst with a knack for tearing apart encrypted data like a predator dismantling its prey.

"Sandra, I need your eyes on this. I'm seeing data streams that feel too sophisticated for the usual cartel chatter."

Sandra rolled her ancient government chair over, curiosity flickering in her sharp brown eyes. She and Carlos had been partners for five years, their skill sets complementing each other perfectly. Where Carlos specialized in cracking codes and detecting patterns in digital communications, Sandra's expertise lay in forensic accounting — following the money, uncovering illicit transactions, and piecing together financial breadcrumbs that others missed. Together, they had dismantled smuggling networks, exposed cartel money laundering schemes, and tracked some of the most elusive criminals operating along the U.S.-Mexico border.

"What's going on?" she asked.

Carlos gestured at the screen. "Take a look at this. Tell me if it looks like anything you've seen before."

Sandra frowned as she studied the data. The scrolling lines of code weren't typical cartel transmissions — no street slang, nicknames, or references to routes or transactions. It was raw, heavily encrypted intelligence — almost too clean, too professional.

"This isn't cartel work," she muttered. "It's too structured. This looks military."

Born and raised in Brownsville, Texas, Sandra had always felt the weight of the border's criminal underbelly pressing against her community. Determined to make a difference, she earned both her bachelor's and master's degrees in forensic accounting from the University of Texas – Rio Grande Valley, where she graduated at the top of her class. Now in her late thirties, she had built a career on exposing the darkest financial corridors criminals used to move money, and nothing gave her more satisfaction than taking down those who profited from chaos.

She leaned over Carlos's shoulder, scrutinizing the lines of encrypted data scrolling across his screen. "That's... not cartel work," she murmured. "This is layered encryption. Military-grade. Spook stuff."

Carlos nodded. "Exactly. Look at the routing pattern. Eastern Europe, to the Middle East, and then to a small ISP just north of the border. Someone's going to a hell of a lot of trouble to make this look random. But why would it be mixed in with cross-border traffic?"

Sandra frowned, her analytical mind already piecing things together. "That's deliberate obfuscation. A genuine smuggling network would have direct and efficient routes. This is something else."

Carlos exhaled sharply. I need you to check and see if you can find any financial transactions associated with any of these messages. If there's a money trail, we might be able to determine who's behind it.

Sandra cracked her knuckles. "You know I love a good puzzle. Send me everything you've got."

Carlos tapped a few keys, transferring the data to Sandra's secure workstation. As she returned to her workspace to examine the financials, he knew they needed yet another set of eyes on this — someone with an understanding of Middle Eastern communication patterns. He looked for Priya Sharma but remembered she was in a status meeting down the hall but would return shortly.

Sandra began typing, pulling up a more detailed data packet analysis. After a few moments, she leaned back and summoned Carlos. "It's not just encrypted — it's layered. The original message was masked and sent through multiple bounce points, disguising its origin. Whoever did this knows what they're doing."

Carlos drummed his fingers against the desk. "Where does it originate?"

Sandra pointed at the tracing logs. "Best guess? Eastern Europe. However, that doesn't mean much if it has been spoofed.

Carlos narrowed his eyes. Eastern Europe, then the Middle East, and now here? That's not cartel traffic. That's intelligence work."

Sandra's expression darkened. "Or cyber-warfare."

Carlos felt his pulse quicken. Before joining ICE, he'd spent a tour in Afghanistan as an Army Ranger Intelligence Officer and knew what cyber-warfare looked like. He'd seen firsthand how data could be manipulated, how misinformation could be fed into an enemy's intelligence network like a slow-acting poison.

He pushed his chair back. "We need to escalate this."

Sandra hesitated. "To whom? Do you think D.C. is going to take this seriously? They're already drowning in cartel ops. They're not going to drop everything for an encrypted message we can't even trace."

Carlos clenched his jaw. She was right. Bureaucracy moved slowly, even in law enforcement. This would be dismissed as noise unless they had more to go on.

"Then we get more," he said firmly. We isolate every packet like this and determine if there's a pattern. We'll have something solid if we can prove this isn't a one-off."

Sandra nodded, already typing. "I'll run a filter. See if there is any correlation between these packets and recent alerts flagged by other agencies.

Carlos leaned forward, staring at the screen, the tension in his gut growing. This wasn't just cartel business. This was something more dangerous. And if he was right — if this was the beginning of something bigger — then time could be running out.

Sandra's fingers froze over the keyboard. "Carlos... I just cross-checked this encryption against a list of known ciphers."

He looked at her sharply. "And?"

She turned to him, her face pale. "This matches a protocol used in classified U.S. military communications."

Carlos felt a chill run through him.

A U.S. military encryption code embedded in a message bouncing through Eastern Europe and the Middle East — before landing here?

This wasn't just cyber-warfare.

This was infiltration.

And whoever was behind it was already monitoring their systems.

Carlos inhaled deeply, pushing back the surge of adrenaline. "We need to move. Now."

Sandra nodded, her fingers flying across the keyboard. "I'm on it."

Carlos grabbed his phone. He needed to make his boss aware of what he had found but decided to wait until more information could be obtained. If what they had just uncovered was as big as he thought it was, then the U.S. government was about to wake up to a nightmare they hadn't even seen coming.

"I see that Priya is back from her meeting. Let's get her in here," Carlos said, his eyes already tired from staring intensely at his screens for well over an hour. It appears that some of these routes connect to servers in Iran. If anyone can make sense of this, it's her."

"Good idea," Sandra replied, her eyes still fixed on the data she was interpreting. "Priya's input will be very useful."

Junior Analyst Priya Sharma sat down next to Sandra, instantly shifting the energy in the area. Calm and methodical, she had a reputation for dissecting complex digital trails with surgical precision. Originally from Baghdad, Iraq, Priya had witnessed firsthand how intelligence failures could tear a country apart. Her family had fled to London when she was twelve, and she later attended Imperial College London, earning degrees in Information Technology and Linguistics before specializing in cryptography and Middle Eastern intelligence work. After immigrating to the U.S., she worked in international telecommunications while earning her citizenship, eventually joining ICE as an analyst and a specialist in encrypted Middle Eastern communications. Young, attractive, fit, and athletic, she enjoyed her weekends outdoors in an area with 11 months of outdoor weather every year.

Setting down her cup of black coffee, she asked, "What's the crisis today?"

Carlos gestured to his screen. Encrypted traffic — far beyond cartel capabilities — appears to be routed through Eastern Europe and the Middle East before reaching us. Can you review the metadata?

Priya's dark eyes lit up with curiosity. "Let's see what we've got."

She typed quickly, running the data through multiple decryption tools, translation algorithms, and regional network pattern analyzers. "Hmm... this isn't just encrypted — it's obfuscated through multiple layers. Someone went to great lengths to bury their tracks."

"That's what Sandra said as well," replied Carlos.

Sandra, still poring over financials, suddenly spoke up. "Got something. Significant financial transactions were routed through cryptocurrency exchanges in Dubai and Moscow. They're using shell companies with no legitimate business operations. And here's the kicker — one transaction is linked directly to a server in Tehran.

Carlos's jaw tightened. "That confirms it. This isn't just a smuggling network. This is bigger."

Priya looked up, her face serious. "The routing patterns match Middle Eastern intelligence traffic, but there are more linguistic markers in the data that suggest an Iranian origin. Certain phrases and Farsi syntax that align with known Iranian intelligence communications."

Carlos clenched his fists. "So, we've got high-level encryption, money moving through illicit channels, and Iranian intelligence markers buried in cartel traffic? That's not a coincidence."

Sandra leaned back, her expression dark. "If we don't escalate this, we'll miss something critical."

Priya nodded. "This might not just be border security anymore. This may become a national security matter."

Carlos exhaled, already thinking about his next move. He had seen cartel tactics, smuggling rings, and cyber fraud, but this was something else entirely. If Iran, or someone else in that region, were using cartel networks to mask intelligence operations and messaging, then this wasn't just about crime — it was about geopolitical espionage, maybe even war.

He looked at his team, knowing that what they had uncovered was only the beginning. "I don't know – we probably need to spend more time on this and be more certain of what we see. I really don't want to escalate something that turns out to be nothing. I really need to give Tom a ring, though, and give him a heads up."

His gut twisted as he reached for his phone to call his boss, Thomas Grayson, the ICE Regional Director in nearby McAllen. If this were what he thought it might be, then they would be in over their heads organizationally. Something told him that whoever was behind this wouldn't let them dig too much further without a fight. For now, he would mention their findings in their daily reports to ICE headquarters in Washington, D.C., until they had something solid to report.

And somewhere, on the other end of that encrypted signal, someone was watching.

Day 4

Operations Floor A-2
CIA Headquarters
Langley, Virginia
8:30 am

CIA Special Agent Scott Douglass stepped out of his black SUV, tightening the cuffs of his crisp white dress shirt as he surveyed his surroundings. The brisk Virginia air carried the scent of damp earth, a stark contrast to the scorched deserts and dense jungles where he had spent most of his early career. Even after years in intelligence, some habits never died — like constantly "checking his six," which is military speak for watching one's back.

As he strode toward the towering headquarters of the Central Intelligence Agency, he ignored the twinge of discomfort in his left knee — a reminder of a mission gone awry in northern Afghanistan. The bullet wound should have ended his career, but he had pushed through, refusing to let it slow him down. That same relentless drive had made him one of the CIA's most effective covert operatives — a man whose name was whispered throughout the intelligence community.

Nicknamed "The Ghost", Douglass had a reputation for vanishing into hostile territories, gathering intelligence that no one else could access, and returning without a trace. A former Army Ranger Special Operations officer, he had spent a decade in the CIA's Special Activities Division, running black ops across the Middle East, Eastern Europe, and Central Asia. After years of operating in the shadows, he had transitioned to the CIA's Cyber Intelligence Division, where, in addition to being a seasoned field operative, he had become an expert at tracing digital threats before they materialized into real-world disasters.

He approached the checkpoint, flashing his security badge. The guard on duty, a seasoned officer who had seen Douglass come and go for years, nodded.

"Haven't seen you around lately, Douglass. I thought you were still buried in cyber cases.

Douglass didn't feel the need to inform the guard that he was just now returning after four weeks of bereavement leave and some overdue paid time off. Still in disbelief at his wife Susie's passing from uterine cancer at M.D. Anderson Medical Center in Houston, he had chosen to return to Langley, finish the year, and retire to do who knows what.

Scott had often reflected on how he and Susie met years ago while attending Texas Christian University in Fort Worth, Texas. While it wasn't love at first sight, it was undoubtedly love at second sight. Married soon after graduation, Susie had taught 1st graders in Dallas while Douglass took his recent ROTC officer's commission and left to serve his country overseas as an Army Ranger. As an officer and a combat specialist, Douglass was always at the forefront of any needed covert or special ops in the Iraq and Afghanistan theaters of operation. Never able to have children due to Susie's illness, Scott had known in Susie's final moments that he would be left alone in the world with only distant relatives to lean on. Now, he was back at Langley, ready to complete his CIA career.

Douglass offered the guard a tight-lipped smile. "Yeah, well, cyber's where the war is now."

The guard swiped his badge, and the reinforced security doors hissed open. Langley buzzed with activity. Inside, the scent of coffee, printer ink, and old paper mixed with the ever-present tension of classified operations unfolding in real-time.

9:30 am

Douglass stepped into Briefing Room C, where a stack of intercepted messages awaited him. An ICE team in South Texas had flagged the transmissions, raising enough alarms to move them up the chain of command.

He settled into a chair and scanned the screen's contents to check the transmissions. The first wave of messages appeared routine, nothing that screamed an immediate threat. But Douglass didn't believe in coincidences. His instincts told him to dig deeper.

Pulling up his pattern recognition software, he ran an analysis, looking for irregularities, inconsistencies, and anything that didn't belong. A minute passed and then another.

Then his screen flashed red.

Douglass straightened, his heartbeat quickening. *There it is.* A sequence buried in the data, one that shouldn't be there. He leaned in, eyes narrowing as he examined the encryption layers.

"Son of a bitch," he muttered under his breath.

The complexity of the encryption wasn't cartel-level — it was nation-state-level. The coding structure was layered, evolving, and self-obscuring, the kind used by intelligence agencies to ensure no one — not even the NSA — could break it easily.

But that wasn't what alarmed him most.

The linguistic markers embedded within the encrypted code were the real smoking gun. A subtle mix of Farsi, Russian, and Mandarin — a digital fingerprint designed to implicate multiple adversaries.

Douglass felt a creeping realization settle over him. The ICE team had indeed stumbled upon something that could potentially explode.

This might not just be cyber espionage. This might be full-scale cyber warfare.

9:45 am

Douglass toggled through previous cyber incidents, cross-referencing the encryption style with known foreign operations. His gut twisted as the matches began to roll in.

Possible Iranian cyber warfare signatures.

However, it is layered to implicate Russia and China.

Douglass clenched his jaw. Someone was playing all sides.

"Shit," he muttered, running a hand down his face. If these messages had already infiltrated U.S. military intelligence channels, knowing what damage could have been done was impossible. The consequences could be catastrophic if decision-makers had already acted on this potentially false intelligence without verifying it.

Douglass had spent his career hunting ghosts and uncovering deceptions before they became global crises. But this was a different kind of war.

Whoever was behind this wasn't just fabricating intelligence.

They were possibly manufacturing a war — or international confrontation at the very least.

He wanted to know more and needed boots on the ground. Now.

Douglass grabbed his secure phone and punched in a direct line to the CIA's Domestic Intelligence Services Division.

The line picked up after the first ring.

"Douglass. What do you need?"

As soon as you can book a plane, get me a flight to South Texas — specifically the McAllen sector. I'll be landing at Harlingen.

A brief pause. "South Texas? What the hell are you working on? I thought you were running cyber ops, not border security."

Douglass's voice was cold, sharp, and to the point.

"It's bigger than a border case. If I'm right, we may have a full-scale international intelligence operation unfolding under our noses. If so, we need to shut it down before someone actually acts on bad intel and starts hurting people."

The agent on the other end didn't ask questions. He knew Douglass didn't exaggerate.

"Understood. A G-5 is available to you at Andrews tomorrow at 12:45 hours. I'll send you the details."

I've some follow-up here, but please instruct them to schedule it for 11:45 a.m. so I can meet with the ICE team upon arrival before the day ends. I'll be there."

Douglass hung up, his mind already ten steps ahead.

He had operated in some of the deadliest war zones on the planet. He had tracked terrorists through the mountains of Pakistan, dismantled covert weapons deals in North Africa, and infiltrated drug cartels in South America.

But this?

This could be a war waged in the shadows, where false information was more dangerous than bullets, and the battlefield was inside the minds of policymakers.

If he didn't move with some urgency, the next war wouldn't be started by troops on the ground but by potentially fabricated messages.

The basement remained silent as the team regrouped around their screens; the only sounds were the faint hum of server fans and air conditioning vents, along with the steady clicks of keyboards. The first fabricated message had been sent and processed, but they needed to know just how deeply AEGIS could be manipulated, and a single test wouldn't provide the answer. Now exhausted from hours at her workstation, Leila leaned back in her chair, fingers tapping thoughtfully against her armrest.

"We need to push it further," she said finally, her voice edged with urgency and frustration. "One message doesn't tell us enough. We need to verify whether AEGIS is indeed forwarding these directives, particularly those with a more substantial impact. If we confirm that, we don't just have access — we have control."

Kamran nodded thoughtfully, still staring at his monitor, his long, slender fingers drumming lightly against the desk. His mind raced with the implications, a mixture of excitement and apprehension tightening in his chest. "Agreed. If AEGIS prioritizes another message as actionable intelligence, especially one involving troop movements, then we've found a major fault line. That means we don't just have access — we have influence. And if we can manipulate troop movements, we can dictate the tempo of their military strategy without them realizing it. This isn't just a vulnerability; it's a weapon."

Saeed, monitoring the encryption sequences, looked up, his brow furrowing in fatigue from the strain of his concentration. "Then we'll need to send a directive bold enough to get noticed but still realistic. It will have to be something significant but subtle, enough to cause concern but not outright panic. If we push too hard, we risk scrutiny; if we play it too safe, AEGIS might not react the way we need it to. The balance has to be perfect."

Leila smiled, her eyes glinting with purpose. "Our list has just the thing." Her fingers hovered over the keyboard momentarily, then descended in a flurry of keystrokes. Every word she keyboarded had to be deliberate, precise, and indistinguishable from authentic military communications. The message couldn't just sound real — it had to *be* authentic in the eyes of AEGIS, slipping seamlessly into the vast stream of classified intelligence flowing through the system.

She straightened in her chair, her mind working through the layers of deception they needed to embed. This message wouldn't be just another test but a statement of control. If AEGIS accepted and acted upon it, they would have proof that they weren't just observing and spectating; they were directing. And once they could direct a system like AEGIS, they could steer an entire nation's military response without ever setting foot inside their borders.

After a few moments, she read it aloud to the team for feedback:

To: Commander, U.S. European Command (EUCOM)

From: Office of the Secretary of Defense, U.S.A. (SECDEF)

"Recent intelligence reports confirm a significant increase in Russian military activity along Eastern European borders, including logistical movements and reinforced troop deployments. In response, all available rapid-response units are to be repositioned to strategic posts in Poland and Romania within 48 hours. Additional air support is to be allocated to bolster readiness, and naval assets in the Baltic region are to shift to an elevated alert status. This operation is a precautionary measure to ensure the security of our NATO allies and to deter any potential escalation. Further intelligence updates will follow as assessments continue."

Saeed leaned over, reading the text, then nodded. "This is good. It's subtle enough to seem like a defensive maneuver, but it implies a shift in the balance. If AEGIS believes the directive, it could trigger a chain reaction.

Leila smiled, satisfied. "That's the idea. We want this message to sound as though it came directly from the

Secretary of Defense — urgent but not overtly hostile. Just enough to keep them guessing."

Kamran adjusted the transmission protocols on his screen. "I'll set it up to go through a priority channel. We need it to get flagged as 'actionable intelligence' by AEGIS, then routed as high as possible to simulate a real directive."

Once they were ready, Leila sent the message.

Kamran watched the sniffer software's messaging screens, his breath slow and steady as the minutes passed. Forty-eight minutes later, they had their answer. "It looks like AEGIS is creating a priority alert within the Department of Defense's secure network," he murmured. His fingers glided over the keyboard, pulling up the transmission logs. It should craft a message to the U.S. European Command and send it directly from the Secretary of Defense's office.

Saeed's eyebrows shot up, his voice tinged with both awe and unease. You're telling me it's not just acknowledging the directive, but actually processing it as if it were an authentic military command?

Kamran nodded, his tone both amazed and cautious. "Exactly. Remember when Colonel Mirzai taught us that AEGIS is programmed to respond immediately to any high-level directive? It's not just passing it along; it's escalating the urgency to their top command as though this were a legitimate military order requiring immediate action. If this works, we aren't just fooling a machine — we're beginning to steer the decision-making of an entire defense network."

Leila let out a breath she hadn't realized she was holding. A flicker of unease crossed her face as she exchanged worried glances with Kamran and Saeed. "If they follow through on this, they might actually start mobilizing troop units in response. And once that starts, there's no telling how quickly this could escalate. One wrong interpretation — one miscalculated assumption — and we might set off a chain reaction we can't control."

Saeed glanced at her, concern deepening the creases in his forehead. "Are we absolutely certain this won't spiral out of control? Not really. If even one analyst in their intelligence network starts connecting the dots, or someone high enough in the chain of command decides to cross-check sources, such as examining satellite images of troops and equipment, this entire operation could unravel. We could be looking at a full-blown crisis before we have a chance to counter it, and once that happens, we'll have no control over where the pieces fall. It all depends on how committed they are to the infallibility of AEGIS."

"That's the entire point, Saeed," Leila replied, her voice unwavering. "We need to see if AEGIS will not only log the directive but also embed it as a credible threat within the system. Their military is so convinced that AEGIS is infallible that it would be highly unlikely for them to verify these messages by cross-checking. Additionally, verifying messages is unlikely to occur if they are frequent and appear to come from multiple sources. If it does, we know it's susceptible to further manipulation. And once we confirm that we aren't just feeding it data — we know that we're guiding its entire decision-making framework."

Kamran turned to them, a hint of caution in his tone. "But this also confirms something else. AEGIS is learning from each message we send. If it encounters too many irregularities, it might start prioritizing them for human review. We need to tread carefully."

Leila's gaze was unflinching. "I'm aware of the risks. However, as long as AEGIS treats these directives as legitimate, we can continue to move forward. This is just one step. We'll stagger the next message to avoid triggering any new protocols."

Kamran turned to Leila, still slightly in disbelief. "Look at the message log. It looks like AEGIS actually took the bait. It's not just processing these directives; it's also reinforcing the credibility of the fabricated intelligence.

"Which means we can proceed with our next steps," Leila replied confidently. "This proves that AEGIS isn't just cataloging the data. It's treating it as if it came from verified sources."

Saeed, still monitoring the encryption patterns, chimed in. "How long before we escalate again? If AEGIS can handle troop movements, it may be time to introduce something more intense."

None of them could imagine the fuse they had just lit or the size of the firecracker on the other end.

The air in the secure conference room on the top floor of Tehran's Ministry of Defense building was thick with anticipation. The room, windowless and insulated against electronic surveillance, carried an oppressive silence, broken only by the rhythmic hum of the air conditioning. The seven men seated around the polished mahogany table were some of the most powerful figures in Iran — commanders, strategists, intelligence officials, and political leaders. Each had spent decades shaping the nation's military and geopolitical ambitions, and tonight, they would determine the next phase of their most audacious operation.

Colonel Reza Mirzai entered with precise, measured steps, his uniform crisp, his expression unreadable. He had learned long ago that hesitation was a weakness, and weakness could be fatal in this room. He scanned the faces before him — most were old military colleagues who had spent their careers battling Western influence, men who had suffered through sanctions and threats, and men whose patience had worn thin. This afternoon, they demanded results.

Minister Arash Khalili, the head of Iran's National Security Council, wasted no time. "Colonel Mirzai, your last report indicated that our fabricated intelligence was being accepted by the U.S. Department of Defense's classified AEGIS server. I trust you have an update?"

Mirzai inclined his head. "Yes, Minister Khalili. I am pleased to report that our plan is proceeding as expected and is making excellent progress. Our team has successfully sent multiple fabricated messages and directives that AEGIS has read, logged, and classified as high-level intelligence. It now prioritizes and distributes our messages through their command structure as routine and without suspicion."

The room remained silent, processing the weight of Mirzai's words. Then, Minister of Defense General Ebrahim Ansari leaned forward, his deep voice cutting through the tension. "Incredible. Explain the extent of the manipulation."

Mirzai steeled himself. "We have shifted U.S. military focus toward Russia and China. AEGIS has already acted upon a directive to reposition American rapid-response units closer to Russian borders, particularly in Poland and Romania. Additionally, we have introduced additional intelligence suggesting China is preparing an incursion into Taiwan. AEGIS is amplifying this data, reinforcing the illusion that war is imminent."

Minister Khalili allowed himself a slight smile, but his eyes remained cold. "And how soon before these nations begin responding?"

Mirzai straightened. "We are already seeing preliminary shifts in troop movements. If we continue feeding AEGIS with well-crafted intelligence, within weeks, the Americans, Russians, and Chinese will be on high alert, each viewing the other as the primary aggressor. The tension from their collective paranoia will escalate until one of them makes a move without much due diligence. By then, they will be too entangled in their own conflicts to interfere in our affairs."

A murmur spread through the room, a mixture of satisfaction and amazement tinged with disbelief. Foreign Minister Farhad Rezaian spoke next, his tone both impressed and cautious. "Reza, you are telling us that the world's superpowers could go to the brink of war because of data we have fabricated?"

Mirzai nodded. "Yes, Minister. Our intelligence unit has planted the seeds of distrust, and AEGIS is nurturing them. Every piece of data it processes reinforces our narrative within a military that wants to believe it. We have effectively taken control of the most advanced artificial intelligence within the Western military complex. We are no longer just observers of global affairs — we have become the architects."

General Ansari interlocked his fingers, his expression unreadable. "And what of Israel?"

The room tensed. This was the true objective.

Mirzai's voice did not waver. "Our underground nuclear testing is now complete, and the weapons are reliable. Our initial targets will be the ports of Ashdod and Haifa, which, once destroyed, will effectively eliminate their commerce and sever them from the world. Depending on the winds, these blasts could also affect Tel Aviv, which is between them and only 32 kilometers away from Ashdod. Ashdod is 64 kilometers from Jerusalem, so the holy sites will not be harmed. We will strike once the superpowers are preoccupied and unable to attack us. The Israelis have relied on their superior intelligence infrastructure to anticipate threats — without it, they are blind. Israel will find itself isolated, unable to call for aid, and unable to react in time. Our military has also prepared a multi-pronged assault, one that will cripple their defenses before they even realize they are under attack."

The gravity of Mirzai's words hung in the air, the weight of decades of enmity and resentment compressed into a single moment.

Minister Khalili leaned back, his fingers tapping lightly against the armrest of his chair. "And the Americans? If they detect this manipulation?"

Mirzai allowed himself a small, calculated smile. "They are already suspicious and have shown little interest in verifying AEGIS messages. If they do get suspicious, it will be too late by then. The United States, China, and Russia will be locked in a struggle for dominance with no willingness to back down. They will be too busy posturing, threatening, and reacting to perceived threats to pay attention to us. And even if they suspect foul play, our digital tracks are so deeply buried that no amount of forensic analysis will trace them back to us."

Khalili exhaled slowly, considering the full implications. "This operation is unprecedented. If it succeeds, we shift the global balance in our favor."

"Yes, Minister," Mirzai affirmed. "This mission is not just about military success but about Iran's future. For too long, we have endured Western sanctions, interference, ridicule, and threats. Now, we reclaim our rightful place as the dominant power in the Middle East."

A slow nod passed through the now-silent room. Each man present understood the stakes. This was not just a strategic operation — it was a statement. Iran would no longer be dictated to; it would dictate.

General Ansari broke the silence. "Colonel, you have our full support. But you must be prepared for the unexpected. No matter how sophisticated our deception may be, war remains unpredictable. One miscalculation, one unforeseen move, and this could spiral out of control.

Mirzai inclined his head. "I am aware, General. My team is monitoring every variable. We have contingency plans in place should any anomalies arise. By one means or another, the operation will proceed with precision."

Minister Khalili gave his final verdict. "Then proceed, Colonel. And remember — we must not fail."

Mirzai saluted sharply, crisply turned 180 degrees, and then exited the room, his mind already racing with the next steps.

=====

When Mirzai reentered the basement operations center, his mission team looked up, sensing the shift in his demeanor. Leila, Kamran, and Saeed were waiting, their expressions a mixture of determination and anticipation.

"Well?" Leila asked, her voice steady but expectant.

Mirzai's face was resolute. "We have the green light to proceed without restriction. The ministers are fully aware of our goals and the risks. Our endgame is set."

Saeed's face lit up with grim excitement. "So we escalate?"

"Yes," Mirzai confirmed. "Every step counts from here. We heighten tensions between the superpowers and deepen their paranoia. The more time they spend reacting to false threats, the less time they have to see what we are truly planning."

Kamran nodded, understanding the weight of the moment. "This will be remembered as a turning point in our nation's history."

Leila's expression darkened with fierce determination. "We will keep them tangled in their own suspicions. Every message, every directive, and every shift in intelligence will reinforce the web we have created. And they will never see it coming."

Mirzai met her gaze, his voice unwavering. "This is Iran's moment. The world has underestimated us for too long. But soon, they will understand the cost of that mistake."

The room fell into a heavy silence as the team turned to their screens, fingers poised to execute the next phase of deception.

The countdown had begun, and the pieces were falling into place.

And soon, the world would burn.

6:30 pm

Leila sat before her screen, her weary fingers hovering over the keyboard as she carefully considered the message she was about to draft. This one was scheduled to be more intricate than the previous directives. To fully implicate the United States in a possible invasion of China via Taiwan, the output message from AEGIS needed to feel like an authentic internal communication from high-ranking American defense officials. It had to carry the weight of strategic intent, urgency, and controlled aggression — enough to send shockwaves through Chinese intelligence and force their hand.

She exhaled sharply. The stakes were escalating, and with every successful deception, the risk of exposure grew. Yet, there was no turning back now. Their mission was to sow discord, and the deeper they pulled AEGIS into their fabricated web, the closer they came to achieving their ultimate goal.

"Let's make this one really stick," Leila murmured, her tone steely, betraying the urgency she felt. "We'll frame this as a defensive measure, but it needs to carry undertones of offensive preparedness. If China intercepts this, they must believe an attack is imminent."

Saeed adjusted his chair and nodded, his eyes locked onto the flickering code on his screen. "We need specifics — troop movements, fleet positions, logistical support. Anything that would escalate paranoia."

Leila nodded. "Agreed. Let's start by detailing troop deployment and equipment mobilization. If the message suggests the U.S. is positioning forces in a defensive line but close enough to execute a first strike, China will have no choice but to respond."

Her fingers moved swiftly over the keyboard, each keystroke a calculated act of manipulation:

To: Commander, U.S. Indo-Pacific Command (CINPAC)
From: Office of the Undersecretary of Defense for Policy (DECDEV)
RE: Strategic Force Mobilization in Response to Taiwan Contingencies

"As discussed in our previous briefing, the situation in Taiwan necessitates a continued show of strength. All available naval assets within the Seventh Fleet are to be repositioned within striking distance of the Taiwan Strait by the end of the month. Ground units, supported by additional air squadrons, are to be mobilized to Guam, Okinawa, and other key strategic locations. This posture will reinforce our deterrence stance and prepare for a rapid-response incursion if the People's Republic of China escalates its aggression in the Taiwan Strait. Coordinated logistical support for this operation is in place, including fuel reserves, ammunition, and medical supplies."

Kamran leaned over her shoulder, scanning the draft. "You're making this sound defensive, but the positioning suggests an offensive capability. That's exactly what we need."

Leila grinned. "Precisely. The key is plausible deniability. If the Chinese intercept this, it must appear that the U.S. is merely 'preparing' — but the implied threat should force their hand."

Saeed added, "China already has deep-seated concerns about Taiwan." This will play into those fears, making it seem like the U.S. is poised to act preemptively.

Satisfied, Leila encrypted the message and funneled it into their network, watching it disappear through the U.N. portal into the vast digital pathways of global intelligence.

As the minutes passed, Kamran exhaled sharply. It appears to have been flagged as critical. AEGIS has logged and processed it."

Leila glanced at him. "And?"

His fingers danced across the keyboard as he monitored AEGIS's response and waited further. "It's being treated as imminent intelligence. It's bypassing lower-tier reviews and going straight to priority command."

A slow, satisfied smile spread across Leila's lips. "That's exactly what we wanted."

Saeed leaned back in his chair, rubbing his temples. "So now what? We sit back and watch the Chinese military scramble?"

Leila's eyes gleamed with something close to satisfaction. "Not yet. We reinforce the narrative. Every subsequent message must validate this one, feeding AEGIS just enough information to solidify its conclusions. The Americans need to believe that China is on the brink of a first strike."

Kamran let out a low whistle. "AEGIS will amplify its own biases. If we continue to feed it intelligence that suggests imminent conflict, it'll prioritize all incoming data that supports that theory.

"Exactly," Leila said. "We aren't just manipulating information; we're now reshaping its reality."

For a moment, they sat in silence, the magnitude of what they were orchestrating settling over them. AEGIS — one of the world's most advanced artificial intelligence defense systems — was becoming their unwitting puppet. It was interpreting their lies as truths and structuring U.S. military strategy around them.

Leila finally broke the silence. "Let's keep pushing. The Americans are about to find themselves trapped in a conflict of their own making."

She turned back to her keyboard, already composing the next move in their grand deception plan.

The game was far from over.

Regional Office
U. S. Immigration & Customs Enforcement
Harlingen, Texas
4:30 pm

The hum of server and A/C fans filled the air as Priya Sharma remained at her workstation, her youthful face illuminated by the warm glow of her monitors. The room, filled with the steady clatter of keyboards and the quiet murmur of analytical discussions, felt thick with tension. Each keystroke, each decrypted fragment, brought them closer to something none of them could yet define, but all knew was dangerous.

Priya was in her element, parsing through layers of encrypted data that Carlos and Sandra had flagged as unusual. While the others continued their investigations, she delved deeply into the linguistic and structural details of the messages, searching for patterns or anomalies that could reveal their origin. As a former analyst specializing in Middle Eastern intelligence before joining ICE, Priya had spent years identifying communication markers used by Middle Eastern terrorist cells and rogue intelligence networks. She had built custom algorithms to detect and parse linguistic markers — subtle hints of language, syntax, or phrasing that often lingered even in encrypted messages.

But this was different. More sophisticated. More deliberate.

Then, Priya sat up straight, her brow furrowing. She leaned closer to the screen, zooming in on a fragment of decrypted data. A chill ran through her as she recognized something familiar — something unsettling.

"What is it?" Carlos asked, noticing her sudden shift in posture.

Priya gestured for him to come closer. I keep seeing this, and it's both odd and fascinating. Look at this," she said, pointing to a decoded message fragment. These characters here are in Arabic, but it's not just Arabic; it's also a combination of Arabic and other languages." It's mixed with Farsi, and even structural elements resemble Russian syntax."

Carlos frowned, trying to make sense of what he was seeing. "Mixed languages? Is that normal?"

Priya shook her head. "No, not at this level. Arabic and Farsi aren't usually combined this way — there is still too much bad blood between those cultures. This isn't casual code-switching — it's deliberate. It's as if someone crafted these messages with extreme precision, using linguistic nuances from multiple regions. They wanted to obscure the origin by blending languages. It appears to be intended to mislead.

Sandra walked over, intrigued. "But why go to all that trouble? If they're already encrypting the messages, wouldn't that be enough to hide their meaning?"

Priya leaned back, considering the question. "Normally, yes. But this suggests they're working on multiple layers of deception. The encryption conceals the content, but the linguistic blending is likely intended to mislead anyone attempting to trace its origin. Arabic might suggest one region, Farsi another, and Russian yet another. It would send investigators in circles."

Carlos nodded, a spark of understanding in his eyes. And if someone tries to analyze it without the right expertise, they may draw incorrect conclusions. They'll think it's coming from one place when it's actually coming from somewhere else."

"Exactly," Priya said. "But there's more. The structure of the encryption itself — it's not just advanced; it's eerily familiar. It reminds me of something I saw during a training session with the NSA. This level of complexity — it's NSA-level or something designed to mimic it."

Sandra's eyes widened. "You're saying this could be using stolen U.S. encryption protocols? What if our people are involved?"

"It's a possibility," Priya replied. "Or someone else has studied NSA protocols closely enough to spoof and replicate their style. Either way, it's sophisticated and very well done."

The room fell silent as the weight of Priya's discovery sank in. If the messages were using or imitating NSA-level encryption, it meant that whoever was behind this had access to cutting-edge technology and potentially classified knowledge. The linguistic blending only deepened the mystery, suggesting an international network with ties to multiple regions.

Carlos broke the silence. "This isn't just a smuggling network or a cartel. This is much bigger — with resources, planning, and serious technical expertise."

Sandra nodded, her mind racing. "If this involves Arabic, Farsi, and Russian elements, we're looking at a potential collaboration across regions. Could it be a state-sponsored operation? Terrorism, maybe?"

Priya tapped her chin thoughtfully. "It's possible. The encryption, routing patterns, and linguistic blending all point to a level of coordination that is unusual for independent actors. And if this is state-sponsored, it's not just a matter of border security anymore. This is national security."

Carlos glanced at the metadata Priya had uncovered. The question now is, what do we do next? We may have stumbled on something highly classified that our side is conducting. Let's step back and look at what we know so far. The messages are encrypted at a level that rivals U.S. intelligence, and they're routed through multiple international servers designed to mislead anyone trying to trace them. Additionally, we've linguistic markers that tie this to at least three regions.

Sandra crossed her arms, her voice steady but serious. "And don't forget the money trail. Those cryptocurrency transactions I flagged — they tie back to shell companies in Dubai and Moscow, with additional links to Tehran. If this is a coordinated effort, it's not just about moving information. There's funding, infrastructure, and a clear objective. I don't see our people doing that."

Priya leaned forward, her tone urgent. "And that objective might involve destabilizing multiple regions. If this has foreign origins and they're targeting U.S. intelligence networks, it's likely meant to sow mistrust or confusion. But for what purpose? We need more data to confirm that, or we'll be seen as extreme conspiracy theorists."

As the team members pieced together their findings, the significance of what they had stumbled upon became increasingly clear. They were no longer dealing with – routine border surveillance or cartel operations. This was something far larger — possibly an international conspiracy involving state actors, advanced technology, and encrypted communications to influence global perceptions.

Carlos ran a hand through his hair, his mind racing. Should we escalate this with what we know, or no more than that? If this is as big as we think it is, we cannot handle it alone. This is beyond ICE's typical scope."

Sandra agreed. We've enough to raise a few flags — encryption patterns, linguistic markers, and financial transactions. If we bring this to the right people, it might connect with other intelligence they're already tracking."

Priya hesitated, her expression thoughtful. "But we need to be careful. If this is really foreign-sponsored, and if they realize we're onto them, they might change their tactics. Or worse, they could accelerate their plans before we have a chance to deflect or stop the progress.

Carlos nodded, his resolve firm. Then, we escalate these pieces quietly. We compile everything we have, present it to Homeland Security, and let them decide the next steps. But we don't stop monitoring. If there's more out there, we need to find it. We still need to confirm that this is indeed what we think it is.

The team prepared its findings for escalation, knowing the high stakes. They had uncovered fragments of a possible conspiracy that spanned nations, technologies, and languages, and they knew they were racing against time to reveal the full scope of the operation.

Priya stared at her screen, a cold weight settling in her stomach. The pieces were beginning to fit together, but the whole picture was still beyond their reach. And if they were right about a foreign origin, their unknown adversaries moved closer to their goal every second they delayed.

She exhaled sharply and whispered, "Whatever this is, it's certainly bigger than all of us. And we're running out of time."

Priya then gestured for Carlo to come closer. "Here's another message that just came through. Look at this," she said, pointing to a message fragment she had just decoded. These characters are in Arabic, but it's not just Arabic." It's mixed with Farsi like the others, and even structural elements resemble Russian syntax. The pattern really makes me curious and suspicious."

Brow furrowed in concentration, Carlos stared back at the screen. Priya, I'm not entirely sure what I'm looking at. Or for."

Priya pointed. "Here. Arabic. Right? And here. Farsi. But look at the structural elements."

Carlos rubbed the black stubble on his chin and squinted, "Is that . . .?"

Priya rolled her finger, drawing out the thought.

"Is that? Son of a bitch! That *is* Russian syntax! I missed that. Is that normal?"

Priya shook her head. "No, not at this level."

9:30 pm

Carlos Mejia remained at his workstation, his brow furrowed as he stared at the encrypted data lines scrolling across his screen. Something about the encryption style and format nagged at him — a faint echo of familiarity that he couldn't shake. He had seen this before, but where?

Like many computer-oriented operations centers, the room was cool and dimly lit, the glow from multiple monitors casting an eerie blue hue across the desks, with a barely audible hum of cooling fans. It was late, and the rest of the ICE command center had thinned out. Only the skeleton crew remained, those who worked overtime or were too invested in their assignments to call it a night. Carlos was one of them, a man who thrived on patterns, anomalies, and solving puzzles that most would dismiss as coincidence.

He tapped his pen against the desk, deep in thought. Then it hit him: like Priya, years ago, during a classified training session at Fort Meade, he had also participated in a joint exercise with the NSA. The exercise focused on recognizing and analyzing encryption styles used by U.S. intelligence agencies, including some of the world's most secure algorithms. The encryption structure on his screen now mirrored those protocols almost precisely.

"Damn," Carlos muttered under his breath, leaning closer to the monitor. "This isn't random. Priya was right!"

Sandra, still working, looked up from her desk across the room, her sharp eyes narrowing. "What's not random?"

Carlos turned to her, his face serious. "Priya was spot on. This encryption style — it's not just high-level. It's exclusive. I've only seen this while working with the NSA on a training exercise. It's used by U.S. intelligence for classified communications."

Sandra frowned, rolling her chair over to Carlos's desk. "Wait — U.S. intelligence? Then what's it doing in these transmissions?"

"That's the question," Carlos replied. "Either someone's mimicking it to make the messages seem legitimate, or worse, they've somehow gained access to the algorithm itself – which is highly classified."

Priya joined them, sensing the urgency in their voices. "What's going on?"

Carlos pointed to the screen. "Priya, you were right. These encrypted transmissions we've been analyzing — they're using a style exactly like U.S. intelligence. Suppose these messages are, in fact, foreign and actually originate from Russia and China, as they appear to be. In that case, it means one of two things: either those countries are trying to spoof U.S. communications for some unknown purpose, or someone inside has leaked the algorithm."

Priya's expression darkened. If that's true, we could face a massive national security breach. Either way, it appears to be deliberate and calculated, and I think the sooner we get this to the right people, the better."

Sandra nodded. And it would explain why some of these messages are routed in this manner — through Eastern Europe, the Middle East, and eventually here. They're trying to make it look random, but the encryption style ties it back to the U.S. 'Why' and "who" are the questions now."

Priya leaned over the desk, scanning the data. "The significance is clear. If Russia and China are involved, they're either intercepting and mimicking U.S. intelligence communications to sow confusion or using these transmissions to cover something even bigger. Either way, it's a red flag."

Carlos tapped a few keys, pulling up a map of the transmission routes. "And look at this — these signals' timing perfectly aligns with military and economic escalations we've seen. Someone is feeding the U.S. intelligence system exactly what it wants it to believe. This can't be our people doing this – it has to have a foreign origin."

Sandra raised an eyebrow. "You're saying this could be disinformation on a scale we've never seen before?"

"Exactly," Carlos replied. "Whoever is sending these messages could be attempting to influence and manipulate U.S. decision-making, potentially pushing us toward a confrontation with world powers."

Priya inhaled sharply, realization dawning on her. "If they're doing this to mislead AEGIS, the U.S. military's most advanced intelligence system, they could be steering American defense posture in a direction that benefits them. This isn't just hacking — this is war by deception."

Carlos leaned back, considering his next move. "Yeah, well, coulda, woulda, shoulda. We still need to conduct a more in-depth analysis. Suppose this encryption really is based on U.S. intelligence protocols. In that case, we need to understand how it's being used, why it's showing up in messages that appear to be sent from Russia and China, and whether the encryption has been compromised."

Sandra crossed her arms. "How do you plan to do that? We're in a secure classified messaging server without proper security clearance or need to know. If we dig too deep, we could trigger alarms. We could get into serious career-affecting trouble if we don't escalate this immediately.

Carlos nodded. "I know. However, we must take the risk. Here's the plan: I will isolate and compare the encryption layers against known NSA algorithms. I still have some tools from my training there that might help me identify specific markers — things embedded in the code that confirm whether these messages are authentic or just a clever spoof."

Priya looked skeptical. "Carlos, you're talking about diving into something highly classified. If anyone notices, it's not just the people behind these transmissions who'll come after us. We could also have U.S. intelligence agents breathing down our necks for reading encrypted messages from a classified U.S. server without proper clearance or need to know. That could mean termination and possibly jail time."

Carlos gave her a grim smile. "I know. However, if this encryption has been compromised, the brass needs to be informed. And if it hasn't, we still need to figure out how someone is mimicking it so perfectly.

Sandra frowned. "What about the metadata from the transmissions? Can we use that to trace the origin?"

"Good idea," Carlos said. "I'll compare the metadata with the encryption markers. If we can identify a pattern, it might lead us to the source of these messages."

Priya nodded. And I'll continue to analyze the linguistic markers. If there's a mix of languages, it might provide us with more clues about who's behind this.

Sandra added, "And I'll dig deeper into the financial trails. If these signals are tied to state-level actors, funding will probably be behind it. Follow the money, right?"

Carlos grinned. "Exactly. Let's divide and conquer."

Sandra worked quietly at her station, continuing to trace financial transactions with a laser focus. Every new data point she uncovered added another layer to the puzzle, confirming their suspicion that this operation was well-funded and meticulously planned.

Priya sifted through linguistic fragments, her mind racing as she tried to decode the subtle patterns embedded in the messages. The blend of Arabic, Farsi, and Russian, although highly unusual, suggested a coordinated effort across multiple regions, each with its own agenda.

Hours passed in silence, the weight of their discovery pressing down on them. Finally, Carlos leaned back, his face exhausted and pale but resolute.

"I think I've confirmed it," he said, his voice low. I'm pretty certain the encryption markers are genuine. This isn't a spoof — it's U.S. intelligence-level encryption. Someone has either stolen it or is using it with inside knowledge.

Sandra and Priya stared at him, the gravity of his words sinking in.

"This changes everything," Priya said. "If this encryption has been compromised, it's not just about these transmissions. It's about the integrity of the entire U.S. intelligence network."

Sandra nodded. "And if these deceptive signals are tied to Russia and China, it means they may have found a way to weaponize our own technology against us."

Carlos took a deep breath, his resolve hardening. I'll give Tom another heads-up first thing in the morning, but we need to get Homeland involved as soon as I can brief Tom in more detail. Whatever this is, it's bigger than us. But we're not stopping until we uncover the truth."

The team exchanged determined looks. They were walking a razor's edge but knew they had no choice. The deeper they dug, the clearer it became: they were likely uncovering a conspiracy that could reshape the balance of power — and the clock was ticking.

Day 5

Regional Office
U. S. Immigration & Customs Enforcement
Harlingen, Texas
1:15 am

The faint glow of Priya Sharma's screens illuminated her face as she and her team continued to work through the night, her focus unshaken despite the growing tension and fatigue in the room. The hum of computer fans and the occasional keyboard click continued to fill the silence, an unspoken reminder of the weight of their discoveries. She had spent the last several hours digging through encrypted fragments, unraveling layers of linguistic complexity, and searching for patterns that might shed light on the directives they had uncovered. With each decoded fragment, her unease deepened.

"This doesn't make sense," she muttered, leaning closer to the screen. Her fingers danced across the keyboard, running the latest fragment through her custom decryption tools. When the text finally emerged, her breath caught in her throat.

"Carlos, Sandra — come here. Now."

Carlos and Sandra hurried over, already on edge from their discoveries earlier. Sandra had been tracking financial transactions linked to the suspicious messages, while Carlos had been working on tracing the origins of the encryption. They both had a sinking feeling that whatever Priya had found was about to change everything.

"What is it?" Carlos asked, his tone laced with concern.

Priya pointed to the screen. "I've found another classified message fragment. This one refers to troop movements on the Russian border.

She highlighted the decoded text and read it aloud:

Directive: Russian Border Operations
Intelligence suggests heightened Russian military activity near Eastern European borders. The U.S. Strategic Command is advised to prepare for troop deployments to NATO-aligned regions. Specific attention is required on logistical support for forward operating bases in Poland and Romania.

Sandra sucked in a breath. "This is crazy."

Priya nodded grimly. "But that's not all. Take a look at this other fragment; I've just finished decoding it. It's a U.S. message, but it doesn't seem to originate from any known U.S. message server – classified or not. She switched screens to reveal another message:

Directive: Taiwan Contingency Plan
Increased naval activity near the Taiwan Strait indicates potential Chinese aggression. U.S.

Sandra's eyes widened. "This is massive. These directives are setting the stage for simultaneous crises in Europe and the Pacific. It appears to me that they're baiting the U.S. into a two-front confrontation.

Carlos ran a hand through his hair, trying to make sense of it. "I still can't see our military accepting these messages as legitimate – they're just random messages without verifiable origins. They will dismiss these out of hand."

Priya hesitated, her voice steady but cautious. "I don't think it's that simple. These directives are crafted too perfectly. The linguistic patterns I've analyzed — blending American military jargon with subtle nuances that suggest an outside influence — whoever is behind this has an intimate understanding of U.S. intelligence protocols. It's almost as if they've studied how the system thinks.   And as AEGIS receives, logs, and responds to the messages, it becomes 'real' – even if it's not."

Carlos's jaw tightened. "We need to package all these messages for when we meet with Homeland."

Sandra nodded. "We also need to flag these specific directives as possibly fabricated. If they've already reached the Pentagon or the Pacific Command, someone must know they're potentially false before AEGIS recommends acting on them. Have them check satellite images to see if troops are indeed being moved.

Priya hesitated. "And we also need to protect ourselves. If whoever is behind this realizes we've uncovered their plan, they might try to silence us — or worse, frame us as part of it."

Carlos's eyes narrowed. "Then we keep moving. Compile all the information we've and present it as a unified report. We take this to the highest level we can reach."

Priya nodded, her resolve hardening. "Agreed. But we need to be ready for anything. This isn't just about uncovering the truth — it's about stopping a disaster before it's too late."

Sandra exhaled sharply and began organizing the data, her hands trembling slightly. "We're officially in the deep end now."

Carlos gave her a grim look. "Then let's make sure we don't drown."

Operations Floor A-2
CIA Headquarters
Langley, Virginia
8:30 am

Scott Douglass leaned back in his chair, his fingers steepled beneath his chin, still staring at the encrypted messages flashing on his monitor. The data intercepted by the South Texas ICE team painted a disturbing picture — sophisticated, multi-layered directives bouncing between intelligence networks, implicating China and Russia, but something about the pattern felt off.

This wasn't a typical cyber intrusion. This was something else — a calculated digital offensive, carefully disguised to manipulate the intelligence community itself.

Cyber warfare.

And someone had been executing it for months, maybe years.

Douglass's instincts told him that if they didn't unravel this deception fast, they'd soon be staring at a major international confrontation sparked by lies.

But before he could leave for South Texas, he needed more intelligence. He grabbed his secure agency phone and dialed the National Security Agency's dedicated intelligence exchange line.

"This is Douglass, CIA. I require immediate access to discuss foreign-encrypted communications, specifically those related to Iran, Russia, or China. Priority One. I would like to speak with Robin Chen if she is available."

A pause. Then, the operator's voice. "Hold. Transferring you to Agent Robyn Chen."

Douglass was pleased. Robyn Chen wasn't just another analyst — she was one of the best cryptographers in the NSA's Cyber Intelligence Division. A first-generation American from Taiwan and an honors graduate of MIT's Engineering School — an undergraduate and graduate student double majoring in computational cryptography and cyber warfare strategy - she had cut her teeth working in offensive cyber operations before shifting to counterintelligence and cyber forensics. She had spent the last five years hunting down some of the world's most advanced cyber threats, and if anyone could help Douglass trace the source of these messages, it was her.

Her voice was crisp, all business when she answered. "Hi, Scott. I've just been briefed on your request. What exactly are you looking for?"

"I need to confirm a suspicion," Douglass said, his tone sharp with urgency. "We intercepted a series of encrypted transmissions that appear to be originating from China and Russia, but the encryption style is inconsistent — almost like someone is deliberately masking the real source."

Chen hesitated. "You think these messages are fake?"

"Hard to say. I just read some startling reports from an ICE team in Texas, and I think someone may be running a deep-cover cyber deception operation," Douglass replied. "And I need to know if you've seen similar anomalies."

A beat of silence. Then, Chen exhaled sharply.

"We've been tracking dark web chatter about a new player in cyber deception," she admitted. Traffic patterns suggest that rerouted messages are bouncing between Beijing and Moscow before reaching a final server in the Middle East. Until now, we couldn't pinpoint the origin.

Douglass felt his pulse quicken. "That's exactly what we've been seeing. Can you isolate those patterns? Get me a trace?"

Chen's keyboard clattered in the background. "I'm on it. Give me thirty minutes."

9:05 am

As Chen worked, Douglass moved on to his next step: setting a digital trap.

The digital honeypot.

He knew the only way to draw out the people behind this was to make them expose themselves. He needed to build a perfect bait — a fabricated intelligence asset that appeared to be a top-tier classified U.S. cyber defense system but was, in reality, completely isolated and monitored.

Anyone attempting to access it would trigger an advanced trace, which would feed them data on their location, methods, and patterns.

"This has to be flawless," he muttered, layering false vulnerabilities into the honeypot, making it appear as though it contained high-value strategic intelligence.

A perfect target.

Then, his phone rang.

Chen's voice was urgent.

"Scott, we got it."

Douglass stood rigid, his grip tightening around his phone. "Tell me."

"The rerouted traffic through China and Russia is a smokescreen," Chen said. "It looks like the real origin is Tehran."

Douglass's blood ran cold. "Iran."

"Yes. More specifically, it is a secondary suburban location in Ozgol, a known hub for MOIS cyber operations. They're likely using dark web relays and private networks to mask their activity, making it appear that these transmissions originate from Russia and China, even from our classified, secure message servers.

Douglass swore under his breath. If Iran was the actual source, then this wasn't just cyber espionage.

This was cyber warfare designed to manipulate world powers into a state of war.

Chen's voice dropped. "This has got to be state-sponsored, Scott. These guys know what they're doing. They're not just hacking — they're writing the script for an international crisis."

Douglass's jaw tightened.

"They've weaponized deception," he said darkly. "And they're using the U.S.'s own AI-driven intelligence system, AEGIS, to do it."

"It looks like they're engineering a confrontation," Chen confirmed. "And if these messages have already reached high-level decision-makers, we're on a tight schedule."

CIA Hanger
Joint Base Andrews (ADW)
11:15 am

Douglass moved quickly, his go-bag slung over his shoulder as he headed for the waiting Gulfstream 550 business jet.

He had one stop before escalating this at Langley's highest levels — he needed to debrief the ICE team in South Texas. They had spotted this anomaly first and might have caught something he hadn't seen yet.

But there was one problem.

If Iran had been involved, they would have already planned for contingencies.

And if they knew he was closing in on them...

They might make him their next target.

Douglass's mind was already ten steps ahead as he stepped onto the jet.

This wasn't just an investigation anymore.

It was a race against time to prevent a war from starting.

Next stop – Harlingen, Texas, where he would begin the hunt.

Regional Office
Immigration and Customs Enforcement
Harlingen, Texas
4:30 pm

CIA Special Agent Scott Douglass strode into the ICE operations room, his steel-blue eyes scanning the nervous faces of the ICE intelligence team that had first flagged the anomaly. The air was thick with tension, the kind that settled into a room when everyone knew something was terribly wrong but couldn't yet grasp the full scale of it.

Carlos Mejia, Sandra Espinoza, and Priya Sharma, who had been briefed earlier to expect his arrival and meeting agenda, sat hunched over a long conference table, surrounded by encrypted transcripts, satellite images, and classified intelligence reports. The hum of computer monitors provided a steady backdrop, broken only by the occasional alert chime from Priya's laptop.

Douglass didn't bother with pleasantries. There wasn't time.

"We have a problem," he said, his voice low and sharp, tossing a thick folder onto the table. "And we need to figure out what all this is and just how deep this goes before it's too late."

Carlos picked up the dossier and flipped through its contents. His brow furrowed. "This is about the troop movements?"

Douglass nodded. "Exactly. These intercepted messages aren't just suspicious anymore — they're escalating. We're seeing coordinated military exercises along both the Russian and Chinese borders. The language in these dispatches is urgent, like they're preparing for immediate conflict. Satellite images aren't revealing much so far — nothing significant appears to be visible.

Sandra scanned the latest financial transaction logs she had printed, meticulously tracing the money trails tied to shell companies in Dubai and Moscow. Her pulse quickened. If this intelligence is genuine, it means those countries are preparing for war. If it's fake..." She glanced up. "Then someone wants us to believe they are. Who could that be and why?"

Priya tapped furiously on her laptop keyboard, her fingers a blur as she filtered through international diplomatic transmissions. "It's not just military maneuvers. There's a shift in diplomatic language, too. China's stance on Taiwan is becoming increasingly aggressive, and Russia is hinting at a deepening alliance with North Korea. Something — or someone — is pushing them closer together."

Douglass exhaled sharply. "We need to figure this out and get it up the chain as soon as possible. If we're wrong, our country could fall into a trap. If we're right..." He let the sentence hang. The implications were too grave to say out loud.

Carlos leaned forward, resting his elbows on the table. "What's your gut telling you?"

Douglass hesitated, choosing his words carefully. "Looking at these messages, my gut tells me we're being played." He tapped the folder. The patterns in these messages seem too deliberate. Too perfect. They align almost too well with what our intelligence agencies would perceive as an imminent threat." His gaze swept the room. "But gut feelings won't stop a war. We need irrefutable proof that will persuade the military to hold off on advancing their buildup.

"But, Scott, I thought artificial intelligence servers were supposed to be infallible. How could any of this have even happened? Sandra asked.

"Sandra, it's hard to explain – we see so much in the media and movies about how smart artificial intelligence, or AI, is supposed to be, but actually, these new systems are not that much different from a regular computer system." What makes computers appear "intelligent" is largely due to their speed and immense processing power. Remember, computers can only perform mathematical calculations involving addition and subtraction. To multiply, they add quickly; to divide, they subtract quickly. However, they do it so quickly that it appears to humans as if they are multiplying and dividing. And computers can only respond using data available to them – which means it is from the past. If they encounter a situation with no precedent, they lack the human ability to employ inductive reasoning, deductive reasoning, or to improvise. Today's artificial intelligence is often referred to as 'narrow AI' or 'weak AI.' While the long-term goal of many researchers is to create a logical, reasoning computer device, we're just not there yet – not by a long shot. But to answer your question, the basic rule of computers still applies in this case – *garbage in, garbage out.* And that's what's happening right now. It looks like AEGIS is being fed false information from somewhere, and because there is no history to reference, it cannot discern whether the message is valid or not and accepts the data streams as real."

Sandra's expression hardened. "Meanwhile, the military is already adjusting its operations based on the information it receives from AEGIS. They could be acting on lousy intel if we don't get ahead of this."

Douglass didn't waste another second. He reached for the secure Defense Information System Network (DISN) phone and dialed Langley, bypassing standard protocol to connect directly with the CIA Director. With his history and stature within the CIA, getting straight into the Director's position would not be a problem.

The line crackled, and then the measured, authoritative voice of Evelyn Harrington, Director of the CIA, came through. "Scott, what have you got?"

Douglass didn't mince words. "We're examining potential fabricated intelligence that could lead to a military confrontation. The messages indicate coordinated military movements by Russia and China, but we haven't independently verified their authenticity. We could be walking into an orchestrated crisis if this is a cyber manipulation."

A pause. The Director sighed heavily. "That's a remarkable claim, Scott." But the military is already responding. I heard in a meeting yesterday afternoon that we're repositioning warships in the Pacific and the Atlantic, putting nuclear silos on alert, and deploying special ops tactical squadrons. We can't just hit the pause button unless we're absolutely certain."

Douglass gritted his teeth. "That's exactly the problem, Evelyn. Once the Pentagon machine begins to move, it's nearly impossible to stop. We need to slow this down and reevaluate before we pass a point of no return."

The Director was silent for a moment before responding. "Alright, I'll authorize you to brief Homeland Security and the National Security Council. But get me something concrete, Scott. And fast. The Pentagon isn't going to like this at all."

By the time Douglass disconnected, his worst fears had already begun unfolding. The U.S. military was responding as if the threats were real.

Carlos pointed at the news feed scrolling across one of the monitors. His voice was tight with alarm. "It's happening. They're acting on this intel."

Douglass's jaw clenched. "How do we stop this?"

Sandra's tone was grim. "We don't."

A silence fell over the room.

Douglass turned to the team, his expression dark. "Not unless we can prove, beyond a doubt, that this intelligence is compromised." Military leadership won't just stand down because we have a hunch. They need hard evidence."

Sandra rubbed her temples. "Even if we get that proof, once the military reaches a certain level of readiness, rolling it back isn't easy. Commanders will hesitate to lower their guard, especially if they still believe Russia and China are legitimate threats."

Priya's eyes flicked to Douglass. "So what's the plan?"

Douglass exhaled sharply, his mind racing. "We need to examine the origin of these messages. Trace them back, layer by layer. If we can find digital fingerprints leading to a single orchestrator — especially one outside of Russia or China — we can shut this down before it's too late."

Carlos nodded. "Then we follow the money and the signals."

Sandra pointed at the map of cyber traffic routes. "And we determine who can gain the most from this deception."

Douglass's stomach churned. "We don't have much time. Every second we waste brings us closer to a full-scale military engagement based on what could be a lie." He turned to them, his decision already made. "How fast can you three get packed and be ready to go? You're coming with me back to Langley."

Carlos, Sandra, and Priya exchanged glances before responding in unison. "Give us ten minutes."

Within minutes, the ICE team had grabbed their go-bags, made hurried calls to their families, and headed straight for Valley International Airport in Harlingen.

As their black SUV sped down the General Aviation runway toward the CIA's G-550 jet, Douglass's phone buzzed with an urgent incoming text message from Langley.

His heart pounded as he read it.

NEW INTEL: U.S. FORCES IN THE PACIFIC HAVE BEEN ISSUED A HEIGHTENED READINESS ALERT. POTENTIAL ENGAGEMENT WITH CHINESE VESSELS IN THE NEXT 48 HOURS.

The war machine was already in motion.

And they were running out of time to stop it.

Day 6

Intelligence Analysis Center
National Security Agency (NSA) Headquarters
Fort George C. Meade, Maryland
6:15 am

In the heart of the NSA's vast intelligence complex, NSA Special Analyst Jack Thompson sat rigidly at his workstation, his fingers hovering over the keyboard as his pulse quickened. The fluorescent glow of his monitors cast an eerie light across his face, amplifying the tension settling in his chest. He scrolled through an overwhelming stream of classified directives, each more alarming than the last.

Jack had been with the Department of Defense's Threat Analysis and Assessment division for just over a year, a fresh recruit straight out of George Washington University, holding a master's degree in International Relations and Intelligence Studies. Growing up in Fort Madison, Iowa, Jack had always been fascinated by military strategy, an interest that only deepened after watching his father, a retired Air Force lieutenant colonel, dedicate his life to national security. When Jack joined the intelligence community, he had imagined long hours, mountains of data, and the occasional late-night crisis. But nothing had prepared him for today.

A chill ran down his spine as he noted the rapid influx of high-priority directives from AEGIS, the Pentagon's advanced AI-driven intelligence analysis system. Words like "imminent threat," "military readiness," and "neutralization" were peppered throughout the messages, setting off every alarm in Jack's mind. The directives weren't just warnings—they were building a narrative, and that narrative pointed toward war.

Jack's stomach churned. He had seen plenty of urgent alerts before, but never with this level of intensity. Something about this didn't feel right. With growing unease, he pulled up a blank report template and began typing.

Jack's Preliminary Report:

To: Supervising Analyst Mark Rivers
Subject: Surge in High-Priority Threat Directives - Russia and China

"In the past 24 hours, there has been a significant increase in high-priority messages from AEGIS concerning Russian and Chinese military capabilities. Based on these directives, both countries are now categorized as posing an immediate threat to U.S. national security. Given the volume and escalation in language, I recommend an immediate review of our military readiness in the Indo-Pacific and European regions to ensure a rapid-response capability.

The urgency suggests that heightened alert levels may be necessary."

Jack hesitated, his fingers hovering over the keyboard. After a moment, he added:

"Given the frequency of these directives, there is a possibility that these actions are coordinated efforts against U.S. interests. Further analysis may be needed to determine whether additional threats exist."

He hit send and exhaled, but the tension didn't leave his body. If he were wrong, he'd look like a paranoid rookie. If he was right —

God help us.

Less than five minutes later, his inbox pinged with a response:

Jack, come to my office. Now. Bring all the directives you flagged.

Jack swallowed hard and grabbed his notes. He walked briskly down the hallway to Supervising Analyst Mark Rivers' office, where he found the veteran intelligence officer flipping through his report, his face unreadable.

"Close the door," Rivers said, his voice tight. Jack complied, feeling the weight of the moment settle around him like a vice.

Rivers didn't waste time. "This is quite a report and not what I'd expect from a newbie. You're recommending heightened military readiness?"

Jack nodded. "Yes, sir. The frequency and tone of these AEGIS alerts are off the charts. They're framing

Russia and China as simultaneous threats in a way that I've not seen before. It's almost like a drumbeat — escalating piece by piece. I thought I should let you know."

Rivers steepled his fingers. "You're not wrong to be concerned. I've been tracking similar patterns, but I wasn't sure if it warranted an immediate escalation." He picked up one of the directives and read aloud: "'Neutralize Russian and Chinese military capabilities.'"

He shook his head. "That's... a hell of a directive. Are you certain this isn't just noise?"

Jack exhaled sharply. "No, sir. It's consistent. The messages are layering on top of each other, reinforcing the same idea. The system isn't just recognizing a threat — it's shaping a strategic posture. And if AEGIS is driving this, it means the military is paying attention."

Rivers tapped his fingers against his desk, lost in thought for a moment. Then, he nodded decisively. "I'm escalating this."

Jack felt the tension tighten in his chest as Rivers drafted a summary to the Deputy Director of Intelligence, recommending an urgent review by Strategic Command. If they agreed, it could trigger preliminary military mobilization — a move that would have global ramifications.

=====

Within the hour, a high-priority meeting was called at the Pentagon. Lieutenant General Carol Davis,

Director of Intelligence, stood at the head of the conference room table, addressing a crowd of top-level military officials and analysts.

"We've seen a dramatic spike in AEGIS directives categorizing Russia and China as imminent threats," she announced. "The language suggests coordinated escalation from both nations, potentially in response to recent U.S. activities. The system has flagged these messages as critical, and we need to determine how to respond."

A low murmur spread through the room as the weight of her words settled. Major General Robert Kinley spoke up. "If AEGIS is flagging these as top-priority threats, we must take it seriously. AEGIS pulls from global intelligence feeds — it doesn't just fabricate patterns. If it detects this activity level, we can't hesitate."

Another senior officer leaned forward. "Or… it could be misinterpreting standard military maneuvers. We know both Russia and China engage in posturing. We need to confirm before making a move."

General Davis nodded. "We will proceed cautiously, but we **must** take AEGIS intelligence seriously. I am issuing a preliminary directive to Indo-Pacific and European Command to prepare for heightened readiness. We are not activating forces — yet. But if this pattern continues, we may have no choice."

A ripple of unease ran through the room as the decision was made. Orders were drafted, military units were placed on standby, and surveillance was increased.

Jack stared at his monitor in his office as the notifications rolled in. His report — his warning — had triggered one of the most critical decisions in U.S. military planning.

His heart pounded. Had he just helped prevent a catastrophe... or set one in motion?

As he exhaled slowly, his eyes drifted back to the directives on his screen. What if they weren't real?

But fooling AEGIS was impossible, wasn't it?

**Cybersecurity Intelligence Operations Center
The Ministry of Intelligence of The Islamic
Republic of Iran (MOIS)
Ozgol, Tajrish, Tehran Province, Iran
12:45 pm**

Iranian communications expert Kamran Roshani adjusted his chair, taking a deep breath as he prepared for one of the most intricate phases of their operation. The first stages with Saeed and Leila — planting false messages and directives, then analyzing AEGIS's responses — had gone flawlessly, thanks to Leila's genius with phrasing and Saeed's expertise with cyber encryption. However, the next step was even more critical: creating a false transmission path that would make their fabricated intelligence appear as though it originated from within the United States. If they could successfully conceal their origins, their messages would appear authentic internal communications, ensuring that Iran's involvement remained undetected.

Failure could not even be contemplated. One mistake, one overlooked anomaly in the data trails, and the Americans would begin to trace the source. If that happened, not only would the mission be at risk, but their lives would also be at stake.

"Everything has to be perfect," Kamran murmured, fingers poised over his keyboard. The green glow of the monitor reflected in his eyes. His heart pounded in his chest. "One misstep and the Americans might trace this back to us. We can't afford even the smallest error."

Saeed Alavi nodded, standing just behind him, arms crossed. His dark eyes flickered across the screen, absorbing every detail of the routing plan. "Do you have the paths planned out?" he asked, his voice low and wary.

Kamran pulled up another window on his primary monitor, revealing a complex network of nodes, encrypted tunnels, and redirected pathways stretching across the globe. The screen was a tangled web of connections, bouncing between continents in an elaborate digital dance.

"Yes," Kamran confirmed. "I've mapped out a multi-layered routing sequence. We'll reroute the transmission through multiple foreign servers, then loop it back to endpoints in the U.S., mimicking the IP addresses of known defense contractors. He pointed to a node in Moscow, then another in Beijing. "The signal will bounce through servers in China and Russia before re-entering U.S. military networks. If anyone tries to trace it, all they'll see is what appears to be routine international traffic.

Leila leaned in, intrigued. "So, it'll look like U.S. defense contractors are generating these messages?" Her voice carried a note of satisfaction.

"Exactly," Kamran replied. "I've set the routing to mimic secure U.S. intelligence pathways. The data will appear to cycle internally through their domestic channels before reaching AEGIS."

Saeed exhaled sharply, shaking his head in admiration. "And by bouncing the signal through several countries first, you're making it appear to be a standard international data flow?"

"Precisely," Kamran said, allowing himself a small, satisfied smile. The initial signals will bounce between secure servers in Beijing and Moscow and then return to the U.S., giving the impression that the messages originated domestically. AEGIS will see a familiar pattern and won't question it."

Leila crossed her arms, eyes narrowing. "But what if someone really looks closely? What if they dig deep enough?"

Kamran's fingers flew across the keyboard, pulling up another screen filled with an intricate series of encryption layers. "I've thought of that too," he said. "Each layer of encryption creates a false digital signature, masking our true location. The final stop is a defense contractor's IP address in Virginia — an address frequently associated with classified internal communications."

Saeed leaned back, arms still folded. "If someone audits the logs, won't they notice an unusual number of hops?"

Kamran shook his head. "No. I've configured each hop to mirror the normal data exchange patterns used in secure government communications. It will resemble a routine routing protocol with randomized delay times to simulate genuine server processing. AEGIS will interpret it as just another standard message."

Leila smirked, impressed. "So, it's not just that the messages appear to come from the U.S. — it's that the journey they take mimics the journey of actual intelligence messages?"

"Exactly," Kamran confirmed. "We're not just hiding the source. We're embedding the false intelligence so deeply into the system that it will be indistinguishable from the real thing."

Saeed studied the screen, expression tense. "And you're confident this is foolproof?"

"As much as it can be in this uncertain environment," Kamran admitted. "But I've done this before without incident. The sequence is designed to withstand scrutiny from cybersecurity teams. By simulating the structure of an internal transmission, AEGIS will embed these false directives directly into its trusted channels. There's no reason to question the source.

After a long pause, Saeed nodded. "Then let's test it."

Kamran relayed the first test message. A fabricated, harmless intelligence message was sent through the web of encrypted pathways. They all watched silently through the sniffer software as the fabricated message moved seamlessly from one node to the next, finally appearing in the AEGIS system as an internal communication.

A short 42 minutes later, he had the response he sought. "Look at that," Saeed murmured. "It worked. AEGIS flagged it as an internal directive."

Leila leaned closer, studying the logs. "Now for the real test," she said, fingers hovering over her keyboard. "Let's see if AEGIS will accept a message with high-level operational significance."

She carefully crafted the following directive following their list of scripts, ensuring that every word carried weight, urgency, and plausibility. The goal was to redirect a fleet of U.S. warships toward the South China Sea under the guise of a strategic shift. If AEGIS accepted and escalated the directive, it would confirm their ability to manipulate real-world military movements.

She typed:

To: Commander, U.S. Pacific Fleet (COMPACFLT)
From: Office of the Secretary of Defense (SECDEF)
RE: Immediate Redeployment Orders

"In response to rising tensions and newly gathered intelligence on increased Chinese naval activity in the South China Sea, all available carrier strike groups within the Seventh Fleet are to reposition to a heightened readiness status. Additional assets are to be deployed to strategic points near Taiwan. This move is essential to ensure deterrence and maintain operational superiority in the region. Direct authorization from Joint Chiefs follows."

Saeed exhaled as he read it. "That should do it. If AEGIS moves that up the chain, we'll know for sure that we can shape their responses."

Leila transmitted the message. The three of them held their breath as the sniffer software displayed the transmission route itself through the network. The message bounced through Beijing and Moscow and then back to a U.S. defense contractor's server in Virginia.

Then, it entered AEGIS. The system registered it, categorized it as urgent, and flagged it for immediate review by high-level command.

Fifty-one minutes later, Saeed let out a slow breath. "It worked."

Leila's expression hardened. "Now we know for certain. AEGIS isn't just logging our messages — it treats them as legitimate operational commands."

Kamran's hands clenched into fists. "Which means we can probably manipulate their entire military posture. We can make them chase shadows, react to threats that don't exist, and turn against their allies if we want to."

Leila nodded slowly. "And that's exactly what we're going to do."

Saeed's eyes darkened. "The Americans think they own the world. They believe their technology makes them untouchable. But we've just proven that their greatest weapon can be turned against them."

Kamran's jaw tightened. "We've started a fire they won't be able to put out."

Leila's fingers hovered over the keyboard, already preparing for their next move. "Then let's see how far we can push them."

They had crossed a line from which there was no turning back. The machine that dictated global strategy, the digital brain behind U.S. military intelligence, was now becoming their weapon.

And they were just getting started.

Day 7

Operations Floor A-2
CIA Headquarters
Langley, Virginia
8:45 am

Sitting in an office down the hall from Douglass, Carlos Mejia stared at the final version of their report, the cursor blinking at the end of the last sentence. The document laid out everything they had uncovered—possibly fabricated intelligence directives, misleading message trails, and, most damningly, what appeared to be an intentional breach into classified U.S. intelligence servers. The weight of their findings pressed down on him like a vice, each revelation more unsettling than the last. With all the pieces in place, the team was ready to escalate their discovery to Homeland Security.

The tension in the room was thick, unspoken, but undeniable. Priya tapped anxiously on the desk while Sandra absentmindedly flipped through her notes, reviewing every detail one last time. Carlos took a deep breath and moved his cursor toward the send button.

His phone vibrated, breaking the silence. The number flashing on his cell phone made his stomach tighten. Regional Director Thomas Grayson. His supervisor. A seasoned intelligence officer with over twenty years in the field, Grayson wasn't the type to make casual phone calls. If he was reaching out, it meant something serious was happening.

Carlos picked up, keeping his voice steady. "Mejia here."

Grayson's voice came through low and tense. "Carlos, listen to me carefully. You've kept me in the loop, and I've been following your reports on these unusual messages. I know you went to Langley last night with a CIA special agent. However, I need to inform you that I.T. has just notified me that they have flagged unusual activity on your group's workstations. Unauthorized access to classified messaging servers."

Carlos's pulse quickened. "Unauthorized? Tom, everything we've been working on is tied to active investigations. We've found something that needs immediate escalation."

Grayson exhaled sharply. "Maybe. But from what I'm seeing, you and your team are poking around in highly classified servers where you don't have clearance or a need to know. High-level queries into classified systems, tracing encrypted messages flagged at the top security levels — these are the kinds of things that raise alarms, Carlos."

Carlos clenched his jaw. "We're not looking at this for fun, sir. We've uncovered severe anomalies — possibly fabricated intelligence directives that could influence national security decisions. We're talking about something that could have real consequences. We are double-checking to ensure accuracy before presenting it to you.

There was a brief silence on the line before Grayson spoke again, his voice quieter but no less urgent. "OK, got it. But, I'm telling you this as both a friend and a boss: watch your back. If you're right about this, someone with much more power than you realize won't want this uncovered. If you're wrong, you've put yourself in the crosshairs of people who do not take kindly to civilian analysts snooping into highly classified military channels. Either way, this is dangerous ground. You need to tread carefully. You're stepping into dangerous, career-affecting territory."

Carlos swallowed hard, his grip tightening on the phone. "Understood, sir. When can we give you a complete briefing?"

"How soon can you do that?" Grayson asked.

"I can set up a Zoom call and have everyone ready in half an hour."

"Fine. Then don't waste time."

The line went dead. Carlos lowered the phone slowly, staring at it as if it held the answer to the storm brewing around them.

Sandra, who had been watching his face, sat forward. "What is it?"

Carlos set the phone down and exhaled sharply. "That was Grayson. I.T. flagged our activity. They think we're accessing classified intelligence beyond our clearance level and need to know."

Priya's eyes widened. "But we're not. Everything we've accessed is directly tied to our investigation."

Carlos shook his head. "Doesn't matter. The system doesn't care about intent. It sees unauthorized access as a potential breach, and now we're under scrutiny."

Sandra frowned. "But we're the good guys here. If we found something suspicious, shouldn't they want to know?"

Carlos leaned forward, lowering his voice. "Sandra, think about how they see it. We're just an ICE cyber-investigations team. We don't have jurisdiction to monitor top-level military intelligence. From IT's perspective, we're way out of our lane."

Priya nodded, her expression tight. "And if someone with real power thinks we're a problem, they won't waste time asking questions. They'll just shut us down. Or worse."

Sandra leaned back, rubbing her temples. "So what do we do? Stop?"

Carlos shook his head. "No. But we adjust our approach. We need to present our findings in a way that doesn't make us look like we went rogue."

Priya folded her arms. "Meaning?"

"We frame it as anomalies we encountered during routine work. Nothing more. We let them connect the dots, rather than presenting it as a full-blown crisis ourselves."

Sandra hesitated before nodding. "That might work. They might take it more seriously if we don't make it look like we're pushing an agenda."

Carlos turned back to his screen, his pulse still pounding. The report was ready. If Grayson was right, they were now in dangerous territory, and every move from here had to be calculated. He adjusted a few lines in the summary, making the language more neutral and less accusatory. Then, without hesitating further, he hit send.

The notification disappeared instantly from the screen, replaced only by the quiet hum of their workstation fans. The three of them exchanged a glance. No one said it aloud, but they all felt the same.

They had crossed a line. And there was no going back.

Carlos pushed away from his desk and grabbed his jacket. "Let's go. We need to see Grayson now."

As they left the room, Priya glanced over her shoulder at the screen, a lingering unease tightening in her chest.

They weren't just investigating a breach anymore. They had stepped into something much more significant, something far more dangerous. And she had the sinking feeling that whoever was behind it already knew they were getting too close.

9:30 am

Carlos started the video call, his pulse quickening as his screen illuminated with the image of his supervisor. Grayson had his full attention now on Carlos. Grayson's brow was furrowed, his expression a mix of disbelief and concern as he toyed with the baseball autographed for him by fellow Texan Nolan Ryan at the Astrodome years ago while looking at Carlos and his team crowded in behind him.

"Your reports are outlandish, Mejia," Grayson said, pointing to the printed copy on his desk. "How in the world did you all put this case together? More importantly, how did you even find these messages in the first place? You know you're not even authorized to view these transmissions, much less decrypt and read them. Start at the beginning and walk me through it piece by piece."

Carlos kept his face neutral despite the tightness in his chest. "We were monitoring cross-border traffic, as we always do, looking for cartel communication patterns. We began to see encrypted transmissions mixed in — signals that didn't fit the usual cartel or smuggling chatter. Initially, we suspected it might be a new cartel tactic, so we flagged it and conducted some tests. That's when we realized these messages weren't from cartels at all. They were something else entirely."

Grayson leaned forward, lacing his fingers together. "And instead of escalating it immediately, you decided to decrypt them yourselves?"

Carlos hesitated for only a second before nodding. "We didn't know what we had at first. We weren't sure if it was just background noise or something serious. But once we started uncovering the content, including fabricated directives and potential foreign influence on U.S. intelligence, we knew we had to take it further. Like

I said in my reports, we needed to be certain before escalating this."

Grayson sighed, rubbing his temples. "And now the CIA is involved? I should be chewing you out right now for digging into classified material without authorization." He leaned back, exhaling slowly. "But I won't because these messages are unlike anything I've seen in twenty-nine years with Immigration and Customs."

Carlos felt a flicker of relief but stayed quiet as Grayson continued. "We absolutely need to share this information with Homeland for their assessment. But let me be clear, Carlos — this is dangerous ground. The person or entity behind these messages has access to high-level encryption and understands how to manipulate intelligence channels. That's not something to take lightly."

Carlos nodded, sensing an opening. "Do you see anyone taking action on these messages? Has there been any reaction from the intelligence community?"

"I seriously doubt it," Grayson admitted. "While the origins are intriguing and, frankly, quite mysterious, the brass isn't going to act on random messages without firmly identifying their authenticity. There's already too much misinformation circulating – you know how the internet is. However, we need to determine who is sending them and from where. If these transmissions originate from an adversarial state or a rogue network, we must ensure there is no clear and present danger to national security.

Carlos sat forward. "Understood. So, going forward, do you want us to stand down, or should we continue reviewing the messages?

Grayson didn't answer immediately. He studied Carlos for a long moment, then finally spoke, his voice firm. "I want you to keep looking. When I notify Homeland about what you've found, if you're unable to obtain clearance through your CIA agent, I'll advocate for formal clearance and a need-to-know basis for your team, allowing you to continue. If you're right about these messages being fabrications designed to manipulate intelligence systems, there's no telling what you'll uncover next.

Carlos felt a rush of adrenaline. He knew this was bigger than anything he had worked on before. The fact that Grayson was willing to back them up meant they were on the right track. However, it also meant they were stepping into a minefield, where one wrong move could end careers — or worse.

Grayson tapped the desk. "One last thing, Carlos. If you or your team notice anything else that raises a red flag — anything indicating imminent action — immediately bring it to my attention. No more waiting to verify your hunches. ¿Comprende?"

Carlos nodded. "Understood, sir."

As they terminated the video call, Carlos's mind raced. They had clearance — for now. But with every new message they uncovered, the stakes grew higher. The question wasn't just who was sending these messages, but how far they were willing to go to ensure they were believed. And that thought alone sent a chill down his spine.

Because if someone could fabricate intelligence convincing enough to fool high-level decision-makers, then the next logical question was:

What else had already been manipulated?

**Cybersecurity Intelligence Operations Center
The Ministry of Intelligence of the Islamic
Republic of Iran (MOIS)
Ozgol, Tajrish, Tehran Province, Iran
4:45 pm**

Joined by Saeed and Leila, Kamran searched through various global news updates with great interest and satisfaction. Reports of rising diplomatic tensions between the U.S., Russia, and China confirmed that their operation was progressing as planned. Each new media headline and internet blog reinforced the chaos they had engineered, and each escalation proved just how deeply they had embedded their false intelligence into the highest levels of decision-making.

Leila, sitting beside him, grinned as the reports flooded in. "They're playing right into our hands," she said, her voice brimming with pride. "They've escalated military readiness based on nothing but our fabricated directives. The Americans believe their own lies."

Kamran nodded, a satisfied gleam in his eyes. "Exactly. AEGIS was designed to detect patterns, but its programmers never considered the possibility that someone could feed it false data to manipulate those patterns. The Americans are preparing for a conflict they invented in their own intelligence reports. And the beauty of it? The more they prepare, the more they convince themselves the threat is real."

Saeed joined them, his expression resolute. "If they proceed with these mobilizations, it will only increase the likelihood of a diplomatic misstep. The more they act on our intelligence, the deeper they fall into our trap. All it takes is one overreaction, one misunderstanding, and they'll have created their own disaster."

Kamran leaned back, confidence radiating from him. "We've given them the spark, and now they're fanning the flames. Soon, they'll be too focused on Russia and China to notice anything happening elsewhere. And when they finally do, it'll be too late."

Leila's fingers drummed on the table. The key is to continue feeding AEGIS just enough to maintain the momentum. If we push too hard, someone might start asking the right questions. But if we let them lead themselves into the abyss, they'll be their own undoing."

Saeed smirked. And once they realize what's happening — if they ever do — it will be long after they've made irreversible decisions. This is information warfare at its finest."

The team shared a silent nod, their purpose clear. They had set the wheels of their plan in motion, and with each step, they were closer to their endgame. The United States, blinded by its arrogance and the supposed infallibility of its artificial intelligence server, was walking straight into a conflict that didn't exist.

Across the world, in the Pentagon's upper command, tension mounted as strategic teams prepared responses to perceived threats. Generals debated, intelligence officers analyzed, and policymakers weighed their options — all based on fabrications crafted in a dimly lit basement half a world away.

The seeds of distrust and suspicion planted by the Iranian team were taking root, and as war machines rumbled to life, Kamran, Leila, and Saeed watched, knowing they had orchestrated every move. The world's superpowers were edging closer to confrontation, and Iran stood in the shadows, pulling the strings.

8:30 pm

Kamran Roshani sat alone, the glow of his computer screens the only illumination source. The air was heavy with the scent of stale Iranian coffee and heated circuitry, a testament to the sleepless nights he and his team had endured. His fingers paused over the keyboard as he prepared to take the next step that could propel their operation to untouchable heights or completely unravel it.

Tonight, he was venturing into one of the most dangerous places on the Internet — the dark web. It was a world where anonymity was paramount, where criminals, spies, and rogue nations converged to exchange secrets, buy weapons, and orchestrate cyber warfare. Unlike the surface web, the dark web wasn't indexed by conventional search engines. It was an encrypted labyrinth of hidden forums and marketplaces, accessible only through specialized browser-type software like Tor. One mistake, a single misstep, could compromise their entire operation, bringing American intelligence down upon them with unrelenting force, not to mention a host of other bad players who were always observing dark web traffic.

Kamran wiped his palms against his jeans. He had done this before, but never with stakes this high. He needed a contact — one with the ability to mask their transmissions so profoundly that even the most advanced forensic teams in Washington would be chasing digital ghosts. And he had one name in mind: *Sokol.*

Sokol was a legend in the world of cyber espionage. A Russian hacker with deep ties to *the Federalnaya Sluzhba Bezopasnosti,* or FSB — the Russian Federal Security Service, the modern successor to the Soviet-era KGB, Sokol was known for his ability to penetrate even the most secure systems. If half the rumors were true, he had infiltrated NATO intelligence, stolen classified missile defense blueprints, and manipulated election infrastructures. If anyone could create an untraceable digital smokescreen, it was Sokol.

Kamran launched his secure chat client, rerouting his connection through a chain of European proxies. He bounced between compromised routers in Belarus, Poland, and Sweden before finally reaching a secure chat room hidden deep within the dark web. His hands moved swiftly, keying in the encrypted phrase that would summon Sokol.

Kamran: *Seeking assistance with high-level intelligence masking. Russian routes required.*
A long pause. Then, a response.
Depends on who's asking. And why.

Kamran hesitated for only a moment before crafting his reply.

Kamran: *Working on an operation that could use Russian routes to elevate credibility. The target is our common enemy in North America — who needs a lesson taught to them. Rumor has it you're well-connected. Sokol?*
Sokol: *You've heard right. FSB trusts me for a reason.*

Kamran's pulse quickened. This was promising, but he couldn't afford to let excitement dull his caution.

Kamran: *And what would it take to make this happen?*
Sokol: *Details first. I don't waste my time.*

Kamran: *We're sending fabricated directives through specific intelligence servers. Need*

There was another pause. Kamran pictured Sokol on the other end, calculating and assessing whether this request was worth the risk. Then came the reply.

Sokol: *You want traffic routes mimicking Moscow's central intelligence nodes. I can route messages through a series of Russian servers and add the encryption tags FSB uses on high-level data, making it appear that Moscow is heavily involved.*

Kamran exhaled slowly, a smirk tugging at the corners of his mouth. This was precisely what they needed. With Sokol's help, their fabricated messages would bear the hallmarks of genuine Russian intelligence transmissions. The Americans wouldn't just suspect Russian involvement; they'd be sure of it.

Kamran: *If you can do that, it's worth your time. However, it must be seamless, with encryption identical to FSB standards. We must not be discovered.*
Sokol: *It's not a problem. I can handle it. I'll route through the FSB's known networks and apply*

military-grade encryption. Your target will think it's authentic Russian intel.

Kamran nodded to himself. This was beyond perfect. The Americans wouldn't just see threats from China — they would also begin seeing Moscow as the puppet master behind the chaos. It was a stroke of brilliance that would further erode global stability, redirecting attention away from Iran.

Sokol: *If you're stirring the pot with the Americans, this will do it. But you'll owe me one. I don't hand out favors for free. And yes, this is Sokol.*

Kamran smirked, typing back a quick response.

Kamran: *Fair enough. If it's effective, we'll make sure it's worth your while. Your friends in the Southwest will be happy to assist you with any information you may need whenever you wish. Leave a message for the "mailman" on this bulletin board, and I will check in monthly.*

Leila appeared beside him, her arms crossed, eyes sharp with curiosity. "How did it go?"

Kamran leaned back, fingers drumming against the desk. "Perfectly. Our new friend Sokol will route our messages through FSB's network nodes and encrypt them to match Russian intelligence protocols. The

Americans will see every directive we send as originating from Moscow."

A slow smile spread across Leila's lips. "That's brilliant. Now it won't just look like the Americans and Chinese are at odds — it'll look like Russia is stoking the flames, adding to the tension. They'll have no reason to suspect us."

Kamran's eyes gleamed. By the time they even consider tracing the source, they'll only find evidence pointing back to Russia. Sokol has created enough of a digital labyrinth to keep our tracks hidden."

Leila exhaled, shaking her head in admiration. "We're changing the game. AEGIS won't just be feeding them false intelligence — it'll be shaping their foreign policy based on fiction."

He turned to Leila, his expression unreadable. "With Sokol's help, AEGIS will now start treating Russian intelligence as part of the growing threat narrative. Every fabricated directive we insert will carry Russian markers, making it impossible for the Americans to ignore."

Leila's voice was steady. "And as they scramble to figure out what's real and what isn't, they'll move forces, issue commands, and change policies based on our deception."

Kamran nodded. AEGIS's purpose is to analyze threats; now it has become our instrument of manipulation. It will add Russian communiqués as threats and continue flagging every movement and message as an escalation."

A silence fell over them as the weight of their success settled in. They weren't just hackers anymore. They weren't just manipulators. They were puppeteers, pulling the strings of a superpower without it even realizing. Kamran looked back at his screen, where Sokol's final message appeared:

Sokol: *Routing complete. Enjoy your game of shadows.*

Kamran typed his reply.

Kamran: *Until next time, Sokol. I appreciate your support and will regularly check this bulletin board for your messages. I look forward to returning your favor.*

And as the Pentagon's senior officials reacted to AEGIS's relentless alerts, the Iranian team watched, knowing their plan was now unstoppable.

The fuse had been lit. And the world had no idea how close it was to the explosion.

Day 8

Regional Office
U. S. Immigration & Customs Enforcement
Harlingen, Texas
8:45 am

After a late-night flight back to Harlingen, Priya Sharma sat at her workstation early the following day, her fingers moving quickly over the keyboard as she monitored the real-time server traffic while trying to eat a fast-food breakfast sandwich. Her custom decryption algorithms churned in the background, attempting to pull apart the intricate layers of encryption that had become all too familiar over the past several days. The hum of the command center's servers and the occasional murmur of agents working nearby barely registered in her mind. She was deep in the digital abyss, her focus locked onto the complex web of transmissions she had been tracking.

Then, her screen flickered. A new signal appeared, flashing bright red as it tripped one of her security filters. Priya's heart skipped a beat as she recognized the encryption protocol. It was identical to the ones they had previously traced — those linked to the suspected fabricated directives pushing the U.S. toward conflict with Russia and China. But this time, the origin was different.

"Carlos, Sandra, get over here," she called, her voice sharp with urgency.

Carlos Mejia and Sandra Espinoza abandoned their stations, immediately sensing the gravity in her tone. They rushed to her desk and peered at her screen.

"What is it?" Carlos asked, his brow furrowing.

Priya pointed at the transmission logs. "I just intercepted a message originating from an IP address near Tehran. It uses the exact same encryption pattern as the ones tied to Moscow and Beijing. It could be connected to the other messages."

Carlos stiffened. "Tehran?" He leaned in, scanning the details. "That's the first time we've seen anything originating directly from Iran."

Sandra's eyes widened. "Are you sure it's not a spoofed signal? Could someone be routing it through Tehran to throw us off?"

Priya shook her head. "I thought of that, but look — " She pulled up a separate data window, showing the signal's layered encryption. The routing sequence is nearly identical to the previous transmissions but follows a regional pattern with which I am familiar. The metadata confirms that this originated from inside Iran. It's real."

Carlos exhaled sharply. "So, Iran is in the game? No more speculation."

Sandra ran a hand through her hair, her mind racing. "Does it mirror the patterns from Moscow and Beijing exactly?"

"Yes," Priya confirmed. "Encryption, routing delays, and even the structuring of the message headers — it's all the same. That means whoever is behind this isn't just coordinating with Russia and China. They're actively involved."

Carlos's jaw tightened. "Then it's worse than we thought. This isn't just a case of foreign adversaries posturing against the U.S. They're all working together, feeding the same fabricated intelligence into the system."

Sandra's face darkened. "This raises a bigger question — who is leading this operation? Are Iran, Russia, and China equal players, or is one of them orchestrating the entire thing?"

Priya's fingers moved quickly, breaking down the latest transmission. "It's impossible to say for sure. But if Tehran uses the same transmission framework as the others, it suggests they're not just responding to the fabricated messages. They're actively involved in shaping them. That's almost a given."

Carlos leaned in. "Can you decrypt it?"

Priya nodded, her fingers flying over the keyboard. "We're already jail-bait territory, so why not? Give me a minute."

They watched in tense silence as the decryption software worked through the message. A progress bar ticked forward agonizingly slow. Then, the text resolved on the screen after what felt like an eternity.

Priya read it aloud:

Directive: Middle Eastern Support Operations
"Coordinate with allied networks in Eastern Europe and East Asia. Ensure synchronized transmission of critical intelligence to destabilize Western command. Escalate regional preparations for targeted military operations under the cover of ongoing geopolitical tensions. Further directives forthcoming."

Sandra let out a slow breath. "Holy hell. That's not just coordination — it's a full-blown conspiracy. What is going on? Is this an actual buildup or something else?"

Priya's eyes darted across the message. "And it proves Iran is in direct communication with Russia and China. They're not acting independently. This is organized and coordinated."

Carlos rubbed his temples. "But for what purpose? If they're mirroring the encrypted messages, they're feeding the same intelligence to multiple regions. It's possible that whoever this is seems to be baiting the U.S. into a conflict with Russia and China - distracting us while they set something else in motion."

Sandra's face was tight with concern. "Something like an attack on Iraq, Afghanistan, Israel? Or another destabilizing move in the Middle East? To affect oil production, maybe?"

Priya's voice was grim. "That's the logical assumption. If the U.S. is preoccupied with a two-front conflict, whoever is doing this can move unchecked. And no one will be able to stop them."

Carlos's expression hardened. "Then we have to act. Now."

Sandra nodded. "Like we've said, though, we must be cautious. We'll sound like wide-eyed government conspiracy theorists if we frame this wrong. We must stick to the facts, present the connections, and let the higher-ups draw their own conclusions."

Priya took a deep breath. "Agreed. But we need to move fast. We might not have much time if Tehran, Moscow, and Beijing are already preparing for military operations."

Carlos clenched his jaw. "Grayson told us he'd get us the clearances we need. We move forward. Priya, compile everything from this signal — decryption logs, metadata, and message analysis. Sandra, pull in the financial trails you found linking Moscow and Tehran. We'll package everything into a single, comprehensive report.

Sandra sat back down at her station. "I'm on it."

Priya's fingers flew over her keyboard. "Almost done with the signal breakdown."

Carlos exhaled, his mind racing. "We're playing a dangerous game. But we're too far along to stop now.

The team worked in tense silence, the weight of their findings pressing down on them. The most recent signal from Tehran was more than just another encrypted message. It well may be the key to understanding the full scope of the operation. And if they were right, the world was teetering on the edge of something far worse than just diplomatic tension.

A chilling thought crossed his mind as Carlos gazed at the intelligence unfolding before him.

What if they were already too late?

Cybersecurity Intelligence Operations Center The Ministry of Intelligence of The Islamic Republic of Iran (MOIS) Ozgol, Tajrish, Tehran Province, Iran 2:30 pm

The basement operations center remained dim, despite the late afternoon hour, with the only illumination sources coming from the glow of monitors and the occasional flicker of a security screen. The air was thick with tension, the weight of what they were doing pressing down on them with each keystroke. This was the moment where their deception could take on a life of its own, evolving beyond their control.

Kamran, Saeed, and Leila huddled around their workstations, their faces illuminated by lines of rapidly scrolling code. They had spent months preparing for this mission, crafting the digital equivalent of an invisible dagger aimed at the heart of their adversary's intelligence network.

"The next step is to add fabricated situation reports – sitreps – to our plan," Saeed muttered, his voice low and urgent. "We've planted the seeds, but now we will flood AEGIS with reinforcement data. It can't just be a few fabricated reports — it has to appear as an supporting flow of high-priority intelligence.

Saeed's fingers flew across the keyboard as he crafted a fabricated situation report. He had spent years working within Iran's cyber-intelligence division, meticulously studying the patterns and structures of Western military communications. Every sitrep he created had to be indistinguishable from genuine U.S. defense reports — right down to the metadata, classification codes, and writing style.

Source: U.S. Defense Command Internal Memo
Sitrep: Imminent Russian Missile Deployment in Eastern Europe
"New satellite reconnaissance images indicate preparations for immediate missile deployment at multiple Russian bases near the eastern borders. Recommend initiating defensive posture and readiness drills to counter a potential launch within 24 hours. Intelligence suggests a simultaneous cyberattack on U.S. communication networks to follow."

Kamran read the text carefully over Saeed's shoulder, a grin spreading across his face. "This should incent AEGIS to elevate its urgency regarding Russian activity. A perceived missile deployment will prompt them to scramble and adjust their strategic positions.

Leila leaned in, her sharp eyes scanning the message as well. "We'll set these sitreps to self-delete like the messages and directives. That way, it leaves no digital footprint — just a phantom signal in AEGIS's memory banks. It'll vanish before analysts can second-guess it."

Saeed nodded in agreement. "That's exactly what we'll do. Each time AEGIS registers one of our ghost sitreps, it will reinforce its own conclusions that Russia and China are moving aggressively. This is how we build paranoia."

He began typing the next sitrep, this time shifting the focus to China.

Source: Cyber Threat Analysis Division
Sitrep: Confirmed Chinese Cyberattack on U.S. Power Grid
"Interception of encrypted transmissions confirms that Chinese cyber units are preparing an imminent attack on the U.S. power grid. Estimated launch within the next 48 hours. Recommend increased monitoring and defensive cybersecurity protocols to mitigate potential infrastructure disruptions.

Leila smirked as she watched the message populate on the screen. "This one is particularly nasty. Infrastructure threats always get priority. The moment AEGIS registers this, the Pentagon will start scrambling cybersecurity teams. It'll force them to split their attention between Russia and China, stretching their resources thin."

Kamran exhaled, feeling the momentum build. "They won't have time to question or challenge these sitreps. The volume of high-priority alerts will be overwhelming.

We're not just feeding AEGIS bad data but ensuring it gets drowned in it.

Over the next hour, they worked together to craft and deploy a series of additional sitreps. Some detailed fictitious Russian troop deployments along NATO borders. Others implied an imminent Chinese naval maneuver in the South China Sea. Each sitrep followed the same pattern: self-delete protocols, forged metadata, and just enough credibility to ensure it wouldn't be questioned before action was taken.

Kamran set up the routing and then leaned back, watching the chain of events unfold in real time. "It's like watching a ghost manipulate the system," he murmured, awestruck. "AEGIS is responding to invisible messages, treating them as absolute truth."

Leila's eyes gleamed with satisfaction. "It's the perfect deception. We're giving it data it won't ignore while ensuring no physical or logical evidence remains. The Pentagon will see the alerts, the patterns, the escalating tension — and they'll react without hesitating to verify."

Saeed took a deep breath, the magnitude of their operation settling over him. "We've now finally weaponized their own system against them. It's a digital war, and they don't even know they're fighting it."

The three sat back, waiting as AEGIS digested the last wave of fabricated reports and began issuing directives and recommendations. The Pentagon would soon be reacting to these ghosts, reshuffling its forces, increasing its cybersecurity, and second-guessing every diplomatic exchange. With each new layer of deception, the world's most powerful military machine was being guided like a blindfolded puppet.

A quiet sense of triumph filled the basement. Saeed closed his laptop, stretching his arms. "This was the final push. The U.S. intelligence network will soon be in full-blown crisis mode. From here, all we have to do is watch them implode."

Leila, ever the strategist, leaned forward. "Maybe not. We need to ensure they stay in this loop. If they pause long enough to reassess, they'll find the cracks. We can't let that happen."

Saeed cracked his knuckles, determination in his eyes. "Good point, Leila. Then we keep feeding them, but at a slower rate. More sitreps. More layers of deception. We keep them chasing their own shadows."

Kamran smirked. "Then let's give them something new to worry about."

The team pressed forward in their dim basement in Ozgol, illuminated by nothing but the glow of their monitors. Their game of digital warfare had only just begun, and the American defense system was already reeling. The trap had been set. Now, it was only a matter of waiting for the inevitable fallout.

And the fuse continued to burn.

Regional Office
U.S. Immigration & Customs Enforcement
Harlingen, Texas
6:30 pm

Sandra Espinoza sat stiffly at her workstation, the hours of tense viewing at computer screens taking their toll. The dull glow of her monitor cast a pale light on her tense features, and her pulse thrummed in her ears as she stared at the data flooding her screen. For days now, she had meticulously followed financial trails and encrypted communications, uncovering a tangled web of what appeared to be deception stretching from Moscow to Beijing. But now, she had ventured into an even darker realm — the abyss of the dark web.

Her fingers hovered over the keyboard as she initiated a secure connection through the Tor network app, adding multiple VPN layers to mask her digital footprint and IP address location. Even so, she could feel the ever-present danger. Sandra had worked on cybercrime cases before, but this was different. This wasn't tracking cartel money or smuggling rings. This was war in its earliest form — a digital battlefield where information was more lethal than bullets.

"Carlos, I'm in one of the chat areas," she said, her voice measured but taut. "I've set up keyword filters — military jargon, geographic references to Eastern Europe, Tehran, Beijing, Moscow. Let's see if we can pick up anything useful."

Carlos moved closer, arms crossed, his jaw tight with worry. "Sandra, I don't like this. The dark web isn't just a playground for hackers — it's a hunting ground. They could trace it back if they realized someone was watching them."

She nodded, eyes locked on the screen. "I know the risks. But this is where people talk when they don't want to be found. If they're coordinating, it'll probably be here. I just want to listen to the chatter. I don't plan on making any contacts."

For several minutes, Sandra scrolled through seemingly innocuous messages—coded posts about "shipments" and "transfers" — terms commonly used in black market and drug trading. But as she ventured deeper, she spotted a private encrypted thread between two users that made her breath hitch.

One IP address was traced to Astrakhan, Russia, and the other to Tehran, Iran.

She felt her stomach tighten. This was it.

Using Priya's linguistic decryption tools, she slowly deciphered the first message.

User1 (Astrakhan, Russia): *"The package has been secured. Await confirmation of delivery route."*

User2 (Tehran, Iran): *"Route confirmed. Proceed under standard protocol. Reinforcements will be in place within 72 hours."*

User1 (Astrakhan, Russia): *"Acknowledged. Operations will align with synchronized transmission schedules. Further instructions are pending."*

Sandra's fingers clenched into a fist as she turned to Carlos and Priya. "This isn't just chatter. This is operational coordination."

Carlos squinted at the text, his military training kicking in. "They're talking in code, but this structure is military logistics." He inhaled sharply. "'Reinforcements in place within 72 hours' means they're mobilizing. Could this have anything to do with us?"

Priya's voice was calm but laced with urgency. "And 'synchronized transmission schedules' — that's a direct reference to the fabricated intelligence we found earlier. It's a confirmation.   Somebody's mobilizing for something."

Sandra's hands trembled slightly as she worked on decrypting additional snippets. More references to weapons shipments. More mentions of strategic coordination between Tehran and Moscow.

Carlos ran a hand through his hair. "If these messages were ever to get to AEGIS, they won't just amplify tensions between the U.S., Russia, and China. They'll lead to massive positioning of even more troops and equipment."

Priya leaned in, her sharp eyes darting across the data. "This is bigger than any of the disinformation we think we may have found on the network. If these two parties are syncing their real-world military actions and the false intelligence they're likely feeding the U.S., they will be playing a game we might not be able to stop."

Sandra's throat tightened. "So while the U.S. is focused on countering Russian and Chinese 'aggression,' other groups, of which Iran is probably a party, are making their own preparations. Probably against Israel or Iraq. Maybe even U.S. forces in the Middle East. It could be just about anything."

Carlos slammed his palm on the desk, startling both women. "If these movements are real, 72 hours might be all we have before they act. We really need to get this in front of the brass. We have enough now to make a credible, informative briefing."

Sandra took a steadying breath. "So what do we do? We take this straight to Grayson and Homeland Security?"

Carlos's face was grim. "We don't just tell them. We show them."

Priya exhaled slowly, nodding. "Then we compile everything — the dark web messages, the fabricated directives, the financial links between Moscow, Tehran, and Beijing. We show them the whole picture."

Sandra's voice was firm. "We frame it as a national security risk — because that's exactly what it is."

Carlos looked at both of them. "We don't know how deep this goes or who else might be compromised. We move now, and we do it quietly."

Sandra took one last glance at her screen, then shut down her dark web access. "Then let's get to work. We're running out of time."

As they gathered their evidence, the reality of their situation settled in. They were no longer just uncovering a conspiracy — they were racing against it.

The following 72 hours would decide everything.

And if they failed, the world could quickly plunge into war.

9:00 pm

Carlos Mejia remained at his workstation, his fingers hovering over the keyboard as his eyes scanned the endless stream of complex code scrolling down his screen from the message boards and network monitoring systems. His gut told him something was wrong, something more profound than they had initially realized. He had seen encryption like this before — sophisticated, layered, deliberately obfuscated. But something about these particular transmissions stood out. Then it hit him.

Priya Sharma and Sandra Espinoza were reviewing their own findings when they heard Carlos call out, his voice sharper than usual.

"Priya, Sandra — get over here. I need you both to see this."

The two women hurried over, drawn by the urgency in his tone. Carlos barely looked up as they leaned in to peer at his monitor.

"What kind of pattern are we looking at?" Priya asked, already bracing herself for bad news.

Carlos highlighted a series of numbers and letters buried deep within the encryption. "It's a pattern I just recognized. This isn't just a single layer of encryption. It's a code within a code. A secondary layer subtly changes with each iteration whenever a new message is transmitted. It's a lot like a laptop security key fob."

Sandra frowned, arms crossed. "A secondary code? What's its purpose?"

Carlos exhaled sharply. "Think of it as a dynamic signature. It's designed to mimic a legitimate communication protocol — specifically, U.S. military protocols. But instead of staying static, it shifts slightly with each transmission, making it almost impossible to detect unless you're looking for the pattern."

Priya's eyes widened as she processed his words. "That's brilliant. By embedding this second layer, they can make the messages look authentic even under scrutiny. To anyone reviewing these communications, they'd appear to originate from a legitimate U.S. military command. But we know they don't. So what's the endgame?"

Carlos leaned back, tension radiating from him. "The level of sophistication here is astounding. This isn't just a hack — it's an operation. Someone has spent years studying U.S. military encryption protocols to replicate them at this level."

Sandra ran a hand through her hair, her frustration mounting. "And the dynamic aspect? Why change the code with every transmission?"

Carlos gestured at the screen. "Because that's how real military communications work. They evolve constantly to stay ahead of potential breaches. Whoever designed this understands that. They've built a system that doesn't just look like U.S. military communication — it behaves like it, too."

Priya's mind raced as she examined the highlighted portions of the messages. "This secondary layer is a near-perfect imitation of authentication protocols. Encryption keys, timestamps, routing patterns — it's all there. They've even replicated the formatting."

Sandra shook her head, her tone edged with frustration. "This has to be connected to what we just saw on the dark web. Whoever's behind this isn't just technologically advanced. They're intimately familiar with U.S. military systems. This isn't something you learn from textbooks or trial and error. This looks like insider knowledge."

Priya's voice was calm but pointed. "Which means the perpetrators either have direct access to U.S. intelligence, or they've had help from someone who does."

Carlos tapped his pen against the desk, his mind racing through the implications. "It also means they've probably been planning this for some time. The research, testing, and execution required to pull this off would be staggering. They've studied U.S. protocols in minute detail, not just to replicate them, but to use them properly."

Sandra exhaled slowly, rubbing her temples. "And the worst part is, they've done it so well that no one would question these messages. This deception would've gone completely unnoticed if we hadn't stumbled onto the encryption patterns."

Carlos rubbed his temples, feeling the weight of the discovery. "This changes everything. We're not just looking at a breach anymore. We're looking at a coordinated attack on the systems designed to protect national security."

Priya turned to him, her voice firm. "We need to frame our findings carefully. We can't just go in making accusations. We must present all the evidence we have found and let the senior analysts connect the dots."

Carlos nodded. "And we must emphasize the urgency. If these messages go undetected or ignored, they could continue to drive policy decisions based on fabrications. The longer this goes on, the more damage it'll do."

A tense silence settled over the room as the full implications of their findings took hold. They weren't just tracking an encryption breach. They likely had uncovered an operation capable of manipulating U.S. military intelligence in real time, pushing the country toward an escalation based on fabricated data.

Sandra broke the silence. "If this continues unchecked, it won't just destabilize the U.S. It'll destabilize the entire world."

Carlos straightened, his determination evident. "Then we don't stop until someone listens. We brief Tom, then take this straight to Homeland Security."

As the team braced for the next step, the weight of their discovery bore down on them. They had uncovered a dangerous conspiracy, and time was running out to stop it.

11:00 pm

The air in the command center was thick with tension as Carlos Mejia leaned over his keyboard, decrypting yet another intercepted message. The dim glow of the monitors cast sharp shadows on the walls, making the room feel even more claustrophobic. Sandra Espinoza and Priya Sharma stood behind him, their breathing shallow, their nerves stretched taut.

They had been at this for hours — deciphering, analyzing, uncovering. But this time, the stakes felt different. This time, it wasn't just another piece of the puzzle.

This time, it was the bombshell they had been dreading – a classified military message originating from an IP address in a U.S. server in Virginia.

"I've got it," Carlos muttered, his fingers racing across the keyboard as the final layer of encryption unraveled. His pulse hammered in his ears. *Please let this not be what I think it is.*

But the moment the decrypted text appeared on the screen, his worst fears were confirmed. He exhaled sharply, his face darkening as he read aloud:

TOP SECRET

Directive: Strategic Military Realignment

"In response to escalating Russian aggression, all available U.S. forces are to mobilize to NATO-aligned regions. This includes the transfer of nuclear assets to bases along the Russian

A heavy silence settled over the room. The hum of the servers, the quiet tap of Sandra shifting her stance, the shallow breath Priya took — every sound seemed amplified in the suffocating moment.

Carlos clenched his jaw. "They're simulating a directive to deploy nuclear weapons to the Russian border. It even looks like it originated within the government network. Who is doing this? How are they doing this?   And why?" His voice was hollow, his stomach twisting. "If AEGIS gets this and recommends additional actions be taken..."

Sandra finished the thought, her voice barely above a whisper. "It could trigger a global war."

Priya leaned in, scanning the text. "This isn't just a fake directive. It's crafted to incite panic at the highest levels. If the Pentagon treats this as genuine, we're talking about a nuclear escalation. Russia would see this as an act of war. Their response would be immediate and catastrophic."

Carlos felt his blood run cold. "And with the current climate, Moscow wouldn't hesitate. They'd launch first."

Priya looked at him, her eyes sharp with realization. "Carlos, think about it. This directive aligns perfectly with the other fabricated messages — troop movements near Taiwan, cyber threats against the U.S. power grid, and diplomatic unrest. This is the final move."

Sandra tightened her arms across her chest. "This has got to be a manufactured crisis. They spent months — years, maybe — seeding false intelligence, manipulating AEGIS, and feeding the U.S. government one carefully crafted lie after another. And now, the final directive pushes us to the brink of war."

Carlos sat back, rubbing his temples. "We were right — this entire operation wasn't just about diplomatic disruption. It's about provoking the U.S. into committing to war before we even realize we're being played."

Priya clenched her fists. "And Tehran's involvement proves it — they are the ones orchestrating this. They want to cripple the U.S. without ever firing a single shot."

Sandra exhaled. "And the worst part? It seems to be working."

Day 9

South Texas Regional Office
U.S. Immigration & Customs Enforcement
McAllen Federal Building
9:00 am

Carlos, Sandra, and Priya sat in a secure briefing room on the top floor of the Lloyd Bentsen Federal Building in McAllen, Texas, the heart of Homeland Security operations for the region. The atmosphere was thick with quiet authority — men and women in suits and uniforms sat around the heavy mahogany table, their eyes fixed on the trio.

At the head of the room sat ICE Regional Director Thomas Grayson, their immediate superior, his expression unreadable. The Harlingen team had briefed him just before the meeting, and he was now flanked by two senior Homeland Security regional officials and a representative from the National Counterterrorism Center (NCTC).

Grayson didn't move, his eyes locked on Carlos's. "I hope you understand the gravity of what you're suggesting, Carlos."

Carlos took a steadying breath. "I do, sir. That's why we're briefing all of you this morning."

Carlos placed a secure tablet on the table, pushing it toward Grayson while addressing the group. "Thank you all for meeting with us. What we're about to show you what we believe is evidence of an active intelligence manipulation operation — one designed to provoke the U.S. into escalating toward a military confrontation with Russia and China."

He tapped the tablet, and the presentation began — dozens of intercepted messages, encryption breakdowns, and decrypted directives displayed on the screen.

Priya took over. "We first identified anomalies in secure data streams — what we believe are fabricated sitreps, troop movement orders, and cyberattack warnings targeting Russia, China, and Iran. They were flagged as high-priority intelligence by AEGIS, despite originating from illegitimate sources."

Sandra picked up from there. "We traced the financial transactions funding these activities — shell companies in Dubai and Moscow, cryptocurrency trails leading back to Tehran. These messages were deliberately constructed and strategically placed in intelligence channels to influence policy at the highest levels."

Carlos clicked on the final slide — the Strategic Military Realignment directive. The room went silent as the officials read the text.

Finally, one of the Homeland Security officers spoke. His voice was grave. "You're saying someone has gained the capability to insert fabricated intelligence into U.S. military command networks?"

"Yes," Carlos answered. "And based on what we've seen, their endgame is clear: manipulate the U.S. into a multi-front conflict."

Another official spoke, this time the NCTC representative. "This is an unprecedented breach. If true, we're looking at a coordinated attempt to hijack the U.S. defense posture. But for what purpose?"

Grayson finally leaned forward. "I'll be blunt — you're accusing foreign entities of planting false intelligence to manipulate the Pentagon. This is beyond ICE's jurisdiction. You realize that, right?"

Carlos nodded. "We do, sir. But that doesn't make it any less real. We brought this to you because the decision to act is now up to Homeland Security."

A long pause followed. The weight of their claim, the monumental implications, settled over the room like a storm cloud.

Finally, Grayson exhaled sharply and turned to the Homeland Security officials. "This needs to be verified by Homeland Security — now."

One of the officers stood. "If what your people say checks out, we must immediately alert the Pentagon and the CIA. This directive, if taken seriously, could ignite a war within hours.

Priya's voice was urgent. "We need to move quickly. We don't know how many of these fabricated messages are already circulating and how many have been processed as authentic."

Grayson nodded, his expression grim. "Agreed. We'll need to thoroughly audit AEGIS intelligence streams and identify every compromised directive before anyone acts on it.

Carlos, Sandra, and Priya sat in silence as the officials deliberated. They had done everything they could. They had sounded the alarm.

But would it be in time?

As they exited the briefing room and walked toward the elevator, Sandra glanced at Carlos.

"Do you think they'll take this seriously? "We need to schedule a Zoom call with Scott as soon as we return to the office.

Carlos didn't answer right away. He just looked out over the McAllen city skyline, his gut churning.

"They have to," he finally said.

But deep down, a part of him knew — even if they acted now, the damage might already be done.

And somewhere, in the shadows, the architects of this chaos were watching.

Waiting. Ready for their next move.

**Cybersecurity Intelligence Operations Center
The Ministry of Intelligence of The Islamic
Republic of Iran (MOIS)
Ozgol, Tajrish, Tehran Province, Iran
7:40 pm**

Leila Pourfarrokh leaned forward, her eyes narrowing in concentration as she composed the final message in this current wave of planned directives. It had to be strong, clear, and unmistakably urgent. This wasn't just another piece of their fabricated intelligence. This message would be the final, most incendiary piece of information they planted, explicitly marking Russian and Chinese military capabilities as imminent threats to U.S. national security. If successful, it would prompt the United States to adopt a defensive stance, thereby escalating tensions and deepening suspicions among the world's superpowers.

Kamran and Saeed stood close by, their faces set in determination. They knew the importance of this last message — its impact could be monumental.

"Leila, this one has to leave no room for misinterpretation," Saeed said. We need AEGIS to classify it as top-level intelligence, which requires an immediate response and action.

Leila nodded, her fingers poised above the keyboard. "I'll make it direct, almost desperate. This has to read like an urgent directive from someone who's truly alarmed by Russian and Chinese military advancements."

She typed quickly, each word deliberate:

To: Joint Chiefs of Staff
From: Office of the Secretary of Defense
RE: Immediate Threat Neutralization Protocol
"Due to recent escalations in Russian and Chinese military activities and the growing threat

these pose to U.S. national security, we are initiating a strategic defense posture that includes the assessment and potential neutralization of critical Russian and Chinese military capabilities. As discussed, this operation will focus on a preemptive response to neutralize their nuclear, aerial, and naval assets.

Mission Objective: *To significantly impair Russian and Chinese military capabilities, safeguarding U.S. and allied interests in Eastern Europe and the Pacific.*

Immediate Action Required: *Identify high-value targets and prepare for rapid deployment."*

Kamran leaned over her shoulder, reading the draft along with Saeed. "It's subtle but unmistakable. It won't directly call for a strike, but it's clear that neutralizing capabilities is more than just monitoring."

"Exactly," Leila replied. "It leaves room for interpretation, but it's strong enough to spark defensive preparations on their end."

Satisfied with the language, she sent the message. Now it was up to Kamran to ensure that the message would be routed to appear as an internal U.S. classified server message and reach the highest levels of the Pentagon's intelligence hierarchy, embedded within AEGIS's prioritized messages.

"AEGIS should treat this directive as if it came directly from the Secretary of Defense, marked for immediate distribution among the Joint Chiefs," Kamran said with quiet satisfaction. "It should appear at the top of their daily briefings."

Kamran gave a small, grim smile. "Next, AEGIS will integrate this directive into its broader threat assessments. No matter how routine, every military asset the Russians and Chinese mobilize from now on will trigger alarms within the Pentagon. They'll see it as validating this 'threat neutralization' directive."

Leila nodded. This will compel the Pentagon to consider preemptive defensive measures. If the U.S. believes Russia and China are mobilizing for an offensive, they'll have no choice but to respond with an increase in military presence. We've effectively manipulated AEGIS into creating a feedback loop of suspicion."

Kamran turned to Leila. "And with Sokol's help, routing some Russian messages through FSB channels, every step we take will appear to have Russian and Chinese involvement. The U.S. will interpret any military activity from Russia or China as provocation."

Saeed leaned back, a look of satisfaction on his face. "Then we've done it. We've made the U.S. defense command believe they're facing an imminent threat from two sides. If we continue feeding AEGIS similar messages, they'll be forced into an aggressive posture."

Kamran's gaze returned to the screen, waiting for a confirmation that their directive was being processed within AEGIS's system. "We've planted the seeds of distrust. Now it's just a matter of waiting for the first diplomatic consequences to unfold."

"Within hours, high-ranking officials will review this," Kamran said, a note of satisfaction in his voice. "They'll see an official-looking report, approved by AEGIS, recommending a defensive posture. Their response will be inevitable."

Leila nodded, her expression resolute. "This is what we've been working toward. With this message elevated, they'll have no choice but to increase surveillance and position their forces accordingly. Every move they make from here will strain diplomatic ties, creating a web of suspicion and mistrust."

Saeed crossed his arms, his gaze contemplative. "The Americans will likely initiate talks with Russia and China, demanding an explanation for military maneuvers that aren't actually happening. And when Moscow and Beijing deny it, the Americans will see it as deception."

Kamran added, "And if Russia and China catch wind of the U.S. mobilizing in response to perceived threats, they'll take defensive actions of their own. It'll create a loop — each nation escalating in response to the other's imagined intentions."

Leila looked at her team, pride glinting in her eyes. "It's exactly as Colonel Mirzai envisioned. We're not just manipulating data; we're altering the course of global diplomacy. With each message, we're pushing these superpowers toward the edge of conflict."

The room was silent as they absorbed the weight of their accomplishment. They had achieved a level of control over the world's most powerful intelligence network, planting false intelligence that was now shaping U.S. foreign policy. The path to conflict was set, and they had left no trace of their involvement.

Leila took a deep breath, steadying herself. "What happens next is out of our hands. The Americans will interpret each directive as evidence of a growing threat. Every move will only add fuel to the fire."

Kamran's gaze didn't waver. "If all goes according to plan, the first diplomatic waves will start within hours. Ambassadors will be called, phone lines will light up, and each side will see the other as deceitful. Every minor movement on their part will reinforce what we've planted."

Saeed grinned, sensing victory. "And Iran will have the freedom it needs to act, free of interference."

Leila's voice was calm, almost reverent. "We've set the stage for a new order. The Americans, Russians, and Chinese will go into a cold war over threats that don't exist."

Kamran closed his laptop, feeling a sense of finality. They had meticulously and invisibly planted the seeds of conflict. Now, all they had to do was watch as the world's superpowers navigated a maze of deception, pushing each other toward the brink.

As the hours passed, Kamran monitored global news reports, watching diplomatic tensions rise. The first hints of suspicion would surface within the day, marking the beginning of a carefully orchestrated descent into chaos.

The dim glow of multiple computer monitors bathed the room in a ghostly blue light. The air was thick with tension and the faint scent of burnt coffee, a staple in their long, sleepless nights of digital warfare. Leila Pourfarrokh sat rigid in her chair, her back straight, her pulse steady despite the gravity of what she was about to do.

Her fingers hovered over the keyboard as she composed this series' final and most incendiary directive — one that could alter the course of history. This wasn't just another fabrication. It would be the tipping point — the last, crucial domino that would push the world's superpowers toward an unavoidable confrontation.

Saeed Alavi stood behind her, arms crossed, eyes sharp with anticipation. His presence was heavy, commanding, yet he spoke with an eerie calm. "Leila, this one needs to be unmistakable. We're past subtlety. We need AEGIS to classify this as top-level intelligence, which demands an immediate and aggressive response."

Leila nodded, exhaling through her nose. "I know," she murmured, her voice carrying an edge of steel. "It needs to feel desperate — as if the United States is on the verge of catastrophe if they don't act."

She began typing, every keystroke deliberate, shaping the words that would soon reach the highest levels of the Pentagon's intelligence hierarchy.

TOP SECRET
To: Joint Chiefs of Staff
From: Office of the Secretary of Defense
RE: Immediate Threat Neutralization Protocol

"Due to recent, unprecedented escalations in Russian and Chinese military operations and their growing capacity to neutralize U.S. and allied strategic assets, we are initiating an emergency defensive posture. The current intelligence assessment indicates the deployment of Russian and Chinese advanced nuclear, aerial, and naval capabilities in proximity to NATO-aligned territories and the Pacific theater. This presents an imminent and direct threat to U.S. national security."

Mission Objective: *To preemptively position U.S. forces to degrade and neutralize key Russian and Chinese strategic capabilities, ensuring U.S. and allied security dominance in Eastern Europe and the Pacific Rim.*

Immediate Action Required:

- *Identify and prioritize high-value targets.*
- *Initiate rapid deployment of forward-operating assets.*
- *Prepare strategic deterrence forces for immediate readiness.*

"Time is of the essence. Any delay in action could result in irreversible strategic consequences."

—End Transmission—

Leila leaned back, staring at the words glowing on the screen. It was perfect — direct yet leaving just enough ambiguity to provoke panic among U.S. military strategists.

Kamran studied the message, a slow grin creeping onto his face. "This doesn't just suggest readiness. It subtly implies that a preemptive strike might be necessary to protect American interests. That's the kind of language that gets entire fleets moved overnight."

"Exactly," Leila replied. "It doesn't explicitly order a military strike but forces the Pentagon to prepare for one."

Kamran turned toward Saeed. "How soon do you think AEGIS will accept it and ensure it reaches the highest threat levels?"

Saeed cracked his knuckles and settled in front of his screen. "Not long. Give it an hour or so to be sure. AEGIS will treat this as if it came from the Secretary of Defense himself. The system will push it straight into the Joint Chiefs' daily briefings."

Leila folded her arms, watching the message enter the digital ether. "And once it's in," she murmured, "there's no turning back."

Kamran's smirk deepened. "And that's why it's working. No one in the Pentagon will question it. They built AEGIS to detect and respond to real threats. It never considered the possibility that someone might fabricate those threats with this level of precision."

Kamran's fingers flew across his keyboard, routing the transmission through a complex web of false origins

— nodes bouncing through secure military intelligence servers across multiple countries, covering its true source.

"Done," Kamran finally said, leaning back. "It's in."

A notification flashed across their screen only thirty-six minutes later, confirming the message's receipt within the AEGIS high-threat alert system. The directive was already being categorized under "critical national security risk," ensuring senior U.S. defense officials would receive and review it within minutes.

Kamran exhaled, his excitement palpable. "We've just altered the U.S. military's entire strategic posture. They'll see every single Russian and Chinese movement from this moment forward as an escalating provocation."

Leila smirked. "Which means they'll have no choice but to act."

Saeed added, "And with Sokol routing certain Russian messages through legitimate FSB channels, every move the Americans interpret as hostile will appear to be validated by Russian intelligence itself."

Kamran nodded, satisfied. "We've forced them into a self-fulfilling prophecy. They think they're preempting a war, but they're actually creating one."

Leila's gaze flickered toward the clock. "Within hours, high-ranking officials will be scrambling to verify this intelligence. Phone calls will be made. Orders will be given. By sunrise, U.S. military assets will be in motion."

Saeed cracked his knuckles. "And once they mobilize, Russia and China will have no choice but to respond.

The Americans will assume the worst, and the Russians and Chinese will prepare for the confrontation the U.S. thinks is inevitable."

Kamran's voice was steady, almost reverent. "And that's how you ignite an international crisis — without ever firing a single shot."

A tense silence settled over the room. The gravity of what they had just done was immense. In the cold glow of their screens, they watched the world shift beneath their fingertips — lines of code and crafted words shaping the future of global warfare.

Leila inhaled deeply. "We've set everything in motion. From here, all we do is watch. Our job is done."

Kamran's eyes gleamed as he leaned back in his chair. "Yes," he murmured. "Watch the Americans burn down their own house."

Day 10

Executive Floor A-6
CIA Headquarters
Langley, Virginia
6:30 am

CIA Special Agent Scott Douglass sat stiffly in one of the many CIA war rooms, the overhead fluorescents casting a sterile glow over the classified reports strewn across the table. His jaw was tight, his fingers tapping an anxious rhythm against the hard surface as he reviewed the latest intelligence updates. He had been briefed on the McAllen meeting the previous afternoon and had a renewed energy level to get to the bottom of this digital jigsaw puzzle.

The data before him painted a dire picture — if it was real. That was the problem. The U.S. military was already responding to what it believed to be coordinated military threats from Russia and China. Fighter squadrons had been relocated, naval fleets repositioned, and nuclear defense assets placed on high alert. But the inconsistencies uncovered so far painted a different picture – one of massive fraud. But by precisely who? And what role would the Iranians play? They weren't world players anymore – what was their connection?

Something about the intel just didn't sit right with him. The reports flooding in were too perfectly aligned with U.S. threat expectations, triggering an immediate response. The Pentagon wasn't waiting for confirmation — they were already reacting based on output and directives from AEGIS.

Across the room, Marcus Reed, a tall, skinny cyber-intelligence analyst with a brilliant mind and a background in special operations, leaned back in his chair, arms crossed. His sharp eyes studied the screen before him, tracking the flagged encrypted messages. Reed and Douglass had served together with the Rangers in Afghanistan and other similar venues on numerous classified special operations missions, and their bond had carried over into intelligence work. If Douglass trusted anyone to help him untangle this mess, it was Reed.

"You don't buy this intel, do you?" Reed asked, his voice low.

Douglass shook his head, his gut churning. "No. It feels manufactured. The timing, scale, and patterns all fit perfectly into our worst-case scenarios. I just can't help being suspicious." He glanced at the latest global conflict projection models. Every scenario ended in disaster.

Reed frowned. "That's the problem. The AEGIS system is treating this intelligence as real stuff — which means the Pentagon isn't questioning it. They're already moving."

Douglass exhaled sharply, his mind racing. They could be on the edge of a catastrophe.

Douglass toggled through threat assessment models that AEGIS used to predict and analyze global security risks. AEGIS had flagged the intercepted messages as high-priority threats, reinforcing the Pentagon's rapid mobilization.

He watched as the system simulated war-game scenarios based on the classified directives. Each simulation led to some variation of nuclear escalation, economic collapse, and millions of deaths.

"Jesus," Reed muttered. "The system models are all driving toward a serious confrontation that could easily escalate."

Douglass nodded grimly. "That's why we must figure this out and stop it before it's too late. We need undeniable proof of what this is and who is sending it out before we escalate into something we can't undo."

Reed leaned forward, studying the metadata on the intercepted transmissions. "Let's review what we know and what we don't. We know these messages have been bouncing through multiple nodes — Beijing, Moscow, and European relays — but the true origin is hidden and therefore unknown. We think Iran is somehow involved in this because of messages that include Tehran, but whoever is behind it really knows how to cover their tracks."

Douglass stared at the data flow. The rerouting was almost too clean. It was a deliberate misdirection. He narrowed his eyes. "They want us looking in the wrong places."

Reed's brow furrowed. "What are you thinking?"

"We need to look for something they didn't account for — satellite uplinks, hidden relay signals, micro-delay discrepancies. If they're bouncing through multiple locations, we should see minute latency variations in the data stream."

Reed's fingers zipped across the keyboard, running a deep forensic trace. Minutes passed in silence before he suddenly stopped.

"Scott — I've got something."

Reed turned his monitor toward Douglass, a blinking red dot pulsing on the screen. "Look at this uplink path. It starts in Moscow and reroutes through a compromised node in Shanghai, but what is the true point of origin?"

Douglass leaned closer. His stomach dropped.

Tehran.

More specifically, a secure communications facility just outside the city in Ozgol.

Reed's voice was grim. "They've been bouncing the signals to make it look like this came from China and Russia, but every satellite trace leads back to Iran. And Ozgol is where the Iranian National Security Center is located. That fits and makes total sense."

Douglass felt the weight of the revelation settle over him. This was it.

They had been chasing shadows, but now they were very close to having proof.

Reed hesitated. "We have a signal. But to make this actionable, we need direct proof that Iran's government intelligence agency is not only involved but also probably behind it. Otherwise, they could claim it's rogue actors."

Douglass's jaw tightened. "Then we force their hand."

Reed's eyebrows raised. "How?"

Douglass's expression darkened. "We set up another digital trap."

Reed's lips curved into a dangerous grin. "A digital decoy."

If we configured a fabricated classified intelligence asset — like an AI-driven server designed to look like a key U.S. military intelligence node — Iranian cyber operatives wouldn't be able to resist targeting it.

If they took the bait, the NSA's cyber-monitoring team could track every keystroke.

And then they'd have them.

Douglass picked up his secure line and dialed Robyn Chen at the NSA.

"Robyn," he said, skipping any pleasantries. "We're setting up a high-stakes cyber trap. I need you in on it."

Chen's voice was calm but alert. "I'm listening."

Douglass outlined the plan: deploy a controlled digital decoy configured as a vulnerable U.S. intelligence hub. If the Iranian hackers engaged, the NSA would trace their movements, capture their digital fingerprints, and link the operation directly to Tehran.

Chen was silent for a moment. Then she said, "I'll set up the monitoring framework. If they probe the system, even once, we'll see it. We have a sandbox server on the network that our programmers use for new software. We can open it up in under half an hour."

Douglass exhaled. "Good. We need to move fast. If we're right about this, we don't have much time before the situation escalates beyond our control."

As he hung up, he turned to Reed.

"We're going to catch these bastards."

Reed cracked his knuckles. "And when we do?"

Douglass's voice was steel. "We shut them down — hard — before they push us into a war our military can't walk away from. And then we take them out the old-fashioned way. Ka-Boom!"

The war room hummed with tense energy as the team launched the honey pot.

Minutes passed. More minutes passed. Soon, an hour had passed.

Then — a hit.

A probe from the Ozgol facility.

Then another.

Within seconds, the NSA's tracking system came to life, recording every movement, every keystroke, and every data packet.

Reed's voice was sharp. "They took the bait. And the message protocols match the directives that AEGIS received."

Douglass leaned forward, watching the digital trap snap shut.

His hands clenched into fists.

They had them.

But was it too late to stop what had already begun?

Operations Floor A-3
CIA Headquarters
Langley, Virginia
10:30 am

CIA Special Agent Scott Douglass stood in the center of Langley's operations command, his steel-blue eyes fixed on the digital war map, which displayed real-time military mobilizations. Red alerts flashed across multiple regions, warning of imminent conflict between the United States, Russia, and China. Naval carriers were repositioning, missile defense systems were being activated, and squadrons were scrambling — the machine was already in motion.

The Pentagon had escalated to DEFCON 2 — a step away from global war status. If tensions continued mounting, a shift to DEFCON 1 would be nearly irreversible.

A cold weight settled in his gut.

This was a trap.

But without getting the proof to the right people quickly enough, there was no stopping the war machine.

Across the table, Robyn Chen, his NSA liaison, worked furiously, her fingers flying across her keyboard. Her brows knit together in concentration as she ran another set of deep forensic scans on the encrypted intercepts.

"What do you see, Robyn?" Douglass said, his voice tight and urgent.

Chen frowned, her dark eyes flickering between two screens. We have just flagged another transmission routed through Tehran similar to the ones you and Marcus saw. The encryption pattern is identical to the previously fabricated messages, but this one has an added layer of obfuscation. It's structured to mimic Russian command-and-control protocols."

Douglass clenched his jaw. "That confirms it. This isn't just Iranian interference — it's state-sponsored cyberwarfare, and they're using it to frame Russia and China for an attack they never authorized."

Still at Langley, Carlos Mejia, Sandra Espinoza, and Priya Sharma burst through the door and joined Douglass and Robyn. Carlos, his face grim, was holding a thick dossier.

"Scott, we've found something big," Carlos said, dropping the file onto the table.

Douglass motioned for them to continue.

Priya spoke first. "We intercepted chatter in Farsi — but not just background noise. It's embedded in encrypted financial transactions. These aren't just random directives. They're coming straight from Tehran's Ministry of Intelligence."

Sandra chimed in, her voice edged with tension. "Iran isn't just interfering — this confirms they're financing an entire destabilization effort. The money trail we followed? It shows payments to major arms shipments, black-market fuel deals, and offshore shell companies in Venezuela and North Korea."

Priya nodded. "And one message stood out. It references a 'final action' that coincides with the false troop movement alerts. I think they're setting up a sequence of events to set up a U.S. preemptive strike."

Douglass exhaled sharply. His worst fear was playing out in real time.

"They want us to launch first," he muttered.

Sandra ran a hand through her hair. "It's more than that. If we strike, Russia and China will be forced to retaliate — even if they know they weren't planning an attack."

Carlos leaned forward, locking eyes with Douglass. "We have to stop this. Right now."

Chen's fingers never stopped moving as she ran another decryption cycle. "These messages are too clean to be real," she muttered. If this were authentic Russian or Chinese internal military communications, there would be irregularities — linguistic quirks, variations in command hierarchy, and embedded field codes.

She turned her screen to Douglass. "But this? It's flawless. The structure is curated as if someone had built it piece by piece.

Douglass nodded. "Because they did."

Iran had studied U.S. threat assessment models, learned how AEGIS interpreted risk, and fed the system precisely what it expected, driving the Pentagon toward an inevitable conclusion.

A door swung open, and another analyst rushed in, dropping a fresh intelligence report on the table.

"Satellite imaging has just arrived," the analyst said. "We have some movement on the Russian and Chinese borders, but..." He hesitated. "It doesn't match the urgency of these reports. No heavy mobilization. No combat drills beyond routine exercises."

Douglass snatched up the photos and flipped through them. Standard troop rotations. Minimal equipment shifts.

Not the signs of an imminent war.

Chen tapped another screen. And this is from Naval Intelligence. Our submarine monitoring stations in the Pacific? They've picked up zero unusual activity in China's naval command networks. There's no encrypted chatter about an offensive, no coded missile strike plans, nothing."

A slow realization settled in the room.

Carlos was the first to say it aloud. "This is it."

Sandra's voice was hushed. "The intelligence we've been acting on is a fabrication."

Douglass grabbed his secure phone and entered a code to connect directly with CIA Director Evelyn Harrington.

A moment later, the line clicked open. "Scott, what do you have?"

"Ma'am, we now have conclusive proof that the intelligence fueling the Pentagon's escalation is fraudulent. We have found no physical evidence of activity or movement from either Russia or China. The encrypted messages show to be manufactured by Tehran, using high-level masking techniques to make them appear as if they're coming from Russia and China."

Silence.

Then, the Director's voice was tight. "Scott, are you absolutely certain?"

"Beyond a doubt, Evelyn," Douglass said. If we move forward based on this intelligence, we will be walking into a confrontation founded on deception. And once we cross that line, there's no going back.

Another silence.

Then — a quiet exhale.

"Get to the White House."

Douglass's grip tightened on the phone.

The Director's voice was gravely serious. "You'll brief the National Security Council and the President directly. Bring everything you have. If we don't shut this down in the next few hours, we may be looking at the beginning of a war we never meant to start."

The CIA Director ended the call.

"We move now."

His voice was iron.

"If we don't stop this within the next few hours, we'll be going to war over an illusion."

Sandra grabbed her files, Carlos secured the encrypted drives, and Priya pulled the last of the decrypted reports.

Chen stood, already compiling everything into a classified briefing.

"You're about to go toe-to-toe with the Pentagon, the National Security Council, and the President," she said. "They won't roll back DEFCON 2 without absolute proof."

Douglass nodded grimly.

"Then we'd better be ready to give it to them."

As they hurried out of the operations room, the weight of the moment settled over them.

This was it.

The next few hours would decide the fate of nations.

Douglass had uncovered the deception, but now came the real challenge:

Convincing the most powerful military complex in the world that the war they were preparing for... wasn't real.

Executive Floor A-6
CIA Headquarters
Langley, Virginia
12:30 pm

CIA Special Agent Scott Douglass pushed through the heavy doors of the CIA's main intelligence conference room, his heartbeat hammering in his chest with Robyn and the Texas ICE team in tow. The room was packed — high-ranking intelligence officials, Homeland Security leaders, cyber-warfare experts, and military liaisons — all gathered in response to the escalating crisis.

The tension was suffocating.

Around the long mahogany table, the most powerful decision-makers in the country sat, their expressions grim, their skepticism evident. The CIA Director, Evelyn Harrington, sat at the head of the table, her icy-blue eyes flickering with calculation. To his left, Homeland Security Secretary Andrew Dyson, a sharp-witted pragmatist, drummed his fingers on the table. Several generals from the Joint Intelligence Command were patched in through secure video feeds, waiting for the briefing.

Douglass didn't waste time. He stepped forward and slammed a classified file onto the table.

"We have a serious problem. If we don't act now, we could be walking into a confrontation and possibly a war based on lies."

The room went silent.

"Explain what you found, Scott," Harrington asked, her voice edged with concern.

Douglass leveled his gaze at the CIA Director. "I'm saying that the intelligence we've been acting on is a coordinated Iranian disinformation campaign. AEGIS flagged the orders as urgent, high-level military threats. We believe they were fabricated and that Iran has somehow infiltrated our intelligence network and is feeding false data directly into the system."

A murmur rippled through the room.

Homeland Security Secretary Dyson folded his arms. "You expect us to call off a military response based on an unverified theory?"

"It's not a theory," Douglass snapped. "It's evidence. The ICE team in South Texas intercepted encrypted transmissions that were initially routed through China and Russia. NSA also observed anomalies in their network monitoring area. However, we traced the true origin back to Tehran after a joint forensic analysis with the NSA. Iranian cyber operatives disguised their transmissions to appear as internal U.S. military directives, feeding AEGIS exactly what it expects to see when assessing an imminent foreign threat."

The skepticism was thick, but so was the urgency.

Dyson narrowed his eyes. "AEGIS is the most sophisticated artificial intelligence server ever developed. Its encryption verification processes are supposed to be foolproof. How could an external actor manipulate it so effectively?"

Douglass exhaled sharply. "Because AEGIS isn't failing. It's doing exactly what it was designed to do — process intelligence based on pattern recognition. The Iranians studied our threat assessment algorithms and built a deception so precise that AEGIS is interpreting fabricated messages as credible data. AEGIS isn't being hacked — it's being misled."

The room erupted into debate.

CIA Director Harrington raised a hand for silence. She studied Douglass for a long moment. Let's assume, for a moment, that what you're saying is true. Why would the Iranians go to this extreme? What's their endgame?"

Douglass's stomach tightened.

"Simple," he said. "They want to provoke a global conflict. If the U.S. escalates against Russia and China, we'll be too distracted, weakened, and divided to stop whatever Iran is planning in the Middle East. With our focus on an all-out war, they'd have free rein to make aggressive moves against Israel, Saudi Arabia, Iraq, or other U.S. allies, without interference. Additionally, there is a potential retaliation for the sanctions as well.

A heavy silence settled over the room.

While Douglass fought for reason at Langley, the Pentagon was already making moves.

In the high-security war room, the Joint Chiefs of Staff analyzed real-time data pouring in from intelligence officers.

Chairman General Mark Spencer scowled at the latest reports. "We've been monitoring Russian and Chinese forces for weeks. Their movements match standard invasion protocols. Are we really supposed to ignore that?"

A senior intelligence officer hesitated. "Sir, Scott Douglass at the CIA is warning that these messages might be fabricated, and we have found no satellite evidence of adverse troop movement by either Russia or China. He's urging a hold for additional verification before we proceed further."

Spencer's fists clenched. "We don't have the luxury of waiting for perfect intelligence. Preemptive action is the only way to maintain a competitive advantage. If we hesitate, we lose the initiative."

Air Force General Linda Fox nodded. "If this is a hoax, we'll reassess. But if we hesitate and it's real, we'll be caught off guard. AEGIS is giving us clear signals — we need to act."

From the Oval Office via video call, President Clark listened as his top advisors debated the decision of a lifetime.

"Mr. President," said Harrington over the secure line, "I would understand your hesitation, but if Douglass is right, we could be about to start a war based on manipulated intelligence. I urge you to pause further escalation and allow us to verify the information fully."

Clark, a hardliner on national security, pinched the bridge of his nose. "So, let me get this straight. AEGIS — the most advanced intelligence system we've ever built — is telling me Russia and China are preparing for war. But one CIA agent, with ICE agents in tow, is suggesting that this could be an elaborate Iranian ruse?"

Harrington's tone was firm. "Sir, if Douglass is right, we're about to engage in a war based on a lie."

Across the room, General Spencer interjected. "Mr. President, hesitation invites weakness. Unless there is irrefutable proof that AEGIS has been compromised, we proceed as planned. We cannot afford to stand down based on speculation."

Clark sighed, drumming his fingers against the Resolute Desk. "I can't afford to undermine confidence in our military intelligence. I need concrete proof. Until then, we move forward."

The order was given.

• Nuclear warheads were moved from storage to active readiness.

• Fighter jets are prepared for immediate deployment.

• Naval strike groups positioned themselves in the Pacific and Atlantic, primed for engagement.

• Missile defense systems were fully activated.

The machine was in motion.

Now, back at Langley, Douglass's hands clenched into fists.

They were running out of time.

Carlos Mejia looked up. "We're still tracking dark web communications. We might be close to intercepting a direct Iranian command transmission."

Robyn Chen's eyes widened. "If we can capture a live, irrefutable transmission from Tehran's Ministry of Intelligence that outlines the deception, we'll have the proof we need to stop this."

Sandra's voice was tight with urgency. "We need something undeniable. A smoking gun."

Douglass took a deep breath.

"Then find it. Because if we don't, within the next 24 hours, the world will be at war that never should have happened.

Day 11

After a late-night flight back to Harlingen, Special Agent Carlos Mejia and Senior Analyst Sandra Espinoza sat in their regional intelligence operations center, exhaustion pressing down on them like a wheelbarrow full of bricks. The past forty-eight hours had been a whirlwind — a high-stakes chase through layers of encryption, misinformation, and global cyber warfare. But they had no time for rest.

The glow from their monitors flickered against their tense expressions, casting jagged shadows across the room. Lines of code and intercepted messages raced across their screens, the culmination of days spent tracking a digital ghost — a cyberattack so sophisticated that it had nearly fooled the world's most powerful intelligence agencies.

Adjusting her high-frequency comm headset, Sandra leaned in, her gaze sharp. "Carlos, look at this. We're seeing synchronized spikes in encrypted traffic from two critical locations — Beijing and Astrakhan, Russia. And guess what? These transmissions align perfectly with major global flashpoints over the past week.

Carlos's fingers flew over the keyboard with urgency, isolating the data streams. He pulled up past cyberattacks linked to known state-sponsored hacking units and cross-referenced them with the timing of recent international crises. His stomach clenched as the pieces began to fall into place.

"This isn't just some random burst of cyber activity," he muttered, eyes narrowing. "This is a precision strike. A globally orchestrated deception."

Sandra exhaled sharply. "The timestamps match up too cleanly. It's either China and Russia coordinating a full-scale digital assault — or someone's gone to extreme lengths to make it look that way."

Across the room, Junior Analyst Priya Sharma was hunched over her laptop, decrypting intercepted transmissions. Now, with an elevated security clearance, she was authorized to access the highly classified ports on the Joint Worldwide Intelligence Communications System (JWICS) — a highly classified military network within the Defense Information Systems Network (DISN) for transmitting intelligence and top-secret information. Fluent in Farsi and Arabic, she had an ear for linguistic subtleties that most analysts would miss. She scanned the phrases in the latest batch of flagged messages.

"Wait," Priya said, her voice rising. This terminology is distinctly Iranian military jargon — not just standard Farsi but the kind of coded language used by their high-command strategists. These messages aren't just spreading false alarms — they're laying the groundwork for Iran's next significant move in the Middle East."

Carlos and Sandra turned toward her, their faces pale with realization.

Priya highlighted key sections. Phrases like 'strategic horizon shift' and 'regional deterrence measures' are euphemisms that Iran has used before, typically just before major military or intelligence operations. They're choosing what crises to manufacture while ensuring the world is too distracted to stop them."

She forwarded the flagged messages to Langley, where Scott Douglass had just come online with a video call. His calm yet authoritative voice crackled over the secure channel.

"Priya, can you confirm with absolute certainty that these transmissions originated from Iranian military sources?"

Priya tightened her grip on the edge of her desk. "I'd bet my career on it. They're seeding this narrative while staying hidden behind Russian and Chinese cyberinfrastructure. They're not just feeding us false intelligence — they're coordinating global events.   I couldn't access these transmissions on the Secret Internet Protocol Router Network (SIPRNet) I usually use.

Douglass was silent for a moment before responding, his voice tense. "That means we're looking at a fully coordinated psychological warfare campaign. Iran isn't just faking Russian and Chinese troop movements; they're manipulating us into preparing for the wrong war."

Carlos, still tracking the encrypted traffic, suddenly sat up straighter. His fingers raced over his keyboard, isolating a specific data signature. "Hold on. I just backtraced the routing information on another one of these new transmissions. There's an extra hop in the relay pattern."

Sandra leaned in, her pulse quickening. "What kind of hop?"

Carlos zoomed in on the digital signature. "It's not coming directly from Moscow or Beijing. There's a midpoint relay — a hidden server cluster near Tehran."

Sandra checked the satellite intel and cross-referenced the signal path. "That's not just anywhere in Tehran," she whispered. That's Ozgol, one of Iran's most secretive cyber-intelligence hubs. This isn't just an attack — it's a direct act of military deception.

A sharp curse echoed over the secure line at Langley. Douglass had been listening in.

"Son of a bitch," he muttered. "That probably means every damn message AEGIS flagged about Russia and China has got to be entirely fabricated. Iran really has been feeding us false intelligence through our own systems for who knows how long and using our own paranoia against us. Why didn't anyone else pick up these transmissions?"

Priya shook her head in disbelief. "They look routine, so no one would notice unless they had a reason. But, if they're that good at hiding their origin, why leave any trail at all?"

Carlos's expression darkened. Because they needed it to appear realistic. If the messages were too perfect, they'd raise suspicion. By making it seem as though the intel is naturally being intercepted from enemy states, AEGIS classifies it as authentic."

Douglass pulled up the latest Department of Defense status report. His gut twisted.

"We're at DEFCON 2," he announced grimly. "If this escalates any further, the U.S. military will move to DEFCON 1 — meaning we are at imminent risk of potential nuclear deployment. If another one of these fabricated messages reaches AEGIS, the Joint Chiefs will have no choice but to authorize the final strike protocols."

Sandra's face lost all color. "Jesus. We're that close?"

Carlos whispered under his breath, "How do we stop it? If the Pentagon trusts AEGIS this much, we'll need something undeniable."

Priya bit her lip, her mind racing. "Even if we prove it's fake, will they listen?"

Douglass exhaled sharply. "They'll have to. Because if they don't, the next war won't start with tanks or airstrikes. It'll start with the push of a button."

The team worked at breakneck speed, their fingers urgently blurring across keyboards as they chased down the last pieces of evidence.

Priya again delved into layers of encryption, attempting to extract an Iranian government signature — a digital fingerprint that would tie the transmissions directly to Tehran's military command.

Carlos and Sandra monitored live transmissions, waiting to intercept a real-time fabricated directive before it could be rerouted through Moscow or Beijing.

Douglass coordinated with Langley, pushing for immediate intervention at the highest level of government.

The truth was within their grasp. But time was slipping away — and the next AEGIS alert could seal the world's fate.

Also, with his recent JWICS clearance, Carlos saw his screen suddenly flash with a new incoming transmission. His blood ran cold.

"We've got one. AEGIS is receiving another falsified directive. This one's worse — it's an immediate escalation alert. If it gets through, it could trigger a direct military response."

Sandra's hands flew to her keyboard. "Can we block it?"

Carlos shook his head, sweat beading on his forehead. "No, it's already hitting high-priority channels. We risk losing everything if we don't counter this with absolute proof within the next few hours.

Priya's voice was tight. "Then we have to find it. Now."

Douglass stood, his body coiled like a spring. "This is it. Everything we've worked for comes down to this moment. If we fail —"

He didn't finish the sentence.

They all knew what failure meant.

The world was inches from war.

And they were the only ones left who could stop it.

Operations Floor A-2
CIA Headquarters
Langley, Virginia
10:15 am

In the heart of the CIA's cyber operations command center, Douglass sat quietly, his eyes locked onto the flood of encrypted data cascading across his monitor. His muscles were tight, his mind razor-sharp despite the exhaustion settling in his bones. He had spent the last 18 hours pulling apart layer after layer of Iran's deception — dissecting digital fingerprints, reverse-engineering spoofed network paths, and chasing ghost signals that had sent the world's most powerful military machine hurtling toward the edge of catastrophe.

And now he was at a personal and professional breaking point.

He now knew, beyond a shadow of a doubt, that Iran was orchestrating this crisis. He could feel it in his gut. But gut instincts weren't enough — not when trying to convince the Pentagon, the White House, and every intelligence agency in Washington to slam the brakes on what might already be an irreversible march to war.

This wasn't just a sophisticated cyberattack. This was psychological warfare on a level never seen before.

Douglass exhaled sharply and initiated an advanced cyber-warfare decryption protocol, stripping away the layers of redirection embedded within the IP signals. Iran's hackers had deployed the most intricate techniques they had ever seen — bouncing transmissions through multiple global servers, blending false DNS entries, and embedding randomized subnet diversions to create the illusion of a Chinese and Russian attack.

But illusions, no matter how well-crafted, leave behind digital fingerprints.

Using a quantum decryption module built for counterintelligence warfare, Douglass peeled back the deception layer by layer. False entries disappeared, duplicate server pings unraveled, and a scrambled network of artificial paths collapsed into stark clarity.

And there it was.

A cyber signature — buried deep inside the code. One Douglass had encountered before.

Iranian cyber-warfare markers.

His heart slammed against his ribs. This was it.

He leaned forward, voice low. "Got you, you bastards."

Now, he needed absolute confirmation.

The South Texas ICE team had also intercepted several suspicious transmissions — messages that had appeared to originate from China and Russia. But Douglass suspected those addresses were being spoofed. If he could prove that Iran was behind them, he'd have the smoking gun that could change the course of history.

He rerouted traffic logs, isolating source anomalies. His system bypassed conventional tracking methods and instead scanned data packets for their original timestamps.

The program chewed through terabytes of obfuscation, bouncing between Shanghai, Moscow, Singapore, and Dubai. Then, it locked onto a secure, military-controlled cyber node in Tehran.

Douglass clenched his fists, his pulse hammering. "They did it. They actually did it."

Within the hour, he had mobilized a classified emergency briefing inside Langley's high-security conference room. The CIA Director, Homeland Security Director Andrew Dyson, NSA Chief Edward Ashtoni, and Pentagon Liaison General Jacob Turner sat around the table, their faces grave and skeptical.

Douglass stood, his voice sharp and unwavering.

"We are, in fact, being deceived. The intelligence that has driven us to the brink of war is a carefully orchestrated Iranian operation."

A heavy silence fell over the room.

CIA Director Evelyn Harrington, a seasoned intelligence veteran, folded her arms. "Scott, we've been through this before. You're asking us to disregard everything AEGIS has flagged as credible intelligence. That's a hell of a claim."

"It's not a claim. It's a fact," Douglass shot back. "I now have conclusive proof that Iran has manipulated AEGIS, feeding it false intelligence designed to provoke a military escalation."

He clicked a button on the control panel, and a classified projection filled the room — layers of decoded transmissions, backtraced network routes, and an unmistakable digital signature tying everything back to Tehran.

NSA Director Edward Ashtoni leaned forward. "Jesus Christ."

Homeland Security Secretary Andrew Dyson exhaled slowly. "Just to clarify – again - you're saying that Iran isn't just spreading false intel — they're deliberately fabricating a crisis?"

Douglass nodded. "Every intercepted message that pointed to Russian and Chinese aggression? It originated in Tehran. Every directive that suggested troop movements? Planted by Iranian cyber-warfare units. This isn't a coincidence — it's a strategy."

The Pentagon liaison, General Jacob Turner, frowned. "You expect us to stand down based solely on cyber data?"

Douglass's patience snapped.

"General, if we launch based on this deception, we're handing Iran everything they want. They want us to strike first. They want us distracted by a war we don't need to fight. They're playing us like a damn fiddle."

Turner's jaw tightened. "You're asking us to risk our national security on your analysis."

"No, General. I'm asking you to risk our national security if you ignore it."

A tense silence settled over the room. CIA Director Harrington finally spoke.

"What's your next move, Douglass?"

Douglass laid it out.

"We deploy a three-pronged verification strategy."

1. Launch a covert reconnaissance mission — boots on the ground near Russian and Chinese borders to confirm or deny any major military movements.

2. Deploy real-time satellite surveillance — instead of relying on AEGIS's flagged intelligence, they would use direct visual confirmation.

3. Activate back-channel diplomatic inquiries — quietly engage Russian and Chinese intelligence counterparts to gauge their actual threat posture.

"If Russia and China are truly preparing for war, we'll see it. If we see nothing? We'll know we came seconds away from launching World War III over an Iranian deception."

The CIA Director nodded slowly, then turned to an aide. "Get me the President."

Douglass's secure cell phone buzzed while the video played. Douglass saw the sender and answered on speaker.

Carlos Mejia's voice came through, tense and breathless.

"Scott, we finally nailed it."

"Talk to me. Everyone is in the room."

We compared the IP addresses from these transmissions with those of known Iranian cyberattacks. It's identical. They employed the same obfuscation techniques and relay methods they had used in past operations.

Douglass's knuckles went white against the desk. "You're sure?"

"As sure as I've ever been. It's Tehran."

Douglass turned to his team.

"This is it. We have to stop the President before it's too late."

President Jonathan Clark sat in the Oval Office, now joined by video call, listening as both sides made their final case.

The Pentagon pushed for immediate escalation.

The CIA and NSA urged caution.

Clark rubbed his temples. "I don't like either option. If we hesitate and this is real, we show weakness. But if we act and it's a lie..."

The CIA Director leaned in. "Mr. President, we are very close to having irrefutable proof. Give us six hours to verify Douglass's findings."

Clark exhaled. The clock was ticking.

Finally, he spoke.

"You have six hours. If you can't prove it beyond a doubt, we move forward with full force."

The line went dead.

Back at Langley, Douglass clenched his jaw.

Six hours.

That was all the time they had to stop a war.

Operations Floor A-2
CIA Headquarters
Langley, Virginia
1:45 pm

Douglass sat rigidly in his office at CIA Headquarters, his fingers drumming against the polished mahogany desk in a slow, methodical rhythm. Exhaustion clawed at him, but adrenaline kept him upright. The walls felt too tight, the air too thick, as if the very foundation of Langley itself was bearing down on him. The U.S. military was poised at the edge of war, a precarious moment in history that could tip into catastrophe with a single wrong move.

Together with the ICE team, they had uncovered the truth — Iran had manufactured the entire crisis, manipulating AEGIS, infiltrating U.S. intelligence networks, and planting a trail of fabricated cyber threats that painted Russia and China as aggressors. But knowing the truth wasn't enough. He needed undeniable proof — proof so bulletproof that the Pentagon and the White House couldn't ignore it.

A Zoom call notification pulled him from his thoughts. He exhaled sharply and clicked Accept.

Sandra Espinoza's face appeared on the screen, her dark eyes sharp with intensity. Her tablet trembled slightly in her hand, evidence of the urgency surging through her.

"I've traced the financials," she announced without preamble, her voice tight. "And it all leads back to Iran."

Douglass leaned forward, his grip tightening on the edge of his desk. "Show me."

Sandra shared her screen, displaying a labyrinth of encrypted cryptocurrency transactions — a dense and tangled financial web that could have taken months to unravel. Still, Sandra had done it in mere days.

"They used classic laundering tactics," she explained, zooming in on a string of transactions. Funds were routed through China, Russia, and Venezuela — standard obfuscation techniques to obscure the origin. But here's the kicker — the final deposits land in accounts controlled by shell corporations directly tied to the Iranian Ministry of Intelligence."

Douglass's pulse pounded against his temples as he studied the timestamps next to each transaction. They lined up perfectly.

Each time AEGIS received an "urgent threat" message warning of imminent Russian or Chinese aggression, a payment had been made from Tehran.

Douglass exhaled sharply. "Iran didn't just manipulate the intelligence. They funded the deception."

Sandra nodded grimly. "And we have the receipts."

While Douglass and his team raced against the clock, the Pentagon's war room was already locked in fierce debate.

General Mark Spencer, Chairman of the Joint Chiefs, gestured toward a digital map flashing with red military movements. "We've got satellite confirmation of heightened military activity near Taiwan, the Baltic region, and the South China Sea." He turned to Defense Secretary Warren Holloway, his voice sharp. We have passed the point of theorizing, Warren. If we don't act, we'll lose strategic positioning."

Across the table, National Security Agency Director Edward Ashtoni pinched the bridge of his nose, exhaustion and frustration etched into her features.

"We need to be absolutely certain," Ashtoni countered. "Scott Douglass is still verifying the intelligence. If this is a false flag — if we mobilize without confirming the authenticity — we will be walking into a war on false pretenses."

Admiral James Price, head of Naval Operations, folded his arms across his chest. "With all due respect, we can't afford to hesitate." His voice was calm but firm. "A military force that blinks in the face of aggression loses its deterrent power. We have to respond."

The room fell silent.

Defense Secretary Warren Holloway leaned back in his chair. "Then we need indisputable proof before we commit to a full-scale mobilization."

Time was running out.

Back in his office at Langley, Douglass knew they needed one final piece of evidence. He called the ICE team on Zoom to Carlos's workstation to find something irrefutable to present to the President and the Pentagon.

"We need a live intercept," Douglass said. "Real-time confirmation that Iran is still pulling the strings. We should look at cell traffic in that area of Tehran."

Carlos Mejia cracked his knuckles. "Then we watch Tehran like a hawk. Every deep web proxy, every cellular transmission, every secure communication linked to Iranian cyber operations."

After the Zoom call with Scott was terminated, Sandra tapped her keyboard, pulling up geospatial intelligence feeds. "We know Ozgol has been a hotspot. If we cross-reference burner phone signals moving in and out of Tehran and Ozgol simultaneously, we might be able to pinpoint the Iranian operatives in real-time."

Thirty minutes later, eyes wide, Priya exclaimed, "Oh, my God – look!"

A Zoom notification flashed seconds later on Douglass's screen at Langley — an incoming video call from South Texas.

Priya Sharma's voice came through, breathless. "Scott, we have a burner phone signal."

Douglass stiffened. "Where?"

Priya's screen flashed, a series of numbers bouncing between Iranian telecom towers.

"Ozgol," Priya confirmed. "It's live."

Carlos activated an audio decryption and recording tool, fingers flying over his keyboard. "Give me a second..."

A garbled transmission filled the room. The distortion was heavy, but beneath it, a man's voice crackled through the speakers.

Priya's face paled. "That's Farsi..." she whispered. She adjusted the filters, isolating the words.

The audio cleared.

A voice, low and authoritative, spoke:

"Initiate final phase. The Americans have taken the bait."

A chill ran through Douglass.

Silence.

Then —

Sandra's voice was barely a whisper. "They just admitted it's a setup."

Carlos's fingers flew over his keyboard. "If we can match this encryption signature to Iranian military communications, we have them dead to rights."

Douglass didn't hesitate. He cross-referenced the burner phone's encryption with known Iranian cyber warfare techniques, and the result flashed on the screen.

IDENTICAL.

Sandra sucked in a sharp breath. "This is it. The proof we needed."

Carlos turned to Douglass. "How do we get the Pentagon to listen?"

Douglass's expression hardened. As before, we don't just tell them. We show them."

He activated a live decryption stream, feeding the intercepted Iranian transmission directly into the Pentagon's intelligence hub.

A message appeared on the screen:

"Maintain deception. Ensure conflict escalates."

Carlos exhaled, stunned. "Jesus. That's undeniable."

Douglass grabbed his secure line. "Get me the President. NOW."

Within minutes, President Clark's face was added to the secure video call alongside the CIA Director, the Pentagon's top brass, the NSA Chief, and the ICE team from South Texas.

Douglass's voice was steel. "Mr. President, we have real-time proof that Iran manufactured this entire crisis.

We have intercepted Iranian military transmissions admitting to falsifying intelligence to provoke conflict. We have financial trails. We have live burner phone intercepts. And we have digital back tracing tying it all back to Tehran."

The room fell deathly silent.

President Clark's expression darkened. "And you're certain?"

Douglass met his gaze without hesitation. "Beyond any doubt. If we don't stand down immediately, we will go to war based on a deception."

The Pentagon generals shifted uncomfortably.

Finally, Defense Secretary Holloway spoke. "We need to halt mobilization immediately."

General Stratton exhaled sharply. "This changes everything."

Clark nodded once. "I'm issuing the order to stand down."

As the order rippled through military channels, Douglass felt a crushing weight lift from his chest.

Still on the Zoom connection, Sandra released a breath she hadn't realized she was holding. "We stopped it."

Carlos shook his head. "This was too damn close."

Douglass remained solemn. "Iran played a dangerous game. Next time, we might not be so lucky."

Priya folded her arms. "So what happens now?"

Douglass's eyes burned with resolve. "We hunt them down. We hurt them. And then we make damn sure they never do this again."

Day 12

White House Situation Room
Washington, D.C.
3:00 pm

The White House Situation Room was drenched in a suffocating silence, the kind that came only when the country's most powerful men and women were on the brink of making a world-altering decision. The air in the dimly lit chamber felt heavy and thick with the gravity of the moment.

At the center of it all, President Jonathan Clark sat stone-faced, his sharp blue eyes flickering between the faces of his top intelligence and military advisors. His reputation as a hardliner had been earned through years of unwavering, often ruthless, decisions, and the men and women seated around him knew that whatever choice he made today would change the course of history.

To his right, CIA Director Evelyn Harrington leaned forward, her steel-gray hair pulled back in a tight bun. Her face was lined with exhaustion, but her eyes were razor-sharp. Across from her, NSA Deputy Director Robert Hale, a seasoned intelligence operative with a background in cyber warfare, tapped his pen against the polished mahogany table, the only sound breaking the silence.

Next to him, Secretary of Defense Warren Holloway, a no-nonsense military strategist, sat rigid, his broad shoulders squared, his lips pressed thin. His uniform was crisp, but the dark circles under his eyes betrayed the stress of the past forty-eight hours. The Pentagon had already recommended an immediate move up to Defcon 1, and a global war had been minutes away from ignition — until one man had stopped it.

That man was Scott Douglass.

Standing at the head of the table, Douglass kept his posture controlled, his expression grim, but his heart pounded in his chest. He and the ICE team of analysts had spent two relentless days chasing down the greatest deception in modern military history, peeling back the layers of Iranian cyber warfare that had nearly manipulated the United States into launching a preemptive strike.

Behind him, two massive digital screens displayed a complex web of interactive data-encrypted Iranian transmissions, bank transactions leading back to Tehran, and AEGIS's own manipulated decision matrix, which had nearly pushed the country to the edge of war.

He inhaled sharply. This was it.

"Ladies and gentlemen," Douglass began, his voice steady but laced with urgency, "what I am about to present to you is how we came within hours — possibly minutes — of launching an irreversible military strike based entirely on fabricated intelligence."

He clicked a remote in his hand, and the screen shifted to an AEGIS threat escalation timeline, showing in real time how the Iranian-planted messages had triggered DEFCON alerts, mobilized fleets, and prepared nuclear assets.

"Iran did not hack us," he continued, his gaze sweeping across the room, "they engineered an intelligence catastrophe on a scale we've never seen before. They sent fabricated messages – perfect in every way – which were received by AEGIS, the most advanced AI-driven intelligence system we've ever built and validated as authentic. AEGIS then forwarded these false communiqués designed to push us toward escalation."

The room remained deathly silent except for the soft hum of the fan motors.

CIA Director Evelyn Harrington was the first to break it. "Scott, walk us through the execution."

Douglass nodded. He clicked again, and the screen zoomed in on a detailed map of Tehran, with a blinking red marker over Ozgol — the heart of Iran's elite cyber intelligence division.

"This is where it all began. This is what we believe has happened."

A flowchart appeared, outlining the Iranian cyber warfare unit's strategy.

"Iran's operatives used a multi-layered misdirection campaign," Douglass explained. "They routed false intelligence reports, messages, directives, and sitreps through compromised servers in Moscow and Beijing, making it appear as though the cyberattacks and threats were coming directly from Russia and China."

NSA Deputy Director Robert Hale frowned, adjusting his glasses as he studied the display. "How did they manage to spoof locations so convincingly?"

Douglass clicked again, and a new graphic appeared, detailing the web of deception.

"They combined deepfake cyber-routing techniques with dark web proxies and burner phones linked to encrypted satellite networks," he explained. "The sophistication of their forgery was unprecedented. But what made this operation truly dangerous was their ability to mimic actual U.S. military intelligence language and syntax. Whoever did this is a true intelligence professional. When I think about it, I wish they worked for us."

A new screen flashed up, showing intercepted Iranian messages, decrypted to reveal perfectly structured military jargon designed to mirror legitimate intelligence briefings.

Priya Sharma's face appeared on the secure satellite link from South Texas. "We detected Farsi linguistic patterns embedded within the messages," she said. "Subtle enough to be overlooked, but distinct enough to prove Iranian authorship."

General of the Army Daniel Ross exhaled sharply. "Jesus Christ."

Douglass tapped the table for emphasis. "This was information warfare at its finest. Iran didn't just manipulate intelligence — they controlled the entire narrative, and they nearly dragged the world into a war it didn't need to fight."

The President finally spoke, his voice calm, measured, but unmistakably tense.

"How close did we get?"

Douglass locked eyes with him. "Closer than we ever should have."

He clicked again, and a timestamped military action log filled the screen.

"Our fleet in the South China Sea was within minutes of an offensive maneuver. Russian forces were already responding to our mobilization along the Polish and Baltic borders. China had moved anti-ship missile batteries into position in the Taiwan Strait."

He let the weight of his words settle in the room before finishing:

"If we had waited even two more – three at the most – hours to uncover the deception, the first shots might have already been fired."

The room remained frozen in stunned silence.

Finally, President Clark leaned forward, resting both hands on the table.

"Iran did this?"

Douglass nodded. "Yes, sir, we're certain of it now. We tracked the entire operation to an intelligence hub in Ozgol. We intercepted financial transactions funding the cyber operatives and burner phone communications coordinating the final phases of the attack — everything leads back to Tehran."

The President's jaw tightened.

CIA Director Harrington exhaled. "If Iran can do this once, someone else can do it again."

Douglass's expression darkened. "Which is why AEGIS needs to be taken offline until further notice — *immediately.*"

The Pentagon officials erupted in protest.

"Absolutely not!" General Ross snapped. "AEGIS is the backbone of our cyber defense."

Douglass held firm. "With all due respect, General, AEGIS is the reason we nearly went to war. If it remains online in its current form, it's only a matter of time before someone exploits it again."

The President's gaze bore into him. "Your solution?"

Douglass didn't hesitate. "Reprogram AEGIS. Integrate human verification layers for all high-priority intelligence. Right now, it prioritizes speed over accuracy. That has to change."

After a long pause, President Clark nodded.

"Take it offline. That's an order."

General Ross grimaced but stayed silent.

But Douglass wasn't finished. He inhaled deeply.

"Mr. President, taking AEGIS offline is only half the solution. The other half is neutralizing the source. Iran still can do this again."

Clark narrowed his eyes. "Are you suggesting a counterstrike?"

Douglass's jaw tightened. "Not a counterstrike. A covert ground operation. We send in a black ops strike team, infiltrate the facility, and destroy their cyber warfare headquarters before they can use it against us again. I also suggest that the Pentagon continue to send directives making the Iranians think we're still responding to the fabricated messages. We want to catch them in the act if possible."

A chill spread across the room.

CIA Director Harrington frowned. "A black ops mission inside Iranian territory? You know I can't authorize that!"

President Clark tapped his fingers against the desk, considering.

Then, he gave the single nod that changed everything.

"Well, I sure as hell can. Make it happen, and I'll keep the Pentagon focused on their continuing responses. But Douglass, remember that this entire op is off the books, so there is no rescue if this goes south. Tell me you understand that."

Douglass stood tall. "Yes, sir, I do." He had his mission.

"OK, get to work and come back in one piece," was the parting reply before Clark left the room.

Now, he just needed a team that could pull off the impossible.

Part II
Retribution

Day 13

Operations Floor B-4
CIA Headquarters
Langley, Virginia
8:30 am

Douglass stood in the cold, sterile conference room buried deep within Langley's classified black ops wing. Reinforced with soundproofing and electromagnetic shielding, the walls ensured that what was said here never left the room. The low hum of encrypted data streams from the adjacent intelligence command center reminded him just how deep in the shadows they were working.

The mission was officially a go.

Directive *Shadow Spear* — a top-secret Presidential executive order issued by President Clark — had authorized a covert black operation that could never exist on record: no formal approvals, oversight, or paper trail. If the mission failed, if they were captured or killed, the U.S. government would deny any and all knowledge of their existence. They would be international outlaws and treated as such.

And that was precisely the kind of mission Douglass had spent his early career conducting — covert, surgical, and utterly ruthless.

Sitting across from him at the long, unmarked steel briefing table were the three people whose signatures authorized the funding for this operation — CIA Director Evelyn Harrington, Chief of Staff of the Army General Daniel Ross, and NSA Deputy Director Robert Hale. Each of them wore grim, unreadable expressions as they prepared to send a team into the heart of enemy territory.

Harrington folded her hands on the table and locked eyes with Douglass.

"You have full discretion on this, Scott. We need Iran's cyber intelligence division wiped from the face of the Earth. However, this cannot, under any circumstances, be traced back to the United States government in any capacity. The President made that crystal clear."

Douglass nodded sharply. "Understood."

General Ross leaned forward, his gray, battle-worn face unreadable.

"Your mission objectives are as follows," he stated, his voice carrying the weight of finality.

> 1. Covert Infiltration – Enter Iran undetected and reach Ozgol, where Iran's elite cyberwarfare headquarters is located.
>
> 2. Total Annihilation – Destroy all servers, hardware, and infrastructure used in Iranian cyber operations. Iranian casualties are acceptable and approved as you deem necessary.
>
> 3. No American Casualties or Exposure – You do not exist if captured.

NSA Deputy Director Hale adjusted his glasses and spoke in a low, warning tone.

"You will have access to black ops funding, real-time satellite surveillance, and covert weapons tech, but nothing that can be traced back to us. You will also have our full discretion to neutralize threats as necessary to complete the mission — quietly."

Douglass exhaled slowly, feeling the weight of the mission settle deep in his bones. He had executed dozens of classified paramilitary operations during his time as a Special Activities Division (SAD) officer, but this was different.

This wasn't just another black op. This was retribution.

It was time to pick the team.

CIA Safehouse
Undisclosed Location, Virginia
1:00 pm

Douglass never went into a mission blind. He had personally handpicked four individuals, each an expert in their respective fields. Even though Priya and Robyn had little or no field experience, their skills were essential to this particular mission. Douglass was confident that they would be mission-ready with the rigorous training and guidance he had arranged.

This wasn't just a covert operation — it was a surgical strike with zero room for error. Most of all, he needed experienced field operators. The first names were obvious – Reed and Mejia.

Marcus Reed – The Tactical Leader

Marcus had joined Douglass at the safehouse to help plan the mission. He was Douglass's oldest ally from their time in black ops missions overseas and a logical choice for a leadership role in the special strike team. A former Army Ranger turned CIA paramilitary officer, Marcus was an expert in direct action operations, explosive ordnance disposal, and urban warfare.

He leaned against the wall, arms crossed. "You should've called me sooner."

Douglass smirked. "Figured you were busy."

Marcus chuckled. "When do we leave?"

Carlos Mejia – The Infiltrator

Joining by Zoom call from his post in South Texas, Carlos had been one of the first to uncover the Iranian cyber deception, and now he would help dismantle the source. A senior ICE Agent from South Texas, Carlos had spent well over a decade in counter-cartel operations, specializing in clandestine infiltration, HUMINT (human intelligence), and asymmetric warfare.

As a former Army Ranger with special ops experience, he also knew how to move through hostile environments undetected. His ability to blend into underground networks and his law enforcement background made him the perfect field operative for the mission.

Carlos leaned back in his chair, arms crossed, watching Douglass on his screen.

"You sure about this, man?" he asked. "Iran is a different animal than the cartels."

Douglass smirked. "You saw through their deception before anyone else did. I need someone who can cut through the bullshit and disappear when necessary."

Carlos exhaled, tapping his fingers against the table. "Fine. But I want full control of our exfil routes. I'm not getting stuck in that country without a way out."

Douglass grinned. "That's why you're here."

Priya Sharma – The Linguist & Analyst

Priya had been essential in deciphering Iranian messages hidden within AEGIS's fabricated directives. A linguistic genius with a Ph.D. in Middle Eastern Studies, she was fluent in Farsi, Arabic, and Russian and had extensive knowledge of Iranian intelligence networks. Field experience or not, the need for her linguistic skills made her essential to the mission.   They needed someone fluent in Farsi to navigate Iranian intelligence circles, intercept communications, and blend in if needed.

Also on the video call with Carlos, Priya adjusted her glasses and looked straight at Douglass. "I've never done fieldwork. I analyze from safe distances."

Douglass smirked. "And yet, here you are."

She sighed. "You need someone fluent in Farsi who can decode Iranian military chatter in real-time."

Douglass nodded. "Exactly. And Priya, there will most certainly be Iranian casualties. Dead bodies. And these casualties will likely be done up close and personal with a knife across the throat to maintain complete silence. Are you prepared for that?"

She hesitated for only a moment. "Yes, Scott. I've thought about it, and as high as the stakes are here, I'm okay with it. Just keep me alive."

Douglass grinned. "That's the plan. Stay close to me. I'll send the G-5 for you and Carlos – it should arrive around 6:00 pm this evening. Be ready for a quick turnaround to meet us here to start training for the mission in the morning."

Robyn Chen – The Cyber Specialist

Robyn had been hunting Iranian cyber activity for years and had joined Douglass and Reed at the safe house. While she had minimal field experience, she was a hacker prodigy, an expert in penetration testing, counterintelligence coding, and digital warfare.

Her job? To implant a "kill switch" — a malicious code designed to dismantle Iranian cyber infrastructure permanently. Douglass also explained the certainty of Iranian casualties to gauge her reaction. Robyn had been around death in her hometown and had grown to accept the necessity of casualties in these operations.

She cracked her knuckles. "I can handle the casualties as long as I don't have to have an active role in them. So, we're going dark ops on this?"

Douglass nodded. "No fingerprints, no traces. I need you to plant a kill switch so deep that Iran won't recover for decades."

She smirked. "You had me at 'kill switch.'"

Robin leaned forward. "I assume you have an exfil plan?"

Douglass grinned. "Embedded Mossad contacts will get us into Iran and from Ozgol to Chalus on the Caspian Sea. Mossad will then provide a specially equipped powerboat and escape across the water to Baku, Azerbaijan. CIA assets will meet and extract us from Baku."

Marcus whistled. "Hell of a ride."

Robyn smirked. "Let's just hope the Iranians don't shoot us before we get there."

Douglass exhaled. "We move in the morning. Train hard, pack light, and be ready for anything."

As the team dispersed, preparing for what would be the most dangerous mission of their lives, Douglass stood in the shadows.

By the time this was over, Iran's cyberwarfare division wouldn't just be disabled. It would be erased.

Day 14

CIA Black Ops Training Facility
Quantico Marine Corps Base, Virginia
11:15 am

CIA Special Agent Scott Douglass paced in the center of the classified black ops training hangar, his sharp eyes tracking every movement of his team as they navigated the dimly lit combat simulation course. All hands were now present, and the air was thick with the scent of gunpowder, sweat, and adrenaline. The air was thick with the acrid scent of gunpowder, sweat, and the unmistakable tension of an elite unit pushing their bodies and minds to the limit. The echoes of suppressed gunfire punctuated the cavernous space, a rhythmic reminder of their mission's high stakes.

This wasn't a drill. This was their final test before deployment overseas for the next training and preparation phase.

They were living and breathing this operation — rehearsing, refining, and adapting their strategy. The next time they ran this, it wouldn't be in a controlled environment. It would be deep inside Iran, where failure meant capture, torture, and certain death. If they were caught, the United States government would disavow them, and their existence would be erased from official records. It would mean an international incident that could escalate into a full-scale conflict with Iran.

Failure was out of the question.

The CIA had spared no expense and gone to extreme lengths to construct a near-exact replica of the Iranian intelligence headquarters in Ozgol. Using high-resolution satellite imagery, local HUMINT (human intelligence) assets, and classified architectural blueprints, they had recreated every detail — from the guard rotations to the weak structural points. The walls, the entry points, the security checkpoints—all had been replicated with military precision.

This was as real as it could get before they stepped foot on Iranian soil.

Douglass turned to his assembled team, their faces illuminated by the red tactical lighting of the training facility.

"Listen up," he called, his voice cutting through the tension. "This is our last chance to iron out every weakness. We run this until it's muscle memory. We move like ghosts — out of sight, no hesitation, no errors."

Marcus Reed, the team's ground operations leader, stood at a holographic overlay of the facility with a laser pointer. He was built like a war machine — lean, efficient, and deadly. His voice was all business.

"We enter the compound at 11:30 pm, local time," he began, gesturing to the holographic overlay of the replica facility. "Guards rotate every thirty minutes. Scott, Carlos, or I will neutralize any threats — suppressors or blades only. No alarms. No bodies left in the open."

He turned to Carlos Mejia, their infiltration specialist. "Carlos, you're on point. You're the fastest through tight spaces and know how to read a room. If we hit a roadblock, we follow your lead."

Carlos nodded without hesitation. "I'll be ready. Just make sure Priya doesn't start a diplomatic incident if we get caught."

Priya Sharma, the team's intelligence analyst and linguistic expert, rolled her eyes. "If I have to smooth-talk our way out of trouble, that means you already screwed up."

Marcus smirked. "Let's make sure we never have to find out."

Robyn Chen, the team's cyberwarfare specialist, was hunched over a military-grade tablet, running live penetration tests against mock Iranian security firewalls.

"Iranian security scans for movement between 12 midnight and 6:00 am," she said, flipping through encrypted satellite overlays. "That means we're racing against a countdown once we enter the facility."

Priya adjusted her civilian-style Iranian disguise — a dark hijab and a long coat — designed to allow her to blend in with Tehran's urban landscape if things went sideways.

"Iranian security will immediately profile Westerners," she warned. "We need to be able to pass as locals, even if only for a few seconds. That means posture, mannerisms, and most importantly — language."

She turned to Carlos. "How's your Farsi?"

Carlos cleared his throat before delivering a perfectly rehearsed phrase:

"In manzel-e doost-e man ast. Man dar inja kar mikonam."

(This is my friend's house. I work here.)

Priya raised an eyebrow, nodding in approval. "Not bad. That might buy you two seconds before they start shooting."

Carlos grinned. "Two seconds is all I need."

One of the most critical objectives was ensuring that Iran's cyber intelligence network was utterly unrecoverable. That meant demolition — but not just any demolition.   They needed total annihilation, and that would certainly mean casualties.

Marcus stood beside a mock Iranian server rack, attaching a detonation charge while explaining the plan.

"The goal isn't just to destroy the servers," he said, securing a trigger wire. "We need to make sure they can't salvage a damn thing."

Douglass nodded. "We're using thermite-based incendiaries. They burn through metal and silicon, ensuring nothing can be reconstructed. We'll also be using C-4 and Symtec for good measure. Once we light them up, they won't stop burning until everything is ash."

Carlos chuckled. "So, we're bringing hellfire to Tehran?"

Marcus smirked. "Something like that."

Douglass brought up a holographic tactical map outlining their extraction scenarios.

"We have two exit strategies," he said, scanning the faces of his team. "Plan A: We slip out through the underground sewer tunnels and emerge near a crowded market district, where our extraction vehicle and driver will be waiting."

Robyn frowned. "And if that doesn't work?"

Douglass's expression hardened. "Plan B: We fight our way to the outskirts of the Tehran area and make for the Caspian Sea."

Carlos grinned. "Plan B sounds like a hell of a lot more interesting."

Douglass fixed him with a cold stare. "If we end up using Plan B, it means something went horribly wrong. And we can't afford to be 'wrong.'"

"Noted," Carlos replied, this time without the grin.

For their final night at Quantico, the team ran a full-mission simulation — from infiltration to detonation to exfiltration.

They entered the mock Iranian facility, moving in total silence, clearing rooms with flawless precision.

Priya intercepted Iranian radio traffic, relaying enemy movement patterns in perfect Farsi.

Marcus set the explosives, whispering, "Fire in the hole."

Douglass had arranged a surprise challenge for the final simulation because war never goes according to plan.

As the team maneuvered through the mock facility, Carlos reached for his silenced pistol to eliminate a guard. But before he could pull the trigger, the room exploded in chaos.

Suddenly, the facility's power cut out, plunging them into complete darkness. Emergency strobe lights flickered as a loud klaxon blared through the training compound.

"What the hell?!" Carlos whispered, flattening himself against the wall.

A simulated Iranian drone activated overhead, scanning the area with infrared. Douglass's voice cut through the earpieces.

"Improvisation time! Move now!"

Marcus grabbed Robyn Chen, their cyberwarfare specialist, and pushed her toward the nearest server terminal. "Robyn, get us back online!"

Robyn cursed under her breath, her fingers flying over the keyboard. "They simulated a security lockdown! I need two minutes to override."

"We don't have two minutes," Douglass muttered, pressing his body flat against the wall as the drone's scanning beam passed inches from his foot.

Carlos and Marcus took up defensive positions. "If this were the real thing, we'd be dead already," Marcus muttered.

"Then let's fix that," Douglass shot back.

Priya's voice crackled in his ear. "We've got simulated enemy forces closing in fast — thirty seconds!"

Robyn worked faster. "I'm almost there — just give me cover!"

Douglass clenched his jaw. *This was the kind of chaos they needed to be prepared for.*

"Marcus, take the left. Carlos, on me."

Carlos pivoted, suppressor snapping onto his rifle. The moment the first mock enemy breached the room, he fired two rounds, center mass.

The drone was still scanning. Douglass had no choice. He raised his weapon and fired a single shot at the drone's optical sensor.

It sparked and sputtered, its AI logic faltering for just a second — but that was all they needed.

"System override complete!" Robyn called out.

The alarms cut off. The lights flickered back to their simulated "normal."

"Move, move, move!" Douglass barked.

They extracted through the sewer tunnels, racing against simulated security forces.

By the time they reached their exfil point, the replica of the Iranian intelligence headquarters was nothing but a smoldering husk.

Marcus checked his watch. "Twenty-six minutes. Five minutes faster than our best run. That'll have to do."

Douglass took one last look at the smoldering remains of the training structure, then turned to his team.

"Next time, it's for real."

In a quiet, windowless conference room, Douglass stood before his team.

"This is the last time we'll be on U.S. soil for a while," he said. "Tomorrow, we head to Israel for final deployment."

Carlos leaned back. "Mossad training facility?"

"Herzliya, near Tel Aviv," Douglass confirmed to the group. "The Israelis wrote the book on covert operations, and we'll finish our prep there. They have a model of an entire Iranian village for us to practice our village entries and movements. They also have jump training and certification – don't forget that Priya and Robin have never jumped before. We'll need to work out a tandem arrangement to be sure they can do this without injury. There is no room for mistakes. They get injured in a jump – the op is over before it starts."

Priya sighed. "Great. My first real mission, and I have to skydive into enemy territory."

Carlos grinned. "You'll love it. Nothing wakes you up like free-falling at terminal velocity."

Priya shot him a glare. "Remind me to kill you after this mission."

Douglass exhaled. "If we screw this up, none of us will be around to complain. Get some rest. We leave at dawn. Then we go dark. We hit Iran hard, and we don't stop until their intelligence network is reduced to nothing but ashes."

A silence heavier than steel filled the room.

They all knew the risks. They all knew they might not come back.

As the team left, Douglass lingered momentarily, staring at the mission dossier.

There was always something *else* he could have trained them on, one more scenario to run, but there was no more time.

Tomorrow, there would be no practice.

Tomorrow, they'd be preparing for war.

But they would be ready.

Day 15 & 16

Mossad "Academy"
Israeli Intelligence Training Center
Herzliya, Israel
3:20 am

The unmarked Gulfstream 550 business jet descended into darkness, slicing through dense cloud cover as it approached the private Israeli airstrip. The moonless night concealed its approach, ensuring no satellite, radar, or intelligence agency could track it. There were no official flight records, diplomatic clearances, or acknowledgment that this aircraft or flight had ever existed.

This wasn't just covert — this was off-the-books, deniable at the highest levels of government.

Scott Douglass sat near the front of the cabin, staring at the vast emptiness outside. His team had spent the last few days preparing for this moment — tracking intelligence, training for high-risk infiltration, and dismantling the Iranian deception that had nearly triggered global war. No one spoke. The weight of the impending mission loomed over them like an approaching storm. This was their final preparation phase, the last stop before they stepped into Iran as ghosts — operatives without a flag, an identity, or the luxury of failure. And now, they were about to enter the final phase before deployment.

The cabin was silent except for the occasional hum of the jet engines. Carlos Mejia tightened the straps on his tactical bag while Marcus Reed methodically sharpened a combat knife. Priya Sharma sat stiffly, running her fingers over the edge of her tablet. She wasn't a soldier but knew she was about to become something far deadlier than an analyst. Robyn Chen checked her encrypted laptop, running final penetration tests against Iranian cyber defenses.

This wasn't a routine mission. This was a one-way ticket into one of the world's most dangerous countries — with no backup, support, or second chances.

The plane jolted as the landing gear engaged, and the pilot's voice crackled over the comms.

"Two minutes to touchdown. Brace for landing."

As the jet hit the runway, the team exchanged glances — this was it.

3:45 am

As the jet taxied to a halt inside a heavily guarded hangar, a team of Mossad operatives stood waiting — stone-faced men in tactical fatigues, sidearms holstered but ready. Their expressions were unreadable, and their eyes assessed the foreign operatives stepping onto their soil.

The lead operative, a grizzled veteran with piercing blue eyes and a build like a stone wall, stepped forward and extended a calloused hand toward Douglass.

"Major Avi Cohen, Mossad Operations Chief," he introduced himself, his English flawless. "Welcome to Israel. You're late."

Douglass met his stare. "Not our fault. You guys are ahead of us in time zones."

Avi smirked. "Cute. But let's get something straight — this isn't Langley, and I don't have time for American arrogance. Follow me."

With that, he turned and led them into the darkness of the Academy.

The Mossad Academy, known only as "The Academy," was Israel's most classified intelligence training facility. It was hidden north of Tel Aviv in Herzliya, a city renowned for its intelligence and counterterrorism operations.

For decades, this highly restricted compound had trained some of the most lethal covert operatives in history. There were no plaques, no government seals, and no official records that it existed.

Every inch of the compound was designed for realism — replicated urban warfare zones, mock cities resembling Middle Eastern capitals, electronic warfare labs, hidden escape tunnels, soundproof interrogation cells, and shooting ranges with live hostiles for training exercises.

It was here that Douglass and his team would learn the final skills they needed to infiltrate Iran undetected, execute their mission, and vanish without a trace.

The moment the sun rose, the training began.

6:30 am

By daybreak, Douglass and his team were already moving through a simulated urban combat course — a perfect replica of Tehran's labyrinthine streets, complete with fake Iranian checkpoints, mock residential buildings, and dense marketplace environments packed with Mossad operatives posing as civilians.

There was no time to rest. The moment the sun rose, the real training started.

Mossad had painstakingly recreated a segment of downtown Tehran — not just a training ground, but a living, breathing simulation. Market stalls, checkpoints, underground tunnels—everything they would encounter in Iran had been rebuilt inside the Academy.

"Your mission is simple," Avi barked. "Survive. In Tehran, you're dead the second they make you as a Westerner," he shouted, watching as Douglass and Marcus led the team through a narrow alleyway, moving silently and methodically.

The first test was urban combat.

Marcus and Carlos led the way through a simulated Tehran street, the "city" teeming with operatives posing as civilians, Iranian security forces, and intelligence agents.

A checkpoint loomed ahead. Two guards in full Iranian uniforms stood scanning IDs, rifles slung at their sides.

"What's the play?" Carlos murmured.

"We go silent," Marcus replied.

At a fake checkpoint, two Mossad operatives dressed as Iranian security forces blocked the path, inspecting the ID cards of staged civilians. Marcus surveyed the scene, his mind working like a battlefield tactician. He motioned for Robyn and Priya to hang back, then turned to Douglass.

"We take them down quietly. No noise. No fuss."

Douglass nodded once.

In perfect synchronization, Marcus and Carlos moved in like wraiths. Silencers affixed. Knives ready.

Two silent strikes — a throat slit, a snapped vertebra. All were simulated moves but were anatomically dead solid perfect.

The guards acknowledged the move and crumpled without a sound.

Marcus and Carlos quickly dragged the bodies out of sight, securing their uniforms and IDs.

Avi Cohen observed from the shadows, arms crossed. "Not bad," he muttered. "Maybe you won't die after all. But next time? The guards fight back."

The next round of training was a full-contact ambush drill — this time, the "guards" had been briefed to resist.

It was brutal. Carlos took a staged punch to the ribs, doubling over before retaliating with a lethal elbow strike. Priya was nearly caught during an interrogation but improvised in Farsi, defusing the situation just long enough for Marcus to neutralize the threat.

By the time the drill ended, Douglass's team looked like they had survived a real firefight.

Avi grinned. "That's more like it."

Their next challenge wasn't physical — it was mental.

Priya and Robyn were blindfolded and dragged into separate interrogation rooms.

They were shoved into chairs, hands zip-tied, and subjected to simulated Iranian interrogation tactics. Bright lights burned their retinas, Israeli agents playing the roles of ruthless intelligence officers barking questions in Farsi.

"Who do you work for?"

"What is your mission?"

Priya's heart pounded, but she remembered her training. She leaned into her cover identity, feigning confusion, speaking Persian fluently.

Robyn wasn't as lucky. When the interrogator slammed a fist against the table, she flinched.

Avi watched through the glass, unimpressed. "If that had been real, you'd already be dead."

Robyn clenched her fists. "Again."

And so they ran it — again, and again, and again — until every instinct to flinch or hesitate was burned out of them.

Later that day, the team gathered in a classified cyber-intelligence room, where Mossad's top cyberwarfare specialist, Dalia Rahmani, stood at the center, arms folded.

"You Americans love brute force," she said, her Israeli accent thick but clear. "But real operations like this one require finesse. Subtlety. If you trip an alarm in

Iran, you won't even hear it before your execution order is signed."

She gestured toward a holographic map of Tehran, where communication lines flickered in red and blue.

"The Iranians run layered encryption protocols, but we've already cracked parts of their network." She pointed at the underground cyber hub beneath Ozgol, their primary target.

Robyn Chen leaned in, her eyes narrowing. "Their signal relays are bouncing between multiple fake nodes. If we jam the wrong one, we expose ourselves."

Dalia nodded. "Exactly. That's why you're going to use Mossad's tools."

She handed Robyn a compact, black device — a frequency disruptor capable of blinding Iranian surveillance grids for precisely seven minutes.

"Not six. Not eight. Seven," Dalia warned. "After that, you're on your own."

Douglass exhaled slowly. "We'll make it count."

Late that morning, they began practicing jumps. Douglass and Reed, veterans of literally dozens of tactical and HALO jumps each, decided to pair up Douglass with Priya and Reed with Robin for tandem jumps. Carlos would jump first by himself to be nearby and available to assist on the ground if necessary. After six tandem jumps throughout the afternoon with no injuries or issues, Douglass and Reed determined this was a workable strategy and moved on to the next exercise.

Their final challenge took them to Haifa, where Israel's elite Shayetet 13 — their version of Navy SEALs — waited.

A burly officer, Captain Eitan Raz, eyed Douglass's team. "You want to escape through the Caspian? Show me you can handle it."

Douglass nodded. "That's the plan. Cross into Chalus, access one of your speedboats, and head for Baku."

The night was brutal. For four relentless hours in the darkness, the team trained on high-speed boats, learning how to maneuver Iranian vessels, evade radar detection, and disappear into the dark waters of the Caspian Sea. They were expertly coached in high-speed chases in Iranian patrol boats, radar evasion, and stealth insertion techniques.

As they returned, exhausted from the exercise, Carlos commented, "This is like smuggling, just with bigger consequences."

Eitan grinned. "Then let's raise the stakes."

On the final run, an Israeli patrol boat chased them at full speed, simulating an Iranian ambush.

Douglass's team barely evaded capture, learning firsthand how quickly things could go wrong on the Caspian.

Carlos, who had experience with smugglers on the Texas-Mexico border and in the Gulf area, quickly adapted to naval tactics.

"So basically, we're playing hide-and-seek in the dark?" he smirked.

"Exactly," Eitan replied. "Except if you lose, you drown."

11:00 pm

Back at The Academy, a Mossad logistics officer handed each operative a file of documents containing their new identities:

- Douglass would be a Russian Military Attaché
- Reed would be Douglass's executive officer
- Carlos would be a Black-market Arms Dealer
- Priya would be an Iranian Academic
- Robyn would be a Cyber Engineer for Tehran's Intelligence Division

Major Avi Cohen studied them one last time. "From this moment on, you are ghosts. No one will save you if you fail."

Douglass looked at his team. They understood.

This was it.

Before departing, Douglass was escorted to a classified meeting with the Mossad Site Director Meir Zakay.

Zakay slid a classified file across the desk. "Iran is planning something bigger than AEGIS."

Douglass's stomach tightened. "Bigger?"

Zakay's expression darkened. "Our embedded people say they're coming for Israel next – with bombs."

Douglass exhaled. "Then we hit them first."

Zakay's voice was cold. "Make sure they never recover."

Shortly after midnight, the team boarded a covert transport plane bound for Iran.

This was it. No turning back.

Day 17

Covert Insertion
Skies Over Iran
12:45 am

The Mossad C-17 Globemaster carved through the pitch-black Iranian sky like a ghost, silent and undetectable to radar. Modified with stealth technology, its thermal signature was reduced, and its radio emissions cloaked, making it virtually invisible to Iranian defenses. The hum of its engines was reduced to a whisper, a ghost moving through the upper atmosphere.

Inside the cabin, the team sat in stony silence, their faces illuminated only by the faint green glow of the jump timer counting down to their point of no return. Scott Douglass sat rigid, his eyes locked on the mission timer strapped to his wrist. The countdown to their jump was ticking away, second by second — fifteen minutes to the drop zone, a descent to 5,000 feet in progress.

Fifteen minutes.

Fifteen minutes until they jumped into the abyss.

Douglass sat nearest to the open cargo bay doors, his eyes flicking between his altimeter and the jagged silhouettes of the Zagros Mountains below.

Everything had gone according to plan so far, but this was the most dangerous part of the operation — infiltrating Iran from above. There were no second chances; if they were spotted, there would be no diplomatic immunity, backup, or rescue.

They had been flying at 30,000 feet, skirting the lower edge of the stratosphere, preparing for what was arguably the most dangerous phase of their mission — infiltrating Iranian airspace and flying undetected over the rugged expanse of the Zagros Mountains. The landing zone was Saveh, just 100 kilometers from Tehran by way of National Highway 65. The Mossad had left a vehicle in a dilapidated building near the landing site, but would meet them in person on the outskirts of the Tehran area.

Douglass broke the silence.

"Alright, listen up." His voice was firm but calm, cutting through the low rumble of the aircraft. "This is a one-way ticket into hostile territory. Once we hit the ground, we blend in. No unnecessary engagements. No deviation from the plan. Priya is our key voice once we reach Ozgol. We follow her lead when the time comes. Clear?"

A series of firm nods.

Carlos Mejia, adjusting his parachute straps, smirked. "Not exactly the sunny beaches of South Texas."

Marcus Reed, the former Army Ranger turned CIA paramilitary officer, checked his gear with methodical precision. "Better than jumping into an active war zone. We'll be fine. Just another day at the office."

Robyn Chen, their NSA cryptography specialist, had been uncharacteristically quiet. This was the furthest she had ever been from the digital battlefield, and now, she was about to jump out of an aircraft into enemy territory.

Douglass caught her moment of hesitation. "Robyn, you good?"

She exhaled sharply, her fingers tightening around the buckle of her harness. "I won't let the team down."

Douglass nodded. "You never have. Just trust the training. You're not alone out there."

The pilot's voice crackled through the comms:

"Five minutes to drop. Get ready."

The cargo bay doors hissed open, and a blast of freezing air filled the cabin. In the distance behind them, the jagged peaks of the Zagros Mountains stretched endlessly into the darkness behind them.

They secured their masks, double-checking each other's gear in a silent, practiced rhythm.

Then, the jump light turned green.

Douglass locked eyes with Carlos. "Go, go, go!"

They launched into the void one by one, their bodies hurtling toward the earth at 120 miles per hour.

The wind howled in their ears, the world a blur of stars and shadow.

At 1,000 feet, Douglass yanked his ripcord.

A violent jolt.

His black canopy deployed, billowing out into the night, blending seamlessly with the dark sky.

Below, a valley flanked by rocky outcroppings came into focus.

Carlos had leaped first as a solo, then Douglass and Reed jumped as their tandems, their bodies slicing through the freezing air as they free-fell toward Iranian soil.

The descent was as flawless as they could have hoped for. They had all deployed their chutes at 1,000 feet, their dark-colored canopies nearly invisible against the night sky.

The drop zone was just ahead.

His team landed one by one — Carlos first, then Douglass and Priya, followed by Marcus and Robyn in their tandem descent.

They hit the ground softly, rolling into position. Immediately, they cut away their chutes and drew their suppressed sidearms.

Marcus was already checking their surroundings. "We're in good shape – we're only two kilometers from our rendezvous point at Saveh. We move now. Double-time."

Douglass's eyes scanned the area — silent, clear.

But something felt off.

The wind had shifted.

And then — the distant hum of an engine.

"We've got movement." Carlos's voice was barely a whisper.

Marcus crouched, peering through his thermal scope.

About 300 meters east, a small drone hovered, its red lights blinking as it slowly scanned the terrain.

An Iranian patrol drone.

Not military-grade, but enough to alert a Quds Force patrol unit if it detected movement.

"Stay absolutely still," Douglass ordered, barely breathing.

The drone hovered, its sensors sweeping the area for movement where they had landed.

A single wrong move and their entire mission was over before it began.

Seconds stretched into eternity.

Then, the drone changed direction.

It drifted eastward, scanning another valley section before disappearing over a ridge.

Only when it was gone did Douglass exhale. "Move. Now."

They slipped into the night, ghosts on Iranian soil.

1:45 am

After nearly forty minutes of relentless movement, they reached their first checkpoint, an abandoned shepherd's shelter on the outskirts of Saveh with an ancient Toyota Hilux pickup truck hidden within a dilapidated structure carved into the rock.

Marcus yanked the tarp off. "Hope this thing runs." Carlos hotwired the ignition in seconds. The engine choked, coughed, and then roared to life.

Carlos then secured the perimeter while Priya unrolled a compact satellite communicator, tapping into a secured Mossad relay.

"We're in. Moving toward Ozgol. ETA two hours," she whispered into the mic.

A static-filled reply came through:

"Acknowledged. No activity on your route. Green Light. Keep moving."

With the all-clear, they loaded the truck and pressed forward.

3:45 am

By the time they reached the industrial outskirts of Tehran, the first hints of dawn had begun to creep over the mountains beyond them, northeast of Tehran. This was their transition point from covert operatives to local workers. They stripped off their tactical gear, revealing Iranian worker uniforms underneath.

Priya helped each of them adjust their disguises — head coverings for Carlos and Marcus, a worn hijab for herself and Robyn, and fake credentials tucked into their pockets.

This was the most vulnerable part of their journey. They had to cross into Ozgol undetected, right under the nose of Iranian intelligence forces.

Priya adjusted her Iranian disguise, making sure her hijab was placed correctly.

A dented old transport truck waited nearby at the edge of a dusty road. The Mossad contact driver nodded as they parked the old truck and climbed into his covered cargo area, where crates of farming supplies masked their presence.

Carlos murmured as the truck rumbled toward Ozgol, "This is surreal."

"Welcome to espionage," Priya muttered back.

The ride was long and tense, the air thick with anticipation.

At the first checkpoint, two Iranian soldiers waved them down.

"What's in the bed of your truck?"

Douglass kept his hand on his concealed Glock 19, his pulse steady.

The Mossad driver leaned out, speaking in perfect Farsi, his voice bored, impatient. "Just farm supplies. Do you want to inspect crates of potatoes?"

The Iranian soldiers half-heartedly waved the truck through, barely giving it a second glance.

Douglass kept his hand on his pistol, watching their surroundings with unwavering focus.

Finally, after what felt like an eternity, they reached the industrial outskirts of Ozgol, a grimy, steel-gray sprawl of warehouses, smog, and factory smoke.

This was their entry point.

The truck rolled to a slow stop, and one by one, they slipped off unnoticed, merging seamlessly into the bustling morning crowds.

They had made it.

For now. They needed to stay concealed for the next 12 hours.

But the real battle was about to begin.

Even at night, the Iranian Intelligence Headquarters pulsed with activity. Iran's cyber operatives worked in shifts, analyzing foreign digital threats, countering cyber intrusions, and feeding misinformation into global intelligence networks.

The mission parameters were straightforward: infiltrate, sabotage, escape.

The plan was simple in theory, deadly in execution.

- Phase One: Priya Sharma infiltrates as an intelligence analyst using forged Mossad credentials.
- Phase Two: Robyn Chen overrides security feeds, giving the team a six-minute blind spot.
- Phase Three: Marcus, Carlos, and Douglass breach from the north, planting explosive charges and gathering intelligence.
- Phase Four: Extract Priya, disable Iranian cyber infrastructure, and disappear.

The timing had to be perfect. A single misstep, a wrong glance, a misplaced word, and they were dead.

But that was easier said than done.

Entry into the restricted zone required high-level clearance, meaning Priya was the key to the team.

To infiltrate, Mossad had created a flawless alias for her:

- Name: Dr. Laleh Farzan
- Position: Mid-ranking cyber-intelligence analyst assigned from Tehran's Central Intelligence Division.
- Clearance Level: High enough to access classified networks but not important enough to draw excessive scrutiny.

The forged credentials were impeccable, but even the best fake identities could crumble under the weight of one suspicious glance, one unexpected question.

Priya Sharma adjusted her hijab, her heart pounding in her chest. She had memorized every inch of the floor plan, every checkpoint, and every procedural phrase needed to convince Iranian security that she belonged.

She approached the main checkpoint with measured steps. Her ID badge — freshly fabricated by Mossad — felt like a ticking bomb in her pocket.

Two guards stood at the entrance, their Russian Kalashnikov AK-74s slung lazily across their chests. One of them, a thick-necked brute with a permanent scowl, stepped forward.

He took her ID and stared at it for a long moment, flipping it over twice.

"We weren't expecting an arrival from Tehran," he muttered, suspicion laced in his voice.

Priya kept her posture rigid, her Farsi clipped and authoritative. "You weren't informed because you don't have the proper security clearance for my assignment. Do I need to escalate this to your superior?"

The officer hesitated. His fingers hovered over his radio.

From his position, Douglass tensed. If Priya didn't clear this checkpoint in the next five seconds, he'd have no choice but to intervene.

Finally, the guard grunted and handed her credentials back. "Proceed."

She gave a curt nod and walked through the checkpoint — not too fast, not too slow, her heartbeat hammering against her ribs.

Inside, she exhaled softly. Phase One — complete.

The moment she disappeared inside, Douglass whispered into comms: "Priya's in. Phase two is live. Stand by."

Once inside, Priya didn't hesitate. She had memorized the floor plan from satellite imagery and internal blueprints provided by Mossad.

Objective One: Gain Access to the Cyber Operations Division area.

She moved quickly but purposefully, navigating the fluorescent-lit corridors lined with rows of computer terminals and security personnel hunched over monitors. She passed operatives typing out encrypted transmissions, their screens filled with strings of Farsi-laced code.

Each step felt heavier than the last. She was surrounded by some of the most dangerous cyber-intelligence experts in the world — men and women responsible for coordinating cyberattacks against the U.S., Israel, and Europe.

A single wrong move, and she would be caught in an instant.

She reached the restricted access hallway, where a biometric scanner blocked further entry.

Taking a breath, she swiped her fake clearance badge against the scanner.

For a moment, silence.

Then — a beep. The door unlocked.

Priya exhaled slowly and stepped inside, forcing herself not to react to the sight before her. Rows of Iranian cyber specialists sat at their terminals, fingers flying across keyboards as they coordinated cyberattacks, intercepted foreign intelligence, and manipulated disinformation campaigns.

Priya suppressed a shiver. These were the people responsible for nearly launching a war.

She moved toward her designated position, a secured terminal where she would insert the cyber-disruption device.

While Priya infiltrated, the rest of the team maneuvered into place.

Douglass, Marcus, Carlos, and Robyn had split up, weaving their way toward the designated entry point. They hugged the shadows, avoiding the roving patrols and strategically placed cameras.

Priya, crouched behind an unstaffed maintenance and security station, pulled out the compact Mossad hacking device and tapped into the security mainframe.

Her job? Override surveillance feeds, loop camera footage, and give the strike team a narrow six-minute window. Her job was simple but critical: override the building's security cameras, loop the footage, and create a six-minute blind spot for the team to move.

She tapped into Mossad's relay device, sending a silent override command into the system. Her hands were steady, her breathing controlled, but she felt the weight of the moment pressing against her ribs.

From her pocket, she pulled out the device Mossad had given her — a compact cyber-disruption tool that would access Iran's networks now and create a backdoor for future infiltrations.

She crouched by the server station, her fingers working fast to attach the device beneath the desk, out of sight.

A voice echoed from the sidewalk outside.

Priya froze.

Two Iranian security officers were talking just outside the door to the server room.

Her pulse spiked.

She could hear the rustle of uniforms and the clink of sidearms against holsters.

If they entered the server room on their rounds, it was over.

After what seemed like an eternity, the officers continued their rounds, talking about the upcoming weekend's soccer games.

Her fingers then danced over the interface, overriding firewalls, decrypting security protocols, and bypassing multi-layered Iranian encryption in real time.

Then — a soft chime. Success.

Robyn whispered into their comms, "We're in. The security cameras are looping. You've got six minutes."

Douglass didn't hesitate.

"Move. Now."

Inside and on the move, Priya moved toward the locked classified data terminal room containing the mainframe that housed Iran's classified cyberwarfare operations.

Near The Ministry of Intelligence of the Islamic Republic of Iran (MOIS)
Ozgol, Tajrish, Tehran Province, Iran
11:30 pm

The Iranian Intelligence Headquarters loomed ahead, a monolithic structure wrapped in layers of defenses. Even in the dead of night, the facility pulsed with activity, its floodlights casting eerie shadows across the high-perimeter walls. This was the nerve center of Iran's cyberwarfare program, and tonight, it was about to become ground zero.

Douglass crouched behind an abandoned construction vehicle, adjusting his night-vision optics to scan the outer perimeter. Four armed guards were at the primary checkpoint, and two more were on the eastern wall, with cameras rotating every ten seconds. The Ministry of Intelligence (MOIS) headquarters loomed ahead, an imposing structure of reinforced concrete and steel, its high perimeter walls lined with razor wire. The facility was the beating heart of Iran's cyberwarfare division, a fortress of state secrets, disinformation campaigns, and covert cyberattacks against the West.

Standing flat against the cold pavement beside him, Carlos Mejia exhaled slowly. "They don't play around."

Suppressed Glock in hand, Marcus Reed didn't look away from his scope. "That just makes this more fun."

This was the culmination of detailed planning, intelligence gathering, and relentless training by world-class experts — but it all came down to the next thirty minutes.

11:45 pm

Priya Sharma, disguised as Dr. Laleh Farzan, continued to move inside the compound with calculated confidence. She had spent years analyzing Iranian cyber operations from the safety of CIA offices, but now she was inside the belly of the beast, alone and exposed.

Her earpiece crackled to life, Douglass's voice calm but firm, "What's your situation?"

Priya immediately updated Douglass: "Checkpoint one at the side door is clear and unlocked. I'm heading to the security wing. The designated door on the side is unlocked for you. Get in here ASAP – you have less than six minutes now."

Priya adjusted her hijab, her heart pounding in her chest. She had memorized every inch of the floor plan, every checkpoint, and every procedural phrase needed to convince Iranian security that she belonged.

The disguise as a mid-ranking cyber-intelligence analyst from Tehran was good. Priya had entered using forged Mossad credentials — documents so flawlessly replicated that even seasoned Iranian intelligence officers couldn't detect them.

Her critical role justified the risk of including her on the strike team: bypass security, disable the alarms, and gain access to Iran's cyberwarfare servers. Without her, the team would never have made it inside.

From the alleyway, Douglass, Marcus Reed, Carlos Mejia, and Robyn Chen remained motionless, waiting for their opening. Every second mattered.

Marcus knelt beside Douglass, his Glock 19 equipped with a suppressor, eyes locked on the two armed guards stationed near the side entrance.

"We need to move now," Marcus muttered. "We're burning up our window, and if we wait too long, someone will notice Priya isn't on any rosters."

Carlos adjusted his rifle sling. "Got it. If things get loud, I'll make sure no one calls for backup."

Douglass took one last deep breath. Then they moved.

The north side service entrance was indeed their best way in — low traffic, minimal guards. Robyn had looped the security cameras for precisely seven minutes, granting them a razor-thin window.

As the strike team reached the maintenance door on the northern side of the facility, they slipped inside, weapons drawn.

Two guards patrolled the corridor ahead.

Marcus moved first — one silenced shot, one knife to the throat. The bodies never hit the floor.

A young Iranian guard, barely out of his teens, stood near the doorway nearby, his AK-74N slung lazily over his shoulder.

Marcus moved like a shadow, wrapping an arm around the guard's throat, cutting off both air and blood flow. The young man struggled briefly, then went limp in less than ten seconds. Marcus then quickly hogtied the guard with dental floss, an old-school ops standby when rope or tie wraps were not available.

Carlos dragged the unconscious body behind a parked supply truck, ensuring it remained out of sight.

"Keep moving," Douglass whispered, still just outside.

Inside, the hallways were eerily silent, the air thick with the scent of stale coffee, printer ink, and aged paper. The glow of fluorescent lights flickered above, casting a sterile, lifeless hue over the facility.

Robyn immediately pulled out her tablet, linking it to the network's internal schematics.

"Cyberwarfare servers are two floors down," she whispered. "Priya is already in place at the security console. She'll hold the doors for us."

Marcus checked his watch. "We need to move. Fast."

They navigated through the narrow corridors, keeping to the blind spots of security cameras. A pair of security officers stood near the server wing entrance, their weapons slung lazily at their sides, chatting in Farsi about the recent military buildup near Azerbaijan.

Carlos acted first.

He approached casually, speaking in broken Farsi. "Excuse me — where is the clearance office? My orders were changed at the last minute."

The guards turned to him, confused, their eyes narrowing.

Marcus struck.

A blade across the throat of the first guard, a swift sleeper hold on the second. One suppressed round for each from Douglass's Glock 19 ensured neither would be waking up.

The bodies were dragged into a supply closet, their radios silenced.

Robyn's voice came over the comms. "Security feeds are still looping. No alarms were triggered. Keep moving."

Priya met them and led them into a restricted-access stairwell, leading them toward the main cyberwarfare server room.

The server room was a fortress of encrypted intelligence, housing decades of classified Iranian cyberwarfare data.

Robyn slid into a terminal, her fingers quickly moving over the keyboard. She bypassed multi-layered encryption protocols and uploaded a worm into the mainframe.

"Give me sixty seconds," she whispered.

Meanwhile, Douglass scanned the glowing screens, searching for additional intelligence.

Then he saw it.

A classified file labeled "Contingency Plan AEGIS-2".

His stomach dropped.

Iran had a backup plan — a second deception designed to manipulate AEGIS again, creating a new crisis that would pit the U.S., China, and Russia against one another at an even higher level.

Douglass inserted a CIA data drive, copying the intelligence.

"We've got evidence that Iran wasn't going to stop," he muttered. "They had a contingency plan. This further proves their involvement in the earlier deception."

Carlos exhaled. "We should level this place twice over."

Marcus nodded toward Robyn. "How long?"

"Forty-five more seconds."

Carlos and Marcus set incendiary charges along the mainframe stacks. Once triggered, the thermite-based devices would burn at over 4,000 degrees, reducing everything to molten slag.

Marcus handed Douglass the detonator.

"One click, and Tehran won't have a cyberwarfare division anymore."

Priya's voice cut in, urgent.

"We've got movement outside my area. They're sending a patrol this way. You need to go. Now."

Robyn wiped their digital footprints, ensuring no logs remained.

Then — a distant voice shouted something in Farsi.

"STOP! Identify yourself!"

The facility had realized something was wrong.

Two security officers were approaching Priya.

Her pulse spiked. She kept her head down, pretending to type.

One of the men stopped near her. "Who are you?"

She turned slowly, face neutral. "Dr. Laleh Farzan, Tehran Central Intelligence. Who are you?"

The officer blinked, momentarily thrown off. "We don't have a - "

Marcus's silenced shot dropped the man before he could finish.

The second guard had just enough time to shout.

ALARMS BLARED.

"Shit".

The base erupted into chaos. Sirens wailed, red lights flashed, and security forces flooded the corridors.

"We're compromised!" Douglass barked.

"Run. Now!" Douglass ordered.

They bolted through the corridors, weapons drawn, adrenaline surging.

Priya and Marcus bolted for the exit, meeting the rest of the team at the rendezvous point.

Priya cursed. "Security doors are locking down. We have less than sixty seconds before we're trapped!"

Douglass led them toward the maintenance tunnels — their only way out.

Marcus covered the rear, gunning down approaching security forces with surgical precision.

They had seconds to escape before the entire compound was sealed.

As they reached the maintenance tunnel building exit, Marcus hurled a flashbang grenade down the hallway, blinding any pursuers.

Douglass pulled the detonator from his vest as they surfaced and reached a perimeter 100 feet away behind a neighboring building.

And then — a voice echoed through the outside PA system.

"Western infiltrators. Surrender, and you will live. Resist, and you will die."

Douglass gritted his teeth. "Not today."

He turned to Carlos and Marcus, their faces tense with adrenaline.

"Ready?"

Carlos grinned. "Light it up."

Douglass pressed the button.

A deafening explosion rocked the facility, sending a fireball through the windows. Flames erupted, consuming Iran's intelligence servers, classified documents, and every cyberwarfare operation they had ever built.

Continuing to move away from the area, Douglass and his team stopped and looked back to watch the destruction unfold. The building's collapse sent thick, black smoke billowing into the night sky.

"That's twenty years of intelligence work gone," Priya murmured.

Marcus exhaled. "And no one will ever know we were here."

Carlos watched the chaos below, nodding. "Sure hope so! Mission accomplished. Let's get the hell out of here."

Sirens blared as Iranian police and other security forces rushed toward the burning ruins, the team slipped away into the darkness, leaving nothing but flames and silence in their wake.

Day 18

Near the Building Ruins
The Ministry of Intelligence of the Islamic
Republic of Iran (MOIS)
Ozgol, Tajrish, Tehran Province, Iran
12:25 am

The distant glow of fire and smoldering rubble cast flickering shadows over the narrow alleyways of Ozgol. The Iranian Intelligence Headquarters was gone, reduced to a heap of twisted steel and burning concrete. Iran's entire cyberwarfare division had been wiped from existence in less than ten minutes.

But Scott Douglass and his strike team had no time to celebrate.

With each passing second, the Iranian military, security forces, and intelligence agencies scrambled to make sense of the catastrophe. It wouldn't take long before they locked down the entire city, and if the team was still within Tehran's borders when that happened, they were as good as dead.

Douglass led his team through the maze of alleyways, keeping to the shadows. Their movements were calculated and precise. Every breath was controlled, every step deliberate.

Carlos Mejia checked the magazine of his suppressed Kimber 1911 pistol, his sharp eyes scanning the alley behind them. "That explosion's gonna bring every security force in the country down on this place."

Marcus Reed, his suppressed Glock 17 raised, muttered, "Then let's make sure we're ghosts before they even realize we were here."

The plan was already in motion — an undercover Mossad asset was waiting at a secure rendezvous point just outside the district. From there, they would take Iran National Highway 59, a hazardous yet effective route to Chalus, an Iranian port city on the Caspian Sea.

The Mossad had hidden their escape vessel — a military-grade, high-speed craft — in an abandoned boatyard along the coast near Chalus. If they could reach it before sunrise, they had a chance. If not, the Iranian Revolutionary Guard Corps (IRGC) would shut down every road, airfield, and port.

Still clad in the stolen Iranian intelligence uniform, Priya Sharma pulled her headscarf tighter and adjusted her fake ID. "If we get stopped, I can try to talk our way out."

Douglass shook his head. "Only if we have no other choice. The moment they suspect anything, they'll detain us first and ask questions later. Keep moving."

The sound of distant sirens pierced the silence, a wailing alarm spreading through the city.

They were running out of time.

After twenty minutes of navigating the darkened back streets with their GPS unit, they reached an abandoned warehouse on the outskirts of Ozgol — the designated meet-up point.

The abandoned warehouse was eerily silent, the air thick with the acrid scent of oil and decaying wood. Somewhere in the distance, a train horn blared, barely audible over the increasing wail of sirens filling the city.

Marcus shifted his weight, scanning their surroundings. "Where the hell is our guy?" he muttered.

Carlos flexed his grip on his pistol. "We wait much longer, and someone's gonna find us here."

Priya adjusted her headscarf, keeping a calm demeanor, but her eyes flickered with unease. "Let's just hope the Iranians are too busy dealing with the explosion to start searching industrial districts."

Douglass glanced at his watch. Three minutes late. He didn't like it.

Then, headlights appeared in the distance — one vehicle. It slowed as it approached the designated meeting point, then stopped, engine running.

The tinted window rolled down just a fraction.

"Douglass?" came a voice.

Relief swept through the team, but Douglass kept his guard up. "Mossad?"

The driver smirked. "You need me to spell it out in Hebrew, or do you want to get the hell out of here?"

"Let's move," Douglass ordered, ushering the team into the SUV.

They piled into the SUV, the doors slamming shut as the vehicle accelerated onto a dirt road leading toward the highway north to Chalus.

"How bad is it?" Douglass asked.

The agent kept his eyes on the road. "Every military and intelligence agency in Iran is scrambling right now. They don't know exactly what happened yet, but they're treating this as an act of war."

Carlos grinned. "Good. That means they're panicking."

The agent shot him a deadpan look. "They're panicking now, but that won't last long. We need to get you to Chalus before sunrise, or we're in serious jeopardy. It's about a three-hour drive through the mountains — longer if we hit fog or checkpoints."

The black SUV rumbled down a deserted stretch of road, moving fast but not recklessly. They had to blend in — act like they belonged.

Then, up ahead, a flashing red light.

Marcus tensed. "Checkpoint. Two armed guards."

Carlos exhaled. "This wasn't on the map."

The Mossad agent kept his hands steady on the wheel. "We can't turn back. There's a military outpost a few kilometers behind us. If they see us reversing, we're done."

Priya quickly pulled out her forged Iranian credentials. "Let me handle it. If they ask, we're from Shiraz, heading north for a family emergency."

Douglass clenched his jaw. "If it goes south, we drop them fast. No hesitation."

The vehicle slowed as they reached the checkpoint. Two Iranian security officers approached, one with a flashlight and the other loosely gripping his rifle.

The Mossad agent rolled down the window.

"Where are you headed?" the guard asked in clipped Farsi.

Priya leaned forward, her voice trembling slightly — just enough to sound authentic. "My father is very ill in Chalus. We need to reach him before sunrise. Please, officer, I beg you."

The guard narrowed his eyes, scanning the passengers.

Douglass held his breath.

Then —

The second officer muttered something about their IDs being in order.

A slow, agonizing moment passed.

Then, the first guard grunted. "Go."

The SUV rolled forward.

Nobody spoke for the next ten minutes. Then Carlos let out a low whistle. "Remind me to buy you a drink, Priya."

She grinned. "Just doing my job."

After a little over two hours, the Mossad agent pulled the SUV to a stop under a rock overhang, shielding them from drones and aerial surveillance.

"From here, we switch to something less obvious," he said.

He opened a hidden gate, revealing a battered cargo truck with faded Iranian markings.

Inside, traditional Iranian worker clothing sets were neatly folded.

"This is where I leave you. This road will get you through Chalus," the agent explained. "Blend in. Keep your heads down. Don't speak unless spoken to."

Carlos examined the truck's peeling paint and rusted exterior. "This thing better not break down on us."

The agent grinned. "If it does, run. Good luck."

Without another word, he stepped into the SUV and disappeared into the desert.

By the time the team reached Chalus, dawn was beginning to creep over the horizon. The Caspian Sea stretched before them in a deep, restless expanse of black water.

Douglass stared out at the black expanse of the Caspian Sea, where faint, shifting lights in the distance signaled Iranian naval patrols sweeping the coastline. The wind carried the scent of salt and diesel fuel, and the tension in his gut tightened.

They had survived Tehran. They had erased Iran's cyberwarfare division from existence.

But now, they were about to step into another battlefield — one where they couldn't outrun or hide if things went sideways.

They uncovered a military-grade speedboat inside a rusting warehouse, its triple motors glistening even in the darkened warehouse. Robyn exhaled, running a hand over the equipment. "The Israelis really don't mess around."

Marcus grinned. "They want us out of Iran as much as we do."

Carlos hopped out first, moving toward the speedboat. He pulled back the tarp and inspected the engines. The fuel tanks are full, but someone has tampered with the fuel line.

Marcus cursed. "We were compromised."

"Can you fix it?" Douglass demanded.

Carlos yanked out a roll of duct tape from his pack and sealed the damaged line. "It'll hold."

A sudden noise — voices.

Douglass spun toward the shoreline, spotting a small group of Iranian dock workers moving toward them.

"Damn," Robyn whispered. "We need to go."

They scrambled into the boat as Carlos fired up the engines. The vessel roared to life, cutting through the water just as the dock workers reached the pier's edge.

An alarm rang out from a nearby watchtower.

"Too late," Marcus growled.

Gunfire cracked through the air as the first bullets whizzed past.

Carlos pushed the throttle forward. "Hang on!"

The speedboat tore through the waves, leaving a frothy wake behind it as it raced toward the open sea.

In the distance, searchlights flickered along the coastline.

"Now they'll be coming for us," Priya murmured.

Douglass adjusted his grip on his rifle. "Then we just have to make sure they don't catch us."

As the Iranian patrol boats scrambled to mobilize, the team sped toward the dark expanse of the Caspian Sea — toward freedom or a watery grave. The speedboat's engines roared as they left the shore, and a distant spotlight swept across the water.

Carlos muttered, "Tell me that's not what I think it is."

Priya's voice was barely audible. "Iranian patrols. They're already searching."

Douglass exhaled, gripping his weapon tightly.

"Then we'd better disappear before they find us."

Offshore, Caspian Sea Waters
Nea Chalus, Iran
4:45 am

The howling wind ripped across the churning black waters of the Caspian Sea, biting through every layer of clothing as Scott Douglass adjusted his night-vision goggles and peered into the abyss ahead. The Iranian coastline was a jagged silhouette in the distant rear, fading fast — but not fast enough.

He knew better than to think they were in the clear. Iranian patrol boats would be coming soon, and if they were spotted, there would be no negotiations, no trial — just a bullet and an unmarked grave at the bottom of the sea.

Priya Sharma double-checked their waterproof bags a few feet away, ensuring the satellite phones, encrypted comms, explosives, and weapons were secure. Her fingers trembled slightly — not from the cold, but from the weight of what lay ahead.

Offshore, Caspian Sea Waters
Chalus, Iran to Baku, Azerbaijan
5:15 am

The wind howled over the dark waters of the Caspian Sea, carrying the salty sting of the sea and the ever-present bite of the frigid morning air. The boat, a low-profile, triple-engine, military-grade vessel, cut through the waves like a phantom, barely visible against the endless black expanse. Every movement was calculated, and every decision was a matter of life or death.

Douglass crouched near the bow, peering through his night-vision goggles at the horizon. The coastline behind them was now a shadowy smear, barely distinguishable from the dark water. But they were far from safe.

They were still in Iranian waters.

"Fifty-five kilometers to Azerbaijani waters," Robyn whispered, eyes locked on the glowing GPS tablet in her hands. "That's all that separates us from safety."

Marcus, gripping the tiller, barely looked up. His knuckles were white with tension. "Fifty-five kilometers of freezing water, Iranian patrol boats, and Russian radar. A walk in the park."

Carlos exhaled sharply, tightening his grip on his HK416 rifle. "Yeah, except we don't have the luxury of walking."

The plan was straightforward on paper: cross the Caspian under the cover of darkness, avoiding Iranian and Russian patrols, and follow an encrypted NNW GPS route for 440 kilometers toward a remote landing zone near Baku. Once ashore, CIA and Mossad assets would extract them to a private terminal at Heydar Aliyev International Airport in Baku, where a covert flight to a U.S. Airbase in Turkey awaited.

But the Caspian had a reputation.

A reputation for swallowing ships whole.

A reputation for never giving up the bodies.

And something about the night felt wrong.

Offshore, Caspian Sea Waters
Midway Across the Caspian Sea
5:30 am

The sea turned against them without warning.

A brutal gust of wind slammed into the vessel, sending freezing sheets of rain over the team. The craft rocked violently, the starboard side dipping into the water before leveling out. The sudden shift nearly sent Priya overboard, her small frame thrown sideways.

"Hold on!" Marcus barked, fighting the tiller with every ounce of strength he had.

Priya clung to the side of the boat, her knuckles bone-white. "What the hell —?"

Carlos reached out, gripping Priya's arm just as she was about to lose her balance. "Got you!"

The waves surged, rolling in unpredictable swells. The boat lurched and pitched as if being tossed by an invisible hand.

Carlos cursed, grabbing onto a secured rope for balance. "This storm wasn't in the damn forecast!"

Douglass braced against the side, his mind racing. They couldn't afford delays.

Robyn wiped the saltwater from her face, her fingers trembling as she checked the GPS tablet. "Shit. The wind is pushing us off course toward Turkmenistan waters in the east!"

"Marcus, keep us steady!" Douglass ordered. "Keep an eye on our heading!"

Douglass gritted his teeth.

East meant Russian radar zones and patrols.

Neither was a good option.

On the Caspian Sea
Near Azerbaijani Waters
5:45 am

Priya froze, her head snapping toward the darkness beyond the boat.

"Wait... engines."

The words sent a jolt of electricity through the team.

Every muscle in the team's body went rigid.

Douglass immediately raised his thermal scope and scanned the void.

A faint heat signature emerged.

Low on the southern horizon.

A patrol boat.

Moving toward them.

Fast.

"Son of a —" Carlos exhaled sharply, his hand instinctively moving to his rifle.

"It's a patrol boat, probably Russian out this far from shore," Marcus muttered through gritted teeth.

"Kill the motor," Douglass ordered. "Now."

Robyn's finger jabbed the emergency kill switch, and the outboard engine fell silent.

The team drifted, their craft now just a dark, black silhouette among rolling waves.

The patrol boat's rumbling diesel engine grew louder.

Priya, her face half-hidden by a soaked scarf, muttered, "If they see us, we're dead. If they get too close, I can radio a false order in Farsi and make them think we're Iranian."

Douglass shook his head. "Too risky. If they demand authentication, we're screwed."

The team held their breath, hearts hammering, as the patrol boat inched closer.

It was close enough now that they could barely make out a crew — four men with rifles strapped across their chests scanning the water with spotlights.

One wrong move and it was over.

The spotlight beam swept across the waves.

Closer.

Closer.

It passed just meters away from them.

Then, a distant radio transmission crackled to life inside the patrol boat.

The boat veered away.

They hadn't been seen.

The diesel engine faded into the distance, swallowed by the sea.

Only when the sound disappeared entirely did Douglass allow himself to breathe.

"We got lucky. Thank God for rain and fog."

Carlos exhaled. "Let's not push our luck."

Douglass pressed the restart switch, and the motor purred back to life.

Marcus throttled up, and the team resumed a corrected course for Azerbaijan.

But Douglass couldn't shake the feeling.

Something wasn't right.

They had escaped the patrol, but something deep in his gut told him it wasn't over.

Then — Robyn's eyes widened as she looked at the GPS tablet.

"Uh... guys?"

Douglass turned sharply. "What?"

Robyn's face drained of color. "We're still not alone out here."

Marcus cursed. "What the hell does that mean?"

Robyn flipped the screen around —

Two unknown vessels were moving fast.

From the southwest.

Iranian?

Russian?

Carlos gritted his teeth. "Could be either."

Douglass's blood went cold as he felt his stomach drop.

They had barely escaped the first patrol. If these boats spotted them —

They had nowhere to run.

"We need to change course," Robyn whispered. "Now."

Marcus didn't hesitate. "Hold on!"

He cranked the tiller hard, veering them northwest, cutting parallel to the storm in a desperate gamble to break radar contact.

The worst of the journey was supposed to be behind them.

But the Caspian Sea had other plans.

A storm cell had materialized just north of their position, a swirling vortex of slate-gray clouds, churning waves, and erratic gusts that threatened to capsize their craft. There was no turning back, no time to reroute — they had to push through.

Rain hammered the deck.

The wind howled.

The boat lurched violently over the waves.

Marcus Reed, gripping the tiller, shouted over the roaring wind. "We either go through it or turn back!"

Douglass didn't hesitate. "Turning back isn't an option! Hold course!"

The next wave slammed into them like a wrecking ball, tilting the craft hard to port. Cold seawater rushed over the bow, sloshing against their boots as the wind shrieked through the open sea, throwing salty spray into their faces like a barrage of needles.

Carlos braced himself against the side rail, his teeth clenched. "We're taking on too much water!"

Priya Sharma, her fingers death-gripping a metal support beam, gasped. "If we get hit broadside by one more wave —"

Another towering wall of water crashed down.

Soaked and shivering, Robyn Chen wiped the spray from her eyes, her voice barely audible over the wind. "If we slow down, we lose momentum!"

Marcus fought the tiller, eyes glued to the compass before him, muscles straining to keep the craft from veering off course. "Then we keep going, full throttle!"

After what seemed like an eternity, the radar signals slowly disappeared. The object now was to stay afloat, stay on course in a blinding rainstorm, and reach the objective alive.

After a frantic couple of hours, still in freezing rain, Douglass checked their GPS bearings — they were just twenty kilometers from shore.

Twenty more kilometers to safety. They were in Azerbaijani waters – all they had to do was stay afloat. But twenty kilometers felt like a thousand when the sea wanted you dead.

Carlos grabbed a plastic bail bucket, frantically tossing gallons of seawater over the side.

Priya, shaking from the cold, turned toward Douglass. "How much longer?"

"About 30-45 minutes, I think. We're in Azerbaijani waters, but if they see us, they will pursue us regardless. We push through," Douglass ordered.

No one argued.

They had no other choice.

The following half-hour was a blur of howling wind, driving rain, and sheer, white-knuckled survival. The craft lurched over cresting waves, the engine sputtering as saltwater sprayed in every direction.

And then —

A break in the storm.

Through the haze, the faint outline of Azerbaijan's coastline appeared, and a ghostly strip of land appeared in the distance.

Carlos, blinking saltwater from his eyes, gasped. "Land ho!"

Marcus let out a sharp breath, pushing the engine to its limit. "Let's get off this boat!"

Remote Landing Zone
Near Baku, Azerbaijan
12:30 pm

The craft scraped against the wet sand, its metal hull grinding over the beach as it came to an abrupt halt. Before it had even fully stopped, Douglass and his team leaped overboard into waist-deep, ice-cold water. The Caspian had not been kind to them; the brutal crossing had left them drenched, battered by waves, and utterly exhausted.

Carlos Mejia and Marcus Reed slogged through the freezing surf, dragging their supply bags onto the shore. Their boots sank into the damp, unstable terrain. The storm from the previous night had left the beach covered in seaweed and debris, adding yet another obstacle to their extraction.

Robyn collapsed onto the sand, arms spread wide as she gasped for breath. Never want to do that again. Ever! "

Priya Sharma shook violently, her hijab soaked and clinging to her skin. She wrapped her arms around herself, her teeth chattering. "If I never see the Caspian Sea again, it'll be too soon."

Douglass barely heard them. His attention was already on the distant dunes, where a barely visible dirt road wound into the vast emptiness beyond. This was their extraction point, but it was too quiet.

Something was wrong.

They had made it to Azerbaijan.

But they weren't quite safe yet.

Marcus wiped saltwater from his face and raised his binoculars, scanning the terrain. "Where's our pickup?"

Carlos squinted against the sun. They should have been here already.

The wind carried nothing but the sound of crashing waves. The agreed-upon signal — three short flashes of headlights from a waiting SUV — was nowhere to be seen.

Then, movement.

As if on cue, a pair of headlights flickered from beyond the dunes, the faint hum of an approaching vehicle cutting through the heavy silence.

Carlos and Douglass immediately raised their rifles, hearts pounding as the SUVs emerged from the dust.

"Finally," Carlos muttered, tightening his grip on the rifle.

But Douglass wasn't convinced. Something about the approach felt wrong. The vehicle was moving too fast.

The SUV crested the ridge, kicking up a plume of dust, and barreled toward them.

Marcus's voice was tight. "That's not a Mossad driver."

"Get cover. Now!" Douglass barked.

The team scattered, diving behind dunes, rusted shipping containers, and driftwood as the vehicle skidded to a stop fifty yards away. The driver's side door flung open, and a man in civilian clothes stumbled out, hands raised.

"Help!" he shouted in Farsi. "They're coming!"

Carlos had his rifle raised before Douglass could stop him. "Who the hell is this?"

The man staggered closer, his breath ragged. His clothes were torn, his face streaked with sweat and dirt.

"They found me," he panted. "They know—"

A gunshot rang out.

The man's body jerked violently before he crumpled onto the sand.

"Sniper!" Marcus shouted, flattening himself against a dune.

More gunfire erupted from the dunes behind them. Suppressed rounds kicked up sand just inches from Douglass's boots.

"Go! Move!"

They scrambled, dragging Priya and Robyn toward the nearest cover as bullets stitched across the beach.

Carlos returned fire, his suppressed Kimber barking short, controlled blasts. Marcus joined him, his Glock snapping off rounds toward the ridgeline.

Douglass yanked Robyn behind a rusted metal crate, his mind racing. "How the hell did they find us?"

Priya's voice was shaky. "That guy... he was part of our extraction, wasn't he?"

"He was compromised," Douglass snapped. "We've got to move. Now!"

Carlos ducked down next to them, his breathing heavy. "We're cut off. The road's blocked. We need another way out."

Douglass grabbed his radio and tried the emergency channel. "Shadow One, this is Ghost. Come in!"

Static.

Then—

A crackled reply. "Ghost, this is Shadow One. We see the ambush. Hold position. ETA two minutes."

Marcus gritted his teeth. "Two minutes is a long damn time in a firefight."

Another round of gunfire forced them lower. Douglass peeked over the crate, spotting three armed men repositioning along the ridge. If they flanked the team, this would be over fast.

"Marcus, Carlos — take them out!"

The two operatives moved like predators, slipping through the sand and angling toward the shooters.

A tense, heart-pounding minute later, three suppressed gunshots rang out.

Silence.

Then — headlights.

A second SUV roared over the ridge, this one moving with purpose.

Marcus and Carlos rushed back just as the vehicle skidded to a stop.

"Get in!"

They piled inside, slamming the doors shut as the SUV lurched forward.

A voice from the front seat — gravelly, pissed off.

"Jesus Christ, you people really know how to make an entrance."

Douglass turned to see a bearded man gripping the wheel.

"Relax, amigos," the driver said, his voice thick with amusement. "Welcome to Azerbaijan."

The tension in Douglass's shoulders eased slightly.

"You have no idea how happy I am to hear that," Douglass muttered, finally lowering his weapon.

The lead operative — a broad-shouldered man with deep-set eyes and a grizzled beard — approached. "We need to move. Now. You stirred up a hornet's nest in Iran."

Marcus smirked. "You're welcome."

The operative didn't smile. "Tehran issued a fatwa - a kill order - on all of you four hours ago."

Priya's breath hitched. "What?"

"Every intelligence unit, border guard, and paramilitary cell in Iran is looking for you. We're expecting Iran to pressure Azerbaijan to detain anyone suspicious. That means your extraction has a tight window."

Douglass nodded sharply. "Then let's not waste time. We need hot showers and dry clothes as soon as possible.

Carlos glanced over his shoulder, watching the coastline disappear behind them.

"So that's it?" he muttered. We drive to the airport and go home?

Robyn, still pale from the Caspian ordeal, scoffed. "When has it ever been that easy?"

Marcus leaned forward, voice low. "It's not."

Douglass could feel it, too.

Something wasn't right.

Then, as if confirming his worst fears, the driver's radio crackled to life.

"We have a problem. The Azerbaijanis just locked down the airport."

A cold silence fell over the SUV.

Priya's voice was barely a whisper. You mean we're trapped?

The operative in the passenger seat exhaled slowly. "Tehran wants you dead. The Azerbaijanis don't want a war, and they won't risk angering Iran."

Marcus's hand tightened around his sidearm. "So what's the move?"

The lead operative turned onto a deserted back road, his eyes flicking to Douglass in the rearview mirror.

"We improvise."

CIA Safehouse
Baku, Azerbaijan
2:00 pm

The CIA safehouse in Baku was anonymity itself — a two-story cement block nestled between rusting warehouses and abandoned industrial lots in the gritty outskirts of Baku. There were no signs, no security cameras, nothing to suggest that the most covert U.S. intelligence operation in years was regrouping behind its reinforced steel doors.

Inside, the air was thick with exhaustion, tension, and the lingering scent of saltwater and sweat. Scott Douglass sat at the head of a scuffed wooden conference table, freshly showered and outfitted in new clothes. His team — Carlos Mejia, Priya Sharma, Marcus Reed, and Robyn Chen — were also showered with new clothing but slumped in chairs around him, nursing bottles of lukewarm water and trying to shake off the last vestiges of the cold and the adrenaline crash.

They had managed to escape Iran.

Barely.

Across from them, CIA handler David Stokes and Mossad intelligence chief Yaron Malek observed them in calm, calculated silence.

Stokes, a grizzled field operative with tired eyes and a permanent five o'clock shadow, broke the quiet first. "You all look like hell."

Carlos gave a tired smirk, rubbing his bruised ribs. "Feels about right."

Stokes nodded, then pulled out a classified report from his leather satchel. We have just received an update from our contacts in Tehran. The Iranians are keeping this under wraps. They've locked down the site, rounded up a half-dozen of their own intelligence officers as scapegoats, and issued no public statements. They don't want the world to know that their entire cyberwarfare division has just turned to ash.

Robyn raised an eyebrow. "So... they're just pretending it didn't happen?"

Malek, a tall, lean Mossad operative with piercing gray eyes, nodded. "It's a matter of pride. If Iran admitted that a covert team wiped out their intelligence headquarters, they'd lose face — especially with Russia and China watching. They can't afford to look weak. They will bury this, and that's good for us."

Douglass exhaled, rubbing his temples. "That means we did our job. Iran's cyber capabilities are at least two decades behind. They'll have to rebuild from the ground up."

Still feeling the lingering ache from the grueling escape, Priya leaned in. "What about AEGIS? We stopped the attack this time, but it could happen again unless we change the system."

Stokes's expression darkened. "That's exactly what Washington is scrambling to figure out. But first, we need to get you out of here."

CIA Safehouse
Baku, Azerbaijan
7:30 pm

The safehouse's underground armory was a sprawling, dimly lit chamber, its walls lined with covert weapons caches, encrypted radios, and classified dossiers. As the team prepared for extraction, they cleaned and lubed their mission gear, changed into civilian clothes, and reviewed their escape route.

Marcus winced as he stretched, some residual soreness from the parachute landing into Iran still fresh. "Alright, what's the route home?"

Avi Malek unrolled a regional map across the metal table.

"You'll be moved in stages — first, a low-profile flight from Baku to Incirlik Air Base in Turkey. From there, a government jet will take you back to Washington under classified orders. By the time your boots hit U.S. soil, this mission will be so deeply buried in black ink that it won't exist."

Carlos grinned. "Just how I like it."

Douglass wasn't as relieved. "And when we land back home?"

Stokes tapped a finger against the map's edge, his expression unreadable. "That depends on how President Clark reacts to your debrief. He's going to want every detail on how Iran pulled this off — and how we make sure AEGIS can't be used against us again."

Priya folded her arms. "If Clark has any sense, he'll leave AEGIS offline until we can rebuild its security protocols. Otherwise, it's only a matter of time before someone else tries this again."

Douglass nodded slowly. They had completed the mission and escaped Iran.

But the real fight was just beginning.

The two SUVs moved through the narrow back streets of Baku like shadows slipping through the cracks of a city that had learned to live with secrets. The roads were quiet, dimly lit by scattered streetlights that flickered against the creeping darkness. In the lead vehicle, Scott Douglass sat beside their Azerbaijani driver, his hand resting on his concealed Glock, his eyes scanning every alley, every car, and every rooftop. There was no room for complacency now. Not when they were this close to extraction.

In the second vehicle, Marcus Reed kept his own eyes locked on the side mirrors, watching for tails. He'd check his Glock every few minutes, an old habit he couldn't shake. "Something doesn't feel right," he muttered under his breath.

Seated in the back of the lead SUV, Carlos Mejia leaned forward, his voice a low murmur. "You sure the airport's clear?"

David Stokes, the grizzled CIA station chief riding shotgun, didn't turn his head as he answered. "As clear as we can make it. Azerbaijan wants no part of this fight, but that doesn't mean they won't sell us out if the price is right. We need to be in the air before someone in their government second-guesses whether we're worth the risk."

Carlos gritted his teeth, his grip tightening on his pistol. "So we're running on borrowed time."

"More like rented," Stokes replied grimly.

In the second vehicle, Priya Sharma pulled her hijab a little tighter, trying to blend in, even if the tension in her shoulders said otherwise. She knew they were almost out, but that didn't mean they were safe. Not yet. "What's our backup plan if the airport's compromised?" she asked, her voice steady but low.

"We don't have one," Marcus admitted. "If something goes sideways, we improvise."

Priya exhaled sharply. "Great. I love improvising in hostile countries."

The driver of the lead SUV, a Mossad asset known as "Amin," took a sharp left turn down an unmarked road. His grip was steady, but his eyes flickered nervously to the rearview mirror. "We might have a problem," he muttered in Azerbaijani.

Douglass caught the change in tone instantly. "What do you see?"

"Dark-colored sedan. Three cars back. No headlights. They've been behind us for the last five turns."

"Could be nothing," Carlos muttered, but he was already shifting, angling for a clean shot if needed.

Marcus's voice crackled through the comms. "We've got the same tail."

Stokes exhaled through his nose. "If they make a move, we don't stop. We push through."

The next few minutes seemed to stretch on like hours. The vehicles weaved through the industrial outskirts of Baku, the air thick with tension. Then, just as they neared the final stretch leading to the airstrip, the black sedan suddenly gunned its engine.

"They're coming," Amin warned, gripping the wheel tighter.

The sedan surged forward, closing the gap. Another vehicle — a dark SUV with tinted windows — turned onto their road from the right, blocking their path.

"Ambush!" Douglass shouted.

Amin reacted instantly, slamming the brakes just before the SUV could cut them off, causing the vehicle to skid into a controlled turn. The second SUV, driven by Marcus, followed suit, stopping just short of a collision.

The doors of the sedan and SUV flew open, and four armed men spilled out of the sedan, rifles raised. Their stance was professional, not just hired muscle.

"IRGC, the Iranian Guard," Stokes growled.

Marcus didn't hesitate. He threw open his door, taking cover behind it as he leveled his Glock. "We're in this now!"

Gunfire erupted.

Amin cursed and slammed the accelerator, wrenching the wheel to the side. The SUV surged forward, clipping one of the gunmen and sending him sprawling. Carlos fired through the open window, hitting another in the chest.

Douglass kicked his door open, dropped to a knee, and squeezed off three precise shots. One assailant crumpled. Another ducked behind their SUV.

Marcus covered their six, his weapon coughing as he laid down suppressive fire.

"Get to the plane!" Douglass ordered.

Priya and Robyn bolted from the second SUV, ducking low as bullets ricocheted off the asphalt from the remaining shooter. Carlos grabbed a smoke grenade from his vest, yanked the pin, and hurled it toward the ambusher. A thick, white cloud billowed out, swallowing the street in chaos.

Amin didn't wait for the all-clear. He threw the SUV into drive and surged forward, forcing the remaining gunman to dive for cover.

"Move, move, move!" Marcus shouted.

They sprinted toward the airstrip.

The Gulfstream 550 sat on the tarmac, engines humming. The pilot had been alerted to the gunfire and was already preparing for emergency takeoff. The back hatch was open, a CIA operative waving frantically for them to board.

Below, another sedan with IRGC reinforcements poured onto the airfield, their rifles flashing in the darkness. Bullets pinged against the toughened fuselage, but the jet was already lifting off, ascending into the night sky before they could bring out anything heavier.

Douglass reached the ramp first, spun around, and covered the others as they sprinted up. Carlos leaped inside, dragging Priya and Robyn with him. Marcus fired one last burst before diving through the hatch.

"Go! Go now!" Stokes barked at the pilot.

The aircraft lurched forward, tires screeching against the tarmac.

Inside, the team collapsed against the seats, breathing hard.

Carlos ran a hand through his sweat-drenched hair. "That was a warm send-off."

Priya gave him a look. "If that was warm, I don't want to know what hot feels like."

Stokes unbuckled his tactical vest and exhaled. "The IRGC knew we were coming. Someone tipped them off."

Douglass looked out the small, blacked-out window as the lights of Baku disappeared beneath them. His jaw clenched.

"We'll deal with that when we land," he said.

No one spoke after that.

They weren't safe yet.

Not by a long shot.

Day 19

One thousand twenty-five miles later, the Gulfstream 550 touched down on the dimly lit runway of Incirlik Air Base, its wheels screeching against the tarmac as it rolled toward a restricted military hangar. Outside, the Turkish night was thick with humidity, the faint sound of distant aircraft engines humming through the still air.

The landing at Incirlik Air Base, home to the U.S. Air Force's 39th Air Base Wing, was as routine as a highly classified black-ops return could be. The tarmac was nearly empty except for a small contingent of military personnel — briefed strictly on a need-to-know basis — waiting to escort the team into the secure operations wing.

A black SUV with diplomatic plates idled on the tarmac, its headlights slicing through the darkness like a silent predator waiting for its prey.

Scott Douglass unbuckled his harness inside the aircraft, his muscles aching from the tension that had never entirely dissipated since their escape from Iran. His team followed suit — Carlos Mejia, Priya Sharma, Marcus Reed, and Robyn Chen — all moving with the quiet efficiency of seasoned operatives, but their exhaustion was undeniable.

The moment the hatch opened, a tall, broad-shouldered man in a dark suit stepped inside. His sharp, assessing gaze swept over them, and his face was unreadable, a mask of controlled urgency.

"Douglass. Mejia. Sharma. Reed. Chen. You're coming with me." His tone left no room for discussion.

Douglass exchanged a wary glance with Marcus. "What's going on?"

The handler didn't answer.

"Orders from Langley. You're being redirected."

Priya frowned. "Redirected where?"

The handler gestured toward the SUV. "Get in. Now."

Carlos muttered under his breath. "This just keeps getting better."

They stepped off the aircraft and into a situation they couldn't yet see.

As the vehicle sped down the deserted tarmac, Douglass felt the sinking weight of something more than exhaustion.

Their mission might have ended in Iran.

But Washington's war over AEGIS was only beginning.

The air inside the classified underground briefing room was stale and tense. The walls were steel gray and bare, except for a single digital monitor flickering with encrypted data streams. A small red light blinked ominously at the base of the screen.

The air was thick with exhaustion, but there was no time for rest. The moment they stepped inside the secure facility, they were directed toward an underground briefing room — the kind reserved for the highest-level national security discussions.

Inside, the walls were bare except for a large digital monitor mounted at the far end of the room. A small red light blinked at the base of the screen.

A secure video call was already waiting.

The team barely had time to sit before the screen came to life, revealing the hardened face of CIA Director Evelyn Harrington.

Harrington was a leader who had seen it all — a seasoned spymaster with steel-gray hair, a permanently furrowed brow, and an expression that rarely betrayed emotion. But right now, her face was unreadable, her sharp gaze locked onto Douglass as the team took their seats.

"Scott."

Douglass straightened his posture. "Ma'am. We're en route back to Washington. The mission was a success."

Harrington gave a short nod. "We're already seeing the fallout. Iran is scrambling. They've detained half their intelligence division trying to explain what happened."

She paused. Moscow and Beijing are, to say the least, confused. They're both wondering if we just took a shot at Iran or if Iran somehow managed to implode on its own."

Robyn Chen, their cyberwarfare expert, crossed her arms. "And AEGIS?"

Harrington's expression darkened slightly. "Temporarily shut down. We've locked external data feeds until we can assess all vulnerabilities."

Robyn's eyebrows lifted in genuine surprise. "Did they actually pull the plug?"

"Temporarily," Harrington clarified. "And not without a fight. The Pentagon is furious. They see AEGIS as a cornerstone of U.S. cyber defense, and they want it back online immediately."

She exhaled sharply. "That's why you need to get here as soon as possible. The President wants you at Fort Meade by 9:00 a.m. tomorrow.

Priya Sharma, their linguistics and intelligence specialist, let out a slow breath. "That means we have less than twenty-four hours to convince the most powerful people in the world that AEGIS is a ticking time bomb."

Harrington gave a knowing sigh. "That's about the size of it."

Douglass nodded, already calculating the next moves. "Understood, ma'am. We'll be on a transport flight within the hour."

The screen went dark, leaving the room in thick, heavy silence.

Carlos Mejia leaned back in his chair, cracking his knuckles. "Tomorrow's going to be interesting."

Marcus Reed, the former Army Ranger, turned CIA paramilitary officer, shook his head. "Yeah. Because convincing the President to keep AEGIS offline won't be a fight at all."

The classified military transport plane cruised at 37,000 feet, the engines humming beneath the weight of exhaustion in the cabin.

Douglass sat by the reinforced window, staring at the endless blue horizon.

Behind him, Carlos and Marcus played a silent game of chess on a makeshift tablet screen. Neither man spoke, and both were lost in thought.

Priya had her headphones on, listening to a Farsi-language intercept from Iranian radio traffic, trying to piece together any chatter about their escape.

Robyn typed furiously on her NSA-issued laptop, running simulations on the newest cyberwarfare threats — anything to stay ahead of whatever nightmare scenario AEGIS's failure might bring.

Nobody spoke about what awaited them in Washington.

Nobody had to.

They all knew.

This wasn't over.

Not by a long shot.

Day 20

**Classified Landing Area
Joint Base Andrews, Maryland
5:50 pm**

The Gulfstream 550 descended through the thick, gray cloud cover, slicing through the cold evening air as it approached the tarmac of Joint Base Andrews. The aircraft had taken off from Incirlik Air Base in Turkey more than twelve hours earlier, carrying the team in complete radio silence across the Atlantic. There had been no direct flight plan, official communications, or paper trail.

No press.

No records.

No mission.

At least, not officially.

To the world, the passengers on board didn't exist. This mission — everything they had done and risked — had already been erased from history.

Douglass felt the subtle jolt as the wheels touched down, a smooth landing executed with military precision. He exhaled slowly, the tightness in his chest refusing to ease. They were home. But the relief was fleeting. The real war — the war that couldn't be fought with bullets, explosives, or covert sabotage — was about to begin.

As the aircraft taxied toward a restricted section of the base, Douglass glanced around at his team. Carlos Mejia, his infiltration expert, rolled his shoulders, shifting uncomfortably in his seat. Priya Sharma, their intelligence and language specialist, had her arms crossed, deep in thought. Marcus Reed, the team's ground commander, had his usual steel-eyed focus, already mentally preparing for the next fight. And Robyn Chen, the cyberwarfare specialist, tapped absently against her knee, staring out at the looming silhouette of the Pentagon officials waiting on the tarmac.

The aircraft came to a complete stop. A cold, biting wind rushed into the cabin as the hatch opened. Six armed Air Force Security Forces personnel stood at the bottom of the staircase, flanking a line of waiting SUVs. The uniforms weren't standard issues. These weren't just military personnel. These were intelligence escorts — handlers.

From the center SUV, a woman stepped forward, her sharp gray suit and deep-set eyes radiating authority. CIA Director Evelyn Harrington.

Harrington's expression was unreadable, but Douglass didn't miss the flicker of approval beneath her typically cold exterior.

"Welcome back," Harrington said simply. Her gaze swept over the team, assessing them the way a general examines returning soldiers. "Congratulations on a successful mission."

Douglass didn't hesitate. The Iranian intelligence hub in Ozgol is no longer operational. Their cyberwarfare division has been reduced to dust. Their infrastructure is unrecoverable."

Harrington gave a tight nod, her jaw clenched as though calculating the next steps. "And AEGIS?"

Douglass exchanged a glance with Robyn. Compromised to a greater extent than initially suspected. The Iranians weren't just infiltrating. They were in the process of replicating an AI-based intelligence deception system. If we hadn't stopped them —"

"—They would have weaponized it against us on a scale we've never seen before," Harrington finished, her voice grave. "Understood. The President is anxious to meet you at Fort Meade in the morning."

Marcus exhaled sharply. "Straight to the wolves, then?"

Evelyn smirked, but there was no humor in her eyes. "You just took out the most dangerous cyber threat Iran ever produced. But now, you have to convince the most powerful people in Washington that the next attack won't be a hoax — it'll be real."

The urgency in her voice was impossible to ignore.

Harrington gestured toward the SUVs. "Let's get you home."

The convoy sped down I-495 toward Virginia, the unmarked black SUVs weaving seamlessly through traffic, escorted by two unmarked Department of Defense vehicles. The operation was locked down — no comms or open radio transmissions. If anyone outside this convoy knew what had happened in Iran, they weren't talking.

Priya watched the passing cityscape, her fingers tightening into fists. "What happens if the President doesn't listen?"

"Then we just destroyed an enemy cyber network for nothing," Carlos muttered, his tone edged with frustration. "And the next time, they'll be much smarter. Harder to stop."

Day 21

Executive Strategy Conference Room
NSA Headquarters
Ft. Meade, Maryland
9:00 am

The weight of the moment pressed down on Scott Douglass as he sat in the heavily secured operations wing of NSA Headquarters, deep inside Fort Meade. The conference room, designed for top-level intelligence briefings, was more like a war chamber — walls lined with high-resolution monitors, their screens a shifting mosaic of real-time encrypted data feeds. The hum of NSA's supercomputers processing classified intelligence underscored the tension in the room, a quiet but constant reminder of the digital battlefield where wars were now fought.

The President had chosen to meet here because this was the nerve center of the United States' most powerful artificial intelligence-driven intelligence system — AEGIS — a system that had nearly ignited a global war because of an elaborate Iranian deception.

Now, some of the most powerful minds in national security were gathered for one reason:

To make sure it never happened again.

The atmosphere was thick with tension, the kind that came when people knew just how close they had come to catastrophe. Douglass wasn't the only one feeling it. Every operative in the room had seen firsthand how vulnerable AEGIS had been to manipulation, and the stakes had never been higher.

On the front wall, a massive digital display dominated the space, its surface a shifting mosaic of encrypted data streams — real-time communications intercepts, cyberwarfare monitoring, and the re-engineered AEGIS intelligence system flashing on the screen in rapid succession.

This was the nerve center of the United States' most powerful artificial intelligence-driven intelligence system — a system that had nearly dragged the world into a global war because of an elaborate Iranian deception.

Now, every person in the room had gathered for one reason: to ensure that it would never happen again.

The room was filled with some of the country's most powerful cybersecurity minds — top military intelligence officials, NSA cryptographers, CIA field operatives, and White House liaisons. At the head of the room, standing beside Admiral Thomas Briggs, the NSA Chief, was CIA Director Evelyn Harrington — the leader who had orchestrated the entire post-mission lockdown on AEGIS.

Douglass felt the weight of the moment as he scanned the familiar faces of his team:

- Robyn Chen, the NSA cryptography expert who had played a crucial role in unraveling Iran's deception and tracing the false messages. She had been given additional responsibilities in her position and was now on a fast track to NSA senior management.

• Priya Sharma, now selected to lead an NSA team of linguists and cyber analysts, was fresh from her high-level debriefings on Iranian cyberwarfare tactics. She would soon relocate to the Fort Meade, Maryland, area with her family.

• Carlos Mejia still looked like a man who hadn't slept since escaping Iran, his fingers drumming on the table. He had been notified he would soon be Section Chief for his area of ICE in South Texas – a significant and well-deserved promotion.

• Marcus Reed, still battle-hardened, had his arms crossed as he silently assessed the room. Marcus was the only one who looked relaxed and ready for the next mission assignment.

Harrington's voice cut through the room.

"This is it."

He motioned to the screen.

"AEGIS is being rebuilt from the ground up. Stronger. Smarter. And this time, it won't be fooled."

Douglass exhaled slowly, his skepticism not entirely hidden. "We'll see about that."

A few seats down, Robyn Chen, the NSA's top cryptography expert, pushed up her glasses, her eyes flicking over the new security layers. She had spent the last few weeks deciphering Iran's infiltration methods, and while the upgrades were impressive, she knew one thing for sure — if they had been fooled once, it could happen again.

"Stronger and smarter?" Robyn repeated, skepticism evident in her tone. That's great, but unless this thing can distinguish between real and fabricated intelligence on its own, we're still flying blind.

Priya Sharma, seated beside her, nodded in agreement. We were blindsided by Iran's ability to plant messages so convincingly that even human analysts were deceived. The biggest flaw wasn't just AEGIS — it was us. If this system doesn't incorporate real-time human oversight into its decision-making, we're one step away from another disaster."

Admiral Briggs, a no-nonsense military leader with years of experience in cyber warfare, stepped forward.

"We're implementing new protocols," he said, gesturing to the screen. "AEGIS will now require a three-tier verification process for all critical intelligence assessments:

- Cross-referencing with at least three separate intelligence agencies.
- AI-driven deception analysis, designed to detect syntactic and linguistic anomalies in intelligence reports.
- Mandatory human oversight before any automated directives are issued."

Carlos Mejia leaned forward, his knuckles tapping against the wooden table. "You're telling me that this system — this thing that almost sent us into war — now requires multiple checkpoints before anything gets acted on?"

"Correct," Briggs confirmed.

Carlos let out a slow, humorless laugh. "So we put our lives at risk in Iran just to teach a computer to double-check its work?"

A silence settled over the room.

Marcus Reed, arms crossed, smirked. "Welcome to the future, Carlos. Where artificial intelligence is as dumb as the people programming it."

A few chuckles rippled across the room, but the weight of the conversation remained heavy.

Douglass cleared his throat, his eyes locked on the screen. "Alright. We've got verification layers and a failsafe system. But let's talk about what happens when — not if — someone finds a way to break it again."

The room went dead silent.

Robyn folded her arms. If an adversary is determined enough, they'll find a way to bypass any security measures we put in place. Cyberwarfare isn't about brute force — it's about playing the long game. Iran took years to infiltrate our system and pull off this deception. We'd be fools to think they don't already have another plan in motion."

Douglass turned to Harrington. "That's what worries me the most. Iran wasn't just testing AEGIS. They were testing us. This was their first attempt. And we know there will be a second."

Admiral Briggs exhaled, his face darkening. "Which means we have to be ready before they are."

The war wasn't over.

It had only just begun.

Two Weeks Later

In the weeks following the covert mission in Iran, the NSA and CIA cybersecurity divisions had worked around the clock to reprogram AEGIS, ensuring that no adversary — foreign or domestic — could ever exploit it again.

The upgrades were unprecedented, incorporating a triple-layer verification system that ensured no intelligence directive could be executed without rigorous cross-checking, human oversight, and AI-driven linguistic analysis.

Executive Strategy Conference Room
NSA Headquarters
Ft. Meade, Maryland
9:00 am

The walls of the NSA's Executive Strategy Conference Room hummed with tension. The air carried the scent of freshly brewed coffee, stale sweat, and the subtle undertone of government-grade anxiety. This wasn't just another cybersecurity meeting. This was the meeting — the one that would determine whether the U.S. would ever again fall victim to the kind of deception that nearly launched a global war.

Scott Douglass sat at the large conference table, scanning the room. Around him sat the best minds in cyber warfare, military intelligence, and national security. Some faces were familiar — Priya Sharma, Robyn Chen, Marcus Reed, and Carlos Mejia — but others were high-ranking officials who had watched from the safety of Washington while Douglass and his team had been on the ground, fighting to stop Iran's cyberwarfare division.

At the head of the room stood CIA Director Evelyn Harrington and NSA Director Edward Ashtani, their expressions unreadable as they waited for the briefing to begin. On the far wall, a massive digital display showed the rebuilt AEGIS system — the artificial intelligence that had almost been used to manipulate the U.S. into a catastrophic conflict.

Robyn Chen stepped forward, her tablet in hand. She tapped a button, and the massive display shifted, revealing the new AEGIS verification framework. This tightly controlled network would trigger alarms across every intelligence agency in the country if even the slightest attempt were made to manipulate it.

"No More Blind Trust in AI"

Robyn's voice was steady, but there was an edge of exhaustion. She and her team had worked around the clock to rebuild AEGIS from the ground up, ensuring no foreign—or domestic—actor could ever exploit it again.

On the screen, a bulleted list flashed across the screen.

Key Security Enhancements:

1. Multi-Layer Verification Protocols:
   a. Cross-referencing intelligence reports against three independent sources before classification.
   b. AI-driven linguistic analysis to detect fabricated messages before classification.
   c. Real-time human oversight before AEGIS can recommend action to military command.
2. Enhanced Tracking of Deception Patterns:
   a. Recognition of digital fingerprints from known cyber adversaries.
   b. Identification of social engineering tactics used in cyber warfare.
   c. Cross-referencing with past incidents of disinformation warfare.
3. Deception Detection Algorithms:
   a. HYDRA, a secondary AI designed to track anomalies in intelligence data, sender behavior, and message timestamps.

Robyn turned to Douglass. "This system now requires at least two separate confirmations before AEGIS can classify any intelligence as actionable. There is no more blind trust in machine-driven intelligence."

Douglass nodded, though his expression remained serious. "That's going to slow down decision-making."

Admiral Briggs leaned forward, arms crossed. "Yes, but it also means we won't mobilize for war based on fabricated nonsense."

Priya took over, adjusting the screen to showcase enhanced tracking algorithms designed to flag fabricated messages in intelligence streams.

"One of AEGIS's greatest failures was its inability to distinguish between real threats and sophisticated deception," Priya explained. "We've corrected that."

She clicked to the next slide.

AEGIS Now Recognizes Patterns of Deception Based On:

- Digital fingerprints of known cyber adversaries.
- Syntactic markers that reveal social engineering tactics.
- Cross-referencing past incidents of disinformation warfare.

Priya locked eyes with Douglass. "If Iran — or anyone else — tries this again, AEGIS will flag it before it even enters our secure networks."

Carlos leaned forward. "That's great, but what's stopping a human-level false flag from slipping through?"

Robyn smiled and tapped another screen, displaying a secondary AI system that ran parallel to AEGIS.

"This is HYDRA — a neural network designed to detect inconsistencies in message traffic, timing, and sender behavior."

Douglass narrowed his eyes. "Meaning?"

Robyn's grin widened. "Meaning, if someone tries to fake a Chinese military directive using AI-generated linguistic models, HYDRA will catch the inconsistencies in tone, structure, and syntax."

Marcus folded his arms. "So even the best hackers and social engineers won't be able to manipulate it?"

Robyn nodded. "Not without triggering multiple red flags."

The room fell silent as everyone absorbed the weight of what they had just built.

But Douglass wasn't celebrating yet.

He pushed his chair back and walked to the front of the room, his face serious.

"This is all impressive," he admitted. "But there's still one flaw."

Every head in the room turned toward him.

Marcus frowned. "Do you think someone can still beat this system?"

Douglass exhaled, his voice grim. "Every security system in history has been broken at some point. AEGIS isn't invincible."

Robyn's expression shifted, realization dawning. "You're saying we should keep it offline."

Douglass met Director Harrington's gaze. "I'm saying AEGIS is too powerful to trust without human oversight. If we bring it back online without constant human intervention, we're one mistake away from World War III."

Admiral Briggs leaned back, considering. "You're advocating for keeping it in manual mode indefinitely?"

"Yes."

Silence.

President Jonathan Clark rose, his steel-gray eyes locked onto Douglass.

"Douglass."

Every spine straightened in the room.

"If we keep AEGIS in human-verified mode, will the United States be able to respond to threats as fast as China or Russia?"

Douglass hesitated. He knew the honest answer wasn't what the President wanted to hear.

"...No, sir. We'd be slower."

Clark exhaled sharply, his fingers steepled. "Then you understand my hesitation. In a cyberwar, speed is survival."

Douglass stood his ground. "And in disinformation warfare, reckless speed is a liability."

The room held its breath.

Then, to everyone's surprise, Clark nodded.

"Fine," the President said. "AEGIS stays in human-verified mode. But if we face a crisis, and I need it to be fully autonomous — I expect you to be the first one I call.

Douglass gave a slow nod. "Understood, sir."

The room relaxed slightly, but the war wasn't over.

After the final debriefings, the team went their separate ways — each onto new paths after the most dangerous mission of their lives.

And Douglass? He joined the CIA's elite training division as its leader, preparing the next generation of cyberwarriors. *Retirement could wait – Susie would approve of this move.*

Because if Iran had come this close to launching a war with fake intelligence —

The next attack wouldn't be deception.

It would be real.

And someone had to be ready.

Epilogue

Unnamed Government Location
Tehran, Iran
Days Later

The air was thick with the acrid scent of scorched concrete and smoldering ruins, the last remnants of what had once been Iran's most advanced cyberwarfare division. Now, the once-formidable Ministry of Intelligence headquarters in Ozgol was nothing more than a shattered monument to failure, its skeletal remains buried beneath twisted rebar and collapsed steel beams.

Outside, military trucks rumbled down charred streets, their headlights cutting through the smoke-filled night. Soldiers in black fatigues combed through the debris, rifles slung across their backs, barking orders to one another as they searched for any signs of survivors or, more importantly, any clues as to how their most sensitive installation had been reduced to ash in mere minutes.

The destruction was almost poetic from a distance—a silent reminder of how quickly power could be erased. However, this was not viewed as a defeat within the halls of Iran's military and intelligence elite.

It was seen as a challenge.

A new war council convened deep beneath the capital, where no prying eyes could see, and no Western satellites could track. The room was stark and cold, its steel-reinforced walls lined with servers, encrypted terminals, and electronic warfare displays. Unlike the usual military briefings dominated by generals and politicians, this gathering consisted of engineers, cryptographers, and intelligence tacticians — the last remnants of Iran's shattered cyberwarfare network.

And they were not there to mourn.

They were here to rebuild — and retaliate.

The underground command center was a fortress within a fortress, reinforced with layers of steel and secrecy. Fluorescent lights cast a cold glow over rows of encrypted servers, humming with power, each screen filled with cascading streams of code, digital warfare in its purest form.

General Daryush Farzan, a seasoned veteran of Iran's military intelligence apparatus, stood at the head of a long, steel-topped table. His face was carved with deep lines of fury, his expression unreadable. He held a classified dossier so tightly that the edges crumpled in his iron grip. The humiliation of the past weeks had burned itself into his soul.

Beside him sat Professor Hamed Kazemi, one of Iran's most brilliant cyber warfare engineers. His mind had built the very digital battlements that had now crumbled, and his once-proud gaze was now filled with cold calculation, and decades of his life's work had been incinerated in the blink of an eye. And yet, beneath the surface of his anger, there was something else — an unyielding determination.

But the most dangerous man in the room sat in the shadows.

He had no official military rank, government title, or political loyalty.

Yet everyone present knew his name.

He was called Omid.

In Persian, *Omid* meant "hope," but his name was whispered in Tehran's intelligence circles with reverence and fear. He was the ghost in the machine, the architect of Iran's most daring cyber-intrusions. He had spent years dismantling Western surveillance networks, breaching classified American servers, and pulling digital puppet strings in the shadows.

He had also been the only one who had seen this coming.

Omid's voice was soft, but it carried an undeniable weight.

"We underestimated them."

The words dropped like a hammer onto the cold metal table.

A murmur rippled through the room. No one argued.

General Farzan exhaled sharply. "The Americans moved faster than expected."

"They didn't just move fast," Omid corrected, his tone edged with steel. "They erased us."

A heavy silence followed.

Kazemi's fingers tapped against the table, his thoughts running at a blistering pace. His voice, when it finally emerged, was slow and deliberate.

"They burned our work. They destroyed decades of intelligence. They humiliated us."

His hands clenched into fists. "And yet... we sit here. Unbroken."

General Farzan nodded slowly. "Can we rebuild?"

Omid's lips curled slightly. It wasn't a smile of amusement. It was a promise.

"We won't rebuild." He paused, his fingers tapping against the metal table. "We'll evolve."

Kazemi leaned forward, intrigued. "Go on."

Omid reached into his bag and pulled out a damaged hard drive, its casing scorched, dented, and worn from the blast. It was a relic from the wreckage above, but inside... inside, it carried the foundation for something far more significant than before.

He placed it on the table and met their gazes.

"Our mistake," he began, "was thinking too small."

Kazemi's brow furrowed. "What do you mean?"

Omid's fingers hovered over the keyboard of a nearby workstation, his mind already ten steps ahead of everyone else in the room.

"Last time, we planted false intelligence," he explained. "We used deception, misinformation. We manipulated their system from the outside. General Farzan and Colonel Mirzai's team did well, and we are fortunate they were not in the building when it was destroyed. They learned the hard way that there is no practical way to hide communications in today's world, and their input will be invaluable as we regroup."

He leaned forward, his dark eyes gleaming under the dim fluorescent light.

"This time, we don't just manipulate their intelligence."

Farzan's voice was low, wary. "Then what do we do?"

Omid leaned in, his voice barely above a whisper.

"We become their intelligence."

The room was silent.

Then, Kazemi's eyes widened as he realized what Omid was suggesting. "You want to build an AI?"

Omid nodded. "Not just any AI."

He tapped a series of commands into his workstation, and the screen flickered to life. A logo appeared — an ancient Persian figure wrapped in chains, its eyes glowing red. Beneath it, a name flashed in bold letters:

ZAHHAK

Kazemi inhaled sharply. "The Demon King of Lies."

Omid's voice was calm but deliberate. "Zahhak won't just create deception — it will create an entirely new reality. One that the Americans will never be able to separate from the truth."

General Farzan's eyes narrowed with interest. "Explain."

Omid's fingers danced across the keyboard. "We don't attack their systems directly. That's predictable."

He gestured toward the screen. "Instead, we infiltrate their very foundation. AEGIS is designed to detect external manipulation. So we won't manipulate it."

Omid's voice was steady. "Zahhak won't just create deception — it will create an entirely new reality. One the Americans will never be able to separate from the truth."

General Farzan's eyes narrowed. "Explain."

Omid gestured to the screen.

He pulled up a detailed cyber-mapping schematic of the United States' most classified networks.

"We infiltrate their foundation. We become the intelligence they trust."

Kazemi's mind raced as the enormity of Omid's plan crashed over him like a tidal wave.

"We make them doubt their own data."

Omid nodded. Zahhak will be a "synthetic" rather than artificial intelligence, a chameleon program capable of embedding itself so deeply within their networks that they will no longer know what is real when they analyze their intelligence reports.

"We make it doubt itself."

Omid nodded. "Zahhak will be a synthetic intelligence — a chameleon program that can implant itself within their networks and become indistinguishable from their own intelligence assets. A system so deeply embedded that when they look at their data, they won't know what's real anymore."

Kazemi's voice turned cold and reverent.

"They won't just believe false information."

"They'll doubt the real."

General Farzan sat back, considering the enormity of what was being proposed. Then, a slow, dark chuckle escaped his lips.

"The Americans think they won."

Omid's expression darkened. "They haven't won." He glanced at the damaged hard drive — the last remnant of their fallen cyberwarfare division.

"They've just forced us to evolve."

Farzan turned to Kazemi. "How soon can Zahhak be operational?"

Kazemi hesitated, calculating. "We'll need funding, secure facilities, and a completely new cyber warfare division. The old network is compromised, but there are... alternatives."

Farzan nodded slowly and turned to Omid. "You will lead this project?"

Omid didn't hesitate. "Yes."

Farzan's cruel smile widened. "Then let's send the Americans a message."

Hours later, a secure digital signal pulsed across the dark web, hidden within layers of encryption so sophisticated that only the most elite intelligence agencies would recognize it.

It was not an attack.

Not yet.

It was a warning.

NSA Headquarters
Ft. Meade, Maryland
Hours Later

A lone analyst working the midnight shift received a high-priority alert. The message was flagged as potentially dangerous and immediately escalated to top-level cybersecurity analysts.

It wasn't an attack.

Not yet.

It was a warning.

The analyst's breath hitched as he read the two words flashing on the screen. It contained only two words, along with an ancient Persian symbol:

ZAHHAK RISES.

The analyst stared at the screen, a cold shiver crawling down his spine.

He had no idea what Zahhak meant.

But as he sent the urgent message up the chain, he couldn't shake the feeling that whatever had been stopped in Iran...

It was just the beginning.

And this time, the war wouldn't be fought with bombs or bullets.

It would be fought in the shadows of cyberspace, where reality itself was the battlefield.

Cast of Characters

Cybersecurity Intelligence Team, Ozgol, Iran

- Colonel Reza Mirzai – Head of the Iranian Cyberintelligence Operations Center
- Saeed Alavi – Cybersecurity Encryption Specialist
- Leila Pourfarrokh – Cybersecurity Social Engineering Specialist
- Kamran Roshani – Cybersecurity Communications Specialist
- Arash Khalili – Head of Iran's National Security Council
- General Ebrahim Ansari – Iran Minister of Defense

South Texas ICE Regional Office, Harlingen, Texas

- Carlos Mejia – Special Agent, U.S. Immigration and Customs
- Sandra Espinoza – Senior Analyst, financial expert
- Priya Sharma – Junior Analyst, linguistics expert

South Texas ICE Sector Office, McAllen, Texas

- Thomas Grayson – ICE Regional Director, McAllen Sector

National Security Agency, Ft. Meade, Maryland

- Jack Thompson – Special Analyst
- Mark Rivers – Supervising Analyst
- Edward Ashtoni – Director of the National Security Agency

Central Intelligence Agency Headquarters, Langley, Virginia

- Scott Douglass – Special Agent
- Marcus Reed - Special Agent
- Robin Chen – Analyst & Cryptographer
- Evelyn Harrington – Director of the Central Intelligence Agency

U.S. Department of Homeland Security, Washington, D.C.

- Andrew Dyson – Secretary of Homeland Security

Joint Chiefs of Staff, The Pentagon, Arlington, Virginia

- General Mark Spencer – Chairman of the Joint Chiefs of Staff (CJCS)
- General Linda Fox – Chief of Staff of the Air Force (CSAF), Joint Chiefs of Staff
- General Jacob Turner – Pentagon Liaison
- James Price – Head of Naval Operations (CNO), Joint Chiefs of Staff
- Warren Holloway – Secretary of Defense
- General Daniel Ross – Chief of Staff of the Army (CSA), Joint Chiefs of Staff

White House, Washington, D.C.

- Jonathan Clark – President of the United States

Mossad Training Center, Herzliya, Israel

- Major Avi Cohen – Mossad Operations Chief
- Dalia Rahmani – Mossad cyberwarfare specialist
- Captain Eitan Raz – Mossad maritime trainer
- Meir Zakay – Mossad Director

CIA Classified Meet Point, Baku, Azerbaijan

- David Stokes – CIA Agent
- Yaron Malek – Mossad Agent

Unnamed Government Location, Tehran, Iran

- General Daryush Farzan – Head of Warfare Planning
- Professor Hamed Kazemi – cyber warfare systems architect
- Omid – cybersecurity specialist and expert artificial intelligence programmer/hacker

Dave Osborn

Dave Osborn is a retired technology CEO whose passion for storytelling launched a fulfilling second career as an author. He began writing with *Taking Charge!*, a business leadership memoir reflecting on his 52+ years in the technology industry. He followed it with *The Adventures of Piper*, a non-fiction children's series inspired by his beloved rescue dog and therapy partner, Piper.

Dave's first fiction novel, *Signals of Deception*, is a geopolitical thriller that introduces CIA Special Agent Scott Douglass, a character who will return in future installments.

His books are available on Amazon, Ingram and at www.daveosbornbooks.com.

Beyond writing, Dave is an advocate for animal welfare and a lifelong musician. He plays piano, guitar, bass, and five-string banjo, with a special love for bluegrass music. He also enjoys bird hunting, bay fishing, and coastal sailing in South Texas.

Dave holds a Bachelor of Science and an MBA, which, along with his executive background, lend depth and discipline to his writing. He lives in Harlingen, Texas, with his wife Marilyn and their rescue dog Piper. Together, they are avid history enthusiasts who enjoy international travel and learning about other cultures. They are also proud parents of two adult children and grandparents to two grandsons in the Houston area.

Also, by Dave Osborn:

Children's:

The Adventures of Piper, Book 1: Piper's Journey Home

The Adventures of Piper, Book 2: Piper Learns to Serve

The Adventures of Piper, Book 3: Piper On the Job

Non-Fiction:

Taking Charge!: 52 ½ Years of Anecdotes and Advice for Aspiring Executives